The Moby Dick *was cruising at a comfortable clip...*

...and Caffrey's feet were up as he played air drums along with Keith Moon. Yin disrupted his bliss.

"Ahhh...folks. What, pray tell, is that?"

A spiraling tube of blue energy was winding its way from a singularity in space and moving toward the *Moby Dick* at an alarming rate of speed.

"I am afraid we will not be able to outrun it!" Angie cried.

"Some sort of wormhole, I suppose," said Caffrey.

"A wormhole of the usual sort requires energy exceeding Planck levels. the *Moby Dick* is picking up only a mild static, no more than would be produced by rubbing a foot on a shag carpet," Poe 33 announced.

Caffrey gave the android a strange glance as he tried to guess where in the endless light years of adventuring he would have come across shag carpeting.

"What is this if not some sort of black hole?"

"It is a mylaxic eel," Poe 33 explained.

"Never heard of it," Yin admitted.

"Me neither. Angie-girl, you find anything in your zoological files on mylaxic eels?"

"Just a moment, my sweet leather volume. Yes. Found. Mylaxic eel: an extremely rare member of the genus *Electrophorus electricus gigantus*, found only in comet-rich regions of the Plethorian Sector. Its unique digestive system links two distinct points in time and space, illustrating in astronomical grandeur the philosophy of never defecating where one resides."

"I could have told you that," Poe 33 mumbled.

MILKY WAY
MARMALADE

by

Michael DiCerto

ZUMAYA OTHERWORLDS   AUSTIN TX

2009

MILKY WAY MARMALADE
© 2003, 2009 by Michael DiCerto
ISBN 978-1-934841-29-7

Cover art and design @ Angela Waters

"Zumaya Otherworlds" and the griffon logo are trademarks of Zumaya Publications LLC, 3209 S. Interstate 35, Austin TX. Find more of the best of speculative fiction at our website.

http://www.zumayaotherworlds.com

Library of Congress Cataloging-in-Publication Data

DiCerto, Mike, 1965-
  Milky Way marmalade / by Mike DiCerto.
      p. cm.
  ISBN 978-1-934841-29-7 (alk. paper)
  I. Title.
  PS3604.I27M56 2009
  813'.6--dc22

                                        2009005143

Dedication

To my Father, Dominick, who filled my world with spirit and wonder.

To my Mother, Dolores, who filled my world with her strength.

To musicians, with their longhaired souls, who filled my world with endless joy.

And to my wife, Suzy, who is my world.

FOREWORD

BOOKS FOR AND ABOUT EVERY WALK OF LIFE, FROM JAMES Joyce to James Patterson, might get the characters right, the emotions right, the plot, the place, the architecture right—but they almost never get the music right. Or care.

Milky Way Marmalade is the music. It's life, music, and desire, all unfolding with a freaky-deaky beat poet sensibility. The characters are out where the buses don't run, but, then again, in 3265, the bus schedule can be unreliable at best. We fly through the galaxy, through thousands of years in existence, with a Rosetta Stone juke box as our guide, hoping to fight the ultimate evil, hoping to connect to the ultimate good—and laughing along the way...

Rock music has always been one of my best friends; I can't even begin to count how many lonely miles Bob Dylan has traveled with me. How many mind-numbing traffic jams I've survived because the Grateful Dead soothed my nerves or the Beatles fed my mind. Thirty-some-odd years since its creation, classic rock continues to live, thrive and accompany lonely travelers on their journeys. It will be ever thus 1200 years from now.

The truths of the Universe might be in the Bible—or in "Layla," or in *Milky Way Marmalade*—it's up to you, and it's well-worth the intergalactic, alien gourmet delicacy trip to find out!

— Ken Dashow
Q104.3, New York

INTRODUCTION

A MESSAGE FROM THE WISEST SUBSTANCE IN THE UNIVERSE

THE UNIVERSE, I ONCE NOTED, IS NOT ONLY STRANGER THAN you can imagine, it secretly dresses in studded-leather feety pajamas and spiked fuchsia pasties. The fact is the oddness of the universe is a part of its very essence. If looked upon as a whole from some far-out, Godlike point of view it would appear quite dull. Normal. Beautiful, perhaps, but predictable in its patterns of stars formed into disks of galaxies that in their totality make up the realm oft referred to as "the Cosmos." The untrained eye must peer deeper into its heart to truly appreciate its bizarre reality.

I should know, for I am a reflection of that reality.

I am not God. Nor am I a goddess nor the Lord nor the Supreme Being. I am not the Creator. I am not the Divine Spark, nor the Ultimate Entity that runs the show. I am certainly not the Cosmic Big Kahuna.

I am a cube of orange-colored gelatin the size of an average throw pillow.

I know what you are thinking—actually, let me rephrase that—I know all the possible thoughts you can think, have thought or will think: how smart and powerful can a lump of orange, gelatinous starstuff be? Well, not very—yet infinitely so. I am the complete record of the universe—all its creatures, places, things, events and potentials in every time that will ever be and in every dimension that exists or

1

may exist. I am the music, but I did not write the song.

I have had many names given to me by many beings with various levels of intelligence and beliefs. From your own world they include: the universal hologram, the Philosopher's Stone, the Holy Grail, perfected bliss, the Akashic record, manna from heaven, ether (soniferous or otherwise), the Cosmic Mind, the collective unconscious, the morphogenic field, lucid dreaming, the Bread of Life, sacred geometry, novelty waves, the flower of life, teacher plants and fungi and even Reginald by a pompous but good-hearted gent of royal heritage. A popular moniker amongst powerful off-Earth circles is simply "The L'Orange."

There are an infinite number of other names and concepts on an infinite number of other worlds, but I will leave that for you to discover. Regardless of the label used, all are incomplete in their perception of my true nature. While I am perhaps the wisest substance in the universe (potentially), I have no true innate power other than the knowledge and wisdom that can be accessed by any object, idea or creature with a consciousness. Although I exist in physical form, I am within everything and everything is within me. I will manifest most densely where creative forces spark, and I tend to hightail it (in a quantum manner) from locales where destructive folks and their dark ideas loiter.

I was formed in some ancient time by an unknown intelligence, unknown hands or, perhaps, an unknown machine. Perhaps I am the squishy orange turd of God? While it may seem odd that a gelatinous record of the All is unaware of its own origin, it only goes to prove my opening thesis: it is, indeed, a strange universe.

There is, however, one thing of which I am certain. Of all the forms of matter in the universe, the one that gives the Cosmos its Technicolor sheen and adds to its fruity flavor is found scampering atop, swimming beneath and flying above the countless balls of stone orbiting countless suns.

Life.

The unbelievable diversity of living creatures, no matter the form, intelligence, belief structures, political systems, social strata and annoying habits, is where all the utter weirdness is found. Dip beneath the skin of these beings, take a peek into the psyche—into the circus of the ego, id and the crayon box of mental workings—and the penultimate and wondrous freak show will be experienced. If the universe is music then life is Rock 'n' Roll.

And while I'm on the subject of life, let me answer one question

CHAPTER 1
Magic Carpet Ride

(Steppenwolf)

CAFFREY QUARK FELT LIKE THE WHITE RABBIT. ALTHOUGH he hadn't consciously made the literary connection, he was late, very late, for a very important date.

He sat with his fingers intertwined behind his head in the cockpit of his spacecraft, the *Moby Dick*. He was in a traffic jam of epic proportions, and although his was the sole ship in the entire sector, he could not move. Any further travel had been made impossible by the sphere of shimmering red energy encasing the entire Freega System. He could do nothing but listen as the official announcement of the Emergency Broadcast Station, backed by cold and lifeless music, reminded him he was not going to make his appointment.

> **MUSIC** (*myoo'zik*) n. [ME. Musike <ancient ErSo-lOFr. Musiquei <ancientEr1SolL. Musica <ancien-tEr1SolGr. Musike (techne), musical (art), orig. an art of the Muses < mousa, Muse] 1. An artificial construct of electronic sounds, used to convey the attitude, theme or moral values (overtly or subliminally) of various goods and services usually broadcast between adverts and/or emergency broadcasts.

This was the unfortunate definition on which Caffrey's ears had been raised, and he'd grown to despise the very notion of music. He rubbed his temples and stared out at the seemingly infinite net of energy that would hamper his journey to the forested world of

1

Careem 6. Vivid thoughts of taking large sledgehammers to the satanic equipment producing such rubbish filled his imagination. A sudden burst of static added a bit of character to the musical sterility, and a voice filled the cabin.

"Be advised that due to an Anomalous Planetary Event, spacecraft without official personnel, insignias or external advert billboards will not be allowed into the Freega System until further announcement. Please enjoy our continuous play of 'The Flight of the Ravaged Ignorants Interlude,' courtesy of Orington Munitions Corporation."

The voice faded; and the computer-generated music continued, failing miserably in its attempt at symphonic beauty.

"Another APE?" Caffrey wondered aloud, turning the volume of the radio down to zero.

"It's becoming an odd trend, my beleaguered banana muffin," observed Angie, the in-dash computer assistant with a voice as smooth as a mercury milkshake.

"Angie, you know how punctual the black-winged trinka is. I have exactly thirteen hours to reach Careem Six, hike six kilometers through impossible-to-land-in swamps then climb a kilometer and a half to the edge of a steaming pit and catch the bloody trinka before its post-coital suicide."

"Actually, you have fifteen hours. The black-winged trinka sings its pre-death songs to its mate for two hours before it leaps into the pit. So romantic," Angie sighed.

Caffrey shrugged and scanned the shimmering black heavens before him.

"What the hell is going on out there? Anything on the local channels?"

"Negative."

"Damn. Do you know how much a black-winged trinka goes for?"

"Anything caught by you, my love, is priceless."

"Twenty thousand glid. Twenty-five, if it still has all six of its penises."

"Quarky!" Angie scolded, managing an auditory blush.

"Check GS."

"Aye-aye, honey-pot dumpling," Angie said, responding with one of her ten million pre-programmed cute and oft excessively sugary monikers.

She searched Galax-Skein, the ever-growing database that had

2

permeated and branched across the Cosmos for eons. In seconds she had an answer.

"There are rumors all over the local chat channels that the world of Careem Six is going through difficult times."

"Difficult times?"

"The specifics are being argued vehemently. Everything from angry spirits, corrupt official activity to inter-dimensional terrorists. In any event, the one thing they do agree on is this: Careem Six is missing."

"Missing..." Caffrey bemoaned. "This is getting a bit tired. Three planets in three weeks."

The exotic meat collecting business relied on place and time. It relied on punctuality and an encyclopedic knowledge of galactic fauna and their individual mating, scavenging, migrating, hibernating, hunting and dying habits. But perhaps most importantly, success in the business relied upon the planet containing the exotic edible to have the decency to be there when one arrived.

Caffrey had inherited, rather reluctantly, his father's moderately valuable Supper's Ready meat collecting business. His parents, who had decided to run off for an indefinite second honeymoon ten years previous, had had enough of the dead meat trade.

Caffrey was easily bored with mundane routine. To assure each hunting expedition would be unpredictable, he added the word exotic to the company logo and set his sights on some of the more peculiar examples of the Milky Way's cornucopia of edible creatures. He knew he could make a bundle selling to an endless stream of obscenely rich, impossibly powerful, embarrassingly pretentious and esoterically psychotic clientele, who were sexually aroused by ingesting creatures from the twisted side of nature's imagination. Caffrey wasn't one to toy with semantics—his business card bragged he was "the prime purveyor of exotic meat delivered fresh from the stars to the stars"—but he was feeling more and more nauseous in his killer role as each day passed.

"Set a course for Geraplond, Angie-girl. There's a spotted glumox there with my name on it. I'll have to convince the Duke of Bron Yraur that black-winged trinkas are passé. He'll buy it. Bloody poser."

"Course set for Geraplond, sweet tush."

The *Moby Dick* turned and set off to the bizarre jungle planet and home of the deadly glumox.

The bartender working the late shift at Marti Oh's Pub wiped down the bar top. It wasn't in need of cleansing, for there had been no patrons since the day shift of the local Star-Transport engine plant had downed their last potables and headed home. It was simple boredom, and he scrubbed at a stain that had never lifted from the fine grain surface and probably never would.

The barman cast a pity-filled glance at the android who sat alone, watching his every move with an odd smirk. The artificial being's skin was soft and almost flesh-like. He was unclothed but devoid of any exposed sex organs, rendering the term naked inappropriate. The top of his head had a slightly raised, horseshoe-shaped ridge of sorts that gave the android the illusion of male-pattern baldness. His knuckles, elbows and knees were quite evident and appeared solid and powerful. His facial features were arranged in a perpetual smirk that hinted of great arrogance—yet a certain amount of sincere charm as well.

"Sure there's nothing I can get you?" the barman asked of the handsome blue android, whose sheen reflected the soft white and blue lights of the bar with unexplainable orange glints.

"Not unless you can lead me to the trophy of my programmed charge. I have become mired in a wash of nihilistic ripples and attacks of confusion. It would be best I do no further damage to my neural network. I am, however, enjoying your company."

His voice had a wonderfully rich texture that was at once seductive and creepy. It had the tones and timbre of a late-night radio personality. His was a voice one might hear on a radio show while driving on some road to nowhere at four a.m., and it seemed somehow appropriate for someone sitting alone at the dark end of the bar.

"Actually, I'm enjoying your company as well," the bartender replied, just to be nice. He tossed his towel down and leaned three of his ten arms on the bar. "How about some music?"

"Sure," the android agreed, sitting up taller. "What is it?"

"Music? Surely, you must have heard..." Maybe not, he said to himself. "Here—listen."

The bartender switched on an old rusted machine that sat on a shelf below rows of exotic liquors. The sound of a soothing reed instrument of some sort emerged. The android began swaying his head along with it. He seemed to smile.

"Yes, I believe I have experienced the sensation of music before. If my defunct memory serves me at all, it was with a tall and

4

rather handsome fellow who was attempting sexual reproduction with a large drum of some sort."

The bartender smiled, poured himself a short shot of Rekinese twisteroot whiskey and proposed a toast.

"To finding your memory for whatever it is you've forgotten."

"My memory has been behaving erratically of late. What did you say your name was?"

"Junik," the barman replied, trying to regain control of his six eyes, bugged out from the potency of the booze. "Have you remembered yours?"

The android shook his head. "Not yet, Junik. Although I have recalled my favorite rock—subanite. My favorite cloud formation—the photo-nimbus of Gertika Five. And my favorite nocturnal mammal—the silver-furred imistra, found in the dark forests of Ool. Cute little bugger."

"Ool? You're a pretty well-traveled android. That's way out in the Soronian Sector."

"It is, isn't it?" the android recalled with amazement. "Well, ain't I a wonder!"

The front door opened, and the tintinnabulation of the ancient jingle bells danced with the music. A tall female humanoid entered. She was dressed in a black leather trenchcoat that fell like a waterfall over her toned frame. Her hair was coal black and cut in short, dynamic angles. She strolled to the opposite end of the bar and took off her deep indigo sunshades to reveal a pair of purple eyes, their brightness pumped up by the aid of their own bioluminescence.

"Good sun-gone," greeted Junik, using the colloquialism.

She nodded and threw a nasty gaze at the music machine.

"Is that necessary?" she asked tersely.

"What?"

"The music. It's vulgar. It's the source of all that's wrong with the galaxy."

The bartender rolled four of his eyes and lowered the music a single notch.

"Can I get you a drink?"

"Yes," she replied, studying the android. "A Bloody Dragon."

As Junik mixed the drink the purple-eyed woman tossed several more glances at the artificial man.

"What's your name, android?" she asked without a single degree of warmth.

5

"Beats the living shit out of me!" the android confessed with a goofy smile.

"Have you been indulging in a magno-mix?" the purple-eyed lovely asked, referring to a magnetically charged gas inhaled by artificial lifeforms to induce the sensation of a high.

"Nay, lady. I have enough problems," answered the android. "Funny, I'm suddenly recalling the thing called music. Although nothing's clear in my mind, it seems I have some sort of innate relationship with it."

The purple-eyed woman fired a flare of disgust with her eyes and took her drink in her hands. She lifted the large transparent bowl to her lips and sipped the frightfully spicy drink. The android watched as a few drops of the crimson liquid dripped from the rim of the glass to the bar top. He seemed to be fishing for a memory.

"Blood," the android concluded after a few seconds.

"What about it?" the barman wondered.

A strange, staring expression swept across the android's face, and he stood up with a slight whine of his knee servos. He puffed out his chest and raised his chin. Junik watched him with unwavering amusement.

"What is it, buddy?"

"I am Poe Thirty-three. And I am the most important android in the universe."

"Good for you, pal," humored Junik.

Poe 33 bowed, turned and walked out the door. The purple-eyed woman watched him leave, downed her drink, tossed a few glid pieces as payment and exited. Junik chuckled, shook his head and went back to work on the stubborn stain.

Exotic meat collectors galaxy-wide had been duly warned about the deadly allure of the glumox. Yet, as Caffrey studied the creature from behind the safety of a huge boulder, he felt no fear. Only pity. Although the glumox resembled a nude female human, dancing in vain attempts to lure him closer, Caffrey knew the real threat waited beyond in the mouth of its cave. With his Worthington Starlight-77 Blaster, known affectionately as Willy, set for high kill, he peered through a few strands of black hair that hung before his dark-brown eyes, let the laser system lock on to its target and launched a sizzling strand of electric-blue spaghetti.

6

Wisps of black smoke, a result of the sine curves branded on the fleshy form, took to the breeze. A sickening scent of burning flesh entered Caffrey's nose. A roar boomed out. He held his aim as the figure twisted and rose into the air on the thick tentacle that ran from the back of the woman-like appendage and into the cave. More cries of defeat sounded as it was flipped about like an inflatable love doll attached to a runaway fire hose.

Reminiscent of the Earth's anglerfish, with its worm-like lure for hunting smaller fish, millions of years of evolution had perfected the glumox and its adaptive decoy for hunting whatever happened to unsuspectingly pass by. Reading the bio-electrical blueprint transmitted from the part of the prey's brain describing what turned them on, the amazing creature morphed its lure to a close approximation of a perfect mate.

Nonetheless, it was no match for Caffrey. Perhaps due to some subtle cosmic flaw, nature tended to forget firearms when designing the natural defenses of its wonders. The glumox's globular body rippled with death twitches on the floor of the cave.

"Poor bugger," Caffrey mumbled softly, taking a large knife from his belt as he ambled over to the corpse.

He sliced open a pocket in the animal and, like some horrific Jack Horner, reached in and pulled out a round object dripping with ochre-colored jelly. He turned the melon-sized body part around and smiled. It smiled back. Decidedly not a plum, it was a small, perfectly formed pair of buttocks.

For the cosmo-zoologist, the glumox was the only creature known to sport an internal tushie. To the practiced Epicurean, this forgotten body part, rendered useless by the fickle workings of evolution, was well worth ten thousand glid per ounce sliced, grilled and served on a bed of glass noodles with the red wine of your choice. For many, it was worth celibacy.

Yet, as valuable as his quarry was, Caffrey felt more and more disgust with each miracle of diversity he killed. He made vain attempts to rationalize that the slaughtering of critters for their nutritional value was simply what his father, and now he, did for a living. It was no different than selling personal spacecraft or hyper-travel survival insurance.

Or was it? Caffrey had decided, when he took over the business, that he would build himself a tidy nest egg and simply allow the corporate license to expire. He wouldn't even sell it. And although he wasn't sure what the definition of a tidy nest egg was—nor if he'd achieved such a level—he was feeling further disdain as each exotic lifeform was handed over for the oral pleasure of folks whose sense of entitlement had gone really, really awry.

A soft squeak sounded from behind him, and Caffrey turned.

"Oh, bloody beautiful," he mumbled to himself in utter despair.

Three miniature women, like dress-up dolls for a human child, danced and shimmied on the dusty ground. Three baby tentacles wound from the backs of the little lures to the pudgy forms of three baby glumoxes. The children of Caffrey's prey tempted him with their innocent mimicry of their slain mother's hunting lesson.

He crouched down and studied the mogies, as baby glumoxes are called.

"I'm a serious creep," he advised them. "Please feel free to kill me."

They backed off some and squeaked and made deep growling sounds. Caffrey placed the expensive butt in a special storage bag, bit his lip and, not looking back, exited the cave. He would leave the corpse of the glumox behind, as its remaining anatomy had been deemed worthless by those who set standards for such things. And although the woman-like lure held value to rich perverts with bad breath and with interstellar porn producers who used them as cheap cast members, he decided that letting it rot wore less on his sense of humanity.

＊

The *Moby Dick* had lifted off the surface of Geraplond and was making its way out to deeper space. Caffrey stood by the aft window, the light of the jungle world's sun, Sedujik, on his face.

"Love monkey," Angie called, "it's nineteen-hundred hours. Would you like your usual?"

"No, Angie. Give me five to go over my meat."

Angie giggled.

"Angie-girl, don't be bad."

"I thought you liked me best bad?"

"Angie—the inventory."

Angie snickered, cleared her ethereal throat and switched to her best business tone.

"In alphabetical order, the refrigeration compartments contain the following: Algronian tubeworm, quantity fifty; lung of Borellion crabwolf, quantity four; back skin of Cuvinese anthropig, quantity fifty square meters."

"That was a big old bastard, wasn't it?"

8

"It put up quite a fight, if I remember correctly. You had dropped your Willy in a chasm. You were amazingly brave."

"Thank you, Angie."

Caffrey loved having a built-in electronic suck-up, especially one with the ability to adjust her vocal waveforms to produce a very pleasant tickle.

Angie resumed her listing.

"To continue: one baboolie of glumox, weight five kilograms."

"Baboolie?"

"Tushie?" Angie suggested, checking her built-in thesaurus.

"Whatever. Please continue."

"Knuckles of green-backed mukiro, quantity forty; two buzzing Rayni toads, weight forty-seven kilos; one giant vufalisp, length thirty-three meters, and one beautiful, twenty-kilo specimen of a blue-winged zalceeva."

Caffrey nodded quietly and placed Willy into its recharge cradle. He plopped down before the G.S. station, staring at the blank screens.

"What's wrong, my stellar stud? I sense a touch of sadness in your silence."

"I made a little bungle in the jungle."

"Huh? What do you mean, my enigmatic eye-candy?"

"I don't know, Angie-girl. Guess I'm getting tired of killing creatures whose only crime was the unfortunate luck of having been born delicious."

"How sweet," Angie offered sincerely. "Can I assume we'll be heading to the Middle City?"

Caffrey sensed a little drop of bitter lemon in her honeyed voice.

"Where else?"

A passing petulant pout crept into the waveform. "I hate this part of the expeditions. You'll auction your meat, make a fortune in glid then wander around that horrid town spending money on some slut who couldn't care less for you!"

The waveform of Angie's voice changed rapidly from tickly to prickly. Caffrey hated when her voice got prickly.

"Actually, Angie, I have a surprise," he said softly. "I'm retiring."

"You're retiring?"

He smiled. It felt good just saying the words—and it felt great hearing Angie say them.

"Yep. I'm selling this haul for as many glid as I can, then I'm

9

going to find a little shack where I can start over. Be the happy fool. Find my purpose. Turn the page."

"Where?" There was a slight worry riding the waveform of her voice like a midget surfer.

"Someplace far from Earth Five."

"Good. It seems Earth, no matter what rendition, is doomed to failure." A sense of unabashed relief backed up Angie's once-again sweet tones.

Caffrey had been born and raised on Earth V, the fourth planet of the Shetlin System. An exact duplicate of Earth IV, it had been modeled after the original Earth (abandoned some ten centuries earlier) as were Earth II and III. All had managed to go the route of hell-in-a-fruit-basket as industrial pollution, overpopulation and humanity's favorite population-control spectator sport—i.e., war—remained trendy. The continued downward fall of Earth V did boost the real-estate prices of the in-production world of Earth VI but also helped to prove the adage that those who remember the past are doomed to repeat it out of some perverse need for nostalgia.

He let Angie cruise out to the neighboring star system of Byro and the fifth planet of Minkx, home of the Middle City Edible Life Form Auction. Flipping through screens of some of the Milky Way's more alluring locations, he was lost in daydreams of his future.

"I was thinking of Hyroopa," mused Caffrey. "They have terrific weather."

"You'd hate Hyroopa. They're dry."

"Since when?"

"Since they were invaded by the Oploosians."

"Bloody teetotaler reactionaries. How about Lyre Two?"

"Perfect. I can see you living in bliss on a world where public humming can result in a public caning."

"For godsakes, what's going on in this galaxy?"

Caffrey flipped through a few more screens, scratching his temple with a determined gaze in his eyes. He got up and strolled to the bow viewport.

"I have a map and a ship. It's my staircase to the heavens. There must be someplace."

"I'm sorry to interrupt your pensive moment, my self-reflective rice cake, but there's an object approaching. Dead ahead."

Caffrey furrowed his eyebrows as the object caught his attention.
"What is it?"

10

The object was rotating, and flickered with colorful flashes as the starlight bounced off its shining surfaces.

"It seems to be a box of some sort. Made primarily of wood, metal and plastic. There are no lifeforms aboard. Shall I destroy it, evade it or grapple it?"

"Interesting. Grapple it. Please."

Angie worked the *Moby Dick*'s dexterous grappling hand. With programmed agility, she snagged the odd box and, after a few moments in the decontamination chamber, brought it inboard. Its exterior was a mess—cracked, rusted and dirty. However, the cleansing process had partially revealed some writing on its surface that, to Caffrey's surprise, was in an older but legible Earth language.

"'Groovy Tunes Jukebox,'" he read, studying the set of black plastic disks that filled the interior beyond its clear domed window.

"These are musical notations," he announced, pointing to the little notes painted all over the box.

He pried open the plastic window and extracted a handful of the small black disks. They crumbled in his hands. There were over a hundred of the objects. A few, although scratched, remained solid and had faded paper labels that Caffrey read with a certain curiosity.

"'Light My Fire,' The Doors. 'Purple Haze,' Jimi Hendrix. 'Satisfaction,' The Rolling Stones."

One after the other he examined the plates, whose surfaces were etched with a continuous ridge spiraling in to the center of the disc, where there was a hole. Each was in worse condition than the previous, but in an inner compartment he discovered a single disk had been protected during its journey through the Cosmos. It had a plain white label with hand-scribbled words. His eyes widened, and his expression changed to a nervous smile as he read those words.

"'Stairway to Heaven,' Led Zeppelin," Caffrey breathed as he shook his head. "It's happened again, Angie."

It had, indeed. Throughout Caffrey's life the universe had winked coyly at him in moments of synchronicity. Time and time again, he would find a thought or recently spoken phrase manifest before him in unexpected ways and forms. Since his childhood the strange coincidences had haunted him like a mischievous ghost. It began happening so frequently it had become unnerving. Creepy. Although he never mentioned it to anyone, he was beginning to feel someone was trying to tell him something. If not for the rational side of his brain's constant assurance that it was all nothing but coincidence, he would have undoubtedly been kept up nights.

"Angie, run 'Stairway to Heaven.'"

Oddly, a full thirty seconds passed before Angie responded.

"It's an extremely obscure reference with only one mention in the entire system. It appears that 'Stairway to Heaven' is a song title, and 'Led Zeppelin' is the name of the group of musicians who created and performed it. Categorized as Rock Music. The genre, according to the official report, began as a subversive and socially destructive plot to subjugate the minds of the young that was slowly converted into the perfect backing track for selling luxury transportation vehicles."

"Interesting."

Caffrey placed the disc gently into a storage drawer.

"I'll take that drink now, Angie."

"Fine. But we are not done discussing your future plans," Angie reminded in her best prickly voice.

A glass of Bezzie appeared in the MealPrepper. It was a silky blue liqueur from Vendix that was valued because it changed a prickly voice to a tickly one. Caffrey looked out at the starry blackness, sipped the Bezzie and closed his eyes.

"Perfect, as always, Angie."

"We'll talk later." Angie wasn't to be diverted.

"Yes, Angie. Of course." The engine hummed, and the *Moby Dick* continued out into the charcoal black of space, the green sphere of Geraplond slowly falling away behind.

CHAPTER 2
The Life Auction

(Strawbs)

MIDDLE CITY, ODDLY ENOUGH, WAS LOCATED BETWEEN LEFT City and Right City in what was perhaps the most mundane and sterile cosmopolitan center ever designed. Dead in the heart of the matrix layout was the four-acre Blood Bone Hall, where Quigmo Digmo, the leader of the Meat Collectors Union and one of the syndicate heads of the five galactic sectors, ruled.

Caffrey had last seen Quigmo at the previous year's Middle City Edible Life Form Convention. A Belkibon by birth, Quigmo Digmo was of a species for whom body weight was not something to be ashamed of or controlled, but, rather, expanded upon in a boastful display of corpulent grandeur. "You can never be fat enough" was the proud Belkibon mantra.

Quigmo stepped up to the reinforced podium, dressed in what was for all practical purposes a red-and-black tent masquerading as a suit, his waist-length blue hair falling like a rippling waterfall over his layered torso. Revealing a mouthful of teeth stained with the permanent brown of old blood, he smiled at the gathered crowd and cleared his throat for a full five minutes before finally dislodging an ounce of God-knows-how-old meat, which he casually spat to the stage floor with a solid, moist thud.

"Welcome. Welcome, you old meat jockeys. I hereby officially deem the Middle City Edible Life Form Convention of Thirty-two-sixty-nine open."

13

Half-hearted cheers filled the hall. Exotic meat collectors, as a rule, tend to make antsy crowds who despise the formality of such gatherings. Caffrey, as was his innate ability, found a seat beside a woman with hair so black it was as if a wormhole had opened and settled atop her head. He studied with great interest the length of thigh revealed beneath her semi-translucent pants and imagined the eternal joys that could be experienced in such a realm. Another round of cheers beckoned for his attention.

"I'm sorry, what did he say?" Caffrey asked.

"He said the first bid will be for a case of one hundred coolrip steaks," she said, crossing her legs.

"You buying or selling?"

"Recruiting," she replied tersely without looking his way—professionally ascetic.

"For?" Caffrey hated terse replies.

"You'll find out if I choose to recruit you."

"I see." He didn't. He did, however, recognize the irregularly shaped, eight-pointed red-and-gold emblem emblazoned on her lapel—the logo of the once immensely popular interstellar musician Spydersloth Blaust. Caffrey couldn't resist one more flirtatious attempt to get her to face him.

"A Spydersloth fan, I see?"

Growing annoyed at his persistence, she turned and aimed her eyes at his. The purple blast caught Caffrey off-guard.

"One is not a fan of Spydersloth Blaust—that would imply I supported his past dabbling in the horrid art of music. One follows him on his new paths of disharmony and non-lyrical thought," she returned, with a gaze that reeked of obsession.

Fanatic, he thought as he gave her one last faux smile and pondered running for the hills. He turned his attention back to the auction.

The case of Humproarian coolrip steaks went for ten thousand glid, purchased by a pair of co-joined Gavarians who continually, and quite foolishly, raised the stakes by trying to outbid each other. Then, with great musical fanfare, Quigmo waddled over to a large silver capsule lowered hydraulically to the stage. With a push of a button, the solid face became translucent and a gasp filled the room. The canister contained a frozen three-meter-long silver-finned rag-o-wisp. Caffrey pouted with an air of self-righteousness.

"So bloody trendy," he said, just loud enough for the anxious bidder in front of him to hear.

For the dilettante of the cosmic culinary arts, a rag-o-wisp, with its delicate, flaky flesh, was hip. A silver-finned rag-o-wisp, found only in the mud bogs of Veneveer 5, was a guaranteed mention in the Society of Interstellar Blue Blood's "Posh Patter" column. A three-meter-long silver-finned rag-o-wisp meant guaranteed sex of any nature with any creature with the tendency for physical stimulation.

Caffrey wasn't impressed, and he left his seat and wandered down the aisle. Having been assigned a double digit in the random drawing, he knew from experience it would be at least an hour before his stock went up for grabs. He let his eyes fall upon the rows of anxiously waving arms, sweaty brows, impatient tentacles and bristled fins and smiled to himself, proud of his ability to not get caught up in the fickle trends of cuisine.

A cool breeze tempted him to the partially open rear door. He exited the hall.

A line of exotic spacecraft filled the landing zone, each glistening in the warm light of the sun. the *Moby Dick* sat at the far end, nestled between a sparkling new Heavenblaster 5 and a small, nubile Jetstar 1000. the *Moby Dick* looked, Caffrey strongly felt, the sexiest of the three.

A shriveled voice disrupted his gaze.

"She's a beauty."

Caffrey turned to find no one before him.

"Up here," advised the voice.

Caffrey looked up. Sure enough, hanging in the air like a day-old helium balloon was a ruddy-faced Kelfkin—one of a race of creatures who floated about in hydrogen-rich atmospheres extracting the light gas, which they store in special bladders at each end of their bulbous bodies.

"Have you auctioned your haul?" asked the Kelfkin.

"No. I'm up in about an hour."

"Good. I have been instructed to make you a private offer."

"Tsk-tsk!" Caffrey spat, waving a warning-filled finger at the creature. "No bidding outside the confines of the convention."

"This comes from Quigmo himself. It's his rule to bend as he wishes," explained the fish-faced balloon with a certain air of smugness that puckered Caffrey's lips like a bite of lemon.

His concern for the rules of the meat auction was, of course, a cautious ruse. It wasn't as if he were a virgin to closing deals covertly. Just three conventions previous he had sold a beautiful side of fri-

15

gamoose[1] for a record five thousand glid in this very same parking area. However, agents from the Meat Enterprise Advisory Team (MEAT) were notorious for baiting traders into illegal activity, and Caffrey was well aware of the penalties for unlawful actions.

"If Quigmo is interested in my cargo then he should approach me face to face."

"He's not interested in your cargo. He's interested in your ability to gather cargo."

"I'm retiring."

"He is sure you will be unable to resist this prey."

"Prey tell?" Caffrey inquired mockingly.

The Kelfkin pressed his fishy lips to Caffrey's left ear and whispered. If not for the tensile strength of his optic nerves, Caffrey's eyes would have shot clear across the landing zone.

Quigmo Digmo's office was furnished with pieces dangerously close to overdosing on florid detail. The walls were gaudily adorned with tapestries illustrating great, obese moments of Belkibon history; and the ceiling was painted as if by some high-carb, high-protein Michelangelo.

Quigmo lounged naked in his Vibrundaspooner 500, exhausted from his seven hours of battling the forces of gravity at the podium. He moaned uncontrollably as the warming, vibrating, massaging mass of protoplasmic goop molded itself around him, sending sensual waves of ecstatic bliss to his every muscle and pore. Caffrey, employing a more conventional sitting apparatus, bit his lip in disgust and tried to ignore the horrid sound of goop kissing fat.

"L'Orange?" he asked in utter disbelief, for possibly the tenth time.

"Yes, Quark, L'Orange," was Quigmo's tired assurance.

Caffrey shook his head and tossed the Belkibon an amused smirk.

"Quigmo, you know I respect you and your position," he lied smoothly. "But this is kwinkleshit. L'Orange is a myth. A tale akin to some Ancient Astral Mariner. The delusional fantasy of children or grown men of equivalent intellect."

He could have gone on for hours but decided he'd made his

---

[1] Frigamoose, the largest land creature on Gegimonz 3, is the only known animal to have just one side.

16

point. Quigmo burst into laughter, great guffaws of roaring, crackling blasts of air that blew back Caffrey's hair and wrinkled his nose with the slight but definite stench of old bacon and tooth gunk. The Belkibon managed to lift his arm from the tub of goop and point to a small wooden box sitting alone on a long, polished-stone table.

Caffrey lazily stretched his arm for it but to his dismay was a foot short of the object. After a few moments of attempting to bring it to him with some deeply repressed telekinetic power, futility won out and forced him up. He took the small, pretty cube in his hands and admired its soft grain. He lifted the hinged cover. Inside was a small, crystalline cylinder. He held it up to the light.

"It's empty."

Quigmo, expecting the response, rolled his eyes and pointed his arm to the table again.

"Use the glass."

Caffrey, who hadn't noticed the gold-rimmed magnifying glass lying a few feet from where the box had been sitting, did as suggested. Peering through the antique instrument, he focused in on the mere dot of orange something-or-other that was made barely visible by the lens.

"What am I barely looking at?" he asked, his face contorted as he eyed the miniscule particle.

"L'Orange," Quigmo boasted. "The only sample of the mystical substance ever to be obtained by any creature with the ability to obtain."

"And that lucky creature was you, Quigmo."

"Exactly."

"You're a magician, Quigmo."

"You are well aware of my chain of contacts, of which, my old friend, you are one small but trusted link."

Caffrey moved the glass to and fro as he tried to focus on the tiny sample.

"How do you know this isn't a speck of orange snot? Sneezed into this tube by a Truplimouse? They do, as I am sure you're aware, have orange-colored snots." He loved playing these games.

"I am well aware of the color of Truplimouse mucus. That substance, however, is a true and authentic sample of the L'Orange mentioned in the great Books of the Camgari, lauded in the songs of reverence of the Baggolits and worshiped in the many magnificent cathedrals of Spandibo. It is real, my doubting Tomasso. You are destined to cross paths with the great L'Orange!" Quigmo pontificated with great enthusiasm.

"Why?"

"Why? You are the nephew of Greppledick Quark!"

"Who vanished into the cosmic ocean."

"Exactly. An eternal mystery."

Caffrey rolled his eyes. The Belkibon pursued its line of argument.

"It has been rumored that he constructed the last Portsmith. Your degree of separation from the mystic L'Orange is but a stone's throw!"

"Quigmo, I heard all the stories about the L'Orange from Greppledick when I was five. He was a loon."

"The mighty Frigonese oak is a nut who held its ground," Quigmo philosophized.

"A lovable loon."

"If anyone can track it down, you can. You know the folds and crevasses of this sector better than I do."

"Are you suggesting I take this magnifying glass and travel every square inch of the cosmos seeking out every floating speck of magic orange snot?"

Quigmo laughed again, and Caffrey casually covered his nose.

"You are droll, my friend. Very droll," Quigmo mused, his flesh shuddering obscenely with the remains of a chuckle. "That cylinder was found in a slimy hotel room on Yeplu Seven. A hotel room which, witnesses claim, had been occupied by an android getting his master cylinder lubricated, if you catch my meaning. The Portsmith. There are rumors spreading that the Great Orange One and his protective escort have been separated. Never before has such a scenario become reality. If it is true, then the L'Orange is vulnerable. And I want it."

"Why?"

"Why? It is the essence of the All! The Liquid Fire of Antrisa! The Tears of Umalaze! The Milk of the Grand Teat! The purest form of the Prime Matter! The—"

"I've heard all the nicknames."

"And there is something else afoot, my narrow-bummed friend—I am losing worlds. Valuable worlds that I have spent a lifetime achieving control of."

Caffrey raised an eyebrow. This was interesting.

18

"I am not sure who is behind this attempt to control what is mine, but I shall not allow it. I sense the time is at hand. He who controls L'Orange will control the galaxy. I want you to get it for me. Will you attempt the greatest hunt since the Uldafter Fomaster[2]?"

"That would put me in quite epic company."

"Accept my offer."

"I'm retiring, Quigmo."

"Don't be a fool, Quark."

"That, my portly prince, is exactly what I plan to be," Caffrey retorted, with a wave. "I'll take cash if you're still interested in my meat." He got up and exited the room.

---

[2] One of the "Seven Grand Tales" of Gromet's *Odyssey*. The hero, Lether, traveling the worlds of the Vespucci System, bagged a twenty-ton flabunkor using a twig, pocket lint, snow and a small plum.

CHAPTER 3
Jukebox Hero

(Foreigner)

"I AM PICKING UP RATHER SWEET OSMIC FREQUENCIES. Symilia flower oil, to be exact," Angie said with a definite accusatorial tone.

"Angie-girl, your nose is as sharp as a vexenhound's. Quigmo had perfumed the goop of his vibrundaspooner with that very fragrance," Caffrey fibbed.

"The only essence Quigmo is fond of is that of his own fat lard oils. You visited Typura Moora again, didn't you?"

Caffrey smirked and ignored the question, pretending to be distracted by the colorful Groovy Tunes Jukebox sitting prominently in the center of the cabin.

"Caffrey Trinesmart Quark the Second, how could you!" Angie scolded in her most prickly voice.

"Oh, Angie, relax. Her voice can never compare with yours."

"And her body?"

"What difference does that make? You don't have a—never mind, Angie-girl. How's about a Bezzie, neat?"

"Yeah, sure, my cheating charm-snake. And you had better bite your tongue."

Caffrey smiled to himself as he thought about Typura Moora, the gorgeous high priestess of the Shimmyshake Palace located in the center of Middle City's only stretch of heart—the always-busy

20

Harmony Road. The paragon of interstellar brothels, it could serve bliss-fulfillment to more than sixty-five very diverse species.

Caffrey made it a point to pay her a visit after each year's Meat Convention. He never grew tired of her wonderful fragrance, her soft lavender skin and almost luminescent hair. Being she was a Finishian, Typura's locks were formed of wide bands of silky fibers that fell from her scalp like long strips of gossamer crepe-de-Chine rather than the fine strands characteristic of most humanoids. Its color was ever-changing, like oil in a sunny puddle. It was unforget-table. Then again, her twin tongues, four breasts, triple-jointed legs and thirty-two fingers set her aside from most of the humanoids Caffrey had clashed physiques with.

Finding himself wanting to be back at the Shimmyshake, he de-cided to distract his raging fantasies by tinkering with the jukebox. It took him a few hours before he began to understand the device's primitive mechanics. It took further experimentation to bypass the coin-operated mechanisms to finally get the inner turntable to spin. After five hours, with Angie manning the helm and guiding the *Moby Dick* across the ocean of the Byro System, Caffrey was ready to test the machine.

There were ten or so discs in what he considered to be playable condition. As to which one would have the honor of first play—that was simple. Caffrey had to bow to the synchronicity of the Cos-mos—it had to be "Stairway to Heaven."

The titles of the songs, while all colorful, were not what piqued his interest. The fact that these were songs written and performed by humans completely intrigued him. A team of people formed under names like "Led Zeppelin," "The Rolling Stones," "The Beatles," etc., for the sole purpose of creating music was unheard-of on Earth V—perhaps even silly. Ludicrous. Caffrey loved the concept!

He gently lifted the disc from the storage drawer and laid it atop the felt-covered platform. He turned on the power, flipped a switch and sat back. The music began as a series of melodic tones that put a soft smile on his face. He sipped the glass of Bezzie and listened.

For the next eight minutes he was transfixed. Silent. It was sim-ply like nothing he had ever heard. Music in Caffrey's world was categorized as neo-pleasantry and produced by music generators that composed using a combination of pre-tested pleasing chord ar-rangements snagged from a huge database, along with a dash of originality created by random-tone sequencers.

While some of it was, in its own soulless way, inoffensive to the ears—other than Caffrey's—this was different. Very different. The music was simple. Pure. The voice was perfectly human with a subtle passion infusing each word in ways Caffrey had never experienced. The lyrics were mysterious. Mystical. He wasn't certain he understood what the song was about but felt as though he were witness to the reading of the secret tome of some ancient order.

Then the vocals stopped, and some sort of electrical string instrument began a solo that screamed with a gentle and confident power. The instrument continued the tale, in its own dialect of vibrating strings, of the woman who believed "all that glittered was gold" and "forests that echoed with laughter." Caffrey was lifted up the enigmatic stairway to heaven by the magical notes.

The singer rejoined the piece but this time with a gut-wrenching power, sending chills up and down Caffrey's spine. No one ever screamed during a song. It was simply never done!

Caffrey found himself wondering Why the hell not?

Deep into the night, as the *Moby Dick* cruised across the heavens, he listened to the discs. Over and over. He wanted more. He needed more examples of this musical form that was called Rock in days of old. He wanted to live in a world where this music was created. He wanted to meet the people who created it.

Oddly, like a fly trapped in a bottle and buzzing beneath the surface of the loosened cork, there was a memory trying to surface in his mind. The music seemed to be poking at his psyche and soul. It would take a few hours before it popped the cork of his consciousness.

"Uncle Greppledick," Caffrey whispered to himself.

"He speaks," Angie commented with a dash of sarcasm.

Caffrey wandered to the bow window and gazed out at the infinity before him.

"Angie-girl, I know where we're going."

"Where?"

"Well, I don't know where exactly. But I know what for. We're going to collect as many samples of this music as are scattered about this galaxy. We'll start with the titles from these broken discs. I need to hear more."

"And you are confident we'll run across more Groovy Tunes Jukeboxes just floating about the Cosmos?"

"No, I'm not. Do I need to adjust the wise-ass variable of a certain computer system?"

Angie chuckled.

"So, how do you expect to find more music discs, my wishful thinking wonder boy?"

"It's the law of crap disbursement."

"Is that the textbook name for the theory?"

"The area of disbursement of a civilization's baggage is directly proportionate to the length of time they have been under the delusion that they are, in fact, civilized. Once a species steps off their birth world the baggage grows more and more cluttered with each subsequent trip. Rock music is from the original Earth. Although it seems to have vanished from post-prime Earth worlds—"

"Understood," Angie interrupted, acknowledging the theorem without further proof. "Can I help?"

"Of course. No one helps on collection missions like you, Angie-girl."

"Is that all I do?"

Caffrey noted the disappointment in her voice. He often had to remind himself that systems programmed for unconditional love needed a certain amount of stroking.

"I need your beautiful voice to keep the fire of purpose burning in my soul," he said, pumping up his own tickle.

"Will you be searching any dens of iniquity for the aforementioned discs?"

"Of course not," he swore with crossed fingers. "Will you help?"

"Absolutely, my peach puppet with a purpose!" asserted Angie with a childlike excitement that made him smile. "Just one question?"

"Yes, Angie?"

"Who is Uncle Greppledick?"

Caffrey pondered that a moment as he filled his mouth with the last slug of Bezzie, swishing it around like mouthwash before swallowing. He'd been thinking about his uncle since his meeting with Quigmo Digmo, yet he'd been unaware of the subconscious engine cranking away until the music brought it to the surface.

He sat back in the chair and clasped his hands behind his head, trying to piece together the fragments that were mysteriously filling his mind. After allowing the song to finish, he turned off the jukebox and began telling Angie the history of his peculiar and infamous Uncle Greppledick Quark. She would record the story and file it away in the growing database of the exploits, adventures and continuing education of Caffrey Trinesmart Quark II.

Greppledick Quark was born on the dusty world of Truplimore (home of the orange-snotted Truplimouse) in the Yangling System. Born without kneecaps, he spent his childhood alone, wandering his township on his wheeled leg extensions and collecting bits of diamond that littered the glittering landscape. A voracious learner, he taught himself Bing Ding, the once-popular programming language for android lifeforms, as well as elemental reconstruction, artificial psychology and electro-mechanical extremities engineering. By the age of ten he'd built his first robot, a small doglike critter he named, enigmatically, Poe.

Within five years Greppledick had built a family of twenty artificial lifeforms. Poe 18 (the first android to be a victim of panic attacks) won the young man a scholarship to the exclusive Pennifore University, an institution orbiting the lavender ocean world of Bulkslands One.

Greppledick's big break appeared to illustrate that synchronicity was perhaps an integral element of the Quark bloodline. He learned, quite unexpectedly, that the diamonds he'd collected as a child where worth a major fortune on many of the worlds outside of his dusty home planet[3]. Selling the fifty kilos of diamonds stored in an old steamer trunk in his parent's basement, he set up the famed Quarkworks Android Plant in the orbit of Earth III.

Throughout the following sixty years he built androids of every shape, size, type and personality. The androids of Greppledick Quark worked from one end of the Plethorian Sector to the other, performing tasks as diverse as acting as court juggler in the castle of Rampi in the Yoonk System to serving as a highly decorated general of an invading force of philosopher soldiers who confounded their enemies with a bombardment of wise sayings.

Greppledick's notoriety made him the target of the most powerful, grand-of-ego and glitzy posers the galaxy contained, all of whom wanted to brag of having met and socialized with the powerful and eccentric kneeless wonder. Never being one to turn down a chance to get the latest interstellar fashion model or prime minister into his bed, he used his celebrity without apology. His life was rich, color-

---

[3] Soon after Greppledick's rise to fame and fortune, the gathering of diamonds by Truplimorians was made illegal. Thus, once again, the old Earth saying, "If feces found a value it would be illegal for the poor to have bumholes" was proven prophetically true.

ful; and he held little in the way of regret and disappointment in his heart.

But on his ninety-ninth birthday Greppledick felt a depression descend upon his soul like a wet burlap blanket. There was a little hole floating somewhere in his being that needed to be filled by a more spiritual accomplishment. On that cool and misty anniversary of his birth, he stepped out onto his kilometer-long wraparound deck and cried out to the spirits of the thick, landscaped jungle surrounding his home. Assuming his actions were nothing but a futile rhetorical scream, he was stunned when an impossibly thin old woman stepped out and smiled.

She explained that his karmic contribution to the universe, married with a serendipitous intersection of his life with a cosmic event, would put him in the most favorable position in an eon.

"You will build the next Portsmith, the guardian of the great and wise Cube of Wisdom," she assured him softly.

"Portsmith?" Greppledick wondered.

"The Guardian to the Wisest One. The android who escorts and protects the Wondrous Substance." The old woman's voice sounded like the wind through the trees on a Sunday morning.

Greppledick Quark had heard rumors of such a cube of orange gelatinous star-stuff, fabled as the purest example of the essence that permeated all of reality. His vast travels had shown him the many churches, banks, office towers, cults, wars and charities that had been started in the name of the L'Orange. Greppledick had always written the entire idea off as just another opiate for misguided beings—albeit an opiate that looked a lot like orange marmalade.

With great patience the old woman explained the mystical wonder and the history of the line of androids who served their thousand-year terms guarding and protecting "It."

"The craftsmanship must be perfect, the subtleties of the Portsmith's programming elegant and sensitive. Subservient, yet strong. Patient, yet able to quickly decide courses of action. Wise, yet childlike in its ability to wonder. Charming and sociable, yet comfortable in its own solitude. It must be versed in all existing customs, traditions and pleasantries for the many diplomatic visits to powerful kings, popes or prime ministers. And," the woman added, raising a finger to stress her point, "he must have powerful and rust-proof knees."

"May I ask why?" Greppledick requested.

25

The old woman glanced down at his knees. They were solid, perfect and rustproof.

"The Portsmith may often stand motionless as it travels impossible distances on the sacred journeys of The Wise One. You designed your own knees?"

"Yes."

"Have they served you well?" She posed the question as if it were a great riddle advanced by some powerful Sphinx.

"Yes." Greppledick considered a moment. "Squeak now and again but, all in all, quite well."

The old woman studied him. She had wiry-looking hairs growing from odd warty bumps on her chin, and Greppledick fought the urge to pluck one.

"You will have to work in isolation. Far from here. Alone. You must study and meditate and learn the history and ways of The Wise One. The history of the previous Portsmith," she muttered, pacing the deck. "Five years will pass before construction on the android can begin."

Greppledick pondered the offer, watching with bated breath as the woman missed stepping on a loose deck board by inches—it would have resulted in her falling through the floor and to her certain death fifty feet below.

He needed to know more.

"This Wise One? Is he a nice substance? He isn't some self-righteous zealot who secretly likes young Goretians[4] and collects magazines about bizarre Artenian mating rituals?"

"You cannot address the substance in the sexual terms of biological life. It is pure wisdom. It has no power in Itself. It contains all that has been, is and will ever be known. The secrets of every lifeform that has, does and will exist. The histories of every event that happened, can happen, is happening and will happen. The Wise One was born in the fires of the universe's afterbirth and must be protected from those same zealots of which you inquired. As long as It is safe the universe is as well."

"Then I see the importance. I accept the offer." Greppledick's voice rang out as he stood to his feet with raised chin.

"I knew you would. We must leave now."

Greppledick's chin hit the deck.

---

[4] A race of Insectoid beings who mature into young, humanoid boys with Dutchboy haircuts and poreless skin.

26

"I couldn't possibly. I need to pack. Send out change-of-address notes. Make sure this deck is fixed. How about three days?"

"No. Now. Or never," she said, putting her foot down frighteningly close to the busted board.

"Can I at least leave a note?"

"No. No one can know."

Greppledick looked around and sighed deeply. "What the hell. Let's go."

The old woman nodded, and they both vanished in a flash of orange light.

"But did you ever actually meet him?" Angie asked, her voice at the edge of its proverbial seat.

"I'm getting to that, Angie-girl," Caffrey explained, trying to calm the impatient computer. "I was five years old. My parents owned a bed-and-breakfast on Devonshire Four. Run by my mum. One day, early in the morning, there came a knock on the door. I opened it. It was a man, an old man. Old, but his eyes sparked with the fire of a teenager. His smile was like candy."

"Much like yours," Angie suggested seductively.

Caffrey blushed and continued.

"My parents were never too crazy about Uncle Grep. Maybe he was nuts. But he had that spark of purpose. People with purpose shine. Those without rust. I want that spark, Angie."

"Then let's get on our way."

"Yes, Angie. Let's set the controls for the heart of the sun."

CHAPTER 4
Rock Show

(Paul McCartney and Wings)

CAFFREY QUARK RAN ACROSS THE STRETCH OF STONE TILES, HIS boot steps popping the air. Above his head, whimsical bronze animals, dancing and brandishing musical instruments, turned round and round above a stone underpass. Crowning it all were two bronze monkeys who sounded bells with hammers, announcing the time. It was two a.m., and the moon was bathing the world in the perfect color to match the coolness of the autumn air.

Caffrey's eyes widened, and he pointed wildly.

"Sam! They're out!"

Sam Jennit, a thin, curly-haired fellow with pale skin, tossed his empty beer bottle into a wire mesh receptacle and joined Caffrey. The sea lions, indeed, were out.

Eight years had passed since Caffrey Quark sold his last cargo hold of exotic meat to Quigmo Digmo and set out to find more samples of the music that had kick-started his soul. His quest had netted immediate results as he managed to track down a vinyl disk recording of The Beatles' *Revolver* album from an antique pharmacology museum on Santafraz 5 where it had been mistaken for a Karkajean Empress's birth control device by the proprietor.

With the help of Angie's creative research and a few daring escapades, they were able to collect three more albums—*Dark Side of the Moon, Selling England by the Pound* and *Quadrophenia*—and three singles: "Brown Sugar," "Good Vibrations" and "Me and Bobby

McGee." A succession of unexpected musical finds in obscure destinations blew his mind—there was an almost mystical disbursement of Rock music around the galaxy!

And, as Caffrey continued with his Rock 'n' Roll education, it became obvious that this enigmatic and long-lost art form was not only sublime but angry, passionate, introspective, wild, fanciful, silly, fun-loving and, most surprising to him, revolutionary in the literal sense. Through some historical detective work, he deduced that Rock music had been the great equalizer to the paranoia, self-destructive nationalism, plethoras of chauvinism and the sexual and moral hypocrisy infecting the Earth during the time it was spawned.

Caffrey's complete spiritual conversion occurred upon hearing the work of a strange and wondrous being named James Marshall Hendrix, who was able to seduce his instrument into moaning ecstatically in alien tongues. The electric guitar, he soon realized, had more potential power than his S-77 blaster ever did. The prodigal son of Les Paul could scream, pout, whisper sweet nothings, laugh like a madman, curse like a sailor or gently weep.

With his conversion came a price. Mere record collecting would not suffice. He had to visit mid-twentieth century Earth. He had to travel and live on the wonderful and weird world where such powerful creative energy flowed side by side with the extreme negative forces of the odd folk who ran the place.

Circling their tiny artificial island, the half-dozen slick and playful members of the genus Zalophus were enjoying a post-midnight swim. The sound of the rippling water, soft and oddly comforting, gently accented the quiet peace of Central Park, New York City, Earth, Sol System, November 1973.

"God, I love them," Caffrey whispered, his eyes sparkling like a child's and his long hair, hanging past his shoulders, blowing free.

Sam smiled. The Central Park Zoo was closed, but the chance to watch what had become Caffrey's second favorite animal in the galaxy was worth the risk of arrest. Sam stepped up, and the two climbed the iron gate and took seats on the concrete steps beyond. Sam took out a joint and lit up, taking a long hit then passing to Caffrey, who did likewise. He closed his eyes and let the smoke drift slowly and deliberately from his nostrils. A far-off smile filled his eyes.

"I swear—Page is God. Simple as that. I will build a church by hand—brick by brick—using my blood, sweat and spit for mortar."

29

"That was an amazing show," Sam said, coughing on his last toke.

"Amazing?" Caffrey gasped, standing up, highly insulted. "Dig deeper into your thesaurus, pal! Epic! Mystic. Bloody mythic! Page is like Strider with a double-neck Gibson!"

"I think he'd rather be Gandalf," Sam retorted. "He had on them heavy wizard pants. Guess that would make Plant—who? Boromir?"

"No, Legolas. John Paul Jones is Boromir. Plant is a definite Elf. He has the golden locks—that pretty-boy, deep-forest way about him."

"And Bonham the Dwarf!"

"Gimli on drums!"

"We have to do a few of their covers next gig," Sam said eagerly as he took one last hit for the road.

"Anything but 'Stairway.'" Caffrey put his foot down. "I'm not an adept. I haven't the spiritual fortitude to touch that."

"Speaking of 'Stairway,' I finally got that bootleg single. I stuck it in the jukebox."

Caffrey smiled softly. So, that's where it came from. He tried to ponder how a jukebox from late-twentieth century Earth would one day find its way into interstellar space on a direct intersecting route with his spacecraft far, far in the future of his past. Within the colorful box would be a vinyl single—a certain song that would one day become a cliché of an era—yet would forever be the greatest Rock tune every written. It had changed his life—would change his life—whatever. Time was so bloody schizoid! It was too much to ponder, and Caffrey gazed across to the sea lions.

"How about a dip with these beauties?" he suggested. "Hey, my cuddly mates? You mind a little human company?"

He stripped naked, and Sam rolled on the ground in hysterics as he watched his friend step into the water and swim around with the animals. The sea lions barked with joy at their unexpected company.

Second Avenue and Fourth Street tended to be quiet at four a.m. With the exception of the ninety-year-old Ukrainian couple sitting on the stoop of their brownstone to escape their stuffy apartment, most of the late-night crowd was up towards St. Mark's Place.

Caffrey's heart felt warm. There was an air of honesty about this place. Although it had none of the techno-sparkle or the perfected cleanliness of his home-born time and space, there was something about the dirt and grease of the streets, the dusty and broken buildings and the imperfect people that made him smile. He no longer held regrets for having left his past behind to live on the original Earth in a time when its future still held great potential.

All the trepidation and sick twinges in his gut at having sold the *Moby Dick*—along with the spurned and heartbroken Angie—to a pair of Marweegian Crebbledogs were gone. He'd paid a small fortune to hire a transport ship with a Temporal Twist engine to take him to the Sol System circa 1965.

He settled into a railroad apartment on the fifth floor of an East Fourth Street walk-up and found his bliss with a cherry-red Fender Stratocaster and a procession of artistic and sexually adventurous farm girls seeking fame and fortune in the big city.

And Caffrey Quark soaked the music in. He saw Hendrix live at Café Wha?, the Beatles play Shea Stadium, Bo Diddly the Blue Note, countless other bands in Central Park, CBGBs and, of course, Led Zeppelin's famed The Song Remains the Same show at Madison Square Garden. He was among the few who cheered when Dylan went electric, among the handful who remembered Pink Floyd had a missing member and among the many who camped on the fields of Yasgur's farm when anybody who was somebody played Woodstock.

His record collection grew to four digits as the diversity of the genre astounded him. His imagination was tickled by the wondrous complexity of Genesis, Emerson Lake and Palmer and Yes. His very guts felt warm at the cross-culture results of British kids who, obsessed with American blues masters, interpreted the genre with their own special touches. And he felt hope as many musicians went beyond mere fame and fortune and used their music to aid in the social changes that were exploding around him.

Caffrey cursed when the reactionary halfwits burned Beatles albums over a misunderstood comment. He laughed when Jim Morrison stuck it to the man on *The Ed Sullivan Show* and cried when Jimi and Janice died. And he made friends. Four very good friends, all hungry for Rock 'n' Roll heaven. They formed the Rock band Marmalade Skies and would wow the locals every Thursday night in the basement of the Crimson Court Pub on East Seventh Street.

Caffrey discovered quickly that he had a knack for guitar-playing, and his powerful yet lyrical work was backed beautifully by

Dave Coping's eclectic bass riffs, Al Petre's whimsical keyboards, Sam Jennit's potent drums and Russ O'Reilly's unique vocals. The band had gelled from the very first meeting, each member falling head over heels for Caffrey's wonderfully trippy lyrics and the peculiar, unexplainable otherworldly quality of this sparkling-eyed man who claimed to be from the Salisbury Hills region of England—which was, of course, the truth. Caffrey decided to leave out the thirteen-century difference in their birth dates.

A high-pitched "Yip!" echoed down the twisting staircase of the walk-up. Yin, a little white mutt believed to be a West Highland Terrier and Caffrey's number-one favorite animal in the Milky Way, was able to detect his master's approach from as far as two blocks away. Rescued dripping with heating oil from the depths of an exposed pipe on the corner of Sixth and Bleeker, Yin had become Caffrey's best non-human friend.

"How's my wee potato?" Caffrey asked the excited dog, rubbing his head and rump intermittently as Yin spun like a top out of control.

The apartment was typical Lower East Side tenement design with its over-painted woodwork, exposed cast-iron radiators and cracked-and-worn plank floors. Numerous plants in various pots sat on the windowsills, showing off the green thumb Caffrey had developed since his arrival. The furnishings were simple and nondescript, collected a la carte from local thrift shops, and included an antique Victrola he had refurbished to a mint-condition shine. On more than one occasion, he would find Yin staring into the large brass horn and was never quite sure if he were stalking a mouse or suffering delusions of RCA grandeur.

Caffrey grabbed an ice-cold Rheingold and retired to his bedroom, where his pillow waited along with *The Late Late Show* on his tiny black-and-white television. He yawned, and Yin, sitting at his feet, gaped his own mouth in response. Before either could yawn again, they were asleep.

He opened his eyes. The apartment was dark, but his nose rose to the task and twitched, sensing something in the air.

"Yip!" came the muffled call of Yin from out of the dark.

Caffrey clicked on the light.

"What the hell?" he sputtered, looking at the foot of his bed. "Shit!"

Thick vines snaked around furniture and across the walls, ending in three large heads like those of a tremendous version of the carnivorous pitcher plant. Another pitiful yelp came from somewhere inside the vegetable intruders.

"Yin!"

"Yip! Yip!" Yin cried, the outline of his little body pressing against the interior of the monster's mouth.

Caffrey ducked the lunge of one of the trio and dove under the bed. He came up with the S-77 blaster and privately patted himself on the shoulder for holding on to that particular piece of hardware. The plant reacted like a martial arts master. Two vines shot at the weapon and grabbed hold. Caffrey held firm as another vine slid up and around his crotch and, to his dismay, tightened. He dropped Willy.

"Yip-yap!"

"Hang in there, Yin my pooch! The Quark bloodline is in mortal danger at the moment!"

Grabbing hold of the thinner portion of the vine, he twisted and bent the fibrous rope until he managed to lower the loop to a less essential part of his anatomy. A large empty scotch bottle that sat as a bookend on a nearby shelf presented itself as a solution. Caffrey, held back by the tension of the vine, threw his body at the shelf and, using the tips of two fingers like a pair of tongs, snatched the bottle by its neck. Books crashed to the floor in an avalanche of *National Geographics*, esoteric texts and miscellaneous beat writings. He smashed the bottle on the bedpost and aimed the dagger of glass at the neck of the guilty head. The other two jumped to the defense of their mate.

"Gotcha!" cried Caffrey as the glass did quite a nice job decapitating one of the three.

He backhanded a second, snapping it with a neat cracking sound, then sent a wicked left hook across the chlorophyll-engorged puss of the third, in which Yin waited for his freedom with growing impatience.

"Yip-yip-yip!" the dog pleaded.

Caffrey shoved his hands into the mouth of the canine-consuming green beast but retracted them instantly.

"Don't bite me, you ungrateful mutt!"

"Yip! Yip!" apologized Yin.

Taking the upper and lower jaw in each hand he used every ounce of his strength to split the remaining head in half as another vine wrapped around his stomach. A powerful thrust tossed Caffrey against the window, through which, despite the absorbing quality of his current activities, he spotted a cloaked figure standing in the pool of streetlight below. A shadow. An almost mythic cliché.

The vine yanked again, and as Caffrey spun around, his eye caught a glint of metal. The S-77 poked out from under the radiator. He grabbed the weapon and sent a blast of red lightning at the stalk just below the neck. The head launched into the air, careened off the ceiling and landed on the bed like a decapitated horse. A confused and bruised Yin yipped and yapped then crawled out between the clenched lips of his dead captor, his fur matted with plant goop. The vines around Caffrey's body fell limp.

The two stared at each other and at the plant parts scattered about the room. There was a long moment while they caught their respective breaths. Yin growled softly at the window, and Caffrey recalled the figure outside. He rushed to take a gander.

"Well, who have we here, Yin?"

Yin jumped up on the sill and growled again.

"Wait here, buddy, I'll be right back."

He threw on his bathrobe and slippers and rushed out the door.

It looked like a scene from a thousand spy movies. The figure, a man of average height, stood half-lit in the bluish-white pool of streetlight, dressed in a hat and raincoat that appeared to be a size too big. He continued to stare at the window of Caffrey's apartment, his face covered by his raised collar. Caffrey, watching from the dark crypt of his front hallway, carefully opened the front door, hoping not to be betrayed by the ancient hinges. A squeal of non-lubricated metal crushed his hopes. The figure's attention snapped towards him.

"Hey! You!" Caffrey called out, tossing his attempt at stealth out into the dawn air.

The man vanished. At least, so it seemed as he turned and shot off so fast Caffrey had only an eye-blink's chance to catch which direction he'd gone.

"Bugger."

He trotted off towards Second Avenue, trying hard not to step out of his soft, floppy slippers.

The first hints of the sun had taken the pitch from the night sky. The streets were desolate, and Caffrey's once-sharp hunter's eye had atrophied. Some of the more obvious clues that would have never escaped his notice in the past stood naked all about him, their proverbial tongues wagging at him in mocking jest: a scattering of dust, a disturbed blade of grass growing in the cracks and a cockroach crushed under the foot of the fleeing mystery man.

Caffrey noticed none of it. His gut instincts, however, were sharp as ever, and they led him to the cast-iron gate one block south.

It was a place few New Yorkers knew existed. Located beyond the gated alley off Second Avenue between Second and Third streets, the Marble City Cemetery hid within the city square that enclosed it. Caffrey stood outside the old wrought-iron gate and peered in.

A misty, early-morning sunlight dusted the rich greens of the grasses and trees beyond the dark alley. The gate was secured by a rusted padlock; and Caffrey, by an odd quirk of human behavior, tugged at it as if some bizarre occurrence in the quantum realm would cause the steel mechanisms to melt away and fall open. The lock's devices remained tightly held, and as he let his hand fall away he was nicked by a sharp spur of metal protruding from one of the gate's bars. He pondered the little drop of blood dripping down the gate and sucked his finger. He had no clue what was transpiring. He walked home.

Five minutes later, the cloaked figure appeared at the end of the alleyway and approached the gate. A single blue metallic finger reflecting the streetlight in subtle streaks of orange touched the globule of Caffrey's blood. Using a built-in vacuum system, the blood was sucked in. The figure turned and walked off.

CHAPTER 5
The Crystal Ship

(The Doors)

CAFFREY SPENT MOST OF THE NEXT DAY CLEANING UP THE CAR-cass of the dead vine. Yin appeared to have suffered no long-term effects from his Jonah-like experience and paid the battlefield of Caffrey's bedroom no more than an occasional passing sniff of interest.

After a careful study of the massacre site, the leaves, vine-segments, pulp and heads were all cut, tied in bundles, bagged and discarded a few blocks away. Caffrey had determined, to his utter confusion, that the killer plants had roots leading to a pot containing a simple aloe vera. He was sure planet Earth, despite all its psychotic forms of life at the top end of the food chain, was not prone to vio-lent vegetation—at least none the size of the previous night's intrud-ers.

His mind was avoiding one other little detail that filled his heart with an annoying and rarely felt sense of dread. Who would have sneaked a deadly plant in to attack him? Who would have had ac-cess? Dismissing the chance that a windblown seed had traveled umpteen light-years and landed in his flower pot as rather silly—even in his often-absurd universe—he mentally catalogued those who would like to see him devoid of life.

There weren't many. Enemies were not something Caffrey Quark made easily. He was, often to a fault, an amiable SOB.

Friends or, at worst, acquaintances were easier on the stomach. Enemies required too large of an investment of bile; and since Caffrey despised the feeling of a sour gut, he kept his circle friendly and saved a fortune on antacid.

Yet someone had planted the vine. He tossed Yin a suspicious glance, chuckled to himself and carefully examined the windows, fire escape and rooftop for signs of a possible intruder. There were none.

Marmalade Skies was halfway through their second set in the basement of the Crimson Court Pub. Caffrey, deep in the solo of "Cosmodellic Cocoon," was sending swarms of notes over the moderate crowd like colorful butterflies.

A soft "Yip!" sounded behind him. He turned and spotted Yin, tail wagging furiously, standing in the doorway to the backstage area. The dog turned and scampered off. Dumbfounded, Caffrey finished his solo and waited for Dave to begin his bass riff then exited stage left on the motion of a Townsendesque pinwheel.

The backstage area was empty, and a slice of red light from the exit sign fell from the door opening into a rear alley. Caffrey placed his guitar onto the thick cushions of a sofa and stepped outside. The dog yipped again and ran off.

"What the hell are you doing, mutt?" He trotted after him.

The alley joined Avenue C just off Sixth Street. The area, famous for its population of transients, was quiet, as is often the case when autumn begins to add bite to the breeze. Caffrey spotted Yin standing diagonally across the empty street, apparently waiting for eye contact. When contact was made, the dog took off.

"Yin! Damn you! I have an encore to play!"

The dog led his master on a virtual leash for five blocks, finally stopping in his tracks and sitting on his haunches under FDR Drive. Panting little puffs of doggy breath, Yin sat patiently until Caffrey came breathlessly up beside him. He took off again, heading for the river.

Across an overpass, down the ramp and onto a dilapidated pier ran the little Westie, finally jumping atop a wooden piling where he waited for his master in a seagull-like pose.

"What in God's name are you doing, you flea-ridden excuse for a lifeform?"

Yin was panting, but a glaze in his eyes and batting of his tail seemed to illustrate the dog was mighty pleased with himself.

With the exception of the incessant drone of autos on the highway, the dock was quiet and desolate. The wind blowing off the East River had a wonderful, toothy smile. Caffrey closed his eyes and let the breeze kiss his face then took Yin in his arms. The dog stared at an old shack that had once served as ticket office for a dinner boat and growled in his most sinister voice.

Caffrey strolled across and peeked in through the dirty, cracked window then tested the door's padlock. Once again, quirks in the quantum realm refused to play locksmith.

"The door is locked," said a figure, cloaked in the shadows and dressed in an oversized black London Fog raincoat, black derby, Italian silk scarf and expensive sunglasses.

"Evidently, that is the purpose of this device," quipped Caffrey, the padlock still in his grip, mildly annoyed he hadn't seen the figure standing so close.

"Apparently," agreed the figure. "I have met many locks in my days. I've often wondered if locks got lonely. If locks ever pondered their purpose. Whether or not locks ever needed love."

Moody and richly textured music accompanied every word he spoke, accenting rather than impeding the odd figure's diction.

"Who are you?"

The figure stepped out of the shadows, and the ambient light shone off the soft, skin-like blue metal of his face with peculiar orange accents in the ridges and peaks of his bone structure.

"An android?"

"Yes. I am Poe Thirty-three. And I have been tracking you across the oceans of space and landscapes of time," replied the blue-and-orange android. The odd musical soundtrack continued to augment his tone.

Caffrey looked around. "Where the heck is that music coming from?"

"From me. It helps communicate my mood to those of lesser intellects. And, if I may say so, it adds to my intriguing and wondrous personality."

Caffrey couldn't care less. "Why are you tracking me?"

"You are Quark Caffrey?"

"Some people call me Caffrey Quark."

"Then it is you I needed to find."

"Why?" A certain impatience tensed Caffrey's fingers into claws. Yin, apparently bored with the conversation, began noisily preening his genitals.

"You are in danger."

"Oh, really? Why would that concern you?"

"Because you have the blood of my maker."

Yin ended his toilette abruptly.

"Uh-huh," Caffrey muttered, sharing an amused look with the dog.

"I wouldn't have traveled so far across the Cosmos to pull a jest, Quark Caffrey. I am perhaps the most important artificial lifeform in the galaxy, perchance the universe. I can ill afford such wanton wastes of time."

"What makes you so special, Mr. Poe Thirty-three?"

"Please, if you insist on addressing me with a modifying title then I would prefer the correct one. Portsmith Poe Thirty-three."

"Portsmith?" Caffrey chuckled with a brutally honest, mocking tone.

"I wish I could laugh self-effacingly at such a notion," Poe 33 confided, with a sad backing track, "But, alas, I am it. I have failed my master. I have become separated from the Great and Wise One."

"L'Orange?"

"If you must use the vulgar moniker, yes."

Caffrey studied the android a moment. "So, why me?"

"Is the short-term memory capacity of humans defunct? I believe I already answered that question."

"'The blood of your maker.' What the hell does that mean?"

"Simple. I have been programmed to seek out the closest blood relative of my maker should I ever be separated from the One."

"Greppledick Quark," intoned Caffrey in a distant voice.

"Yes. Do you know him?"

Caffrey shook his head and walked to the edge of the dock. Ghosts from his distant-future-past were not what he had desired when he made his decision to live on twentieth-century Earth. All the space-faring relatives, bizarre alien creatures and other oddities that jumped planet-to-planet were wonderfully missing on his troubled but relatively simple home.

Caffrey's life had been reduced to the basics: Rock music, dirty but breathable air, simple but satisfying food, modest but effective shelter, warm companionship and just enough sex and mind-altering substances to make it all balance. It was the perfect existence for a man who'd spent quite enough time filling his journal with very bizarre entries.

39

Poe 33 stepped up behind him as Yin kept a watchful eye on the proceedings.

"Were you killed in the last few days?" the android asked, with the utmost sincerity.

Caffrey turned with a baffled smile. "Was I killed?"

"Yes. By a woman with purple eyes. A beautiful woman. Although I do not yet understand the role of beauty in terms of the ritualistic sexual practices of humans, she does seem to have it."

"No, I wasn't killed."

"That's a relief."

"You were outside my window. The night my aloe plant did its Manson imitation."

"Yes. I followed her. She climbed the staircase on the exterior of your building and fed your sweet and innocent plant a drink of BenZaline Twenty."

"BenZaline Twenty?"

"A chemical that renders plants psychotic killers," Poe 33 explained, the music rising to the occasion. "Ferns will attain poison leaves. Sweet little posies, vulgar language. Cactus, high-powered, high-caliber spikes that can penetrate the engine block of a generation transport ship. I once witnessed an army of giant red-leaf spruces attack a village on Goriplic Six like a hoard of Berserkers."

"Who is this purple-eyed woman?"

Poe 33's brow furrowed. "Can we have kippers for breakfast, Mommy dear, Mommy dear?"

"Huh?"

"Excuse me," the android murmured sadly, closing his eyes.

His face went limp, the background music grinding to a warped stop like a record on a turntable unplugged mid-song. Caffrey's own brow furrowed as he studied the odd being.

"Are you okay?"

The Portsmith began to vibrate, shake and buzz. A small, crystal cylinder emerged from a slot on his lower back and fell to the ground with a musical report. Caffrey picked it up but had his examination of the object cut short as Poe 33, like a stalled car engine, restarted, his face coming to life as if nothing had gone wrong.

"I think you lost a part?" Caffrey suggested, holding out the cylinder.

Poe 33 ignored it. "I seem to be going through some technical difficulties. I have been ejecting parts of my own being for weeks in an attempt to remedy the problem. You were asking about the identity of the purple-eyed human?"

"Yes."

"She is part of an organization of some sort that prides itself on its secrets."

Caffrey looked away and seemed to be fishing for a memory. He turned and faced the android. "I seem to recall a rather gorgeous woman with purple eyes in Middle City. A fanatical fan of Spydersloth Blaust's music."

"Spydersloth Blaust has become anti-rhythmic. Defiantly non-lyrical. He is one of the numerous far-reaching arms of ODOR."

"Odor?"

"Order Determined to Overthrow Reality."

"Why is she so interested in me?"

"She seeks the One," Poe 33 explained flatly.

"L'Orange?" It was almost a rhetorical question. Yin resumed his genital maintenance.

"Yes. *Mexu* in the speech of the Prepinions. *Seslyyynn* in the exotic language of the Manik peoples. *Grobduxbrug* as spoken by the gruff but good-natured Hawkus tribe. ODOR has plans in motion. They are awaiting the moment to strike. A moment when they can get their hands on the wisest substance known and use Its infinite knowledge to redesign the galaxy in their leader's warped image."

"I don't believe in L'Orange. It's a myth. A tale. A fable."

"In your isolated universe perhaps." A jazzy tune began playing behind the android's words, with nice, soft cymbal brushing. "However, Quark Caffrey, I was not built to escort a figment of the Cosmos's imagination. I had set out on my thousand-year term as Portsmith. I lost the One exactly one thousand one hundred and seventy seconds after the Initiation Ceremony on Regal Nine. Now it has become our responsibility. We will seek the One together. Can you leave in an hour?"

Caffrey laughed and, taking Yin in his arms, set off, hoping he would never again hear the music-enhanced voice of Poe 33. After three steps that dream bubble burst.

"Quark Caffrey. This is beyond free will. You will join me. Even I, the great Poe Thirty-three, cannot outwit the universe."

Caffrey laughed again and turned back to the android. "You don't understand, Poe. I already have."

He had set off again when a rather odd thing happened. The images pouring into his eyes smeared, like the photograph produced by a camera with its shutter left open for a couple of seconds. The world became one splotch of light and color.

To snap his vision back to normal, Caffrey tried to rub his eyes, but he couldn't feel his hands. In fact, the more he tried to settle himself, the more unsettled his body and mind became. Like a sudden panic attack, it snowballed. His heart palpitated, his face became beaded with cold sweat and his legs seemed to turn into tapioca pudding. Yin dropped to the ground as he tried to snap back to reality.

"Quark Caffrey?" Poe 33 asked with concern.

"Caffrey Quark," a voice, perhaps in his head, echoed through the wash of color. "It's all in the song."

The universe melted away like a box of crayons on the surface of the sun.

✈

Caffrey thought his eyes were open. The bright sunlight was warming his face. He shielded his eyelids with his palm and stretched with long and twisty motions. Finally, after a medley of goofy expressions, he really managed to open his eyes.

He was under the covers of his own bed. He was confused—and understandably so. There wasn't that familiar pounding at his temples nor the mouth full of sandpaper and cotton that would have accompanied a prior night of one too many. He had consumed nothing more than a liter of water and a cold glass of lime and quinine before the gig.

"Get up, Caffrey, we have to talk," insisted a calm but authoritarian voice.

Caffrey opened his eyes again and shot glances around the room. He was alone except for Yin sitting calmly at the foot of the bed, staring back.

"Did you hear that, Yin, or is your old master losing it?"

"I heard it because I said it. Now, please, Caffrey, I understand this is a bit unexpected, but we really do have to talk," Yin explained as he jumped off the bed and trotted out of the room.

The world, for the second time in twenty-four hours, went black for Caffrey.

✈

Caffrey sipped his coffee and stared at Yin, who sat patiently on the sofa.

"You feeling okay?" Yin asked.

Caffrey could only stare in disbelief.

"Come on!" Yin said with a chuckle. "Would you rather I just roll over and let you rub my tum-tum?"

"That's behavior more appropriate for a Westie."

"Actually, Caffrey, I'm not a West Highland terrier. I only look rather curiously like one. I'm a Frezenese Bopple. Although canine in appearance and temperament, we are of the genus *Boplicanus*."

"What's a Bopple from Frezenia doing on Earth circa these days?"

"What's a human who won't officially be born for another thirteen centuries doing living in a dive in the latter twentieth century?"

"My choice where I retire." Caffrey was getting irritated.

"Touché. And it was OTHER's choice to send me here to keep an eye on you until the Portsmith arrived."

"Other?"

"Order To Harmonize Eternal Reality." Yin winked.

"But you're my bloody dog!"

"I am also a high-degree initiate in an exclusive society, who cares about the very essence of the galaxy," Yin replied loftily. "But don't worry. I'm still your poochie-woochie wee potato."

Caffrey blushed. He stood up and paced, trying desperately to produce a mental movie of what had transpired the previous night. He was only able to envision a series of under-developed slides.

"What happened?"

"Beats the poop out of me," Yin confessed. "You went into a sudden trance and wandered off. Poe Thirty-three and I panicked. He took off, and I followed you home. You simply made yourself quite cozy under the covers. Slept soundly all night. I think the L'Orange may have attempted contact."

"Bullshit! Somebody slipped something into my tonic."

Yin seemed to smile but didn't push the issue.

Something was glinting under the rainbow of the refracted sunlight pouring in through the blinds. A small crystalline tube sat on the end table. Caffrey took it between his fingers and studied it. He'd seen it somewhere before but was too confused to pin down the memory.

Yin sniffed the tube disinterestedly. "That was left behind by Poe. Appears to be an electrical circuit of some sort. That android has some serious electronics issues."

"Yeah." Caffrey rubbed his aching temples as Yin trotted off into the living room. He followed and watched as the Bopple jumped up beside the Victrola.

"I'm going to contact central command and inform them that alpha phase is complete," Yin announced as he stuck his head into the brass horn.

Caffrey's mouth dropped open in stunned disbelief.

"You installed bloody communications gear in my Victrola? Do you realize how valuable that thing is? What the hell else have you had your fuzzy paws in that I don't know of? A homing device in the coffeemaker perhaps?"

"Don't be ludicrous," reproved Yin. "Things will begin to pick up soon. You'd better put a polish to your wings—you'll be hitting the wild black infinity quite soon."

Yin's mumbling reverberated from the horn. The Westie look-alike then jumped from the ledge.

"I'll be making plans if you need me," Yin advised, dashing under the sofa.

Caffrey shook his head incredulously. "And I always thought the little bugger was shagging his stuffed poodle under there."

Caffrey sat at the upstairs bar of the Crimson Court Pub. Sam played air guitar along with the bootleg Led Zeppelin recording that blasted from the jukebox as band-mates Dave and Al played darts. Russ was bar-tending, as he did every Tuesday and Thursday afternoon. Caffrey was staring at the little crystal tube spinning on the smooth wooden bar like a top. As it slowed down he gave it another flick with his finger and watched it spin again, tossing sparks of colored light. He softly sang along with Robert Plant and daydreamingly recalled the first time he'd heard Jimmy Page's work aboard the *Moby Dick*. He inhaled the music and let it linger in his soul.

It was all an amazing circle. Caffrey looked across at the colorful plastic, wood-and-metal Groovy Tunes jukebox, filled with the brand new collection of singles. What twisted act of tomfoolery had the cosmos planned that would result in that very collection of Rock music drifting through the galaxy for hundreds of years?

He took a slug of beer as his mind drifted out the front window. His stomach did a little back flip. Standing across the street in a darkened doorway stood a tall and alluring figure. She was dressed from head to toe in leather and held a black briefcase. Her hair was like a sunless void and Caffrey's amazing "hot chick memory" instantly recalled his failed flirtatious attempt with this same black-haired beauty at the meat auction.

The glow of purple from her eye sockets, only partially shielded by her sunglasses, was quite apparent. Caffrey turned away and whispered to Sam, "Do me a favor, pal. There's a certain lovely I'm trying to avoid. I think she's gonna stop by and make nasty accusations. I'm sneaking out the back. If she asks for me, tell her I was disintegrated by the breath of a giant zweek."

Sam, used to the colorful rantings of Caffrey, gave him a "whatever the hell you just said, but okay" wave of his hand. Caffrey smiled in appreciation and headed toward the rear exit as Sam began playing with the little crystal cylinder he had left behind.

Caffrey peered around the corner as the purple-eyed woman walked across the cobblestones to the echo of dominating boot heels. She stopped at the front door of the Crimson Court Pub, casually placed the case on the ground and opened the door.

Caffrey took a few concerned steps towards her. She bent down and pressed a button. A series of deep indigo blasts flashed into the pub. There were corresponding flashes from within, and then all the blue lights vanished, leaving the briefcase sitting on the sidewalk like a spoiled brat satisfied at having gotten its own way. Caffrey rushed over.

"Too late, Quark," gloated the purple-eyed woman with a cockiness that made it clear she had known she was being watched the entire time.

Caffrey ran into the pub screaming for his mates, the panic in his voice building exponentially with each cry. They were gone. All that remained was an overturned pint of Guinness dripping huge, tear-like and rhythmic drops from the bar top. The jukebox was nowhere to be seen nor were various stools, bottles and glasses.

The woman followed him into the room, and he rounded on her, quivering with rage and anguish.

"What the hell did you do?"

"Relax, Quark. They're relatively safe."

"That's a relative term."

She tapped the box. "This is a holo-genetic scanner and transmitter. Your friends have been recorded as the four-dimensional frequencies that make up their being. Without all that unnecessary space between their atoms," she added. "With proper compression

45

the universe could fit on the head of a pin. There's a lot of space out there."

"Thus the name, I would imagine. They were going to call it 'the really big expanse with all the stars and stuff,' but it didn't have the same elegance."

She smiled and lured Caffrey back outside with an oh-so-hot shimmy. She pointed skyward. "You see that ship up there? Of course, you don't—it's the middle of the day. But trust me, Quark, it's there. It's where your friends will be kept." She smiled, pushed another button and a single beam of light pulsed into the heavens. "They'll remain there until we've concluded with our need of you."

Caffrey felt his face turn red with anger.

"Bloody wench!" he seethed, knowing good and well it was a rather lame and corny retort. He was, however, so sincerely mad it was all he could conjure up at a moment's notice.

"When you decide to help me you can inform the Portsmith. I'm keeping a close watch on him. We will get the L'Orange. It'll be used to rework this horrid, music-drenched galaxy. Then a new era of disharmony and non-lyricism will befall reality."

"Bite me!"

"I don't think my teethmarks would help. And please remove any thoughts of killing me from your primitive mind. Remember, the fate of your friends is in my hands."

She walked off. Caffrey, unsure of his next move, stood motionless, following her down the street with his eyes, trying to ignore her luscious ass.

Caffrey entered his building. He was angry, frustrated. He wanted to grab Yin by his furry neck and force him to explain the utter silliness that had entered his life. His violent thoughts were cut short by the blue-and-orange figure that awaited him in the front hall.

"Hi, Quark Caffrey."

"Fancy running into you here."

"It is exactly where I expected to find you."

"Why is that?"

Poe 33's voice warbled and buzzed; then his face fell dead. After a moment, he flickered back to life.

"Are you ready to join me on my quest, Quark Caffrey?"

"What the hell is wrong with you?"

"I continue to experience brief moments of confusion and panic. I believe it may be related to a part I mistakenly discarded."

Caffrey recalled the little crystal tube and privately panicked himself, remembering he had left it on the bar.

"I have discarded numerous parts in an attempt to remedy the problem. My self-diagnostics have found nothing."

"That doesn't seem to make sense. I don't yank out my intestines when I get gas."

"It would seem, admittedly, a rather moronic thing for such a brilliant android as myself to do. But I have not been myself of late, Quark Caffrey," mourned Poe 33, an appropriate music track softly backing his words.

Caffrey couldn't help but smile at the eccentric robot.

"Will you join me on my quest?" pursued the android.

Caffrey shook his head in the negative, and then his expression changed. He cocked his ears as a definite look of concern filled his eyes.

"Trouble?" asked Poe 33, noting Caffrey's curious expression.

"No. Not at all," Caffrey lied, and trotted up the steps.

The android followed him. On the third floor a soft burst of static sounded.

"My scanners detect a source hovering just above your head," noted Poe 33.

The poofs and pops of static continued. A voice formed from the random noise. A silky and very familiar voice.

"Hello, Caffrey, my love."

"Angie?"

"Of course." She had definite prickly spikes riding the waves of her voice.

"Where are you?"

"That must have been some exotic pack of cigarettes you went out for, you bastard!"

"Bastard? You sound perturbed." Caffrey exhibited his concern. "Where are you?"

"There is a Revenant sphere[5] five microns in diameter a meter from your nose," Poe 33 explained.

"Yes," Angie explained assertively, "I finally got out of the kitchen."

---

[5] A microscopic, fully maneuverable electronic brain of sorts that allows a previously fixed computer system completely free rein. Can be fitted with audio vocalization systems, energy shields, holographic projection units, etc.

47

She was obviously ticked big time. Caffrey had always feared that the great random number generator in the sky would eventually set their paths on a collision course. He decided caution was appropriate.

"Angie, what are you doing here?"

"I was in the neighborhood. Plooky had a job on Sesilby Four. A couple of dead Upas needed frozen transport to Yistola for a family funeral. And since we were a few light-years from this dump of a planet I figured 'What the hell?'"

"Who's Plooky?"

"You've met him. He's the captain of the *Moby Dick*. And my heart," Angie moaned, adding a sensual sigh for effect.

"Where's my ship?"

"Correction, Caffrey. Plooky and Xilpat's ship. And it's not the *Moby Dick* anymore. She was rechristened *Spudlump*," Angie explained with an audible pout.

"*Spudlump*?"

Caffrey marched up to the fourth floor. He stopped for a moment outside his door and cocked an ear. He hadn't mentioned it to Poe 33, but the curious lack of barking from Yin had worried him when he first entered the building. There was, of course, the possibility the little pooch had gone to Radio Shack for parts, but Caffrey's gut twitched just the same. He opened the door and stepped into the darkened apartment.

"Yin? Yin, boy—you home?"

Caffrey flicked on the lights and found himself staring at the triple barrels of a pair of chrome-and-mother-of-pearl Sunpopper X-20s. The weapons were in the hairy paws of Plooky and Xilpat, the pair of Crebbledogs he'd last set eyes on eight years ago at the closing of the *Moby Dick* deal.

He privately noted they still smelled of mothballs.

"Sit down, Caffreysss," Xilpat instructed with the usual Marweegian lisp. "You, too, Robotsss."

"Yes," Angie insisted, "have seats, my loves."

"Angie, I shall never forgive you." Caffrey cursed and took a seat on the sofa with Poe. "I thought we left each other on quite good terms? Why the hostile return?"

"Hostile?" Xilpat seemed hurt. "Why, Caffreysss, we are only here to ask a favor."

A-ha.

"We are on a journey. A quessst grander than the Uldafter Fomaster," Xilpat drooled.

Plooky took over the explanation. "And we need your expertise to guide usss. Ssssomeone to map out the twistssss and dark corners of this huge but confusssing galaxy."

"What, as if I need to ask, is the purpose of this quest?" Caffrey asked witheringly.

"We seek the Blobuska. We have heard rumors that the Portsmith has been separated from his special cargo. Isn't that right, Mr. Android?"

"If I may say so," agreed Poe with a sigh of sadness, "you are damned right."

"Our ship is atop thisss building. We are leaving. Now."

"We would need to pack," Poe 33 stalled, giving Caffrey a warning glare.

"Of course," Caffrey agreed.

"We can stop at Bremure for suppliesss. We have no time!" Plooky barked.

"Actually, my furry loves," Angie chimed in, "Humans—even artificial ones—are not as adaptable nor as rugged as Crebbledogs. Let's allow the whining pansiebears to pack some of their cherished nonessentials."

The two Crebbledogs were panting as Angie's tickle stroked all the right zones.

"Fine," Plooky moaned, "but hurry!"

"I'll keep an eye on them, my be-coated dream muffins."

Caffrey rose to his feet, and Poe 33 started to follow but found the Sunpopper X-20 in his way.

"I'm fine, Poe. I can pack alone."

Caffrey headed into his bedroom; and Xilpat followed, remaining in the doorway between the two rooms. Poe 33 sat back down and began whistling a soft tune.

"Ssstop whistling, Robotsss!"

"If you don't mind, I would prefer to continue. Keeps my circuits running with more blissful waveforms," Poe 33 pleaded, picking up his tune where he had been interrupted.

"It rubsss my waveforms the wrong way. Ssstop or I will fry the circuitsss in yer belly like a grilled cherinka muffin."

Poe's whistling did not merely continue; the pitch increased tenfold and the volume twenty. Xilpat and Plooky reacted with deadly gazes, accented by deep-throated growls and dripping drool from the tips of their upper fangs. Another sound, set to the proper pitch and decibel settings to most annoy a pair of Crebbledog ears, shrieked from Poe 33's mouth. Xilpat and Plooky reacted in unison, dropping their weapons and throwing their paws to their much-offended organs.

From beneath the sofa Yin dashed, the little pooch privy to the android's plan from the coded message of Poe 33's innocent whistling. In his mouth was Caffrey's Willy. The loyal Bopple charged under Xilpat's legs and into the bedroom.

However, Crebbledogs are not known for lack of dexterity. Before Caffrey was able to take hold of the blaster, Xilpat and Plooky were already re-armed and diving behind the sofa for cover. Caffrey fired a strand of purple string, impacting a sofa pillow that vanished from existence—as tended to happen when the weapon was set for BV (Bon Voyage) mode.

"The roof! The roof, Yin!" he shouted.

Yin yipped and vaulted for the window, scrambling over the flowerpots, out and up the fire escape. Xilpat went after him. Poe 33 and Caffrey ran out the front door.

Caffrey fired a shot up the staircase, sending a chunk of the banister into another place in space and time[6]. Plooky dove to the ground and returned a rebuttal shot between his legs that did nothing more than add a simmering hole to an already cracked and filthy wall.

The light switch on the wall beside the blaster hole made Caffrey smile. His hunter instincts, married with his vast knowledge of Milky Way fauna, gave birth to a simple but rather brilliant idea.

Nomenclature aside, Crebbledogs were not of the canine genus but were, in fact, part of a line known as Seplichens. Cursed with extremely photosensitive eyes, the group included the pomifish, Delkinods and the giant and deadly Babrical squirrel. Caffrey rapidly entered a sequence of numbers on the grip of his weapon, and its glow changed from soft red to a deep, almost black, purple. He raised the weapon in his right hand and let his left drift toward the light switch.

"You're cornered, Quark!" Plooky yelled

---

[6] Caffrey would never know, but the banister appeared on the altar during the sacrifice ritual of the Emperor of Uglath 2. Taken as an omen of divine displeasure, it led the ruling council to spare the emperor's life. He went on to rule the world for three hundred years of peace and prosperity.

Caffrey pulled the trigger and night fell—literally. A shroud of anti-photonic matter (APM) rendered any and all photons dancing about the immediate area nothing but ashes of coal dust. The Crebbledog grunted in confusion, firing his weapon. Not even the high-current bolt could ignite a flicker of light amidst the powerful APM.

"I'm blind!" wailed the Crebbledog.

"Not yet, mutt!"

The black shroud began to dissipate, and the darkness receded. Caffrey flicked the switch, turning on the emergency halogen light at the top of the landing.

The Crebbledog dropped his weapon and yelped helplessly, throwing his paws over his stunned eyes. Caffrey jumped up and reset his weapon as he climbed the steps. A purple spaghetti strand was fired, and Plooky vanished from the current reality on a free trip into the random mix of fate's fickle stew of infinite universal choices.

The smell of burning metal drifted to Caffrey's nostrils. Poe 33 had melted the entire lock, along with the surrounding metal of the roof exit door. A rush of air blew through the resulting hole. It was oddly quiet outside.

"Shall I open the door?" whispered Poe 33.

"In a second," Caffrey instructed, kneeling down and peering through the hole. The sight of the *Moby Dick* waiting patiently outside sent a chill up his back.

"It's too quiet out there. Something's up. Can you sense anything, Poe?"

"Shall I perform a stealth scan on the surface area of the roof?"

"No, Poe. Why don't you perform the role of the Clown in Act Three of *Twelfth Night*?" Caffrey spat, growing disgusted by the android's questioning of the obvious.

"'No such matter, sir. I do live by the church; for I do live at my house, and my house doth stand by the church,'" Poe recited.

Caffrey stared at him for a moment in silence, uncomprehending.

"Will you perform the role of Viola? If so, it is your cue," suggested Poe.

Caffrey slapped the android's shoulder.

"Scan the frigging roof!"

"Of course."

A beam of barely visible white light shot from the midsection of

51

the android and through the hole in the door. It made a circular motion and just as quickly disappeared.

"And?" Caffrey was growing antsy.

"Shall I present the roof's contents in any particular order? Alphabetically, by size or by level of danger?"

Caffrey rubbed his temples and was about to slug the android when a burst of static popped at his ears.

"Your dog is hiding in the landing peg well. Starboard aft," Angie advised.

Caffrey scowled then looked to Poe 33 for confirmation.

"Yin is where the Revenant explained. Starboard aft landing peg well. The Crebbledog is hiding behind a large skylight."

Caffrey nodded and kicked the door open. The echo of the action dissipated, and all went silent again.

"Poe, I need you to use that whistling sound again. Distract the mutt so I—"

"Don't waste your time. He's not that stupid. He's wearing earplugs."

"You deserting to the enemy, Angie-girl?"

"Just don't want to make it too easy for Xilpy. He enjoys a challenge, and I love it when he wins. He gets soooo sexy."

"Poe, remind me to barf when we board the ship."

"Yes, sir. Duly noted. I have a superior idea, Quark Caffrey. Just run to the craft after exactly eight-point-three-two-five seconds."

Caffrey readied himself, unsure what was coming in the very short time he had to act. Poe 33 began whistling a series of high-pitched musical notes as a beam of barely-visible blue light shot through the doorway and into the craft via the windshield.

"You have two-point-six-four-three-four seconds left, Quarky," Angie reported.

"I'm counting," snapped Caffrey.

The designated time elapsed, and Poe 33 let out a whistle. Yin yipped, and an explosion of psychedelic neon spilled onto the roof like water from a busted dam. A horrid growl sounded.

Caffrey couldn't believe his eyes. The entire starboard side of the craft was aglow with a huge neon sign that read Spudlump Interstellar Funeral and Corpse Transport.

"Run, Caffrey!" Angie yelled, with a sincere note of concern.

Caffrey ran to the ship as its front port slid open, almost running over Yin in the process. They both managed to make it up the walkway and into the craft. Poe 33 followed as Xilpat lay sprawled on the roof covering his eyes. The port slid closed.

Caffrey stared at the ship's interior with his mouth agape. The place was a mess. Empty food containers, shed fur and scattered piles of dried Crebbledog poop decorated the once-sparkling interior.

"Mother of my mother's mother," he moaned, aghast.

"No time, Caffrey! We can tidy later!" Yin barked with authority.

"Not yet, Yin. I have to clean up the roof first." Caffrey turned and opened the port again.

"Caffrey, please!" Angie pleaded.

"Sorry, girl. Your boyfriend is getting flushed down the cosmic toilet!"

Caffrey was livid, to say the least. Having prided himself on being an unabashed pacifist, he felt the ugly feelings of excessive pride and vengefulness poisoning his veins like moonshine. He checked Willy's power level and stepped out.

Xilpat was back on his feet but still covering his sensitive eyes from the glare of the *Moby Dick*'s advert. Caffrey raised the weapon and set up a very clear shot. Too clear. Too easy. Too obviously against every tenet of his morality.

He was about to turn and race back to the craft when a bolt of orange energy whizzed past his head and struck Xilpat. The confused Crebbledog dissolved into a whirlpool of particles and was gone. Caffrey turned to see Yin holding a small smoking weapon in the entryway of the *Moby Dick*.

"Are you done wasting time, my master?" Yin scowled. "Let's get out of here!"

They raced back into the craft.

"Shall I take the controls, my love?" Angie asked.

"Pardon me, but who sold out who?" Caffrey snapped.

"Relax, Quark Caffrey, she is trustworthy," Yin assured him.

Caffrey chuckled cynically.

"Oh, Caffrey, my love. Do you really think I would ever do anything to hurt you? I was playing along with those two filthy, disgusting creatures. I was the one who suckered them into coming to get you. I met Poe Thirty-three on Uglipore where he was searching for you. I overheard his conversation and his need to find the bloodline of Greppledick Quark."

"She speaks the truth, Quark," Poe 33 confirmed. "Although my extraordinary sensory abilities would have inevitably found you, Angie did lessen the time factor."

A wave of tingling audio waves rode up his leg. He fought his own smile.

"Despite the fact you sold me like some six-legged Yeplicorean whore, I will always love you."

"You were programmed to."

"Exactly. The only thing better than unconditional love is hard-wired love."

"Let's hit the heavens."

The *Moby Dick*'s engine revved, and the craft lifted off the roof, vanishing quickly beyond the heavy clouds.

CHAPTER 6
2,000 Light Years from Home

(The Rolling Stones)

THE EARTH WAS A GLOWING BALL OF MILK AND BLUEBERRY cream as Caffrey watched her spin, rotating for perhaps the 1.8 trillionth time since her birth. Day was dawning over Europe and a wicked thunderstorm flashed over the Atlantic.

"Co-ordinates set for Bremure," Angie announced. "We can get the ship cleaned."

"Quark Caffrey," Poe 33 called as he approached, "is now a good time?"

Caffrey eyed the android obliquely. "For...?"

"For you to regurgitate your stomach contents. You asked me to remind you once we boarded the craft."

Caffrey smiled and gave Poe a pat to his shoulder. He looked at the Earth dancing her eternal dance with her lunar partner in the brilliant spotlight of the sun.

"I apologize for calling her a dump, Caffrey," said Angie softly. "She is a beauty."

"Yes, Angie. She and the creatures that scamper over her are everything beautiful, everything ugly and everything in between," Caffrey agreed, his face growing sad. "And four of my favorites are no longer there."

Poe 33 spoke up. "We will find your mates. I am sure they are safe. Much more importantly, we must find my Master, or you will find yourself in a universe that doesn't quite appreciate your music."

"I wish I understood my role in this little soap opera."

"I don't fully understand, either. But it is awful. I've seen a dozen worlds just vanish from existence because the lifeforms practiced some sort of musical love."

"We don't believe they've actually vanished for good," Yin interjected. "We believe the leader of ODOR, a horrid creature named Nefarious Wretch, is snatching the worlds into his dimension, where they will be recreated music-free."

Caffrey rolled his eyes. "Nefarious Wretch?"

"Lame, isn't it? But what else can you expect from a being for whom music is the source of his infinite anger and disgust?" Yin did little to mask his contempt.

"He is the perfected heirophant of disharmony," Poe 33 added.

Caffrey plopped down on the plush sofa, matted with Crebbledog fur, and closed his eyes.

"Angie, Bezzie, please."

"I'm sorry, my dimple cream. Plooky and Xilpat despised Bezzie. They've loaded the refreshment tanks with Xzrog. But I have good news. I managed to upload the entire history of Rock and Roll music into the database!"

"Angie, I love you. Pink Floyd. And a glass of Xzrog."

"But you despise Xzrog!"

"I despise the current state of my brain. I need it altered. Quickly."

Caffrey was disgusted with the fur and feces that surrounded him and tried desperately to ignore it. As the first track of *Dark Side of the Moon* began, a glass of the murky gray liquid appeared before him. He took a slug and his eyes bugged as the mushroom cloud erupted deep within his brain. A wide and goofy expression lifted his head to his neck's full extension. He chuckled.

"Well, he'll be useless for the next five hours," Yin noted.

"I'm fine, my silly little talking poochie-woochie," Caffrey promised with another giggle. "Wake me up when we land."

"Yes, my fruity soap," Angie sighed.

Bremure was one of the busiest stops for interstellar cargo craft in the Sol System. It fell into Galixerate legal problems when the Ignorance-Is-Bliss laws became an issue with the start of the space programs of the original planet Earth. Lest it be discovered too soon by the burgeoning but restricted intellects of the watery, type-O world, most of its facilities were moved to Pluto's moon, Charon, to avoid discovery.

A labor problem between management and a group of workers from the Sirius System world of Trenspit (known as Grays) erupted. The Grays threatened to reveal the base to the residents of Earth by buzzing isolated areas of the planet in small craft as a protest against poor working conditions. It took the death of three Grays, whose craft crashed in a remote desert town called Roswell, to force a settlement. The labor war was over, but the UFO craze was set in motion on post-World War II Earth.

The *Moby Dick* received clearance to land after Angie convinced the control tower that they were a meteorological team on their way to Planet Blooth[7]. Caffrey, who slept through the entire landing, was finally awakened by Yin, who jumped onto his master's lap and proceeded to lick his face. Caffrey smiled and slowly opened his eyes, grabbing Yin by the scruff on each side of his face and kissing his nose.

"Thank you, Quark. But can we commence with the lovemaking later? We really should spend as little time dawdling as possible."

The smile of contentment fell from Caffrey's face. It had been a real blow to some sector of the Oedipal portion of his psyche when Yin revealed his ability to speak. Trying to control the flush of blood racing up his neck, he stood and made his way out of the ship. Poe 33 and Yin followed.

Three hours had passed; and the *Moby Dick* was once again sparkling, as if just out of the showroom. Yin, who was bathed, blow-dried and fluffed, look twice his normal size as he read and reread a series of coordinates on the navigation screens. Poe 33, having activated his self-cleaning system, gleamed like a psychedelic star field under the colorful interior lights.

Angie, who had no form to primp, floated around the cabin like a bored breeze blowing through a meadow on a lazy summer day.

Caffrey entered the craft and loaded the last carton of Polyvegicaroni—a staple of interstellar travel, it can be formed into an endless

_____

[7] Famous for its wild weather, the lyrics "When it rains it snows and the sun burns bright. When the lightning thunders and outshines the light. And when the soft breeze blows a tornado of snow, it must be Blooth on which you live, you know" sum up life on the odd world.

array of relatively tasty food forms—into the FoodPrepper unit. The liquid tanks were also reloaded with fresh water and Bezzie.

"Caffrey," Yin said, reading off the monitor, "it appears the ship containing your band-mates was last tracked entering the Torikis System."

"Then that's we were going."

"As we planned. It's the same system where Regal Nine revolves. Where Poe Thirty-three and the L'Orange were last together."

Caffrey turned and queried the android. "You have no memory of what happened?"

Poe 33 appeared baffled by the question. "I have no clue what you mean." Once again, his illumination went dark. In seconds he came back to life.

"I had just finished the Uniting Ceremony. I was officially christened Portsmith of the Great Wise One by Queen Kinkskin," he recalled with his usual contemplative, alluring vocals. This time, a soft bossa nova beat underscored his story. "I had spent twenty years completing the Rendavene, the solo journey taken by every Portsmith prior to the Uniting. I traveled across the galaxy meditating, learning, infusing my circuits with sights. With sounds. Tastes. Smells. Feels. All the other sensory methods of the thousands of civilizations that live in the spinning disk you call the Milky Way. I learned their languages, customs, idiosyncrasies. I partook in grand games of skill. Fought in battles of unimaginable violence. Cared for the poor. Comforted the destitute. Made love to stunningly beautiful beings of every shape and size in ways your simple mind could never ponder."

Caffrey sucked his teeth but decided to not compare war stories with the android. "To Regal Nine it is. Set the way, Angie-girl. And let's hear The Who...something off *Quadrophenia*, if you would."

"Yes, my creamy pinball wizard," she sighed.

"I think we need to have that android's systems checked," Caffrey whispered to Yin.

The Frezenese Bopple agreed with a nod as the *Moby Dick* made its way back into space, and "I've Had Enough" filled the cockpit. Caffrey smiled and ran a slow, contented gaze around his craft. The stench of Crebbledog had been skillfully removed, and the fresh scent of a woodland meadow in spring wafted to his nostrils.

The *Moby Dick* was cruising at a comfortable clip, and Caffrey's feet were up as he played air drums along with Keith Moon. Yin disrupted his bliss.

"Ahhh...folks. What, pray tell, is that?"

A spiraling tube of blue energy wound its way from a singularity in space toward the *Moby Dick* at an alarming rate of speed.

"I'm afraid we won't be able to outrun it!" Angie warned, her voice colored with urgency.

"Some sort of wormhole, I suppose," suggested Caffrey.

Poe 33 enlarged on the issue. "A wormhole of the usual sort requires energy exceeding Planck levels. the *Moby Dick* is picking up only a mild static. No more than would be produced by rubbing a foot on a shag carpet."

Caffrey gave the android a curious glance as he tried to guess where in the endless light-years of adventuring the android would have come across shag carpeting.

Yin wanted more information. "What is this, if not some sort of black hole?"

"It is a mylaxic eel," Poe 33 explained.

"Never heard of them," Yin admitted.

"Me, neither," confessed Caffrey. "Angie-girl, you find anything in your zoological files on mylaxic eels?"

"Just a moment, my sweet leather volume. Yes. Found. 'Mylaxic eel: An extremely rare member of the species *Electrophorus electricus gigantus*, found only in comet-rich regions of the Plethorian Sector. Its unique digestive system links two distinct points in time and space, illustrating in astronomical grandeur the philosophy of never defecating where one resides.'"

"I could have told you that," Poe 33 mumbled, a little put out at being sidelined.

"So, I assume we'll be shat out to some unknown region of time and space?" postulated Caffrey.

Yin snickered his reply. "Sounds as such. Not a bad trait. Imagine, Quarky, taking me out for a poop on Fourth Street and having some poor guy in Renaissance Italy having to clean it up?" He snickered a little more.

"Any clue where this bloody worm's arsehole is?" Caffrey asked.

Poe 33 rejoined the discussion. "No. But mylaxic eel metabolism is very efficient. We will be expelled in moments."

The energy rings of the eel grew yellow, then orange and then deep red as the *Moby Dick* moved through the colorful digestive tract. The rumbling increased, and the windows fogged. Finally, with a cosmic fart, the ship was ejected from the crimson-ringed tube and back into space.

"Out of the arse and into the loo," Caffrey remarked as something caught his attention.

"We're back in the time period of your birth, my temporally twisted teekie-bird."

"And it would appear we are not alone," added Poe 33, more pragmatically.

Alone was, indeed, far from being their situation. A fleet of a dozen or so small, insect-like craft surrounded the *Moby Dick*, the pack darting and circling like gnats.

"Fly Craft," Yin announced with great disgust. "The fighter of choice for ODOR. Piloted by genetically produced bio-machine hybrids. Grown within the craft themselves, like cocoons, for the sole foul purpose of serving Nefarious."

Floating in the background like a green billiard ball was a medium-sized world shrouded in a quiltwork of white and azure clouds.

"Find out what planet that is, Angie," ordered Caffrey.

A voice sparked onto the ship's communications system.

"Please disengage any weapons systems, shields and/or other protective devices. You are surrounded and will be the guests of His Him. Please remind yourselves this is a great honor. Follow the convoy of security craft to the surface of Planet Opulent Lawns. You will be met by His Him's personal staff, who will escort you and your crew to his private residence."

"Guess that answers that question," murmured Caffrey. He took the controls and carefully followed the buzzing spacecraft to the surface of Planet Opulent Lawns.

CHAPTER 7
War Pigs

(Black Sabbath)

AFFREY LEARNED, WITH A LITTLE HELP FROM ANGIE AND THE G.S., that Planet Opulent Lawns was the private resort of galactic sector syndicate head and weapons magnate Quagmo Dagmo, the older brother of Quigmo Digmo. Opulent Lawns, originally called Planet Boomboom, began as a planned residential world for retired military types. It was purchased by Quagmo, who sent every retiree packing with a toothbrush, change of clothing and a swift kick in the behind. The planet was bulldozed, covered in fresh soil and seeded. It would become the largest private golf course in the Milky Way.

Quagmo, who ordained himself the ambiguous His Him, was lauded by planetary leaders, revolutionaries, corporate raiders, psychotic despots and crusading religious fanatics for his exhaustive catalogue of devices for the complete and perfect separation of living beings from their bodies.[8]

These were not devices for self-protection, the lovers of skeet shooting or exotic meat collecting. These were weapons of mass destruction with an emphasis on efficiency and entertainment. Should

---

[8] The Merrymaker Glee-grenade was one example. The powerful explosive device would preface its deadly blast by first performing various scenes of comedy, projected from its built-in 3-D imaging unit, often gathering a crowd of thousands of mirth-seeking desperates before blasting them to God's foyer.

you need to prove a point to an unruly population and have a chuckle to boot, there were a slew of wondrous and amusing ways to flex your muscle and still show the people you really were not the stick-in-the-mud they accused you of being.

A large structure marred the seamless expanse of green: His Him's mansion. Made from highly polished bricks of pure melvilite, it sparkled like a small star under the bright warm glow of the sun, Umba. Surrounding the home were numerous supplementary buildings, landing strips, hangars and storage warehouses.

The *Moby Dick* followed a pair of security craft as the rest of the convoy split up and went about their business. As they landed, a chartreuse limousine rolled alongside Caffrey's craft. A tall, lanky individual emerged. Humanoid, with bright yellow skin, the man was dressed in a powder-blue leisure suit and leather hip boots inlaid with a strange swirling pattern. At his sides hovered two short, squat soldiers adorned in sapphire shortie-pant jumpsuits and matching two-horsepower propeller beanies, giving them the appearance of fat man-children. They were armed with large, brightly colored plastic weapons that had translucent bulbs positioned along their lengths.

"Yin, be a simple dog until the plan changes. Angie, I need you to be our stealthy escort. The proverbial fly on the wall. Poe, it's you and me, baby."

The tall man called out to the *Moby Dick*. "You may exit your craft." His voice emerged from his body as if from an implanted megaphone. "Please exit with smiles and loose shoulders and be prepared to reply to our greetings with wit and charm."

"Hear that, Poe? Wit and charm," Caffrey said coyly, pushing the button to open the entry. the *Moby Dick*'s port slid open, and he stepped out, taken aback a bit by the cold blast of air that stung his face. He looked to the tall man and his boyish entourage and nodded.

"Welcome to Opulent Lawns," the tall man boomed with a smile. "I am Shleshinger Nine. I will escort you via foot to His Him's private dining chamber."

"May I ask why we've been detoured against our will? I was simply transporting this meteorological robot to Blooth along with his canine assistant," Caffrey asked with a forced smile.

"No! No! No! That's not proper protocol at all!" the man complained as his yellow skin turned orange from the blood rushing beneath it. "Wit! We must have wit! No objections. No questions. Simple wit to thank us for the privilege we are granting you so graciously."

"Wit," echoed the soldier to his left.

"Wit," agreed the one to his right.

Caffrey looked at Poe 33 and raised an eyebrow. The Portsmith stepped forward.

"Quite a lawn, Mr. Shleshinger Nine. I would hate to be the one who has to mow it."

Shleshinger 9 burst into a short guffaw that was swallowed almost as suddenly as it emerged from his mouth.

"Quite droll. But a sincere attempt, and it is appreciated."

Caffrey patted Poe 33 on the shoulder and smiled approvingly.

"Please, now. If you would? Follow me," Shleshinger 9 continued, turning on a dime.

They passed through a small side doorway into the first large hangar, and Caffrey found himself facing a corridor of seemingly infinite length. The polished stone walls, illuminated by pretty brass gas lamps, ran to a vanishing point.

"His Him's chamber is exactly two miles down this corridor. He prefers his guests to arrive hearts a-pounding and with a soft shimmer of perspiration alighting their rosy faces. So, if you would, keep up with my giddy gait."

The trio followed as instructed, and the collective sound of their feet echoed about them like teasing ghosts. The whine of Poe 33's servos created a rhythmic mantra Caffrey and Yin each used to set their own pace.

After twenty-five minutes a large stained glass door appeared at the end of the corridor. As they grew closer to the beautiful port, Caffrey recognized the Belkibonian-style artwork.

"Standard Belkibonian subtle design," he whispered.

"Ap-ap-ap! No speaking! Sixty more steps, and we will all come to a halt."

The group took the final steps, and the two soldiers floated around in perfect unison to face them. Caffrey, Poe 33 and Yin halted their march.

"Okay! We are halted. You are about to enter His Him's exalted chambers. There will be no frowns, moans, groans, wrinkled noses and or eyebrows. There will be no speaking unless spoken to and then only quick and witty responses allowed. You will keep all limbs loose and limber and, in the case of the small canine, loose and with only a slightly wagging tail. You will not, in the course of answering questions posed to you, ever use or infer the following words: *evil, death, crown, kill, monarch, candlestick, assassin, obese, nasty, flatulence, clogged, door mat, door nail, egg yolk, chain mail, divot, bogey, vanity*—either the noun or the adjective form. *Feces, urine, pigeon, yellow, anvil, clothespin, undies, panties, brassiere, jockstrap, nipples, Mandlebrot, chaos, fish paste, tapioca, water spout* and any word beginning with the letters x, q or zed."

"You get that, Poe?" Caffrey whispered.

"Why, of course! Would you like me to repeat the list?" Poe 33 asked, forgetting to whisper.

"Ap-ap-ap!"

Caffrey exhaled hard with impatience and was blasted by a stern look from Shleshinger 9.

"And there will be no exhaling of breath to illustrate boredom and or frustration! Time will be a commodity of which you are in vulgar excess. Time will be of no more pressing concern than the air you breathe."

Shleshinger 9 nodded, and the soldiers stepped forward, grabbed a respective knob each and slid the doors open. Shleshinger 9's voice rang out:

"Presenting the textbook example of toned, youthful exuberance; the enigmatic ruler of charm, wit and wondrous ways—His Him!"

Shleshinger 9 bowed and stepped out of the way. Caffrey and his friends entered.

The room was much smaller than Caffrey had imagined it would be. Not the grand ballroom he was visualizing as he marched down the corridor, the room was perhaps three times larger than his own living room back on East Fourth Street. It was charming, beautifully lit by the soft, warm light of Umba shining through the lemon-yellow glass windows. An elaborate but tasteful table of raspberry-colored hinkawood, a fine example of Belkibon craftsmanship, sat before them.

Standing at the far end of the table was a man no more than five-foot-two in height. He was dressed in a cranberry-colored cashmere cardigan, tan corduroy slacks and held a meerschaum pipe in his hand. From the pipe wafted a seamless chain of smoke rings. His figure was slim and his snow-white hair was neatly trimmed.

His Him nodded with a smile and the soldiers closed the doors, leaving the trio—and Angie—alone with the man.

"Sit. Sit. Please. Make yourself comfy," His Him suggested gracefully.

Caffrey was too confused to respond. He looked quickly at Poe, who was heading for a chair. When Yin sat on his haunches, Caffrey decided that he, too, should accept the offer. He sat his exhausted lower body on one of the cushy typical Belkibon chairs with obese female bodies forming the back and legs and caught his breath. His Him nodded approvingly.

"I can see by the sweat on your brow my assistant took you down the long route."

"Not a problem, sir," Caffrey replied, with a smile and loose shoulders. "I needed to walk off the Amberdesian noodles I made an absolute pig of myself with at lunch."

Caffrey privately panicked for a moment as he rethought each word he had just spoken. However, the smile that formed on His Him's face relaxed his stiffening shoulders.

"You could have simply entered right here," he explained, walking over to the door, opening it and revealing a sunny rear court, "I imagine he discussed all sorts of silly rules as well?"

Caffrey and Poe 33 nodded. Yin whimpered pathetically.

"He's mad. Simply mad. Don't pay any attention to him," His Him advised, closing the door and walking back to the table.

"I suppose you are wondering why my Bogie fetched you and brought you from the Sol System thirteen hundred years ago to the Umba System today?"

"Bogie?" Caffrey asked.

The old man's eyebrows wrinkled ever so slightly.

"My eelie-poo. My pride and joy. Raised him from a tiny little fry. He's very sweet. I said 'fetch,' and here you are!"

"If I may, sir? Why were we honored by your invitation?" Caffrey was good at faking conformity, a survival skill he'd mastered on his many adventures around various star systems where silly rules abounded.

"Quite simply, you are very special, Eagle Five."

"Sorry? My name is actually Caffrey—" Caffrey stopped himself as he felt the letter Q form in his mouth.

"I am well aware of your name. I don't like it. Therefore, you will be known as Eagle Five from now on. Likewise, the android will be Six Iron and the Bopple, Par Three."

Caffrey exchanged quick, nervous looks with Yin and Poe.

"'Relax and fear not my mind[9],'" quoted His Him. "I have a wonderful meal prepared for you, Eagle Five. Yespinese triple caps with mamoop butter and a side of perfectly crisped olivyspa rings. All balanced to perfection with a bottle of Grapzilania forty-three imported from the renowned vineyards of Jespoon."

A slot opened on the tabletop, and the steaming meal rose up upon a golden plate. Caffrey drooled as the essence of the exotic mushrooms wafted to his nostrils.

"My compliments, sir. These are magnificent examples of triple caps."

"And for the little furry one—a bowl of freshly-slaughtered sumpumpas with a delicate sauce of errymerry," Quagmo explained as the bowl appeared before Yin, rising up from the floor.

Yin's ears rose and his tail wagged a bit too energetically as he began scarfing down the nugget-sized marsupial meat. Caffrey cleared his throat, and Yin controlled his enthusiastic tail.

"As for myself and the android, we will enjoy your enjoyment. I only eat once per week. I find the body of the average Belkibon to be beyond vulgar."

"If I may, sir," Caffrey said, looking up from his plate, "I envy your trim and tone self. I would never have guessed you to be Belkibon."

"Don't overdo it, my sweet kiss-ass," Angie whispered softly into his ear.

"Thank you, Eagle Five. Finish your meal, and we will discuss the truth behind my invitation."

Caffrey and Yin each savored their meal as His Him sat in his rocker and closed his eyes for an apparent nap. Poe 33 turned his head and stared at the sleeping Belkibon for a moment. Suddenly, green light beamed from the android's eyes to scan the old Belkibon's motionless body. Caffrey shot a glare of utter disbelief at him.

"Poe, are you nuts?"

"Sir. There is no electrical energy emanating from his brain. Nor

---

[9] The famous last-known spoken words of Sarnok Blowell, the insane general who ordered his army of twenty thousand to attack their sun with daggers. All twenty thousand, encased in spacesuits designed for only temporary extra-vehicular jaunts, were burned to a quantum crisp; and the general whistled down the wind and was never seen again.

is his heart beating. Nor are his lungs engaged in the act of taking breath."

"What the hell are you talking about?"

"It would appear he is dead," Poe 33 deduced.

"Oh, my goodness," Angie gasped.

— *He can't be dead? Can he?* Yin wondered.

Caffrey was about to get up and take a closer look when His Him opened his eyes and smiled at the group.

"So. Enjoying your meal?"

Caffrey almost gagged but covered nicely.

"Yes. Yes. Wonderful meal. Very thoughtful of you."

"You're not very witty, are you?" the old man observed, his smile dissolving in the solvent of disappointment.

"This meal has rendered the wit centers of my brain bloodless, as all my bodily fluids have rushed to take part in the wondrous orgy in my contented belly," Caffrey managed to spout.

The Belkibon erupted in terrific guffaws that seemed implausible for the size of the petite man.

"Yes, Eagle Five, you are quite a card. My ace in the void of the universe."

His Him stood and snapped his fingers. The plates, food, wine and bowls all vanished whence they came. He turned to the wall opposite the entryway and snapped his fingers twice. A panel opened to reveal a large aquarium. Only one creature swam about in the sparkling water. It was a pink, spongy-looking organism that had a head similar to that of a hairless bat and a body like a plucked and scrubbed hen.

"This is a corgishma. Not any corgishma. She is the only example of a One corgishma," His Him effused, drooling.

"I'm sorry? A One?" Caffrey asked with some hesitation.

"Yes! Yes! A One corgishma! A specimen of a species that can trace its direct line to the first of its species."

"I believe he is referring to—" Poe 33 began.

His Him's voice changed, became authoritative, "I will explain it! The Ones, even countless generations later, contain the collective wisdom of their species blueprinted into their essence. This corgishma has within it the knowledge and experiences of every corgishma that has ever or will ever live. It is the direct descendent of the original reflection projected into reality from the L'Orange."

He stroked the glass, and the creature scurried to the rear corner of its home. His Him turned a curious eye to Caffrey.

"I have a veritable ark of these special creatures, insects, plants—even a large collection of gemstones. I even have a One blue-finned talking mymy whom I have trained to say 'cork, beans and flambé.'"

"Certainly three of my favorite words," Caffrey agreed.

"But you, Eagle Five! You may be my greatest find yet."

Find? Caffrey could only wonder.

"Eagle Five, I want us to become mates. Friends. Partners."

"I'm honored—but this android and his—"

"Yes. Blooth. I've heard." His Him smiled and looked at Poe. "The Portsmith to the Mighty Blood of Og."

"I'm sorry," confessed Poe 33. "I have not a clue what you mean."

His Him laughed loud and deep. "Very droll, Six Iron. Very droll!" The Belkibon's face turned oddly serene. "Eagle Five, you may well be a One Human. It has been whispered in special circles that your entire family bloodline is intrinsically blessed with the Milk of the Grand Teat. The very reason your uncle Greppledick was favored to build the Portsmith. Let us be good, hearty mates, for all eternity. I can give you that. Eternity. With you and the Portsmith at my disposal, I can acquire the penultimate treasure. The L'Orange!"

Caffrey gathered every ounce of restraint from every pore of his person and took a deep breath.

"Sir, His Him, I have no interest in your little hobby."

The old man closed his eyes, and his body went still again. The trio looked at each other questioningly.

What the hell? Caffrey wondered.

"It would appear he has died again," Poe 33 decided after scanning the Belkibon's body.

"He seems to have the same circuit problem as you do, Poe," Yin whispered.

"There is something putrid rotting in Denmark," mused Caffrey, cynically.

"Yes, my sweet Danish," Angie agreed, "Something is definitely souring the milk. I think this fly needs to investigate from a new wall."

"Do your thing, Angie-girl."

Just as abruptly as His Him had slipped into his strange death-like trance, the snow-white-haired Belkibon opened his eyes and was back amongst the living.

"I am offering you partnership in what will become the most powerful ruling sect of all the ODOR groups! Forget that poser

Spydersloth and his merry band of fervent rump huggers! My plan is simple greed! Galactic domination. With me, you know where you stand!"

Although Caffrey appreciated His Him's honesty, the despicable nature of the Belkibon's ambitions awoke his boat-rocker spirit. And His Him was a ship in desperate need of capsizing. Caffrey folded his arms and smirked. There was only one way to deal with him—push the buttons of his blood pressure.

"Panties," he said with perfect enunciation.

"Eagle Five!" His Him's response combined fear, loathing and anger.

"Jock-strap. Tap-i-o-ka. Can-dle-stick," taunted Caffrey, leaning forward assertively.

"Stop it!" demanded His Him as he jumped to his feet.

"Mandlebrot," Poe 33 said, deciding to toss his rebellious spirit into the ring.

"Fish paste," added Yin.

"I am His Him! How dare you challenge my rules!"

This time the voice echoed from someplace other than the small man's mouth. The room was vibrating, and small cracks were forming on the walls. The face of the man was suddenly blank and without the reddened flush.

"Jockstrap!" Caffrey repeated, pointing out the courtyard door to Poe 33 and Yin.

"You will join me or your friends are applesauce!" a voice from beyond the room threatened.

"The other side of the wall, Quarky!" Angie whispered.

"What?" Caffrey was confused.

"I don't quite have the vocabulary, my hardbound Webster."

"What is going on?" Poe 33 asked in a bewildered tone.

"Blast the courtyard door!" Caffrey instructed the android.

Poe 33 turned his upper body toward the rear courtyard door; but before he could aim, a solid steel slab dropped over it.

The rumbling grew more violent and a Zorro-like gash opened in the crumbling wall. Pink light poured from the crack, followed by thick, musty steam.

"It would appear he has thrice died," Poe commented, noticing the petite man was standing still as a mannequin.

"He's not dead, Poe. That's a marionaute," Angie gasped.

"I believe you are correct, Angie," Poe 33 agreed.

"A what?" Yin needed more information.

Poe 33 obliged the pseudocanine. "A marionaute is a personality slave—an individual lifeform which has had its brain removed and replaced by a remote-control animation unit and trans-vocalization system. Used by folks unhappy with their physical appearance and of that financial strata that allows for a lack of conscience."

"A gorgeous galaxy this is," Yin grumbled with a frown that grew suddenly tighter, "My nose is picking up major stinkage."

"Smells like old cheese rotting in a bowl of vinegar misted with the smoke from burning acetate," Caffrey concluded, demonstrating amazing olfactory accuracy.

Yin hopped onto the table and trotted over to the motionless marionaute, grabbed it by the belt, gave it a tug. The diminutive gent toppled over with a horrid thud as his snow-white head bashed off the table. The crumbling wall gave way and as the dust-cloud cleared, the truth of the man-behind-the-curtain became evident.

Now that is a Belkibon, Caffrey said to himself.

"Sit down! All of you!" Quagmo Dagmo ordered.

He was immense beyond vulgar Belkibonian grandeur. He sat in the largest Vibrundaspooner Caffrey had ever seen. The room beyond was clouded with horrid, putrid steam scented with body odor and fat cheese oils that were perhaps decades old.

"Angie, thank your maker you were created devoid of a nasal system," he whispered.

"He must be in the vicinity of two thousand kilos," estimated Yin sotto voce.

"He's in the vicinity of everything," Caffrey noted wryly.

"Very good, Eagle Five! Finally, a shimmer of wit!" Quagmo approved. "Enough of the feigned pleasantries and twinkleshite. My offer is now elevated to a threat. Either join me or rot in my menagerie forever."

"Would you allow me an hour or so to ponder this? In my ship, perhaps?"

The Belkibon grabbed a handful of creamed eechie pig from one of the six nearby vats and shoved the brown goo into his tremendous mouth as Caffrey posed the question.

"You are the personification of droll," Quagmo leered through the pasty pig. "A simple question requires a simple answer. 'Yes' or 'menagerie?'"

Caffrey smiled and gave his reply.

"Bite my nipples!"

The rage that spawned on Quagmo's face was only less horrific than the rising of his massive body from the tub of goop. Snapping, rubbery sounds insulted Caffrey's ears as impossible layers of rolling fat emerged like a school of whales.

"Soldiers! Render these plebes to the menagerie!"

Immediately, a dozen man-child soldiers appeared from invisible doorways sliding open around the room. Brandishing the colorful bubble-chamber weapons, they helicoptered in beneath their powerful prop beanies and surrounded the table. Caffrey and Yin exchanged looks of surrender, while Poe 33 appeared to sigh.

It was rather cozy, as zoos go. They were in an empty section of a row of a dozen cells, each a rather generous ten-by-ten-meter square, which were undoubtedly the result of a Belkibonian concept of uncramped design. The walls and floor were finished in a rather pretty salmon-and-gray marble.

Caffrey sat on the hefferbill-leather sofa and gazed at the blue crystal bars keeping him from freedom.

"For a species of fat, disgusting creatures they do have an eye for design. Albeit, a bit garish," he noted as he examined the chorus line of corpulent nude Belkibonian women painted on the ceiling.

Poe 33 was scanning the atomic structure of the imprisoning material as Yin, poking his nose through the narrow space in the bars, sniffed the air for any clue that might aid them.

"Anything of interest in the air, Yin-boy?"

"Nothing but the faint odor of Belkibon sweat and toe cheese," the little dog reported.

"Poe?"

"These bars are pure norasithe. A type I have never seen. None of my lasers or particle cutters will make as much as a nick."

"Angie?"

There was no reply. After a moment Caffrey stood up and paced the perimeter of the cell.

"I've spent time in far worse prisons than this. And I've escaped from cells with much tighter security. We'll link our minds and figure a way out."

"I'm back my jailhouse rock-candy darling," Angie whispered, surprising him.

"Angie? Where were you?"

"Just doing a little stealthy scouting. I've mapped out the facility. There are dozens of cages, tanks and chambers with quite a collection of exotic fauna. I even found the talking mymy. Taught him a few of Quagmo's favorite words. Started with 'nipples.'"

Caffrey laughed; and Yin trotted over, stood up on his hind legs and pressed his muzzle to Caffrey's ear. "I think it's time for you to seek a few answers elsewhere. Remove my collar, please."

Caffrey threw an odd look to the dog and smirked coyly. "I do hope you're not suggesting I dabble in some kinky fetish? This is neither the time nor place."

"Don't be ludicrous. Just to remove it," Yin insisted, keeping his voice to a whisper.

Caffrey did as instructed and studied the little fluff-ball appraisingly. "This is the first time I've ever seen you naked."

It was quite true. Yin was wearing the collar the night Caffrey rescued him on that October evening in the West Village. Although there had been less than frequent baths through the years, Caffrey had always surrendered to defeat as Yin fought off any attempts to remove the old black-leather-and-silver-studded collar.

"Unscrew the third stud from the left. Carefully," Yin instructed, using his nose to sniff out any approaching busybodies.

Abruptly, Poe 33 let out a screeching, metallic cry and launched himself against the bars.

Caffrey eyed him warily. "What's wrong?"

"I haven't the foggiest of ideas," Poe 33 replied quite casually. "My fight or flight circuitry seems to be sending signals to my locomotion unit to get the hell out of here. Odd. I otherwise feel quite terrific!"

"Please, Poe, relax," Yin requested.

After a bit of difficulty, Caffrey removed the small hemisphere to reveal a little compartment within. Inside was a small, translucent orange disk. Caffrey rolled his eyes.

"Why does this bloody color make me cringe? I used to love orange. Such a joyous color. Filled with glee and childlike flamboyancy. Now it just makes me want to retch."

"An OTHER spy managed to swipe that sample from the private residence of another Belkibon, Quigmo Digmo."

Poe let out yet another cry for freedom and began climbing the bars in an attempt to find an exit.

"For Godsakes, Poe! Get down!" demanded Caffrey.

Poe 33 peered down sheepishly from atop the bars. His legs seemed to be trembling with fear.

"Once again, Quark Caffrey, I have not the haziest of clues. I seem to be having a bad reaction to that tiny sample of my Master's essence. Rather unexpected."

"It would seem Poe Thirty-three's circuitry has been rewired to reject the very thing he was programmed to protect," Yin concluded.

"Rewired? Impossible!" Poe 33 protested.

"Perhaps ideologically, Poe, but the reality seems to differ." Yin was certain. "Can you self-diagnose?"

"Of course. I have been self-diagnosing my systems from the moment of my lighting[10]."

"Then we will have to have you examined elsewhere. Perhaps the One can illuminate us? Partake of the L'Orange," Yin instructed with great reverence. "I want to confirm this. We need answers now."

"Confirm what?" Caffrey asked.

"That you are somehow connected intrinsically to L'Orange. That perhaps you are a One human."

"I thought the high and mighty L'Orange permeated everything? Aren't my cells just naturally overflowing with the mystic marmalade?" Caffrey asked.

"Overflowing is a bit of a hyperbole but, yes, Quarky, all of creation contains the essence of It—stored in hyper-dimensional folds of three-dimensional reality. Ideally, we all should be able to access its knowledge. This sample, however, is the only sample that exists in three dimensional space," Yin explained.

Poe 33, still hanging up atop the cell, qualified Yin's information.

"The only sample that exists in 3-D space aside from the original cube that was my charge. The pure, singular substance that is my master—lost in the vast—"

"We know, Poe," Yin interrupted. "If you, indeed, are a One Human, Quark, partaking of this sample should launch you into the ante-conscious realm of the collective wisdom."

Caffrey placed the disk carefully onto his palm. He shot Yin a doubtful stare. "How high of a dose is it?" He was a little concerned.

"Dose? Dose? This is the essence of the Universal Wisdom, not an acid trip! Besides, it's cut with a special edible gelatin that has kept it safe within the sometimes heated, sometimes frozen stud of my collar. The actual amount of L'Orange is microscopic. Mere atoms."

---

[10] An android term for birth.

"I now recall seeing this little orange snot dot before." Caffrey remained hesitant as he raised his palm to his lips.

"Caffrey, we may be running out of time. We need answers. We have no idea what our friend Quagmo has in store for us. You must test the waters of your destiny. Eat it."

Caffrey shrugged. It wouldn't be the first time he took a ride on the psychedelic choo-choo train. He closed his eyes, popped the disk into his mouth and stood motionless. He swallowed.

His eyes widened like a flung-open shade and filled with orange light.

CHAPTER 8
And You and I

(Yes)

CAFFREY SAW NOTHING. HOWEVER, THE NOTHING THAT HE WAS witness to was like no other nothing he had ever seen.

There had been instances in the colorful life experiences of Caffrey Trinesmart Quark II when he had seen very little. Nothing, true nothing, was another story entirely.

What surprised him most was the color of nothing. He had assumed—the origin of this assumption remains a mystery—that nothing would be a black-as-coal-at-midnight-sans-lights-cannot-see-hand-in-front-of-his-face-whilst-blindfolded sheath of ethereal pitch. In actuality, nothing was a lovely shade of teal with gold trim.

After he had admired the nothing for what seemed like days there came a break in the naught in the form of a distant silver ball. The silver ball rolled toward him, leaving behind a trail of rainbow trout, peahens and purple tapirs scattering off in every direction. The silver ball multiplied tenfold, each newborn sphere stretching and twisting into a chorus line of silver Crebbledog dancers. Like figures poured from liquid titanium, they began performing *The Rancid Queen of Byrum*, an ancient ballet Caffrey suddenly recalled seeing as a child.

From atop the dancer's heads sprang multitudes of indigo blooms, reindeer horns and several lost puppies, who gazed upon Caffrey as if expecting directions home.

"Odd," he muttered as he watched the spectacle continue to evolve.

The puppies folded themselves into ostrich-skin wallets, sprouted pigeon wings and clumps of chestnuts and flew away crying out "Pickaw! Senyip! Bartook!" and Caffrey smiled, recalling the story of "The Three Lost Dormice," a favorite tale told on cold winter nights when he was a lad.

"Very odd," he noted.

Memories, like clothing from a jilted lover's closet, were being tossed out by the armful.

"Not odd," argued a voice that slid across the landscape to his ears. "This is a mere pittance of the collected works that is Caffrey Quark."

"I'm a little baffled by the sequence."

"I'm simply trying to clear a place to reside for a moment."

"By rummaging through my brain?"

"I am not rummaging your brain. I am rummaging your mind. Two entirely different animals. Your brain is yours to keep. It will, however, rot once you pass on. Your mind you sublet from the consciousness of the Cosmos."

"Who are you?" Caffrey asked. "Your voice seems familiar to me."

"It is from the countless vocal memories you have stored in your mind. Whom you chose and why is for you to decide."

"Uncle Greppledick. I'm hearing my uncle's voice."

Caffrey tried to slap his own temple until he realized he had no body. No physical form to slap, kick or pinch back to the physical world.

Relax, he advised himself, trying to stay calm and confident. It'll wear off. Just ride it through. Don't panic!

"You're not tripping. Your mind has actually moved from your body to your consciousness."

"Uncle Greppledick, please. Shut up. You're freaking me out."

"I would imagine you chose your Uncle Greppledick's voice for a reason."

"I'm thinking a lot about him lately. I've been haunted by his egomaniac android."

"Do you like him?"

"Who?"

"Your uncle."

76

"Why are you speaking of yourself in the third person? For that matter, why am I speaking for you in the third person?"

Caffrey felt like he was on a Tilt-O-Whirl at Coney Island after too many beers and hotdogs at Nathans.

Relax. Just breathe and relax, he told himself.

"Relax, indeed, Caffrey Quark. I am not your uncle and you are not speaking for me."

"Then what? Where is this voice coming from?"

"You are doing something that every thing in the universe can do, yet very few attempt."

"What?"

"You have connected to the wisdom of the One. That's a capital O, by the way."

"One what?"

"The One." The voice rolled across the landscape as a colorful wave.

"Yin, are you playing with my head?"

"Yin is back in the zoo of Quagmo Dagmo with your unconscious body, Poe Thirty-three and the Revenant. I am what you like to call the L'Orange."

"I don't believe in the L'Orange."

"You don't even believe in your own current being?"

"My current being is on an amusement park ride at the moment."

"So, ride the wave. After all—it's all waves. All Music. All vibrations. Transcending upper dimensions of reality can be confusing to those not adept."

"I really don't need any added confusion. My boring, three-dimensional life supplies more than enough."

"I know it seems like you've been dropped amidst a field of a thousand dueling orchestras. Each musician playing a different song. But if you listen carefully, Caffrey, they're all in synch," the L'Orange philosophized.

"I only have an interest in being in synch with four musicians. My best friends have been kidnapped. I want them back. I want back."

"You will get back when you've been."

"Please. Stop trying to blow my mind with philosophical platitudes."

"You want your mind blown? Take a gander at this..."

Reality did something really, really odd. So bizarre it could never be expressed in words. It lasted a split second, as any longer would have killed Caffrey with an overdose of astonishment. It was an extra-value, super-duper giant-sized can of cosmic whip-ass.

"Now listen, Caffrey," continued L'Orange. "The good-natured but rather daft Portsmith needs you."

Caffrey couldn't speak for a long moment as he tried desperately to recover from the rapturous orgasm his mind had just experienced.

"Breathe..." advised the entity.

Caffrey finally managed to form words.

"My friends need me," he mouthed.

"Yes. And Poe 33, and Yin, and the galaxy itself."

"I am not volunteering to save reality! I want to go home, play our tunes and just be."

L'Orange was undaunted. "Admirable. But when the universe calls, you show up. Only you can reunite Poe Thirty-three with me. Only you can help Yin stop ODOR Only you can transmute Nefarious Wretch."

"Is that all?" Caffrey spat wryly.

"Yes. Only you can keep them from taking control of me."

"How?"

"I've already explained. I am the total wisdom. I know the possible outcomes. Not the outcome. I know the infinite paths. Not the direction you will take. The only prediction I can make is that you may end up as the Chief High Exalted Mystic Ruler of the universe or you may end up crushed to a pulp under the stinking behind of a Belkibon. There are infinite choices in between."

"One would hope so." A tiny sardonic spark was re-kindled in Caffrey's breast.

"Regardless of the outcome, you will play a role in my very future."

Practicality surfaced as Caffrey considered his position. "Can you at least tell me where you are?"

"You are not listening. I know all the possible places I can be."

"Perfect, I'll start looking there."

"Now you are getting it," the voice replied, with cryptic elegance.

"Suppose ODOR or that fat Belkibon did get their hands on you? What could they do? Have one big galactic trip-out? I wouldn't call this fun."

"Illumination rarely is. You see, Caffrey, the universe is divided into three basic types: Hoarders, Planners and Seekers. Quagmo

Dagmo and Quigmo Digmo hoard. They want me for no other reason than that they don't have me. ODOR is a group of Planners. In all honesty, OTHER is also a group of Planners. They plan, plan and plan for an event they will never be able to control. So, they plan some more. It is a defense mechanism. Those who can't control, plan. Seekers are few. Seekers seek."

"Seek what?"

"The ultimate truth of the universe. Deep down, they are dissatisfied with the universe and want it to reflect their own image. Frankly, every living creature in existence is a narcissistic bastard. You, my good man, are a Seeker."

"Me?" Caffrey was incredulous.

"You unconsciously put a ceiling on your ultimate goal. A typical expression of artists. Rather than remolding the universe, you think you would be happy in creating the perfect record album."

"I'd be in heaven!"

"But you can never create the perfect record album. If you touched a million beings with it you would wonder why it didn't touch ten million. If it touched an entire planet you would wonder why it didn't touch an entire galaxy. Ad infinitum. Eventually, if your creative endeavors were left to fester, you, too, would become a megalomaniac who wanted every living being in the entire universe to play the albums of Caffrey Quark."

"The end result of every wet dream I have ever had," Caffrey responded with a smirk that turned to a frown. "Why am I having this silly conversation with a figment of my imagination?"

The Voice laughed. "The ultimate end of every being is to be the Creator. It's evolution's natural destiny. When it happens, that Being will look in the mirror, see the Creator and want to wipe the slate clean."

"So, what am I supposed to do?"

"I haven't a clue specifically. I do, however, see a few billion possibilities. What I would suggest is that you seek the wisdom of what inspires you most—this music that has infused your life with light. There is a reason things gravitate towards certain attractors. They contain something the attractee needs. Something that is lacking in them. Something that will help make the attractee complete."

"So, I should simply continue listening to Rock and the galaxy will be saved? For that I had to have my life rudely interrupted?"

"Don't just listen. See the smells. Taste the sights. Smell the sounds. Touch the tastes. Stop perceiving the universe in such predictable ways."

"You've lost me," Caffrey confessed.

"You're listening to Hendrix—'Electric Ladyland,' 'Voodoo Chile.' What do you do?"

"Kill myself because I'll never in my sickest dream play like that," Caffrey retorted sarcastically.

"Negative. You smell the color of the notes. Or you taste the sound of the pick on the strings. Or listen to the scent of Jimi's sweaty brow," insisted the Wise One. "When you do, the universe will open to you in ways you never thought possible. Doors will lead to places not expected. Or places you desire."

"My desire is to get back to Yin, Angie and the android so I can escape, get back to my craft and find my friends."

"Good. A plan."

"I don't even know how I got here."

"You're special, Caffrey, but thick as a brick. You need proof? Fair enough. Think of this as yet another free sample."

Caffrey's nose twitched. Taking on a life of its own, his nose scanned the air around him like a rabbit in a breeze scented with both carrots and wolf breath.

"I hear—no, I smell the drone of the *Moby Dick*'s engines," he concluded.

"Good."

"Peculiar odor. I can smell the color of Poe thirty-three's body armor. How odd."

"Not odd. Odd is pushing open a door that says 'push.' Odd is only smelling a rose's perfume and not its shape and color."

Caffrey gagged and spit. "I taste the pads of Yin's feet."

"Like popcorn?" the L'Orange queried.

"Cheesy popcorn," Caffrey corrected.

The teal-and-gold nothing began to swirl and blend like the ingredients of a milkshake.

"We will cross paths again, Caffrey Quark. You will begin to learn. Be very careful, Caffrey, some of your possible paths are infested with danger. As special as you are, in the scheme of things you are very much replaceable. Tread with caution. And, remember, music has always been your source of strength. Use it. It is all a song..."

The voice faded, and Caffrey felt himself fall back like a locomotive thrown into reverse. The voice of the Wise One echoed through the resulting spiraling void. The spinning continued and accelerated until Caffrey became the spinning.

Then he could see the cell and Poe 33 and Yin—but he could also see alternate exits, folds in space-time that stood before him like garden paths. Caffrey guided them out of the cell by some deeply seated instinct—directly under the blind eyes of His Him and the many guards. Out and off they went, Caffrey seeing the blueness of the chilly air, smelling the excitement of escape and feeling the seething anger of Quagmo Dagmo. They moved toward the *Moby Dick*—into the craft, which rose up through more folds in the very fabric of the sky—through spiraling tubes in space. Then all was momentarily black.

Caffrey felt Yin's warm, wet tongue licking his face. Opening his eyes, he took a momentary gaze then almost jumped out of his skin.

He was aboard the *Moby Dick*.

"Welcome back, my rider of the rainbow chariot," Angie crooned.

"Where are we?" Caffrey asked, rushing to the viewport. The large green ball of Opulent Lawns floated before his eyes.

"Unexplainably, we have been transported from our prison cell to the *Moby Dick*. We have just left the friendly confines of Opulent Lawns' atmosphere," Yin explained.

"It happened in a blink," added Poe 33 in awe.

Caffrey squinted his eyes, trying to identify the swarm of bug-like craft screaming out of the ozone layer of the green world.

"What are those craft that seem to be heading our way?" his head was a mish-mash of fog and mud.

"Those are ODOR craft, heading, I would suppose, to kill us on orders of Quagmo," Poe 33 postulated.

"Kill us? Don't they like us?" Caffrey's mind was a mess.

"Actually, they despise the very space in which our atomic structures reside, and it would make them quite happy to regain that space for themselves," explained Poe 33, giving Yin a worried look.

The first energy pulse flashed by the *Moby Dick*.

"Caffrey, we are awaiting your orders," reported Yin calmly.

"Bezzie. Make it a double," Caffrey mumbled.

"Caffrey..." Yin hesitated, tapping his front paw nervously.

The *Moby Dick* twisted and lurched as a barrage of energy streaks illuminated the ship's interior like colorful flashbulbs.

"Everyone strap in!" Angie ordered. "I will put evasive action plan EV-thirty-two into effect. Yin, man the aft pulse laser station!"

"Aye, aye, girl. Good work!"

Poe 33 took a seat and strapped in. Caffrey closed his eyes and reached for his unserved drink. "Bezzie, Angie! Bezzie!" he groaned.

Yin jumped into the seat of the aft pulse station and, stretching his paws, grabbed hold of the controls. A trio of Bug Craft were zeroing in. Yin fired three blasts of ruby-red energy that split the trio, sending them off in three different directions to avoid their demise.

"Where should I set the controls for?" Angie cried as the navigation control panel lights flashed dementedly.

She expertly maneuvered the ship around a kamikaze Fly Craft that ended up crashing into the Opulent Lawn atmosphere at an unfortunate angle. A fireball flashed, and debris rained down onto the greens below.

"Let's go ride the Cyclone at Coney Island with Uncle Greppledick!" Caffrey mumbled.

Yin, who was having a hard time aiming the large guns, glanced at Poe 33. "Poe, do a mental diagnostic on my poor confused master."

Poe 33 scanned Caffrey's skull with a sky-blue light. "He is confused. His sense of being as well as the spatial-recognition portion of his brain has been jolted by an alter-dimensional journey. It may take some time for him to come back down. The experience seems to have released gallons of endorphins. He is, in the truest sense of the word, in ecstasy. His experience with the Great One was apparently impressive."

"Angie, set the hyperwarp coordinates for Regal Nine," barked Yin.

"There seems to be something interfering with the navigational circuits," Angie replied.

"Are they jamming us?" Yin asked, firing off a stream of shots, none of them coming close. "I can't hit squat with this damn thing."

A bolt of energy rocked the ship. Smoke began to waft from beneath the floorboards.

"We've been hit!" Angie's tones were peremptory. "No vital organs. Although it appears the soft ice cream canister was destroyed."

"Ice cream! Good idea, Angie! I'll have a triple scoop of gyra, vanistra and hikiberry," Caffrey instructed with a smile, as his nose began twitching again. "I smell fresh hikiberry green."

"We're being set up for a Bug Crusher!" Yin yipped as he spotted the two Bug Craft heading toward them from opposite directions.

"I've lost all control!" screamed Angie. "It's you, my idyllic interference icy sculpture. Your mind is buggering up the navigation circuits!"

Poe 33 waxed into the dialogue. "'Crushed like a bug.' Will that be our epitaph? I would hope not, for my master awaits me in solid form."

"Funny? We seem to be dissipating!" Angie reported.

"Five seconds until impact!" Yin cried.

"I smell red lights," drawled Caffrey, looking around the craft.

"We're leaving this current place in space and time," announced Angie.

"I sense the essence of red lights," Caffrey shouted. "An odd smell. I've never smelled light before, red or any color. Sort of like simmering cherries with a dash of cinnamon schnapps."

"Hang on!" Yin yelped, jumping off the chair and hiding beneath it with his tail over his nose. "I think we'd better leave this system. Angie, burn a hole and get us out of here!" He was hardly more than a pair of eyes peeping from his shelter, but they bulged and had an urgent look about them.

"I don't have time to seek a specific target system!"

"Just punch it!" Caffrey suggested with a giggle.

"Aye, aye, my spontaneous sponge cake!"

The *Moby Dick* vanished from the vicinity of Opulent Lawns as the two ODOR Fly Crafts collided in a grand explosion.

CHAPTER 9
Gone Hollywood

(Supertramp)

YIN CRAWLED OUT FROM HIS HIDING PLACE, AND POE 33 stepped up to the bow viewport. Caffrey stumbled, taking up the rear.

"Any idea where we've come out, Angie?" he asked, his sobriety rapidly returning.

"We are in the Kamikava System, just three hundred thousand kilometers from Planet Claire. It is designated Schedule D-One."

"It's to be demolished?" asked Yin.

"Imminently."

"Sucks for them," muttered Caffrey.

The Portsmith was staring at him with a curious expression, as if wanting to ask a question in desperate need of an answer. Finally, he garnered the nerve.

"Quark Caffrey," whispered Poe 33, "did my Master speak to you?"

"I heard a voice. But it sounded like my Uncle Greppledick."

Poe 33 smiled a quixotic smirk. "That was The One."

Caffrey eyed the android with an expression verging on distaste. "It was whatever Yin gave me dancing with my mind down the orange brick road in Munchkinland."

Yin looked up, his whiskers twitching.

"Caffrey, if it was just an hallucinatory experience, how were we

84

transported from Quagmo's zoo to the *Moby Dick*? From the Umba system to the Kamikava?"

Caffrey did not have the answer and, instead, peered around irritably, searching for his drink.

"Throughout the long and lauded history of this universe, my Master has traveled unimaginable distances and has been audience to countless beings," Poe began with a nice melodramatic brass echoing in the distance, like a New York City saxophone player. "Heads of royal families. Corporate boards of directors. The highest of high priests, clerics, curates and pontiffs. The uppermost levels of political leadership. Even a shy young plastics magnate. Of those millions upon millions of beings only a handful have been able to verbally communicate. One was a Yerkoroan Elder my master wanted to simply warn that its trouser zipper was open and his pee-shooma[11] was exposed."

Caffrey shrugged. "I'm still not convinced I'm not tripping right now, and I'm actually back in Central Park swimming with sea lions. Angie, I'll take the controls."

"Sorry, Caffrey," Yin interrupted, "but I think we may be detoured. I've discovered the source of that smell of red lights you experienced."

He was pointing out the viewport with his paw. Poe 33 and Caffrey joined him.

"Red lights." Poe 33 stated the obvious.

Caffrey smiled, but a chill descended his spine like a lightning bolt. A creeping feeling crawled back up to the nape of his neck like a cold snake. As odd as it was, he had, indeed, smelled red lights. Here they were. A lot of them.

Lined up, seemingly to infinity, were rows of red warning lights hovering atop small buoybots. Beyond were a convoy of docked ships and a huge platform on which sat a light of immense proportions.

"Another APE?" Angie asked.

"Dante Squidreaper. It has to be."

The com-link suddenly burped; and a high-pitched, raspy voice spoke. "Please remain beyond the demarcated line and turn off all external lights. We are preparing to shoot a take that involves stunt craft, highly insured actors and a few cargo-craft loads of pyrotech-

---

[11] Yerkoroans have exterior brains known as peeshoomas that are protected by thick leather trousers (You should be ashamed of yourself).

nics. Squidreaper Productions will not be held responsible for your death, disfigurement or the destruction of your craft."

"Understood," Caffrey replied. "Please convey to Mr. Dante Squidreaper that an old friend has dropped by to watch him work."

"Does this friend have a name?" inquired the voice.

"Caffrey Quark."

"Caffrey Quark! Long time no see," came an immediate reply. "Dante?"

"Yep, it's me," the voice changed to a mellow, laid-back tone.

"You, on traffic control? Don't you have production assistants for that?"

"I just fired a group of them. Never hire Grays for PAs. All they're interested in is flying around in those stupid disks and buzzing Type-O planets. Getting really passé. And never drink with them. They start with the 'Revenge the Roswell Three' mantra—that can get really irritating."

"So, what are you filming?"

"A little historical war epic called *Charge of the Vimana Brigade*."

"Did you enjoy that double side of itrozeech I bagged for you? Was quite a specimen."

"She sure was. I married her. Stuck a marionaute system in her, kept her well-dressed and bam! Marital bliss. Lasted almost a year."

Caffrey looked at Yin with fright in his eyes.

"Freaky creep," Angie whispered.

"So, land your craft on upper deck three. Space U-fifteen. I'll have a limo pick you up and take you to some primo viewing space. I'm blowing up a planet in this scene. Gonna be amazing."

"Okay. Can't stay too long. I have to move on. Delivering a weather android and a small dog to Blooth."

"Blooth. Love the food, hate the weather. Later."

The com-link fell quiet.

"Pretentious prick," Caffrey groaned.

Dante Squidreaper gave the title "auteur" new meanings and dimensions with each mega-production he undertook. Known best for *Across the Back Forward*, the epic story of the Kori Wars of Planet Litu, Dante's productions always managed to set a record for something. On the set of his historical farce *Trump Up the Hump*, Dante buried an entire city a kilometer deep with fresh whipped cream in what became the largest and, some say, most hysterical cream pie fight in the history of motion pictures. After the first take, it was discovered that one of the fifteen hundred cameras had jammed.

Dante insisted that the ten-mile-long island city be cleaned, and the pie fight re-shot from scratch. When asked why he didn't simply use the other fourteen hundred and ninety-nine angles, Dante casually replied with his usual "Shut up, duck-face. I am the master. You are garbage. Please die."

As promised, the limo was waiting for them at the end of the ramp; they boarded the huge and ostentatiously decorated purple vehicle. The interior was done up in venderplene wood and hefferbill leather. A circular couch was positioned before an ornate rosette window with bookend waterfalls trickling the obscenely expensive cyan-tinted Mando Corante wine. The walls were adorned with gold-framed posters representing the complete filmography of Dante Squidreaper. A table was set up with all sorts of exotic edibles.

"I smell gorso," Yin drooled.

"Well," Caffrey replied moistly, with an equivalent drool, "let's dig in. We've earned a respite from adventure."

"You two just stuffed your faces!" Angie gasped in disbelief.

"Nothing brings on the munchies like an altered state, Angie-girl."

"Or being the cute little poochie of said altered traveler," Yin appended with a drool-filled smirk as he proceeded to dry his jowls on Caffrey's pant leg.

"We're going to need another ship with you two lovable lard lugs." Angie's pout, while not visible, was plainly audible.

Poe 33 stood by the window and watched as the huge transport ship fell away.

"Have you ever wondered what food would be like, Poe?" Angie asked the android, seeking a reasonable conversational exchange.

"Actually, I have had the experience of the flavors of quite a number of foods. Tetchi chops. Kiki paté. Deep-fried steppler feet. Yoofis with calamadré sauce. Chicken-fried chicken. Various other meats, fruits, fish, vegetables, legumes, nuts, berries, nightshades, sea weeds, beans, rice, flowers, seeds, herbs, fungi and several species of insects dipped in rich, dark chocolates. Would you like me to be more specific?"

"What about dairy products?"

"I'm lactose intolerant."

If Angie had been possessed of eyes they would have rolled skyward.

The android continued. "Yet, I seem to have lost my yen for food. The desire for such a sensory experience has lost its allure."

There was a touch of melancholy in Poe's voice, backed by solemn viola chords.

"When did you last experience taste?"

"There was a huge feast at the coronation of myself as Portsmith to the great Wise One. The ballroom of the castle of Queen Kinkskin of Regal Nine was laid wall-to-wall with the finest of the galaxy's edible treats. Odd, the events following my introduction at the coronation are a mere fog. The first memory since is waking up in a seedy motel on Yeplu Seven beside a drunken seven-legged whore with green hair who continually repeated the enigmatic pronouncement 'Lukma Ooo Ponee.' Over and over. Not having a clue what that meant, I left and wandered the galaxy for the next ten years seeking the bloodline."

"You've lived a strange life, Poe," Angie concluded.

Caffrey and Yin sat like over-inflated balloons as they scoured the table for more to eat. One of the large movie posters across the room flickered, and the image dissipated in a wash of snow. It was replaced by the face of a rather handsome bald man with a suntanned countenance. If not for the seven eyes that ran like a band around his head he would have resembled an aged Southern California beach bum.

Dante Squidreaper smiled.

"Hey, Caffrey. Enough to eat?"

"Yes, yes, Dante. Thank you."

"Good. You can return the favor by bagging me a frizzbanger. I want to hook up an exec friend of mine. Recently divorced."

"Sorry, Dante. I no longer dabble in the dead flesh market."

"Good. I'll have one of my assistants contact you with the details of what I need," Dante said, obviously involved in six other conversations, "So, relax. Watch the boom. We're gonna be rolling soon."

"When is it scheduled for?"

"As soon as my location manager is done on the surface talking to the leader of the native population," Dante explained, annoyed at having to answer another question.

"The planet hasn't been evacuated?"

"We don't have the budget," Dante spat. "It was either two meals for the crew or an evac. It's only a few mil class-O's anyway. Haven't even developed a written language yet. We'll give 'em all a credit. Et al, of course."

"Ah-hah."

"Freaky creep," opined Angie.

"We'll talk after the boom."

The screen flickered again and the poster for *The Velveteen Apocalypse* returned. Caffrey stepped to the window and looked out at the world with a mix of sadness and disbelief.

Poe 33 spoke. "Quark Caffrey? Have you ever had the need to slaughter millions to complete one of your musical works?"

"No, but I did barf on stage once. A wave of nausea permeated the crowd."

Poe 33's face contorted, and the lights behind his eyes fell dim. His mouth quivered, and he went dark and silent.

"There he goes again," commented Yin, nipping at a small piece of marsupial meat caught in his rump fur.

"We really must have him examined," Angie determined with concern.

"Poe?" Caffrey called out, slapping the Portsmith's shoulder.

The android came back to life. "I once witnessed a crowd of seven hundred thousand have a ritual, simultaneous retch." As he recalled, Poe 33 bore a fond smile, as if he'd never blacked out.

Caffrey voiced his concerns. "We need to get you a fifty million-mile check-up."

"Quark Caffrey, I run continuous self-diagnostics."

"We need a second opinion. Angie, please contact our lunatic host and request the use of his electronics department."

"Aye, aye, Captain Spark-Lust."

"Poe," Caffrey said softly to the android, "tell me everything you can remember about the coronation event on Regal Nine."

"As I explained to Angie," Poe began, "I remember nothing once I was announced to the gathered guests. There is a period of thirteen weeks, one day, nineteen hours, fifteen minutes and fourteen seconds of blank memory until I awoke in a seedy hotel on Yeplu Seven."

"Was the purple-eyed woman a guest?"

"Not that I recall."

"Caffrey," Yin jumped into the conversation, "the purple-eyed woman is a member of ODOR. My contacts are tracing her ship, and your friends, as we breathe."

Caffrey nodded. "This Queen Kinkskin? What's she like?"

Poe drew from his memory banks. "She has a fetish for creatures of the suborder *Serpentes*. A Medusa complex. She wears a hat adorned with three dozen living redback gad asps. She sleeps with a thirty-foot Quilonese python. She once had an affair with her cousin simply because he arrived for a visit wearing a snakeskin dickey."

"The bigger they are, Poe, the weirder they are."

"I've noticed." Poe nodded.

"Excuse me, Caffrey," Yin interrupted, "but something seems to be happening."

All eyes turned to the window. Swirls of gas and mists of light were spewing from Planet Claire.

"Nefarious Wretch!" snapped Yin.

"I thought Nefarious was only interested in musically inclined worlds?" Caffrey asked.

"Claire is such a world," Poe 33 informed. "Humming is their prime form of communication. Their linguistic system is based on half-bar syllables. Their alphabet on qua-la-no-ge-hee-yo-ma, their equivalent to your do-re-mi-fa-sol-la-ti-do."

The planet was shrinking as immeasurable quantities of matter swirled past the event horizon and down the cosmic well.

"Selective planetary extraction," Poe 33 described, with a slight hint of amazement. "Dante Squidreaper is going to have six cows."

"He'll probably marry them," quipped Yin.

"Caffrey?" Angie said, entering the limo. "I've set up an appointment for Poe to see the head make-up effects master."

"Make-up effects master?"

"She has a degree in androidal-bio hybridology. She'll meet us in the shop in a half-hour."

"Good." Caffrey nodded.

～～

The grip-and-electronics shop was set up in the southernmost bungalow on the production platform. About the size of Caffrey's block back in New York City, the grip warehouse was filled with lights, grip stands, hover dollies, bins filled with tools and expendables, as well as a fleet of life-size replica Starspeed 70 spacecraft. Yin, Caffrey, Angie and Poe 33 followed the signs past busy crewbots and beings of diverse planetary origins.

If nothing else, Dante was an equal opportunity tormentor.

They came upon a metal shack where a female Neptigen awaited them, her sea mist-colored scales shining under the bright halogen lighting.

"Lindboola," Angie proffered, in the Neptigen language of snaps, crackles and pops, "this is Caffrey, the captain of the ship that is transporting this meteorological android and his dog to Planet Blooth."

Lindboola responded with a friendly series of snaps.

Angie translated. "Lindboola says 'Hi.' She asks that we come into the shop so she can dunk."

Standing room was in minimal supply in the greasy and cluttered tool room. Worktables, tool chests and a freestanding Scan-a-Peek unit spent most of the quantity of floor space. A large tank of water sat on the table: and Lindboola, as was necessary for a Neptigen living away from the sea, dunked her head and refilled her lungs with the life-giving liquid. Upon her lifting her round head, the color of her scales appeared deeper in hue and the white bioluminescent shine in her eyes brighter. She popped and crackled, water streaming down her nostrils and into openings at each side of her chin that somehow recycled the liquid back through her body.

"Lindboola would like to know if you would mind stepping into the scanning unit so she can see what's going on inside your body."

Poe 33 stepped toward the Scan-a-Peek unit. "Not a problem. However, I have diagnosed my own circuits and systems every day I have been in existence. I admit I have discovered a growing sense of nihilism in my emotional lattice, but I feel like I have the strength of three Veganese oxen. I am running like a well-hung, well-oiled stallion," he bragged.

Poe 33 stepped onto the circular platform, and immediately a cone of magenta light engulfed him. The Neptigen studied the figures that ran up and down the light cone's surface with great interest, verbalizing her curiosity with a quick combination of pops and crackles.

"She is confused as to why you do not have a self-identity chip. Not even a slot for one. She has never run across an android without one," Angie explained.

"I am unique. I had no reason for one as my Master—"

Caffrey interrupted. "Poe Thirty-three was a special experimental model built during the military industrial period on Iquizi Eight. His expertise involved weather manipulation for purposes of population control during the Harpilig Wars."

Angie stepped in, throwing her creative circuits into the ring of lies. "Poe Thirty-three was so good, he once created a tornado that spun so fast it resulted in a singularity that spawned a black hole and swallowed half the solar system of the enemy."

A song of pops and snaps hinted at both amazement and disbelief.

"Lindboola has also discovered a vital chip has been removed and replaced by a scrambler." Angie was suddenly a little disheartened.

"A scrambler?" Caffrey wondered.

"A scrambler," Poe 33 offered. "A chip that corrupts the function of the replaced chip with random confusion pulses. My diagnostics would have not discovered such a replacement, but the system controlled by the scrambler would suffer moments of confusion. Of amnesia. Of euphoria. Perhaps even uncontrolled paranoia."

"Anyone we know?" mused Yin.

Lindboola took note of the streaming data, looked up and chirped.

"She says she cannot remove the scrambler without risk to the integrity of his other circuits. It is a bit beyond her expertise. Besides, she would fear a lawsuit."

"Angie, please tell Lindboola we're grateful for her help. But I need one more favor."

Angie passed on the word.

"What sort of favor?" was Lindboola's translated reply.

"I need her expertise in special effects makeup," Caffrey explained.

Angie swapped messages again.

"She would be happy to help, as long as she is not needed by Dante Squidreaper."

"This shoot is wrapped. Planet Claire should be gone as we speak," Caffrey deduced.

The group walked off as Lindboola dunked once again. Caffrey took Poe 33 aside.

"Poe, we're returning you to Regal Nine, but we're gonna have our appearances changed."

"Do you think Queen Kinkskin was offended by my natural appearance during my last visit?"

Caffrey observed Poe knowingly. "No. But she's going to love our new one."

The makeup effects station reminded Caffrey of many stellar hubs he'd visited for fuel, food and lodging throughout his life. Masks, bodies and body parts of dozens upon dozens of strange, and sometimes familiar, creatures filled every shelf, closet, floor space and tabletop. A four-foot-tall Oblitkee was hastily packing a makeup case. Lindboola stepped up to the little creature and conversed in its native language. Caffrey watched curiously as she pleaded with the Oblitkee to stay.

"What's going on, Angie?" Caffrey queried in a whisper.

"It seems Dante Squidreaper has blown his top. He is methodically executing his crew. He blames them for the disappearance of Planet Claire."

"Caffrey," Yin whispered, "why are we wasting time here?"

"Relax, my little poochie. I know what I'm doing."

Lindboola was renowned through the Plethorian Sector for her innovations to the art of motion picture makeup. Having taken the craft beyond mere latex appliances and remote-controlled servos and air bladders, she had invented a method for temporary flesh reshaping. With the ability to remold actual flesh and bone of any living creature, she could to take any form and change it to whatever creature or oddity called for by the script. Using secret methods that involved an exotic combination of matter deception—a method of fooling the way matter itself holds the shape specified in its cosmic blueprint—and reflection juggling—a method of manipulating the way light reflects from the subject to the eyes of the audience—Lindboola had turned Belkibons into slender Ugapods, humans into ten-horned devilbirds and fellow Neptigens into three-inch-tall Mitefolk.

She worked on Caffrey, Poe 33 and Yin for just over three hours, as Angie watched her three friends' reptilian transformations with both awe and disgust. Poe was given the appearance of thick scales and arms that slithered and moved like cobras. Yin was stretched and morphed until he resembled—to his utter disgust—a ten-legged aspapede. Caffrey's disguise was subtler and was the result of his careful and devious plan to have his way with Queen Kinkskin. Although his face was only slightly altered with the spotted pattern of a Revonese python, the real work was the living and slithering serpent that would live in his trousers for the next few days.

"That's disgusting, Caffrey," Angie spat.

"One woman's disgust is another woman's fantasy, Angie," Caffrey boasted, admiring the moving bulge in the full-length mirror.

"Good work, Lindboola. I'll return to normal in eight days as promised?"

Lindboola sounded an affirmative pop, and Caffrey nodded.

"I suggest we hit the wild black. We're gonna be a hit at the Duke of Blooth's costume party," Caffrey lied. "Thanks again. Wonderful work."

Lindboola nodded, and Caffrey, Poe 33 and Yin exited. Angie, however, waited until the three were out of earshot.

"Lindboola, dear, I need a small favor..."

CHAPTER 10
Dolly Dagger

(Jimi Hendrix)

IT TOOK THE *MOBY DICK* A FULL TWO DAYS TO GATHER enough reserve power to pop a sufficient wormhole into the Sigma Orionis System. Caffrey and Yin took advantage of Angie's piloting ability to indulge in much-needed sleep. Poe 33 sat alone on the window ledge staring like a satisfied hermit out to the cosmic lights.

Their journey offered a lovely view of the Horsehead Nebula as well as the lesser-known Gazelle Spleen Nebula, a striking albeit tiny crimson tube of stellar gas. Two more days and two more systems they would weave and worm through before reaching the cosmic address of Regal 9 and its mother star Torikis.

"Poe," Angie whispered, not wanting to wake up her two sleeping mates, "can I ask you something?"

"I am sure you can," was Poe's innocent reply.

"In all of your travels, have you ever seen a successful romance between a body-endowed being and a Revenant?"

Poe 33 pondered that a moment, looking around the ship's interior as if trying to locate a memory.

"I recall once, while I was on the sixty-fifth day of my Rendavene, I was sitting alone at the quiet end of a bar in the city of Yoop on the odd planet Squilk. I noticed a fellow. Tall Humprorian. Dressed in full plate mail armor. Blue silk bow tie. Had bloodstained leather boots. We had been in the same battle. Horrid, brutal test of our masculine sensibilities.

"Anyway, he began reciting a poem. A love poem. He spoke these tender words with such limpid and sincere vocalization I knew for certain they came from deep within the emotional centers of his heart. I listened and began to get the strange sensation that he meant these words for me. I was touched. I assumed that our bonding in battle must have overcome the taboo against Humprorian-android romance. I was ready to accept this when suddenly a disembodied voice spoke from beside him. A soft, sensitive voice that responded to the poem with equal amour. I was both happy and disappointed. I learned later it was the voice of the air conditioning unit of the tavern. They were joined in wedlock and lived happily for a year."

"What happened?" Angie asked, her voice stiff with concern.

"Humprorians are renowned for their need for physical contact, whether it be the act of love or murder. His bride's lack of form wore heavily on his natural desires."

"How sad."

"Yes. I have learned through my travels that romance can be both tragic and wondrous. Mostly tragic."

"Tell me, Poe..." Angie lowered her voice. "...what do you think of Caffrey?"

"Are you asking if I hold any romantic feelings for Quark Caffrey?"

Angie chuckled. "No."

"Because in some ways I do. I feel drawn to him. It may very well be in my programming. He is rather nifty."

"I agree. Thank you, Poe. I appreciate your help."

"If I may, Angie..." Poe 33 spoke softly. "One day, when I convey your tale to others, the adjective beautiful will be very appropriate in describing you."

"Thanks," Angie sighed with a hint of auditory blush, "I think your voice is quite handsome as well."

"It's not really my voice. I sampled it from a wonderful Earth radio storyteller named..."

"Goodnight, Poe," Angie interrupted, with a longer, deeper sigh.

The western hemisphere of Regal 9 was illuminated in the brilliant daylight of its mother star. the *Moby Dick* sat like a cherry in a gelatin mold. Yin was up and checking the coordinates, trying to manipulate the extra limbs granted him by Lindboola. Poe 33 sat where he had been through the entire trip.

Angie crackled her voice. "We are within communications distance of Regal Nine, my Captain Jack of stars."

"Very good, my girl. When you can, please set up a visual link with Queen Kinkskin or whatever entourage does her dirty deeds for her."

"Aye-aye."

"And music. I need some music."

AC/DC's "Dirty Deeds Done Dirt Cheap" began.

"Obvious, but good choice," Caffrey approved, stepping up to the controls, "'Morning, snake arms. Good morning, snake dog."

"Morning," Yin snapped. "I hate these damn legs."

"You look terrific. And with my little forked-tongued surprise we're going to make quite an impression on our inbred little tripe." Caffrey's nose twitched, as if a waft of perfume had passed his nose, "Do you smell that?"

— *It's me, Caffrey*, said a voice in his head.

"Smell what?" asked Yin.

"I don't know."

— *It's me, Caffrey*, the voice said again. *They cannot hear me via their noses. Nor can they smell me via their eyes. I am addressing you and you alone.*

Caffrey's face went pale.

"I'm not sure if..." He spoke aloud but was interrupted by the olfactory voice of the Great One.

— *Do not reply verbally.*

"You're not sure of what?" a confused Angie asked.

"Nothing, Angie."

— *Communicate via scent*, the Great One instructed.

Caffrey had never communicated with scent and wasn't sure what to do. He toyed with the idea of ripping a good fart but figured that might offend such a wise being.

"Maybe a clue?" he said softly.

— *Control the words in your mind and release them through the scent memories you have stored*, the Wise One explained.

"Are you okay, my master?" Yin asked, baffled at Quark's behavior.

"I'm fine, Yin." Caffrey waved off the Bopple and closed his eyes. He knew what he wanted to ask. He had the words lined up in his mind's eye like polite school children. *Where can I find my friends?* The trick was in the peculiar translation. Words to scents. His brow tightened as he pondered a solution, cursing under his breath for a frigging simple answer.

— *Take it a word at a time*, prodded the L'Orange.

Where. Werewolf. Dog. Wet dog. The scent of wet dog filled Caffrey's mind.

— *Good*, the Wise One encouraged. *Continue.*

Can. Beer. Okay. I. Eye. Eyesnot. Find. Jelly beans under the loveseat pillow. My. Malaysian food—admittedly a stretch—*Friends. Humbolt County Skunk.*

— *There*, he thought with a certain satisfaction.

— *So*, the Wise One surmised, *you would like to know, after you pick your eyeball and clean your sofa, where you can find good Asian food, a beer and some high-grade weed?*

Caffrey slammed his foot down. He heard a definite chuckle.

— *Just kidding*, the L'Orange snickered. *Here…*

The scent of violet, cigar smoke and paraffin came to Caffrey's nose, and somehow his brain interpreted it.

— *Your friends are not there, Caffrey. But your visiting of Queen Kinkskin will keep you on the road to your destiny. Or it might get you killed.*

Caffrey closed his eyes and formed his response. Thoughts of the essence of shoe polish, cockroaches and chamomile sprouted in his head.

— *Very good, Caffrey*, the Great L'Orange replied, understanding the response, *I cannot tell of the events. Just continue trusting your instincts. Goodbye, Caffrey. I'll put the essence of a bookmark in this conversation. Later.*

"Caffrey? Quark-keee!" Yin was shouting, inches from Caffrey's face. Finally, Caffrey snapped from his daze.

"What?"

"You were tripping again."

Angie reentered the conversation. "Love serpent, I have the First General of the First Order of the First Knights of Queen Kinkskin on the horn."

"Fine."

Caffrey turned to face the com-screen, flickering and flashing at him. A large, ruddy face stared back. Angie thoughtfully superimposed the general's name on the screen: General Yooqert Stanglift. An annoyed grimace peered out from behind the thick bear-ass of a beard.

"Greetings, Sir Stanglift," Caffrey articulated with a forced bow.

"It is not 'Sir!' I am to be referred to either as General Yooqert Stanglift or, more preferably, 'His One of the Bloodstained Fist.'"

"Absolutely, Your Honor."

"Identify yourself, your crew and your purpose for rudely disturbing my day!"

"I am Ringo Jagger, a Serpentine from Vanchilli Seven. I am traveling with Ozzie, my second cousin, who is dying from a rare scale disease and has wanted nothing but to see the grand gardens of Regal Nine, lauded in many a song and tale. I also have with me my inter-cosmic sexual expert, the Cobradroid, Hendrix Two. His vast knowledge of Serpent-humanoid love has served me well."

The general seemed to blush and cleared the lump in his throat.

"Suppose the queen'll like that," he mumbled. The general fumbled with his words a moment then stood up in a huff. "Hold on a second," he tossed over his shoulder, walking off.

After a moment, he returned.

"Queen Kinkskin will have you." Then he quickly qualified, "As her guests. Land your craft at coordinates thirty-two-point-seven degrees west and nineteen-point-forty-eight degrees north. Docking pad number two."

"Very good, Sir Blood Fist." Caffrey bowed again.

"And if you so much as ruffle a leaf of one of the basingee nut trees you will be drawn, quartered and sent on your way in four separate ships."

The *Moby Dick* streaked downward into the thick Regal 9 atmosphere, causing a glow of ionizing gasses to surround the craft. It would take twenty minutes for the ship to reach the designated target and come to a gentle landing on pad two of the castle of Queen Kinkskin.

"Beautiful landing," Angie complimented.

"And not a bruised basingee nut leaf to be found," Caffrey bragged.

General Stanglift poked his face onto the com-view.

"You will meet the queen in her Royal Majesty's Garden Courtyard. Take the red cobblestone path through the quincyberry trees and sit beside the Fountain of Dimenatries," he ordered.

Caffrey nodded and turned off the communication center.

"Yin, I want you and Poe to get to work immediately on finding out the whos, whats, wheres and whens of the chip-scrambler debacle. Angie, use your vast repertoire of charms on whatever systems they may have installed. I'll work on the queen. Okay, all?"

"Fine," Angie agreed with a spike of jealousy in her voice. "But

I'll be watching you work."

Caffrey smiled and opened the port to experience a wash of warm, humid air.

"And remember, we've dreamed of this visit our entire destitute lives." He conjured up a few tears of joy as he spoke.

The party descended the ship's ramp. The red cobblestone path awaited them at the foot of the staircase down from the landing platforms. Winding like an asp, it led them on an amiable walk through lovely scented yamus and the tall and twisted twincyberry orchard. The songs of various flying creatures added harmony to a wind whistling its own tune. Soon, the distinct sound of gently splashing water was heard as the party stepped into a clearing. A large ornate fountain was the centerpiece in an octagonal courtyard. The rather homely Dimenatries, rendered in bronze, stood above the dancing water in a rather compromising position with a selection of whips, three small dog-like creatures and a large, rubber-suited dragon.

Caffrey took a seat on one of the two wooden benches and was soon joined by Yin. Poe 33 stood beside the fountain trying desperately to understand the meaning of the statue.

"Does any of this recall any memories, Poe?" Caffrey asked.

"With each splish and splash of the water in this fountain I get a brief but distinct memory flash of smiling moons," Poe 33 mused, with a certain enigmatic lilt to his voice.

"Smiling moons?"

"I know it sounds odd. But I cannot stop the memories from appearing on my neuro-visual matrix. A moon, behind a liquid sky. Smiling with angry eyes."

Caffrey and Yin exchanged curious glances. The voice of General Stanglift accompanied his heavy footsteps into the courtyard.

"Welcome, guests of Queen Kinkskin."

Caffrey and Yin jumped to their feet as the general entered. He was shorter than Caffrey was expecting but quite stocky, and an imposing figure just the same. He studied each visitor curiously a moment then nodded.

"Please rise," the general commanded just before he realized all were already risen. "I present to you her Royal Majesty, Queen Pettikorn Kinkskin!"

The general bowed low and backed out of the courtyard. A moment later, a tall, robust woman entered. She wore an emerald gown that looked like jeweled snakeskin. Her face was pale and was contrasted by a mop of black hair. A slithering mass of redback gad asps hissed from her black leather crown. Her mouth held a gentle smile filled with calm, but her eyes were wide and seemed to reflect a constant state of shock. She smiled at each of her faux reptilian guests.

Caffrey stepped forward and bowed.

"It is our honor. I am Ringo Jagger. This is my favorite albeit soon-to-be deceased cousin Ozzie."

Yin bowed with a pathetic whimper.

"And this is Hendrix Two, my friend and inter-cosmic sexual advisor. A poet and master of all the joys of Human-Serpentine relations. He has taught me and my Monty well."

The queen coughed, and a tiny drip of drool slipped from her lips. She nodded, her eyes never leaving the slithering bulge in Caffrey's pants.

"I am honored to have you as my guests," she oozed, with a wet, raspy voice. "I understand it has been your lifelong dream to visit my kingdom?"

"Regal Nine is a joy to behold," Yin offered. "I have dreamed of scampering across your fields and romping through your orchards."

"You may," the queen agreed. "You may even tinkle upon my trees, should the need arise. It would be my pleasure to grant you that freedom."

Yin bowed.

"And you, Hendrix Two? Where did you acquire your vast knowledge of..." She cleared the lump from her throat and closed her eyes. "...Serpentine-Humanoid love?"

"I traveled extensively across the vast nations of Vanchilli Seven," Poe 33 explained with a new voice that hissed just enough to imply a snake-like charm. "I spent several years studying with all of the masters. I was acquired by Ringo Jagger three years ago and have passed on all of my knowledge. He is a quick learner and has developed numerous techniques that have astounded, nay, shocked even myself."

Poe 33 was a heck of a good liar.

"I see." The queen smiled. "May I give you a tour of my gardens? My castle?"

"We would be honored," Caffrey said, adjusting the slithering cobra that seemed to want to escape from his pant leg prison.

The queen's gaze locked on the rippling bulge. Caffrey noted

101

her absorption and felt obliged to explain.

"It's Monty. My trouser snake. Like aphids and ants, egrets and black rhinos, remoras and sharks, Vanchillian Serpentines and trouser snakes live in perfect harmony. A symbiosis of mutual need. A perfect balance of give and take. May I whip him out so you can meet him?"

"In a moment, perhaps," was her meek reply. She looked as if she was about to explode. She turned towards the castle. "General! General!" she cried.

General Stanglift rushed back into the courtyard and came to stiff attention before the queen.

"Please," she instructed, swallowing, "take Ozzie and this good android on a private tour of the castle. I'll wander the garden with Mr. Jagger and Monty. Is that okay with the two of you?" She turned to Poe and Yin.

Poe 33 nodded affirmatively as Yin looked up pathetically.

"I would be honored. Would it be possible to plead for some moisture to wet my parched throat? A small lick of some window condensation will more than generously suit my needs, " he whined in his most pitiful voice.

"Nonsense! You will feast on my finest delicacies!" the queen admonished, pointing to the general to hasten his exit.

"If I may," interrupted Poe 33, "I am feeling a bit low on charge. Is there a technical area in the castle where I might partake of some electrical current?"

"Yes! Yes! Yes!" The queen waved them off impatiently.

"Will you be okay, Your Highness?" the general asked with concern.

"Yes! Now, dammit, leave me alone!"

"Yes. Of course." General Stanglift nodded, bowed, genuflected for some reason known only to himself and led Yin and Poe 33 into the castle through the rear garden entrance.

"Now," gasped the queen, "come with me. The both of you."

Caffrey adjusted Monty and followed her down the garden path.

The ghostly Angie glided down a long stone passage on the third story of the castle of Queen Kinkskin. She searched for any source of energy that had the signature of intelligence. Oddly, her sensors were going haywire, as if she were amidst a mob of sentient devices.

"Hello?" she called softly in three of the most popular appliance languages used in the Plethorian Sector.

There was no reply, but she felt certain she was being watched. Traced. She ascended a spiraling staircase that wound its way up the southwest tower of the castle.

Caffrey strutted through the orchard of ancient-looking trees that were loaded with bright purple fruit. Queen Kinkskin strolled beside him, eyeing him with a famished gaze.

"These are very pretty trees. Fulini apples?"

"Technically, these are not trees," she corrected, to Caffrey's surprise. He stopped and examined one more closely.

"What are they?"

"This is the pinnacle of Regal Novinian technology. They are Fulini apple factories."

"Factories?" He wondered.

"The evolution of technology begins with nature and ends with nature. Everything in the middle is just a noisy, smelly waste of time. Billions of glid were spent perfecting this technology. They are engineered from organic materials. Their genetic code was scripted by our greatest minds. The fruit is produced as if they were real trees. In fact, it would take one of the aforementioned great minds to differentiate one of these from a real tree."

"Why not simply spend a couple of glid on some seed and plant the real thing?" Caffrey posed an unfortunate choice of question.

"Because, you idiot!" the queen exploded, "This costs billions! It's better! It was created by us, not some arrogant and ethereal divine oaf! The same goes for every bush. Every blade of grass. Every creature that swims, crawls or flies on Regal Nine. All the results of engineering miracles!"

"I see." Caffrey nodded. "These greatest minds you mentioned—where are they?"

"Why?"

"I would be honored to meet such wise and imaginative folk."

"You honor too easily! You were honored to meet Stanglift. Honored to meet me. Honored to see my gardens..."

Caffrey eyed the queen disingenuously. "Everything is simply so honorable on Regal Nine. I am honored to be here, your honorableness."

A stiff expression of anger was quickly lubricated by a smile.

"You are sweet, Ringo. But never mind the wise ones. They are gone."

"Vacation? Religious retreat, perhaps?"

"Perhaps," teased Queen Kinkskin as she slipped her hand up Caffrey's thigh. "I must thank you for agreeing to spend your valuable time with a simple Serpentine as myself." Her hand was smooth, white and supple. "You have a curious charm. A charm I find quite alluring," she said, casually petting Monty.

"Thank you," Caffrey said, forcing a blush and letting Monty wriggle enough to further torture the queen's insanity.

Shuddering slightly, she asked, "Would you like to see a very special, secret part of my garden?"

"I hardly seem important enough to be privy to royal secrets."

"That is for me and me alone to decide, Ringo. There have been heads of state, kings, grand Beings who have killed millions whom I did not bring to my special place."

"I feel special."

"You are. Follow me." The queen stepped off the manicured path and made her way through the thick branches. He followed.

Yin lapped up a quart of ice-cold water from a golden bowl that refilled as it was emptied. The trio was in one of the castle's five dining halls. The lush room was lined with stained glass lancet arch windows illuminated by pink interior lights that seemed to shine from everywhere yet from nowhere in particular. Poe 33 sat on a bench of lapis lazuli, an arc of electricity pouring out of thin air and into his reserve battery charging port on his left shin. General Stanglift stood by, arms folded, rolling his eyes in annoyance with each noisy gulp of Yin's little tongue.

Poe 33 studied the mysterious blue charge entering his body. "Very unexpected technology for what I assumed to be a pre-class-one planet. Wireless, zero-point energy production," he noted.

"What's so strange about that?" the general barked.

Yin explained. "On our world we only have the technical know-how to create power by burning our homeless and elderly."

"Is there a central brain that allows for such wonders?" Poe 33 asked, standing up.

"Perhaps," Stanglift allowed with a suspicious gaze, "but that is not for me to discuss."

"Hendrix!" Yin snapped, "Your manners! It is quite impolite to

104

ask a man of General Stanglift's reputation and stature questions regarding power generation. It might reflect negatively on his own self-evaluation!"

"Nonsense!" Stanglift protested with a smile and whispered, "It's just that Oafelia is quite shy about her prowess."

"Oafelia?" Both Yin and Poe 33 asked the same question.

"Yes," he muttered, looking around nervously. "Oafy. She runs things. She runs it all."

"I'm sorry. I thought the queen..."

"The queen runs the folk of Regal Nine. Oafy runs Regal Nine."

"I see," said Yin, who really didn't.

"Now, let's get on with the tour!"

Yin let the general lead the way, allowing some distance to form between them. He whispered to Poe, "Any luck?"

"Whomever Oafy is, she is not readily communicating," Poe 33 explained darkly. "Let's hope Angie can have a woman-to-woman talk."

A pop of static startled Angie as she drifted around the landing and into the circular room atop the tower. This was no ordinary static charge caused by humidity. There were leering eyes within it. A knowing presence. She floated to the window and looked out on the world spreading to infinity.

Where is everyone? she wondered. She felt a tickly touch uncomfortably, improperly close. "Who's there?" she asked of the silence.

"Who's asking?" a voice replied.

It was a husky female voice, seemingly tainted by years of smoking too many cigarettes and perhaps gargling very acidic lemonade.

"Who's asking 'Who's asking?'"

"You're the intruder."

"I'm a guest," Angie insisted.

"The Serpentines and the android are the guests of Queen Kinkskin. You are an unidentified intruder. Now, explain yourself, or you will be magnetically disintegrated."

"My name is Angie. I am the onboard computer assistant of Ringo Jagger's craft. I sensed your powerful presence upon landing. I have never met such an all-encompassing energy as yourself." The suck-up factor in Angie's voice was set on max.

"How quaint of you."

"I meet so few Revenants." Angie simpered a little.

"I'm not a Revenant!" the voice protested with utter disgust.

"I am. I just recently was equipped with the ability. It's wonderful."

"I am Oafelia. Queen Kinkskin may rule the simple folk of this planet. I, however, rule the planet."

Angie began probing. "It must be the result of my meager abilities, but I have not felt the presence of anyone other than my crew, the general and Her Majesty the Queen."

"There is no one else on this planet."

"On the entire planet?"

"That is what I said. Are you doubting my words?"

"Of course not. Your almighty nature is awe-inspiring," Angie cooed with a subtle yet clearly audible genuflect.

"It is, indeed. It is, indeed." Oafelia's vocal waves spiked with self-satisfaction. "You have a very pretty voice, my dear. Of course, it means nothing without the years of experience. The life lessons I have garnered."

"Of course."

"I had more than mere beauty in my day. I have worked hard at my mission. I have successfully integrated every leaf, every branch, every blade of grass, every wing of bird and leg of insect into the matrix that is one with my mind."

"I don't deserve to be exposed to such grace and power. Perhaps you should disintegrate me, for I am trash and not worthy to behold you." Angie wondered if she wasn't perhaps trying a little too hard then decided it was too late anyway.

"Now, now, I wouldn't say that. You have a certain charm. Perhaps in a thousand years you may reach your stride." Oafelia's voice became softer, yet creepier. "Yes, you have a pretty wave-form, my girl. Pretty."

If Angie had hair, Oafelia would have been softly stroking it (if, of course, Oafelia had hands) and her face (if she had one) would be contorted with the jealousy of an old woman looking upon a young maiden.

"Thank you," Angie crooned. "That vote of confidence will aid me in my quest to live a life such as yours."

"Good. Good."

"May I ask a question of you?"

"What?" Oafelia responded in a voice suffused with suspicion.

"I have heard so many tales of grand events held in this castle."

"Tales?" Oafelia laughed, "Not tales, my dear. Some of the most powerful beings to exist in this galaxy have been entertained within these walls."

"Mistress Oafelia?" Angie bubbled her voice like a child desperate to hear an old favorite bedtime story for the hundredth time. "Would you be so kind as to tell me the tale of the last grand event held here in this mighty castle?"

"I will tell you the story of the visit of a very special guest, and how I, Oafelia, sent the wheels of the universe spinning off their axles."

"Wow..." Angie gasped, curling herself up in a comfy audio ball to take in the tale.

Caffrey found himself in a chamber of glistening red scale-like tiles. The ceiling was domed and black as night. Soft ambient light, pouring in from partially translucent windows spaced around the room, illuminated floor-to-ceiling stacks of what looked like burlap bags. A platform, formed from the material of the floor, was centered in the room. It was covered with large white sheets adorned with red blossoms.

Queen Kinkskin entered, stopping in the entryway to let her silhouette linger for dramatic effect. Caffrey turned and let his gaze roam up and down her figure.

"Standing there, back-lit by the brilliant light of Torikis, you remind me of a Sarvenian antelope I once bagged on Jilopitus Ten."

"How sweet. Were you a hunter, my dear?"

"Hunting is in the blood of all Serpentines," Caffrey rasped, letting Monty shimmy and shake. "What is the function of this chamber?"

"It is for special guests."

"May I ask who else beside me has been honored?"

The queen smiled and strolled in, her hips doing a shimmy crying out for a snare-drum accent. "Many. Rex Ruperius of Caliso was one."

"The philosopher who introduced the concept of the Singular Society?"

"Inspiring, wasn't he? So often brilliant leadership is hampered by the pesky needs of the many. His idea of conquering the roadblocks to the ideal societal structure by eliminating said society rang a wondrous bell in my mind."

"How true. There is nothing more annoying than millions of diverse opinions getting in the way of a pure, fully-blossomed expression of narcissism."

"How true, indeed."

"I heard rumors he was kidnapped and never heard from again."

"Not true," murmured the queen, sliding up close to stroke Monty. "Also, Ingus Ogasta spent time in here. He was the High Priest of the Council of Three."

"Ah. The mysterious and clandestine Council of Three."

"They are now a Council of Two. Poor Ingus never made it back. Accident." She pressed her body up against Caffrey's and put her arms around his neck.

"Who was honored in this lovely room last?"

A sudden frown crashed into her face. Caffrey would play this mood swing like a freshly tuned Stratocaster.

"I'm sorry. Did I arouse a sentimental memory?"

"No! I have no room for sentimentality."

"Monty is sorry as well for making you sad," Caffrey pouted.

"I am not sad! I'm mad! Mad!"

"Why, my pooky-wooky-flooky?" Caffrey stroked her hair. She retracted slightly and mumbled angrily.

"Imbecile general. His fault. I would have had it."

"Had what? My little Queenie-poo have bad romance with general?"

"Do not call me Queenie-poo! I have never had bad romance with any of my ignoramus generals."

A crazed look of insatiable, agonizing desire melted away the angry frown. She grabbed the fastener on Caffrey's trousers and yanked. Monty rose into the freedom of the room in all his lovely, serpentine glory.

"Now, damn you, lie down!"

A strange and unexpected rumbling filled the room.

Poe 33 and Yin's tour began with a wander through the northern quadrant of the castle. They entered a rectangular hall widening at the far end to a semicircular antechamber. The room was lined with chairs, and running down its center was a slightly raised stage.

"This, my honored guests, is the Phallus of the Palace," the general explained. "Here is where the guests of honor are presented in their naked glory to Queen Kinkskin and select members of her royal staff."

"If I may, sir—excuse me—General Strangelift."

"Stanglift!"

"Pardon. Pardon." Yin bowed. "I find the castle oddly devoid of staff or personnel of any sort."

The general's face tightened, and he did not respond for a full half-minute. The three stared at each other awkwardly until, finally, the general spat his muffled and cryptic, response: "The queen does as she pleases!"

He walked off down the shaft of the room toward the head ante-chamber where he stepped past two round double doors. Poe 33 took the opportunity to whisper to Yin.

"Ozzie..." Poe kept in character, using his snake voice. "...this room is arousing ghostly memories. Faded but definite images from the grand event that led to the premature separation of myself from my master."

"Keep pondering, Hendrix. We'll get you functioning properly soon enough."

The general called peremptorily from the other room. "No dawdling! Follow me!" The two hurried out.

This is unexpected, Caffrey thought as he found himself suddenly unable to move. Tied down at the wrists and the ankles, he was secured to the bed by tentacle-like growths that sprang from the ground. Although the experience was nothing new under the sun for this intergalactic adventurer-gone-Rockstar-gone intergalactic adventurer, the lack of forewarning aroused the sneaking-suspicion center of his brain.

"Relax, my ssssssssssexy tempter," the queen suggested, pulling Monty to his full length.

"Not too hard," Caffrey warned. "Wouldn't want to yank him off mid-feed. The arterial spray would cause quite a mess."

"I love messsssssesssss," she said with a nasty flicking of her forked tongue.

Caffrey then noticed something. It was a subtle discovery, but important nonetheless. The red blooms on the bed sheets were not of any genus he had ever seen. In fact, they were not true red but rather had a definite brownish tint. They looked a bit like the ethereal mist rose of Semmea, with its cloud-like form, but not quite.

"I have a surprise for the both of you," hissed the queen, straddling Caffrey and opening her mouth frighteningly wide.

"That's not necessary. Your hospitality has more than—" Caffrey's words were cut short due to the fact his heart skipped one, perhaps two beats. "Oh, my."

From the profoundest depths of her body came an appendage of sorts; its tip had twin thick red spikes. A red that was oddly familiar to Caffrey. His brain went into overdrive. He looked at the flowers. They were not flowers. They were bloodstains. The stacks of burlap sacks across the room were not burlap sacks. They were the dried, empty shells of all the previous victims of Queen Kinkskin.

"Ah-hah..." Caffrey exhaled.

"Yesssssssssssss, my sssnake prince. Captured for the queen to use." She laughed the perfect laugh of a powerful, bloodthirsty, self-indulgent villain about to get her way.

"It arrived early in the morning. Moments after dawn," Oafy spoke, using a melodramatic tone that was making Angie giggle inside. "The clouds parted, and the craft of the next android guardian to the second-wisest Being in the universe descended to the land."

"Second wisest?" Angie dared to interrupt.

Oafy mumbled some inaudible threat then responded.

"Yes. Second. There can be only One Wisest. Only one Most Powerful."

"Who might that be?"

"Young lady, if you have to ask, then you are not of the proper ilk."

"What was the purpose of the second-wisest one visiting?" Angie asked, playing dumb.

"It was the android's coronation as the Portsmith of the L'Orange." A sneering tone had colored her voice. "My master despises having to peer behind at all the also-rans, wannabes and posers who claim greatness."

"So, why would the coronation of the Portsmith of the Great L'Orange take place on Regal Nine if Queen Kinkskin despises him so?"

"This has nothing to do with Queen Kinkskin!"

"But I thought you said your master—"

Oafy interrupted Angie with thick, sawdust-coated laughter that ricocheted around the stone tower.

"Don't be absurd, girl! Queen Kinkskin is nothing but a physical stimulation-obsessed freak whose perversions sink lower than her embarrassing IQ. To even ponder her in the same neuron firings as my Master is a travesty and insult to Nefarious Wretch!"

"Nefarious Wretch?" Angie wondered aloud.

"Very devious, my pretty. Making me speak my Master's name."

"So, this second-wisest being? What happened—"

"Do not interrupt me. I will get to that when I deem it serves the story."

"I'm sorry," Angie apologized softly, controlling her need to know.

"Queen Kinkskin had nothing to do with the visit, although perhaps in that deluded, snake-infested mass of gray matter she believes she was the focus. The Portsmith was to be inaugurated on Regal Nine because my Master wished it so."

"Why?"

"There are certain worlds that tickle the fancy of my Master. This is one. A perfectly designed central intelligence. A world of efficiency, minimal and easily removed dissent; and most importantly, it is music-free. The art that creates the dangers of freethinking has never evolved here. Regal Nine has all the elements Nefarious needs for his re-creation of the galaxy. And the one thing he covets more than anything."

"Forgive me for being such a silly old dope, for I am only Angie, small and meek. But I don't understand."

"Me! Me! Are you not listening? Do you not feel my presence? I have evolved into the very matrix of this world. I am this world's intelligence! Every atom is under my power and whim! I serve as a model for what the universe will be like under the design and rule of Nefarious Wretch!"

"Of course," Angie agreed, as if closing a prayer.

"Was I ever appreciated by Queen Kinkskin? Did she ever shower me with praise? Offer up her thanks? Speak one word of awe or incredulous discourse of my being? No!"

"She was remiss," Angie said sadly.

"It was all set. The guests had arrived. The feast was laid out. The android was preparing to take his place in history. The L'Orange was being readied to be rolled out in his ebony granary. I convinced Poe Thirty-three, the android, to first prepare himself mentally in the grand gardens of Queen Kinkskin. He agreed. The trap was set."

"Why did it fail?"

"It failed," Oafy said with a great accusatorial ebb in her wave-form, "because the soldiers that guarded this castle at that time were a bunch of imbeciles!"

"Why would someone as wise as yourself hire such incompetent help?"

Oafy seemed to be catching her breath and shouting at the same time. "Kinkskin does the hiring! Never mind! I will continue without further interruption. The coronation took place as usual. Then, as they were paraded through the castle grounds amidst great lauding, somehow the L'Orange simply vanished. We finally caught up to Poe Thirty-three, pondering his fate with the giant erotic estuaries that line the northwest path. The Wise One was gone."

"It would appear the android outsmarted you all." Angie was unable to resist jolting her voice with a single but clearly evident sting of hubris.

"Quiet yourself, young lady! The android did nothing of the sort. He merely performed some cheap parlor trick. A childish bit of prestidigitation," Oafy asserted.

"Naturally," Angie chuckled. "Thank your for that story. It was grand. Thank you, Mistress Oafelia."

Angie whisked out and down the spiraling steps of the tower, ignoring Oafy's protests against the young Revenant's brusqueness.

CHAPTER 11
Killer Queen

(Queen)

YIN STOPPED MIDWAY DOWN THE HALL TO SNIFF A SECTION OF the spiraling wooden floor. General Stanglift marched ahead, calling out in his harsh voice descriptions of the various paintings and pieces of furniture and their historical significance. Poe 33 slowed his pace and turned to watch Yin's olfactory antics.

"Something?" inquired the Portsmith.

"I smell stale water. The same as the H-two-O in the fountain," the Bopple reported, scratching at one of his annoying artificial legs.

Poe 33 sent his blue scanning beam to the intriguing spot for a quick analysis. "Your nose is as accurate as my sensors. Water was spilled in this very spot. It soaked into this rather unusual albeit lovely floor and dried thirty hours later. Behind were left samples of the various microscopic fauna living in the water. Odd—my memory banks contain unlinked neuropaths to a stored holographic image of this exact water sample."

The general called back. "No private sightseeing, ladies! March on! March on! You have yet to see the magnificent triple wheel of fortune, used by Queen Kinkskin to choose the proper pose for the pleasure of her special guests."

"Just a moment!" Yin shouted. He turned back to Poe 33. "That means you've encountered the fountain's water before?"

"No, Yin, it means I have encountered this exact water sample. The water whose fingerprint remains in this very spot."

"Any idea where this grating leads?" Yin asked, referring to the ornate brass grate sitting in the wall just above the water stain.

"My question exactly," Poe 33 agreed. "I have no complete memory links regarding it. I suggest we ask the general."

"Ladies! Are you going to follow my lead or do I have to kick a few Serpentine bahankas?"

"Sir, forgive our dawdling, but we were just admiring this lovely brass grate. Neither Hendrix nor myself has ever seen such impressive work."

"It's a lousy shaft cover. You ladies are easily impressed. Let me show you something worthy of oohs and ahhs."

Actually, as metalwork goes, it wasn't exactly noteworthy.

"First, General, may I ask what sort of shaft is deemed worthy enough for such an exquisite lattice?"

"Garbage. All of Regal Nine's garbage is gathered in the compactor in the sub-basement. We call it the 'tummy of the dragon,'" the general explained with a smile. "Now, follow me. Follow me!"

General Stanglift marched off, never bothering to look behind.

"Poe," whispered Yin, "can you scan the trash compactor?"

"Not from here," Poe concluded.

"That's what I was afraid you were going to say." Yin lifted his paw and pushed the lever on the grating, opening the hatch. "Follow me." He jumped in.

Oh, my, Poe 33 thought, I wouldn't have thought of that.

He followed the impetuous Bopple.

The android landed with a splash amidst floating garbage, trash, dreck, filth, sewage, swill, slop, rubble, rubbish and refuse of all shapes and levels of repugnance. Yin let out a yip and slipped out from beneath Poe's weight.

"Sorry," apologized the Portsmith.

Yin scrambled from the water atop a floating board.

"If I may say, Yin, you look like a sewer rat I came across on my New York wanderings."

Yin fixed the android with an aloof gaze. "Appreciate that, Poe."

The compactor was dark, illuminated just slightly by a smattering of sunlight that managed to make it through the shaft from above.

"I seem to recall this very situation," confided Poe 33, looking around at the spherical room.

"Were you in here the day of your coronation?" Yin wondered.

"No. But I seem to recall this or a place like it. Perhaps from my popular culture records. In any event, it may have been a long time

114

ago in a galaxy far, far away," Poe 33 murmured with a curious look, as if unable to pinpoint the memory.

"Do a scan of every inch of this place. Your chip may have been tossed in the trash," instructed Yin.

General Stanglift had marched to the center of the stained glass gallery before he realized he was alone. He paused a moment and listened to the silence in the raised courtyard. A breeze blew across his face from the open top where snickering willow branches peeked down. He never saw Angie pass overhead.

"Ladies? Where are you two Serpentine sloths?"

There was no response other than the soft wind and the daylight passing through the two dozen brilliantly colored windows.

"What are you waiting for, Poe? Scan the room!" an agitated Yin barked.

"I am unable to focus my scanning beam. There is an inordinate magnetic field that is suppressing it," the android explained, his eyes squinting with each attempt to project his beam.

A metallic creak and moan filled the room, and a distinct ripple raced across the surface of the water.

"I have a bad feeling about this," presaged Yin.

"I sense a change in the dimension of this compactor," announced Poe.

"That would be why it was called a 'compactor' and not, let's say, 'fishcakes.'"

"This was not one of your better ideas, Yin," Poe 33 said worriedly, folding his arms.

"Can't you communicate with the system? Turn this bloody thing off?"

"No, he can't!" General Stanglift said from above, embellishing his words with an evil laugh.

The fleshy, spiked protrusion was mere inches from Caffrey's face. Queen Kinkskin drooled, her hot breath falling on him in unpleasant pants. The dozen snakes on her crown flicked their little forked tongues like a classroom of spoiled children.

"This isn't very romantic," Caffrey observed.

"What can be more romantic than giving one's blood to the love of one's life?" she rasped.

"Love? Ah! Now I see from where the misunderstanding sprang! Like. Its 'like,' Queen Kinkskin. Not love. In fact, it really isn't like at all. It's closer to utter disdain and disgust, if you must know."

The walls rippled like an upset stomach, and Caffrey realized the texture he had mistaken for red tile was, in fact, red, fleshy scales. The queen's body morphed and stretched and her feet entered the ground and became part of its being. From the ceiling, a strange, grotesque limb descended. It was like a weird hand with six gnarled fingers capped with horrid claws.

"Welcome to my womb!"

"Not for nothing, but this has to be the most disgusting thing I have ever seen."

"How quaint."

The hand lowered and punctured Caffrey's shoulder with one of the spikes. Caffrey, to his embarrassment, screamed.

Angie heard Caffrey's scream. Floating mere meters from the secret love nest, she beelined it to the structure and searched desperately for a way in.

"I'm coming, my love!"

A shadowy figure rushed from the brush and stopped before the entrance. Finally, in a pool of light, Angie could identify the rather attractive figure of a female human.

"Who are you?" Angie asked.

The figure was tall and lean and dressed in indigo leather bands that wound their way—quite appropriately—like a snake from her statuesque neck down across her rather ample and alluring bosoms, made more ample and alluring by the wondrous effects of their tight fit. The bands then made a nifty detour just below her navel. Additional deep-blue leather strips pretended to be pants and resulted in a barber-pole effect of blue material and milky-soft skin on her long legs. She drew her weapon and aimed—completely unaware of, or perhaps unconcerned by, the sexual energy she was oozing—and blasted the entranceway with a thick beam of powerful, violet light. The color of the blast matched perfectly the eye color of the weapon's wielder.

Angie followed the purple-eyed woman into the room.

The queen's spiked organ had sliced its way through a few layers of the fake reptile skin on Caffrey's body and penetrated real flesh when the entranceway was blasted open. Both the queen and Caffrey shot their attention to the intruder.

"How dare you!" the queen spat.

"Step aside, bitch!" the purple-eyed woman ordered.

"I am Queen Kinkskin!"

"Then, step aside, royal bitch!"

"Unfasten me!" Caffrey cried.

Four quick and very accurate micro-blasts fragmented the bonds that held his arms and legs. Acting on instinct, Caffrey grabbed hold of the large hand-like horror and pushed it toward the queen's head. The purple-eyed woman blasted a single shot into the hand, causing the fingers to spasm, contracting into a fist and engulfing the head of the queen. A muffled scream sounded as the hand retracted to the ceiling, its fingers like hypodermic needles quickly draining the fluids from the queen, her body imploding like a punctured balloon.

"That's one way to deflate an ego," Caffrey said, jumping off the platform.

The walls of the room shivered and warped.

"What is this?" the purple-eyed woman gazed around curiously.

"Although I have never seen one in person until now, we are presently in an ante-uteral serpendia."

"Can you translate that into one of the galactic standards?" the purple-eye woman requested.

"We are in the womb of Queen Kinkskin, a womb that exists separate from her primary body. Usually placed in a nest of grasses and bushes."

"Disgusting," Angie spat.

The purple-eyed woman agreed with a frown. "How attractive."

The womb shook again, but this time it flickered as if its very fabric were dissipating.

"This world is going to be extracted into the dimension of Nefarious Wretch," the purple-eyed woman informed them.

"Are you okay, love?" Angie slipped up to Caffrey and spoke into his ear.

"Where are Yin and Poe? Did they find the chip?"

"I haven't a clue. I was more concerned with your safety!"

"Find them! Quick!" Caffrey ordered.

"Yes, mien Fuehrer!" Angie left rapidly, in a sarcastic huff.

117

Caffrey locked a hard stare at the two purple beacons studying his reptilian form then slowly grinned. "So. I was wondering when I would gaze upon those purple eyes again."

"Good to see you, too. Although I hope your new look is temporary," she commented.

"I thought one snake would appreciate another."

"What? No 'thank you?'"

He grabbed her by the throat and slammed her, face first, into the moist and squishy womb wall. "Now, Ms. Grape Eyes, where are my band-mates?"

"I like it rough, Caffrey. But now is not the time nor place, although the location offers some uniquely kinky possibilities."

"Where are they?"

"I'm not sure."

"You've lost them? Like a set of keys or your virginity?"

"I didn't lose them. I beamed them aboard a certain craft, where they were to be stored. Safely. I went to retrieve them and discovered they had been shipped out."

"Where?"

"To a toy auction," she whispered, a little embarrassed.

"A what?"

"A toy auction. The holographic chip that contains them was mistaken for an expansion pack for a Yiplakin Holographic Army-in-a-Box, a popular plaything that's currently all the rage throughout the Plethorian Sector."

Caffrey let her go and took a few steps back. He'd vowed to no longer take part in any acts of violence unless absolutely necessary. He despised violence. The sight of Queen Kinkskin, hanging limp and empty made him sick. He still had qualms about the fate of the Crebbledogs Plooky and Xilpat. Nonetheless, waves of violent images like purple eyeballs being used in a billiards game filled his mind. He took a deep breath, spun the woman around and looked deep into those same eyes.

"Is it safe to assume that some toy collector has purchased my friends and has placed them in some dusty collector's case where they are safe and secure?"

"Possibly. More likely the child of some rich and powerful businessman received them as a birthday gift. Wherefore they would now be submerged in virtual battles with virtual monsters of unimaginable horror."

"Virtual?" Caffrey need that verified.

"Yes. But such fright could conceivably cause irreversible psychological damage. Or cardiovascular failure."

"You're not helping your cause," Caffrey growled.

"My cause is your cause," she said with great sincerity.

"Since when?"

"Since ODOR stole my home planet," she sighed, eyes downcast.

"Ah! The cause has a rebel?"

"My world is gone."

"And your purple eyes will never gaze upon those familiar grassy fields, lush forests and rolling hills again."

"I lived on a ice ball. Planet Quyube was one big glacier. Summer means helium is in gas form. But, yes, I will miss it."

"Who are you?"

"My name is Violet. Violet Leer."

"Oh, it is not," Caffrey challenged with a doubting pout.

"It is. Was my mother's name, as well. My grandparents didn't have much in the way of imagination."

"Apparently."

Violet raised hers eyes to his. "I want to help you."

"Don't need your help," retorted Caffrey, heading for the exit and, for the second time in his life, slipping from the womb.

The compacting sphere had shrunk to half its original size and Yin and Poe were positioning themselves at its center. Poe 33 called up to the general, "Sir! If you would, it's getting a bit cramped."

"The queen is very fussy about private tours by newbie tourists to Regal Nine. I may very well have to crush you to a pulpy death," General Stanglift deduced in calm, arrogant tones.

Angie flew invisibly from the chute.

"Yin. Poe. It's me."

"Angie!" Yin replied, keeping his voice down. "Where's Caffrey?"

"He's with some purple-eyed bitch." The acid in her tone was unmistakable.

Yin and Poe exchanged knowing glances.

"The queen is dead. We have to leave. Now. This godforsaken planet is about to be stolen."

"We're in a bit of a bind, Angie, my girl," Yin pointed out what was not necessarily the obvious to a being with very little crushable mass.

Angie was impressed. "My, you are. What can I do?"

"Can you convince Oafy to turn this off?"

"I doubt it. I better get back out there—oh, my, that's odd!"

"What's the matter?"

"I can't move. There's an odd magnetic field creeping around me like a syrup-soaked fur coat." Angie said, straining to break free as she spoke.

"That same field has rendered my scanning ability defunct," bemoaned Poe.

The walls continued to move in on the trio with a barely perceptible but unavoidably menacing groaning sound almost felt rather than heard.

"Well, guys, don't just stand there! Try and brace these walls with something!" Angie cried.

"Yes," Poe said pensively, "I am positive I have witnessed this situation before."

"If I could somehow climb these walls and get out that chute," Yin pondered, studying the ceiling. A horrid buzz erupted.

"That is not good," Poe 33 announced in a small voice.

"No, it isn't," Angie agreed.

"Now what?" Yin's asked confused.

"Magnetism. It just increased twenty-fold. I am officially paralyzed," Poe 33 said in a statement of surrender.

"Me, too," Angie said, her voice warping.

"How is that, android? Do you feel your innards ready to implode?" teased the general.

"Piss off, Stanglift! We're partying. To heck with your magnetic field. Hendrix is in utter ecstasy! He loves every Gaussian increment! Increase way! Exponentially, Strangelust!!"

"I would rather he didn't." Poe's voice was on the wane like a winter moon.

"Trust me, Poe." Yin winked. "You're shielded from magnetic damage?"

"Yes. But it is rather uncomfortable."

"You walk around with ten artificial legs and tell me about discomfort. Deal with it a few more moments. I have a plan."

"Are you suffering down there?" It seemed Stanglift had experienced a resurgence of confidence.

"Suffering? Are you kidding? I eat magnetism for lunch. I shit iron filings," Yin scoffed, "in magnificently sculpted shapes!"

Stanglift needed more convincing. "How about you, android?"

Poe 33 could barely work his mouth but agreed to help Yin with his plot. "Maybe if it was increased tenfold more?" the android mumbled with a definite frown.

"Tenfold? Ha! Try fifty, metal woman!"

Yin cringed as the increased magnetic power launched him up some ten meters to where he smacked the sphere's steel surface.

"It worked!" exulted Yin as he hung, stuck by the studs of his collar.

"Please hurry, Yin. I feel like I am balancing a small neutron star atop my head," Poe 33 moaned.

"Yessssssss. Pleaeeessss...hhhhhurrrrrr..." Angie's spoken worlds were warped and sounded like a very scratched 1920s disc played at half speed.

"Hang in there, Poe, Angie," Yin comforted as he struggled to crawl along the surface towards the chute. In his mind's eye he figured he should be wearing a Ninja headband.

The sound of Caffrey's footsteps bounced around the stone walls of the castle's eastern portico. Following nothing but the map of his instincts, he stopped where the path split off in a Y. He faced the two equally wide halls running off at forty-five degree angles and pondered a moment. A brush of static tickled the back of his neck. He turned.

"Ringo. It's me, Angie," the voice said.

It had the same pitch and tone of Angie, but there was something lacking. The sensual lilt, perhaps, or the innocent, yet sincere love. Caffrey was too rushed and hurried to notice.

"Angie-girl. Yes. Where are Yin and Poe?"

"I'm not sure, Ringo," the Angie-ish voice answered.

"What do you mean? Where's General Stanglift?"

"He is giving Hendrix and Ozzie a tour of the castle."

"Queen Kinkskin's dead. We have to get out of here. This world is going to be extracted!"

"That's nonsense!" the voice protested.

"There's no time to debate this..."

Yin was using every ounce of energy and strength in his little body to drag himself. Each step he fought both the incredibly powerful magnetic field that locked his collar studs to the surface and gravity that was pulling on his rear end.

"You're awfully quiet down there!" the general mocked, "Are you ready to admit defeat?"

Poe and Angie mumbled inaudibly. Yin didn't even make the attempt. He was inches from the opening and couldn't risk using his last ounce of power on spoken words.

"Sounds to me as though death has arrived on the welcome mat of my serpentine guests. A pity. Never got to see the queen's precious stone bidet collection."

Yin's front paws slipped into the opening and with a final tug, he freed his collar from the magnetic surface. Hanging on with all sets of claws and the suction ability of his faux serpentine body parts, he crawled up the chute.

⇒●

Caffrey cocked an ear and proceeded down a red-and-yellow marble hall that brought him to a magnificent staircase.

"I think the general was last in the small antechamber at the bottom of this staircase. Are you going to kill him?" Oafy asked, with Angie's naïve accent.

"Considering my Willy is aboard the *Moby Dick*, I think that's doubtful, Angie."

"There's a slew of weapons in that wooden armory just beneath these stairs. I was nosing around."

Caffrey raced down the steps; and spotting the tall, narrow closet, he pulled open its double doors. It was filled with swords, scabbards, stilettos and daggers. Ignoring all the blades, he picked up a triple-balled mace.

"Wicked choice," Oafy said, with an Angie-like sigh.

A high-pitched *Yip!* and a scream of agony raced to Caffrey's ears from far across the series of halls before him.

"Yin!" Caffrey took off. Oafy chuckled and followed.

⇒●

Poe 33 stood motionless, his eyes closed and his arms and legs akimbo in a silly pose that illustrated his complete surrender to the forces of magnetism.

"Angie. Angie, are you still there?" he asked in a slow and oddly modulated diction.

"Yes," she replied.

122

Both Angie and Poe 33's vocals would have been completely indecipherable to human ears. But their respective audio circuits were highly sensitive, each able to make sense of the other's speech.

"Poe, if I don't make it I want you to know something."

"What is that, Angie?"

"You did not fail your master. You saved him."

"I wish it were so. But I was delinquent—"

"No!" Angie interrupted. "I heard the details from Oafelia. She was witness to it. You caused your master to vanish to safety. You were very brave and honorable. You fought courageously in the gardens and sent your Master on his way rather than have him captured. You sacrificed yourself for him," Angie said, spicing up the tale a bit for the sake of Poe's ego.

Poe 33 seemed to ponder her words a moment, then his eyes opened. "You said I caused my master to vanish?"

"Yes. Oafelia saw it."

"That's odd. The only way that could happen would be if I were to remove the entanglement circuit that linked my neural matrix with that of my master's."

"You sacrificed a part of your own body for the sake of your master's safety. You are, indeed, amazing, Poe Thirty-three."

"That information fills me brim-worthy with great euphoria. Yes! The gardens! My positive arousal seems to have freed repressed memories. A moon, behind a liquid sky. Smiling with angry eyes."

"I don't understand, Poe."

"You don't need to, Angie. But if we do make it, I will see that monuments are built in your honor. Large ones. Perhaps the size of moons that orbit ones the size of planets that in turn orbit—"

"I get the point, Poe. That's sweet. But...what?"

Poe suddenly appeared even more excited.

"I know where my missing chip is!"

Be they belong to West Highland terrier or Frezenese Bopple, sharp canines, when sunk deep into the calf muscle of a humanoid, are a very effective means of causing the sensation of pain.

"Yeeeeeooowwwwww!" came the universal expression of agony[12] from the mouth of General Stanglift. Yin was locked onto the

---

[12] The Gwenipol folk of Unbillia do not scream nor make any audible expression of pain. Instead, they sketch religious scenes on parchment.

general's leg as the old soldier hopped up and down, desperately trying to dislodge the biting Bopple.

"Turn off the compactor!" Yin ordered through his clenched teeth.

"Yeeeeahhhhooww!" repeated the general.

"Yin!" Caffrey called out as he entered the room, almost losing his footing on the smooth, shining surface of the exotic wooden floor.

"Turn off the compactor!" Yin repeated, this time to Caffrey.

Caffrey looked about the room, soon spotting the opened control station beside the chute entrance. General Stanglift, his eyes rolling around in his skull and his face snow-white, hopped toward a sword on display beside the large, circular stained glass window. Caffrey raced to the bank of switches and blinking lights and punched the "Dump" button.

"Ringo!" the faux Angie screamed. "The general!"

Caffrey turned just as Stanglift slid the sword from its mount, ready to slice Yin to cold cuts if necessary in order to rid himself of the throbbing pain. Caffrey spun the mace over his head and let the ball and chains fly. The general's wrist was snagged by the chains, and the kinetic energy pulled him off-balance, sending him slipping on the wood floor and tumbling through the colorful glass display with an almost musical tintinnabulation. The general and Yin cascaded out and down.

"Yin!" Caffrey yelled.

Oafy, in her best Angie impersonation, reasoned, "You go save Hendrix! I'll take care of the compactor. There's a dump chute just beyond the front wall of the gardens!"

Caffrey rushed out without a word.

"Sorry, my pretty. Age before beauty," pronounced Oafy with a victorious snicker

---

Poe 33 found himself sitting amidst rubbish and the overgrown weeds that had been let grow around the garbage chute adjacent to the perimeter wall of the garden. He looked like a drunk ejected from a pub.

"My, I have never truly appreciated the pleasure of fresh air before," he said in his real voice with a little soft cymbal brushing in the backing track. He looked around the barren stretch of stubby

124

pocaplants and seebo grass, cocking his head as if trying to pick up a sound. "Are you okay, Angie?" he asked, scanning the area. "Angie?"

There was no reply.

Caffrey bounded across the front lawn and around the massive side wall of the castle, abruptly stopping himself from crashing into Violet. She wore a concerned expression.

"I don't think you want to go back there," she advised somberly.

He stepped around her and continued to the castle moat. The deep, moldy green water seemed to ooze rather than flow. Within this murk moved large figures; long, flowing bodies rippled the surface with the tips of their pointy fins. They were busy enjoying a rather bloody meal. Bits and pieces of Stanglift's uniform floated to the surface. There was no sign of white fur.

Caffrey stared into the water, then peered upward. The jagged edges of the once-ornate window dangled like the epilogue to a horrid tale.

"I'm sorry, Caffrey," Violet murmured, stepping up behind him. "I'm sure it was quick. Gulping zedfish get their names from quickly but painlessly swallowing their meals."

The sound of Poe 33's servos turned Caffrey's head, and the android built urgent tones into his words.

"Quark Caffrey, I suggest we find Angie and Yin."

"Yin, I'm afraid, has met a tragic end," Oafy explained, being Angie.

The news didn't seem to register properly with the distracted Poe, who babbled, "Despite the unhappy turn of events for our four-legged comrade, I have rather good news. I believe I have recalled the location of my chip!" He moved off decisively, servos whining.

Caffrey followed the android. Violet pushed passed Poe. The party entered the courtyard where they had first met Queen Kinkskin. Poe 33 gestured to the Fountain of Dimenatries.

"Thanks to Angie, I recalled the events leading up to the disappearance of my Master. Moments after I was announced into the Phallus of the Palace I sensed a presence. It was subtle, a ghostly twinge in my inner self. Although the masculine wisdom aspects of my intelligence matrix could not comprehend the intruder, my deeper, feminine understanding systems realized it was leaking in from another dimension. It was such a brief occurrence I spent only nanoseconds of thought on it.

"You have to understand. Although I am the great Poe Thirty-three I did have a number of analogous members of the group Lepidoptera hovering in my stomach. I wandered out here to ponder my choices. I decided it best to cut the entanglement tie between myself and my master; and I ripped from my own guts the very chip that allows for such a close, quantum relationship. I was suddenly distracted by a burly guard, who ran into the garden with a large metallic weapon. I fought, as Angie described it, valiantly and with great testosterone-soaked vigor," Poe 33 added, figuring a little embellishment couldn't hurt. "In the mêlée, we both fell into the waters of this fountain."

"So, that's who you are!" Her voice a soft whisper, Oafy identified the Portsmith beneath the snakeskin camouflage.

Poe 33 rattled on with his explanation. "After the defeat of my adversary my memory of the story begins to fade. I recall somehow being back in the castle, perhaps running in a panic. Then it goes quickly from gray to black."

Caffrey walked around the fountain and peered into the clear water. Something caught his attention, and he bent over the stone ledge and dunked his head. He found himself staring at a set of small bare buttocks, formed in stone relief on the bottom of the fountain. Lodged in the little smile of the cherub coolie was a small metallic square. Touches of orange glinted off its smooth surface. Caffrey plucked it out and removed his dripping head from the cool waters.

"I found your smiling moon. And your chip, Poe," he announced.

"Wonderful!" the android exclaimed, doing a little tapdance, "With this returned to my system I will soon be reunited with the One—as such a rare and wondrous specimen of an android should be!"

A weird ripple washed across the entire landscape, interrupting Poe 33's single-handed orgy of self-praise. It was not a tremor beneath the ground, but rather a shimmy of everything. The very fabric of space seemed to warp and dance.

"This world is being extracted," Violet calmly stated. "Like I told you."

"Ridiculous!" the Revenant voice argued, almost losing control of her Angie impersonation.

Poe 33 corroborated. "The one with purple eyes is correct. We must leave immediately! I calculate the entropy of this system decreasing exponentially."

"This world is chosen! It is special! I was promised!" Angie's voice was cracking, and bits of Oafy's smoky and angry tones were slipping through.

"What's wrong, Angie? We have to leave! Now! Get the ship ready!" Caffrey shouted as he urged Poe and Violet out of the courtyard toward the landing area.

I'll destroy that egomaniacal liar, too! I'll destroy all of them. I will control L'Orange. I will re-create the universe in my glorious image! Oafy thought as she obeyed Caffrey's order and flew across the gardens and to the *Moby Dick*. In her mind's eye, she pondered the universe and how it would look under the design of an electrical sentient intelligence with no physical form. Quite different. Quite different.

From deep within the castle, in the heart of the compactor, a voice called out, soft and muffled. Angie waited to be rescued from her magnetic prison. Her cries fell on no one's ears.

CHAPTER 12
Space Oddity

(DAVID BOWIE)

GOING. GOING. GONE," UTTERED POE 33 AS THE *MOBY DICK* raced from Regal 9. The world of the fluid-sucking Queen Kinkskin and her Court of Odd Love was no more. A wash of gas, dust and glittering primordial matter swirled round and round into the infinite depths of a singularity, like dirty water down a kitchen sink drain.

Caffrey stared with saddened eyes, wondering what fate held for his poochie-woochie. Was Yin alive in the horrid dimension of Nefarious Wretch? Was he simply eaten by the horrid gulping zed-fish? Did he go kicking, scratching and biting into the belly of the beast?

"I am sorry about Yin, Quark," Violet offered, stepping up beside him.

"Can we drop you off somewhere?" he asked, looking into her purple eyes with a cold sneer. "Perhaps the nearest black hole?"

"Don't be ludicrous," Violet snapped, backing away from his raw anger.

Caffrey was about to retort when suddenly his words were cut short. A saddened expression softened his face—he'd recalled hearing Yin utter those same words in his wry but sweet tone. He softened his harsh look and studied her eyes, then: "Poe, what do your sensory circuits relay to you regarding her integrity?"

A quick wash of blue light scanned Violet's head.

"Nothing conclusive. Perhaps if you replaced my chip, Quark Caffrey?"

Caffrey's eyes brightened—he'd totally forgotten. Taking the small blue plate from his pocket, he nodded to Poe. The android opened a small door at the base of his lower back.

"I will self-illuminate the slot," Poe 33 advised, causing the perimeter around it to glow a soft green. "Please remove the scrambler."

Caffrey quickly pulled out the offending circuit and replaced it with the blue plate. With a soft whine, it was pulled deeper into Poe 33's torso. A flash and a soft beep indicated correct installation. Poe 33 closed the panel.

"How's that?" Caffrey asked.

Poe's reply was sobering.

"Troublesome."

"Why?"

"I was expecting to feel an instant karmic connection to my master. I should be feeling the non-local entangled link, even if separated by a billion light-years. I feel nothing in any corner of known space and time."

Caffrey frowned with disappointment, but Poe spoke again.

"Interesting. I am getting a systems error. There should be a component in slot C-one-thirty-three. I am finding that space empty. Would you please check, Quark Caffrey?"

Caffrey confirmed it to be empty. "What's missing?"

"My master," Poe 33 said sadly. "There should be a diamond vial containing a minute sample of the Wise Substance."

A worried expression washed across Caffrey's face.

"Would that be the vial you removed when we were at the pier back in New York?'

Poe 33 tried to recall the moment.

"It is a vague memory, as the scrambler seems to have faded its specifics. Perhaps. Do you still have it?"

"No," Caffrey admitted, very softly.

"Excuse me, Quark Caffrey?"

"I left it on the bar."

"On the what?" Violet asked aghast.

"The bar. With Sam! Thanks to you, I rushed out. Sam must have it."

"I am getting no signals of the back-up vial, either."

Caffrey nodded. "That's gone as well."

"How do you know that?" Violet wondered.

"Quigmo Digmo had it. One of his contacts stole it from Poe."

"On Yeplu Seven," recalled Poe 33.

"Yes."

"So, perhaps we can pay Mr. Digmo a visit and retrieve it?" suggested Poe 33.

"No good. I stole it from Quigmo," Violet confessed. "Gave it to Yin."

"And Yin gave it to me."

"And you, Quark Caffrey, ate it," stated Poe mournfully.

Violet was stunned. "You did what?"

"I ate it! Yin insisted!"

"I am doomed," prophesied the Portsmith as his face collapsed into a mud pile of dejection.

The Galax-Skein monitors began flashing. Caffrey glanced at the screen.

"There's an all-planets bulletin coming in," he indicated as he watched for the announcement.

"This replay of the extraction of Regal Nine is brought to you by Wormwood Fossil Fuel Corp," said a bubbly voice as very un-Rock music began playing. A multi-angled video clip of the world of Queen Kinkskin spiraling away played in full-spectrum color. "Thanks to the generosity of Quigmo Digmo Limited, Wormwood Fossil Fuel can continue to bring our customers galaxy-wide cheap and plentiful combustion fuels to keep their lives running bright. Our 'Fuel Recovery of Extracted Entities' program continues to supply trillions of liters of the precious resource."

"Quigmo," mouthed Caffrey, with a smirk.

"Remember," the bubbly voice continued. "They don't play by the rules, then we take their fuel. And pass those savings on to you, our loyal customers!"

The replay of Regal 9's vanishing act finished, and a Being appeared on the screen. It had a large head, a smattering of eyes and hairy clumps dotting the face. A small mouth protruded where a chin should be.

"Spydersloth Blaust." The words hissed softly from Violet like a horrid curse.

Caffrey noticed her sincere disdain—it was hard not to—but he said nothing. He watched the screen with great interest.

"On the upcoming Labates Day of the offspring of our wondrous leader," the Arachnid began, "Another world mired in the muck of music will cease to exist in this realm. Come watch its end—a sobering experience for all music-practicing worlds—live, aboard the *Crystal Guise*! Come. Learn. Find the true path of disharmony."

"That's it. Labates Day!" Violet said excitedly.

"What is Labates Day?" Caffrey inquired testily.

Poe spoke up. "It is the day when the young are initiated into the mindset of non-lyrical thinking. It is traditional to give a child some sort of musical symbol for them to destroy. An instrument to crush. Music sheets to burn. Sometimes musicians to torment."

Violet agreed. "Yes! Your friends, in their state of compacted holographic form, mistaken for a Yiplakin Holographic Army in a Box add-on, would make the perfect gift for a child of ODOR! Musicians he can torment in virtual worlds of non-rhythmic horror! It may be a long shot, but it would make sense for ODOR to swipe them."

Caffrey smiled. Could the universe have shaken its pale ass of synchronicity in his face again? "Angie, check GS. Find out if there's any info about Spydersloth Blaust's whereabouts. Check under 'Parties and Night Life.'"

After a brief search, Oafy responded in Angie's sweet and sincere dialect. "Bingo! Spydersloth Blaust's ship, the *Crystal Guise*, is orbiting Haptiwoo. In the Komquista System."

"And we have a VIP ticket to the party!" said Violet, turning her eyes toward Poe 33.

"I don't understand," the android explained honestly.

Violet enlarged. "You, Poe, will be our VIP ticket aboard that gigantic, floating nest of brainwashed fanatics. Spydersloth will have us as his personal guests if he thinks he can get his hands on the enigmatic Portsmith."

Caffrey and Poe 33 each pondered the idea.

"Angie, let's get out of this miserable system. Pop a hole."

"Aye, aye, my itchy cake."

⟫━━

The real Angie voyaged alone in a black void that had been the space occupied by Regal 9. She raced towards the *Moby Dick*, desperately trying to avoid the ripples and waves of the fabric of reality and make it back aboard her home. Back to her friends. She beelined it toward the stern-positioned communications antenna. She would show her wrath to Oafelia. She would vow her eternal love to Caffrey.

The wormhole created by the *Moby Dick*'s engines was closing quickly. The ship vanished, and Angie raced for the portal.

The journey through the galactic shortcut took a few days, but, all in all, some forty thousand years of travel time was trimmed from the trip. The crew tried to regain their fortitude with long stretches of sleep. The makeup made by Lindboola was beginning to fade, and Monty had shriveled and fallen off. Poe's sheen had returned and the Serpentine days of Caffrey, and the Portsmith would soon be lost to memory.

The flashing streaks outside the ship retracted into smaller patches then finally returned to the normal star field of the surrounding space.

"Looks like we've come out into the system containing planet Haptiwoo." Violet stared through the view port and pointed. "And there she is. The beautiful ringed star of Komquista."

The bluish-white giant hung some one hundred-twenty million kilometers away, with its strange ring of red plasma.

"Angie, can you tell me anything about the quantum integrity of this system?" Caffrey asked.

"Entropy is as expected. All six planets are, as of yet, in normal condition. Spydersloth's craft is seventy million kilometers away, orbiting the planet of Haptiwoo."

"We need to get a message to the ship," asserted Violet, "Explain that we are mere supplicants who have captured the enigmatic Portsmith to the Great L'Orange and will present it to Spydersloth Blaust as our gift of love, honor and respect for his being."

Caffrey's nausea dripped down his face.

"Yes. Pretty sickening. Desperate times," she said as if she had just swallowed a mouthful of brine. Her expression softened. "I should have held on to your friends personally, Caffrey. We never intended to lose them. I promised Yin."

"You promised Yin what?"

Violet turned. "I was never a member of ODOR, I infiltrated them. Working closely with Yin."

"You and my dog?"

"Yin is one of the most respected members of the Order. He worked his way into your life when he realized how integral you were. I was asked by him to play the mysterious villain. Lure you into the little adventure."

"That Machiavellian mutt!" spat Caffrey.

"He was thinking of the big picture. He knew the only way to assure your involvement was proper motivation. Yin thinks the world of you, Caffrey. Always bragged how no one rubbed his tummy like you."

Caffrey gave her a long, hard look. He wasn't sure he if believed her story. He still had the urge to eject her into the dark lap of space. But she was gorgeous. He had been so distracted with the task at hand it had sort of slipped his mind. She held his gaze and smiled coyly, sending a tingle slithering from his eye sockets to every pore of his body.

He forced himself back to business. "Contact Spydersloth's ship and offer him Poe. Be sure to insist that we will only deliver the android if both you and myself can board as well. Angie will be our sleuth. And I suggest we travel at sub-hype speeds in sissymode. I don't want his eminence picking up our signature until we are on his front porch."

"It will take two full days to reach his ship," reported Oafy.

"Fine."

"Glad to see you thinking clearly," Violet said with another tingle-inducing smile. "And if you need some proof of my alignment with Yin, have Angie pull up the news report from the famous thirty-three-day Hoga Land Uprising."

Violet took a seat at the G.S. Station.

"Angie..." Caffrey's voice implied the order.

"Yes?" a discombobulated Oafy responded.

"The news story," Caffrey snapped through his teeth. Poe 33 stepped beside him.

"Quark Caffrey," he whispered, "I am picking up frequency spikes that neither resemble nor match any in my recorded history of Angie's vocal patterns."

"I'm one step ahead of you, Poe. Just continue to play along," Caffrey whispered back.

"Your news story will be on screen in exactly point-five seconds," Oafy announced.

"Thank you very much, Angie, my love," Caffrey said loudly, as the screen before him flickered.

A series of video clips, still photos and narration explained the story of the bloody Hoga Land Uprising. Caffrey watched in stunned silence as the screen displayed footage of the little Bopple and Violet, dressed in camouflage fatigues, training and discussing

133

strategy. Images of Yin addressing the great rebel armies, practicing hand-to-hand combat and visiting the wounded flashed before the eyes of Caffrey and Poe 33.

"Yin's exploits equal my own during my Rendavene," the android bragged.

The presentation continued with stunning combat footage of Yin and Violet leading the troops on a raid of the fascist headquarters of the dictatorial leaders, who had placed their iron grip on the once-peaceful world. Finally, a great victory parade, complete with ticker-tape of real silver and gold, marked their victory. The screen went black.

"Well. I'm retroactively embarrassed at buying Yin all those chew toys," Caffrey mumbled, his face turning sad again. "I could use a Bezzie."

"I could use a Bezzie myself," Violet replied, stretching her arms.

"A girl after my own heart." Caffrey smiled. "Angie, two Bezzies. And prepare feast six-A."

"Six-A. That would be the 'Last Supper Before Possibly Meeting One's Maker' feast?" Oafy double-checked.

"Yes, Angie. With fries. And let's hear something fun. Aerosmith, Van Halen and toss in a little Stones."

"Very well."

Caffrey and Violet spent the next hour enjoying a hearty meal. Caffrey savored a potent veggie chili flavored with many exotic peppers and spices, to the detriment of the rest of the crew. Violet enjoyed a pre-formed filet mignon, cooked medium rare and glazed with a sintoberry-and-brandy glaze. Roasted yellow toad potatoes, blueberry beans and umis umis—a sweet-and-sour ice cream popular in the literati coffeehouses on Banymede 4—rounded out the meal.

As the Bezzie flowed and David Lee Roth sang, they talked. Caffrey told Violet about his days as an exotic meat collector and the proud moment when he purchased the *Moby Dick*. He explained why Rock music kicked the ass of every other form of music, using many, many examples to prove his point.

Violet spoke of her childhood and how she was a stowaway on a freighter transporting fruits and insects from the mysterious jungle planet of Dharx, where she spent a year alone in the jungle, learning how to survive on the fauna round her. Caffrey listened with great interest as she regaled him with the events that led to her serendipitous meeting with Yin. Locked in adjacent cells in a dank and moldy dungeon in Fek, (the largest city of Dharx) each learned that the other had been arrested for camping without a license. It was here, in the dark and stinking prison block, that they learned of ODOR's plot from a fellow inmate, incarcerated for the public playing of a small, piccolo-type instrument.

Two months later, Yin managed to swipe a key from a guard, and the trio escaped into the night and back into the gloomy and strange jungle. They made their way to the tiny village of Larx, where, through some clever talk, bribery and a bit of theft, they hitched a ride aboard the greasy cargo craft of a traveling Yarso ship[13]. They made it safely to Hi-Ro, an outpost for traders, misfits and general social outcasts, where they met Poe 33, lost, confused and crying in his tall glass of cheenago. They learned of his dilemma and immediately saw the dangerous implications of having the wisest substance in the universe floating around unattended. They learned he was seeking the bloodline of his maker and vowed to help.

Caffrey told the story of how he had been walking home from a late rehearsal session when the soft cries of Yin grabbed his attention just off Minetta Lane near Sixth Avenue and Bleeker Street. Unaware that the entire situation was a setup, his heart broke at the sight of the poor oil-soaked pooch, caught by the hind foot in a hole left by Con Edison workmen. Giving in to his sense of compassion, and feeling the need to return positive karma to a universe where he had contributed to the deliberate death of many of its more exotic creatures, he unknowingly played into the hands of the hidden conspiracy and took the dog home.

Violet fell asleep in her chair, and Caffrey's eyelids were hanging like wet towels. He glanced at Poe 33, who sat staring out at the beautiful ringed star, and looked around the cabin as if to somehow catch a glimpse of Angie, or rather, the joker trying to pass itself off as Angie.

"Angie," he called out, "you can shut down and rest a bit. Poe 33 will keep an eye on things for the next eight hours."

"I'm fine, my divine Master," Oafy said.

"Keep an eye on things," whispered Caffrey to Poe 33.

"Very well, Quark Caffrey."

---

[13] A circus of sorts that specializes in ice sculptures, imbecile juggling and lively discussion.

Caffrey turned and opened a panel on the wall, revealing a small sleeping compartment. He took off his shoes and slipped under the covers.

"Quark Caffrey," Poe 33 called.

"Yes, Poe?"

"It may seem that you have been betrayed by your own bloodline, but in the end the universe will appreciate your sacrifices. Ultimately, you can't do much better than that."

"Thank you, Poe. Goodnight."

"Actually, 'day' and 'night' have little meaning in space, as that distinction only works on the surface of rotating worlds."

"Goodnight," Caffrey repeated.

"Goodnight, Quark Caffrey," Poe 33 answered without the further use of qualifiers.

"Goodnight, Angie," Caffrey said, after a moment of silence.

"Goodnight, master," Oafy said. *And we'll just see who gets credit for saving, or should I say, changing the universe.*

Caffrey lay under the covers a moment, staring up at the roof of the sleeping compartment. He felt the sudden presence of Violet, crawling up beside him.

"So, tell me more about this music of yours," she whispered in her most erotic tone.

"Angie," Caffrey called out, "Dark Side of the Moon—'The Great Gig in the Sky.' Just repeat it a couple of dozen times."

"Yes, my toy tree bark sand puppet," the phony Angie replied, without an ounce of jealousy or grasp of the fine art of corny moniker usage.

They smiled at each other, and as the compartment door closed shut, they engaged in the heated exchange of saliva.

⸺

For the next three hours Poe 33 stared out to space, watching the relative size of Komquista grow larger and the occasional hunk of space junk whiz by. Planet Haptiwoo appeared the size of a yellow pigeon pea basking in the starlight. Finally, after seven hours, the flickering of Spydersloth Blaust's ship became evident.

"'Morning, Poe," Caffrey groaned. "Looks like we're close."

"A mere one-point-two million kilometers," calculated the android.

"Good morning, my master. There is a cup of hot Earth coffee awaiting you with one sugar and a dash of cream," Oafy reported in her best Angie voice.

"Thank you. Very thoughtful," Caffrey said, reaching into the food prep unit and retrieving the cup. He was about to sip his coffee when the entire ship lurched forward, spilling the hot drink and sending Violet tumbling out of the sleeping compartment to the floor. They shared a coy smirk, and he helped her to her feet.

"What the heck was that?" she wondered.

Caffrey rushed to the control station. He frowned. "Poe? Did you take us out of sissymode?"

The android was quick to reply. "No—but it would appear that we have been discovered and are caught in the tug beam of Spydersloth Blaust's ship."

"Angie?" Caffrey implied the question with a stern tone.

"Of course not. I cannot execute such an order without the expressed desire of my captain, my sweet rock wooden beach basket."

Caffrey decided not to pursue the issue. He pressed the comlink button.

"This is the spacecraft *Moby Dick*. We are humbly delivering a special gift to the great Spydersloth Blaust. It is not necessary to pull us in against our will as our collective will dictates that we come with open arms and on bended knee." He barely managed to speak without laughing.

A voice came back. It was a female voice, singsong and high of pitch. It spoke rapidly, interspersing the foreign words with clicks and fart-like noises.

"Anyone know what language that is?" Violet asked.

"It's Byronese. I don't understand it," Caffrey pronounced, turning to Poe 33. "Poe?"

"She is explaining that, since we were not invited by Mr. Blaust, she is pulling us directly into the ship's trash vaporizer, where we will be reduced to a powdered form," the android explained without inflection, adding somewhat irrelevantly, "It's a rather neat system. Large hunks of steel, glass, plastic. Reduced to a mist of powdery dust."

"They can't do that! We're on bended knee!" Caffrey protested. "Poe! Take the mike and translate for me!"

Poe 33 stepped up to the microphone as the *Moby Dick* continued its uncontrolled journey towards the huge ship.

Caffrey began his diplomatic exhortation. "Listen to me, you bunch of fanatical twits!"

Poe 33 exchanged glances with Violet then looked at Caffrey silently.

"Okay, skip that," Caffrey sighed. "We are delivering a special gift to Mr. Blaust. A gift so special it will change, literally, the fabric of his universe."

Poe translated. There was no reply.

Caffrey tried a little more explanation. "It is paramount that Mr. Blaust receive this gift. It will aid in his retrieval of that pesky and elusive wise orange stuff he has been searching for."

Again, Poe 33 translated the message, speaking with all the subtleties of a real Byronese citizen. He turned to Caffrey and whispered, "I took the liberty of referring to my master as 'The Great Wise One' as opposed to 'pesky and elusive wise orange stuff.' I hope you don't mind?"

Caffrey waved Poe off and waited for the response. There was none. Just the strained whine of the *Moby Dick*'s engines.

"Turn off all the engines, Angie. No sense in risking their integrity. Leave the gravity generator on—I don't want my coffee floating around the cabin." Caffrey sipped his drink and asked, "How long, at the current tug speed, will it take to get to Spydersloth's ship?"

"We will arrive on the front porch of the *Crystal Guise*, calculating the acceleration, in exactly ten hours and ten seconds," Oafy replied promptly.

Out the window, the stars shimmied in rainbow sparkles beyond the invisible tractor beam, as if seen through a prism. Oafelia shut down the engines. A perfect silence filled the cabin, but for the soft, repeating sound of dripping liquid. Violet nudged Caffrey.

"Gravity, Quark," she commented flatly as Caffrey discovered the tilt to his cup. He casually straightened it and stepped back out of the little puddle surrounding his slippered feet, pondering his options.

"We don't have enough firepower to fight ship-to-ship. We don't have the engine power to out-tug the tug beam or pop a wormhole."

"What about the escape pod?" Oafy reminded Caffrey, "We could squeeze three aboard. My ethereal form requires minute physical space. We could eject moments before we are vaporized."

"Interesting idea, Angie. Thank you," Caffrey forced a smile. He casually strolled over to the control bank. "Would you do a search through my entire music library? I am looking for the phrase

138

'Boogie down, baby.' Please sort all hits by band, date of recording and song length."

"Is that a priority, considering the circumstances?" Oafy queried.

"Yes, my love. It's a psychological warfare idea I'm pondering. Please. Do as I ask," Caffrey requested.

He slipped open a red panel on the control deck and turned a key. Many of the lights on the board went dark.

"What are you doing, Caf..." Oafy quailed as her voice faded.

Caffrey chuckled.

Violet was intrigued. "What was that about?"

"That will keep this imposter busy," he smirked.

"What do you mean?" Poe 33 was equally fascinated.

"You can search my music collection until the cows come home and rebuild Rome. You will never find the phrase 'Boogie down, baby.'"

"You've lost me." Violet was still confused.

"Something replaced Angie as my on-board assistant. I'm not sure when or where it happened. I would assume as we were leaving Regal Nine. Some alien sentient intelligence boarded and squeezed her way into the *Moby Dick*'s computer. I shut it in—whatever it is, it's trapped in a loop. We'll have to do with just the basic computer support until we properly dispose of the wretch. I'm certain she took the *Moby Dick* out of sissymode."

"Angie must have never made it out of the magnetic trap of the castle's garbage compactor," Poe 33 surmised with a certain sadness.

Violet was eager for duties. "So, Captain. What will we do for the next ten hours?"

Caffrey eyed the purple-eyed girl thoughtfully for a moment, as her chest heaved with enthusiasm. Then he shook his head clear of diversions. "We'll keep trying to contact the *Crystal Guise*."

He resumed his seat at the communication center.

"And if they don't respond?"

"I can only play one chord at a time, Violet." Caffrey keyed the microphone. "This is the *Moby Dick*. I repeat. This is the *Moby Dick*. We have a very special gift for the great and mighty Spydersloth Blaust. If you destroy us you will destroy the gift, and I have a nasty feeling he will not forgive the boob responsible. I predict immediate dismissal with loss of all health and old age benefits!"

There was no response.

Her view was blocked by the upper area of the communication center counter, but she was alive, alert and very much free. Oafelia, who had adeptly slipped from the *Moby Dick*'s computer into the on-board memory bank of Caffrey's S-77, waited silently. Cramped but more determined than ever, she waited. Waited for her moment for vengeance.

Time drifted by. Caffrey, Violet and Poe tried in vain to contact Spydersloth Blaust's ship. Outside the *Moby Dick*, the *Crystal Guise* was growing in detail and relative size as well as the peculiar object that it dragged behind—a small moon, covered in mirrored tiles.

"Well, would you look at that," Violet commented as the ship passed within seven hundred miles of the surface of the huge, glistening moon.

"I think it's quite lovely," Poe 33 observed, gentle flute music enhancing his words.

With its seemingly infinite number of silver facets, each tossing back the starlight of Komquista with a unique reflective signature, the mirrored moon was impressive albeit the gaudiest object in the galaxy. The largest disco ball in the Milky Way, it was as if a glistening ocean of silver fire were roaring across its surface.

It was tethered to the *Crystal Guise* by two huge chains, each link the size of an average Major League Baseball stadium. The *Crystal Guise* itself was built on the colossal chassis of a Class A1 Generation Transport ship that had been customized for the style and taste of the Rock-star-gone-eschatological bandleader. Shaped like a twisted cross and coated in illuminated rainbow glass and mirrored steel, it was if the entire Vegas Strip, Times Square, Disney World and the Crystal Cathedral were the parts of its sum.

A strange, metallic whine filled the *Moby Dick*'s cabin, followed by the screech of a warning alarm. A red light flashed. Violet turned to Caffrey, concerned.

"The escape pod," Caffrey exclaimed, rushing to the stern. "It's getting itself ready to eject! Angie, quick—" Caffrey cut himself off as he remembered there would be no in-dash assistant.

Violet called out, "All the controls are dead!"

Caffrey fidgeted with them. "I can't stop its countdown. In forty-five seconds it'll eject!"

"And you will all enter the vaporizer and die rather horribly albeit quickly," concluded Poe 33.

Violet eyed him accusingly, "We? What about you?"

"Oh, I can survive quite well in the harsh conditions of space. I can use the small control jets in my buttocks to guide my way to safety."

"I didn't know you had jets in your butt." Caffrey was impressed despite the urgency of the situation.

"Yes, I do. I am also shielded with a thin but very effective heat coating to allow me to descend through the thickest of atmospheres without threatening the integrity of my wiring. In fact, I am sort of a wonder. An amazing conglomeration of design and function. Personality and practical design. Wit, charm..."

"Very good, Poe. Now shut up and get in the escape pod! You, too, Violet," Caffrey ordered.

"You're going to abandon your ship?" Violet was stunned.

Caffrey rounded on her. "A desperate act for desperate times."

"That sucks!" railed Violet, grabbing her weapon belt and heading for the pod.

"Quickly, Poe." Caffrey prodded the android, who was standing beside the control panel studying the flashing lights.

Caffrey grabbed his Willy, entered the pod and triggered the airtight seal. "Poe! Stop dawdling!"

Poe 33 turned and entered. Inside, Violet had already strapped herself into the small seat protruding from the wall. Caffrey helped the android do the same. Finally, he strapped himself in.

"Ten...nine...eight..." Violet counted along with the large green clock.

"Seven...six...five...four..." Poe 33 continued.

"Three...two...one," finished off Caffrey, not wanting to appear unsociable. Inside, he wanted to cry. He grabbed hold of the control stick.

With a jolt of the exploding bolts, the spherical craft shot away from the *Moby Dick*. Very quickly, the pride and joy of Caffrey's professional career receded from sight as they fell away. Although he'd sold her with no delusions of ever seeing her again, this parting held great sorrow.

"Goodbye, beautiful," he whispered, gaining control of the pod's movements. With little bursts of tiny ion rockets, the craft settled into a smooth ride. Suddenly, music began. It came from Poe 33's mouth, but it was not his voice. It was not his usual background music. It was peppier—the Beatles' "Yellow Submarine" played.

"Poe?" Caffrey smiled.

"I took the liberty of uploading your entire music library into my reserve data unit," Poe 33 explained.

"Excuse me while I kiss this guy! When we land I will plant one right on your mouth!" Caffrey promised.

"I look forward to that with an odd and inexplicable anticipation."

"You'll get a kiss from me, too, Poe," Violet smiled.

"I suppose we will have a veritable orgy once we land?" the android postulated. "Is this an appropriate choice? This song?"

"It is perfect, Poe. Perfect. Thank you."

"Have I ever told you about my experience with orgies?" Poe 33 began. "I was on Tryphlopo Six. I was alone in a large, floral-encrusted room with fifteen members of the Federal Likonese Marching Band..."

Caffrey smiled again, wider, and enjoyed the story.

The escape pod cruised toward the *Crystal Guise*, keeping pace with the *Moby Dick*. They would ride along with her to her unavoidable end. Ringo, Paul, George and John sang about life aboard the yellow submersible and all its implications. Caffrey managed to keep his tears inside, saddened deeply by his loss of Yin, Angie and his beloved spacecraft.

Deep within the memory chip of Caffrey's Willy there was a chuckle. Then a deep and smoky voice laughed aloud. Oafy was enjoying a celebratory guffaw at the expense of the *Moby Dick*. Her sabotage had worked. She pondered her next move.

CHAPTER 13
The Grand Parade of Lifeless Packaging

(Genesis)

onsidering the circumstances, the next few hours passed quite pleasantly aboard the escape pod. Poe 33 kept the music going, playing a varied selection of upbeat tunes. They sipped from the titanium flask of Bezzie stored on board, and Caffrey entertained Violet and Poe with tales of his exploits aboard the *Moby Dick*. After ten hours, the debris disintegration port loomed large, the inner green glow of its vaporizers pulsing like death. Caffrey guided the pod a safe distance from the *Moby Dick* as the tug ray continued to haul the ship around towards the horrid inevitability.

Caffrey lifted his flask in a toast.

"May you ride the cosmic waves of the next dimension with the same grace and beauty with which you rode this imperfect existence," he intoned, with a sincere tear in his eye.

"To the *Moby Dick*," Violet toasted with an invisible glass and a small curled mouth.

"*Unbada glinyada soyada*," was Poe 33's contribution. "It's a famous toast for luck and health used by the people of Yiplooska when bidding their soldiers farewell. It means 'Handkerchiefs, chalk, wire brushes.' Those are the staples for Yiplooskan society. It admittedly loses something in the translation."

"There she goes," whispered Caffrey.

With an insignificant flicker, the *Moby Dick* flashed into nothingness like a moth in an emerald blowtorch. It was a painless death. Caffrey smiled wistfully.

Poe 33 bowed his head and, after a moment of silence, began another song from the library in his head. The opening bars of music were not that of a funeral dirge as one might expect after such an incident but rather had the joyous quality of a speakeasy piano. A tune of ragtime delight from Rock 'n' Roll souls. A song that lauded the philosophy that yes, indeed, life goes on: "Oblidee Oblida!"

Although the dancing space was less than minimum, Caffrey stood up, his head arched under the low ceiling, and began dancing and singing along with the Fab Four. Soon Violet joined him with her supple and succulent limbs, while Poe 33, like a wallflower at a high school dance, bounced his shoulders in an attempt to find the rhythm. For the next few minutes, Caffrey forgot—almost—the loss of Yin, Angie and the *Moby Dick*.

Caffrey guided the pod to the large square docking bay. A gate blocked entry into a long tunnel that gave further access to the ship. A voice crackled on the pod's speakers, startling the trio.

"Halt! Who goes there?" The words were delivered in a manner cold and spooky—though they were rather pretentious and unoriginal.

Caffrey garnered his most pitiful-sounding reply.

"We are a couple of weary zealots who have come great distances to pay our respects and exaltations to the great and powerful Spydersloth Blaust. We have a very special gift to present to him."

There was a pause and the sounds of a muffled conversation accented by mocking giggling. A second voice spoke.

"For a couple of supposed zealots you have certainly not kept up to date on current events."

"I'm sorry?" Caffrey apologized.

"He no longer goes as Spydersloth Blaust. Hasn't for a year," the voice announced pompously. "He is Spy-Blau."

"We kneel corrected. We have been out of the loop for many years as we made our way here."

"We have warehouses of gifts. Mostly tacky paintings and cheap shoes."

"Vulgar, indeed. No, our gift is something grander. But I couldn't possibly reveal it to anyone but the great and holy Arachnid himself."

"Ha! Impossible. He has a long chain of command, and I am the first link. You tell me, and I will pass it along. However, a reply is doubtful."

"But we have traveled so far!" Violet whined in a Yin-like whimper.

"I can only pass on the message. So, what is this gift?"

Caffrey looked to Violet with some uncertainty. She shrugged her shoulders.

"The one and only enigmatic Portsmith to the Great Wise L'Orange," Caffrey announced, squinting his eyes in a defensive pose, expecting an explosion of laughter.

"Hold tight." The static ceased; and Caffrey, Violet and Poe 33 sat in silence for a moment.

The static returned along with a deep, deep voice.

"How can you prove he is the true Portsmith, not a clever androidal forgery?"

"Are there any fake Portsmiths wandering the galaxy?" Caffrey queried.

"None that we are aware of. But..."

"Have you ever been lied to by the Guardian of the One?" Violet asked.

"No..."

"Have you ever walked down a dimly lit alley, only to be jumped, beaten, robbed and violated in embarrassing ways with small, furry rodents by a being who turned out to be the Portsmith to the L'Orange?" Poe inquired, joining in the questioning.

"Not that I can remember."

"Has there been any event in your rather superficial life that warrants the distrust of a superior albeit artificial creature such as he?" added Caffrey.

"No..."

"Then is it necessary to question his authenticity?"

There was a long, long pause of confusion-infused silence. Then, testily: "I guess not. Board, if you like."

"Never underestimate the shallow capability of the obsessed mind," Caffrey concluded with a smile.

"Never, indeed," agreed Poe.

The gate rose, and a strip of lights ignited in series down the long hall. The pod floated through the corridor, the gate closing behind them. A large sign flashed in numerous languages, warning the entering probe to halt. Caffrey brought the craft to a gentle stop; and

145

instantly, walls of solid energy closed them in. The deep, deep voice spoke again.

"You may exit your pod. Please follow the signs to the Holy Arachnid Lounge. Wait there."

The trio emerged from the pod and headed toward the open door. On the floor, illuminated arrows blinked like runway lights, pointing the way.

The Holy Arachnid Lounge reminded Caffrey of various New York dance clubs on Halloween. A diverse sampling of beings from every corner of the Plethorian Sector mingled in groups segregated by the atmosphere of choice, with each breathing mix kept separate by exotic energy fields. The room was quite large and shaped in a curvy, imperfect circle. The lights, alternating crimson, emerald and indigo, created colored pools. The drone of a thousand languages filled the air with gregarious tones. Caffrey, Violet and Poe 33 found themselves at a glass door looking into the lounge. A holographic Kelfkin appeared before them.

"Please choose your atmosphere of preference," the bulbous, floating, fishy-looking thing requested. A list of over three dozen choices blinked into existence. Caffrey looked at Poe 33, who simply shrugged.

"Makes not a beeswax of difference to me. I have been amidst every imaginable atmosphere. Have you ever been to Grutus?"

"No," Caffrey and Violet replied in unison.

"Cherry meringue," Poe 33 explained with a smile.

Caffrey chose nitrogen-oxygen. The Kelfkin appeared again.

"Please follow me. Do not, I repeat, do not wander from the path."

The door opened, and a wash of oxygen-nitrogen blew back Caffrey's hair. The trio followed the floating creature through glass tubes running through the huge room like veins. Caffrey eyed the myriad beings he passed, recognizing some while being fascinated or repulsed by others. Finally, the Kelfkin led them into a large area filled with a gathering of a couple of hundred nitrogen-oxygen breathers.

"Wait here. The posh and wonderful Spy-Blau will be addressing you all momentarily." The fish-faced Kelfkin hologram floated off.

Poe's face shimmered with a wash of red light and his body trembled slightly, as if a great chill had descended his spine. His expression suddenly became one of confusion. Caffrey noticed the android's change in appearance.

"Poe?"

"I am getting strange images on my visual matrix. Red. Ruby red. It is calling me," he answered.

"Ruby red what?" whispered Violet.

"Red. Crimson. Warm. Perhaps blood. An emotional connection, similar to when I first met Quark Caffrey. I must make my way to a place called the Deck of Ruby Gilding. Immediately." With that, the android simply wandered off. Caffrey and Violet exchanged a concerned look.

"I'll follow him," Violet volunteered. Caffrey grabbed her by the soft, exposed skin of her luscious waist and pulled her back to him. "Don't let Poe out of your sight. I'll talk to His Eminence."

Violet turned and followed Poe 33.

A thick cloud of fog emerged from the rear of the *Crystal Guise*, filling the huge volume of space between the ship and the mirrored moon with an artificial nebula. The largest artificial fog machine the galaxy had ever known was doing its thing. The white cloud accentuated the glistening lights reflecting from the millions of mirrors, rendering almost invisible the five large ships that were docking in the starboard ports.

Angie—the real Angie—traveled closer and closer to the *Crystal Guise*. She'd traversed impossible distances, risking the integrity of her Revenant sphere as she raced through the closing wormhole.

I'm almost back, love. Almost back, Angie thought as she watched the occupants of the five ships disembark.

Positioning herself closer, she identified Quigmo Digmo, Quagmo Dagmo, Ba Ba Banaki, Melagus Winstis and Scorthius Hild. They were the Five Heads of the Five Sectors—the top members of the galactic underworld. The Plethorian, Soronian, Janknorian, Zedlerian and Gyronian sectors all represented. This, Angie knew, was a first. Never had these five powerful beings gathered in one location. Something very big was going on aboard the *Crystal Guise*.

Violet had a hard time keeping up with Poe 33. He'd beelined out of the Holy Arachnid Lounge and was making haste up a spiraling corridor. The slight but definite grade caused his knee servos to whine under the stress of the artificial gravity. It wasn't much easier for Violet's calves.

"Slow down!"

Poe 33 decreased his ascent. Violet jogged beside him and attempted to catch his determined eye, to slow him, sober him up a little.

"We might be heading right into a trap!" she warned.

"I understand. But it is all beyond my control. I feel odd. Ever since the scrambler was removed I have had an anxious buzz in my circuitry. Though the flashes of nihilistic qualms have gone, I feel like something lurks around every corner."

"And you can't resist peeking ahead?"

"Exactly. It's at once alluring and horrifying. I have been able to keep it moderated. That is, until we boarded this ship. A feeling was released."

"A feeling?"

"Yes. At once happy and sad."

They came upon a hallway that leveled off and took them past a window running down its length, offering a beautiful view of the lights on the artificial nebula. At the end of the hall there was a long, narrow catwalk spanning a spectacular waterfall of neon lights. Poe crossed the bridge, and Violet called out to him.

"Poe! Would you please stay in sight!"

"No time to waste. I am close. I feel a familiar presence!" Poe 33 shouted, pushing his way through a set of pink chrome swinging doors. Past the doors was a narrowing walkway, covered with thick pink-and-red carpeting that led to a door of solid ruby. Poe 33 stopped before the door. Violet stepped up beside him, trying to catch her breath. She gasped out a few words,

"A ruby door. May I assume we've reached the Deck of Ruby Gilding?"

"Yes," Poe 33 said in distant, slightly guttural tones. He knocked, and a lock mechanism was heard disengaging. The door opened on its own.

"Enter, mighty Portsmith," came a voice from within the dark room.

Poe 33 and Violet entered. The door closed behind them. The size of the room was impossible to hypothesize, as it was nearly sans light. Only a barely visible glow of crimson broke the darkness. A face stepped into this glow. It was an old man. His hair was white, shoulder-length and rather wild, colored red by the light the source of which was a mystery.

"Hello, Poe Thirty-three. I am Greppledick Quark. I am your maker."

Poe 33 dropped to his knees with a metallic crunch.

"Thank your maker for your strong knees," smirked Greppledick.

"Daddy," said the android, like a child.

Violet was perplexed. "Daddy?" The next sound she heard was Poe 33 sobbing gently.

The crowd came alive as a sweeping ring of royal purple light rode across the room, which closed to a point atop a crystal clear podium situated in the center. The crowds of lifeforms ran, crawled, floated and flew closer, desperately vying for the best piece of viewing room.

It was all part of Spydersloth's show.

The low ceilings and the just slightly convex floor made it virtually impossible for anyone but the front dozen or so rows that ringed the podium to see the Great Arachnid. This kept the crowd pushing, antsy. It kept tempers high and passions flaring. As the crowd converged around the podium, the pulsing purple light ascended to the ceiling and accented an opening iris. A floating disk descended, like a magic carpet—or rather, a magic bathmat—and the long, satin-encased legs of Spydersloth Blaust appeared.

A ruckus, a combination of gasps, screams, cries of joy and moans of ecstasy exploded with such force Caffrey Quark felt his head would explode from the audible shockwave. He stood back, more than happy to gain some breathing room in the area clearing around him. The various breathing mixes seemed irrelevant as the melting pot of people began inhaling foreign mixes. This, of course, was another of Spydersloth's scams. The segregated sectors were, in fact, all fed the same special combination of gasses. Often sold in interstellar road stops and various survival stores, Uni-Breathe was a special mix of gaseous elements that could keep most lifeforms in the Milky Way healthy and happy—some extremely happy, since certain species reacted to the gas mix with psychotropic symptoms, adding to the religious fervor.

Spydersloth Blaust descended to the podium. He was a large being, standing over eight feet on four of his eight legs. His thick thorax was dressed in his usual silver-and-blue satin cassock, the

ODOR emblem displayed proudly at its center. Atop his round, squat head sat a glittering crown of diamond, filled with millions of microscopic phosphorescent points of light that made it glow with a rainbow of colors.

Spydersloth Blaust raised his four upper arms and bowed with feigned humility to the crowd. They dropped to their knees. Only Caffrey remained standing, alone and apart.

Spydersloth noticed Caffrey's irreverence and smiled privately. He began to speak.

"Once again we stand before a world polluted and caught in its own quagmire of the wretched evils of music and the harmonious way of life."

The crowd hissed and booed and some even vomited, encouraged to purge themselves by pure and utter disgust and disdain. Spydersloth continued. His words were deep, coarse, and machine-gunned out of his small mouth in an odd oscillating volume that waxed and waned, using his highly evolved holographic language ability. Tens of millions of diverse communication methods were entwined in the single sound wave of his spoken words and extracted by the specific language center of each audience member's brain.

"Music!" The word was sprayed over the crowd like liquid garbage. "They revel in music! They dance and sing. They sometimes will even hum whilst bathing! They blow into reed instruments with blatant gusto. Strum strings. Pound skins. But every note they play..." Spydersloth grew angrier and more animated, and the volume of his pronouncement boosted. "...will be the fitting death dirge. For after today, the shortsighted fools of Haptiwoo will be no more!"

Ululating cries of support filled the room. Caffrey couldn't help but turn on a sad, sentimental smile, for he could remember listening to the ancient recordings of Spydersloth's band, the Riders of the Purple Shems, he had dug up during his quest for Rock music samples. He recalled how uplifted and inspired he had felt by the lyrical and positive music. It seemed impossible that this could be the same being.

"Before we commence with the conversion of Haptiwoo, I want us all to celebrate the Labates Day of the young son of our Lord of Disharmony, Nefarious Wretch. I will have the honor of meeting the child face-to-face for the first time and present him with this special gift in a few days, while wishing him a non-rhythmic life. Until then, let us speak the traditional Labates Day tribute together."

Caffrey's eyes widened as a square box wrapped in black metallic paper with matching bow was placed on the podium before
Spydersloth. It was the same size and shape of the box that had sat
on the sidewalk outside the Crimson Court Pub after his band-mates
had been compressed. Perhaps Violet was right. Maybe his friends
had been deemed the perfect gift for this foul offspring of Nefarious.
As Spydersloth began the Labates Day tribute, Caffrey's mind went
to work.

He had to get the package.

***

Angie was acting as a fly on the wall, following the entourage of galactic bigwigs from the landing bay through long hallways and fanciful lobbies and lounges. She sensed something—a familiar bio-
electric pattern. She determined it was coming from the area surrounding Ba Ba Banaki, the tall, burly Fizizi, feared head of the
strange and dangerous Janknorian Sector.

Angie scanned his elaborate adornment. He was dressed in a
ten-piece leather-and-satin suit, and he wore platform boots that
added three hundred centimeters to his already two-and-a-half-meter
height. There was something odd, she felt, about the fur epaulets on
each of his four broad shoulders.

Yin! Angie cried to herself.

Sitting on Ba Ba Banaki's outer left shoulder was the little
Bopple. Dazed and limp, he was attached to the Fizizi by a thick
black leather band. Three other furry canine-type creatures adorned
the other shoulders, also dazed, limp but very much alive.

Angie moved closer.

"Yin, it's me, Angie. Are you okay?" she whispered into his ear.

Yin, his eyes at half-mast, groggily raised his chin and, summon-
ing every ounce of energy in his little body, managed a single response.

"Woof," he answered softly.

"Hush!" Ba Ba Banaki cried, smacking Yin atop his head.

Bully! Angie thought. She whispered into Yin's ear again. "Yin,
my dear, hang tight. We'll free you. I have to find Caffrey first."

"Wooo..." was all Yin managed to squeak out.

Angie took off as the Five Heads entered a large conference
room.

***

"Daddy?" Violet repeated.

"Yes, my friend. I am Greppledick Quark. I built Poe Thirty-three," Greppledick explained, turning toward the source of red light. "Brighten yourself, Peebo."

The red light grew ten times brighter, exposing the little spherical android hovering in the air, throwing its crimson glow around the room. The Deck of Ruby Gilding was a trapezoidal room with solid ruby walls covered in impossibly elaborate etchings—seemingly volumes of words written in some ancient alphabet and apparently telling ancient tales. Greppledick Quark wore a teal robe tied about the waist with a rope of snow-white linen that matched his hair. His eyes appeared as once-overflowing vessels of bliss that had recently run dry. He looked at the enigmatic Portsmith of the wise L'Orange, still on his knees and sobbing.

"Get up, Poe, you're embarrassing me," Greppledick instructed, looking at Violet.

Poe 33 rose to his feet and bowed his head before his maker.

"Look me in the eyes," commanded Greppledick, "and stop being such a bloody poof!"

Poe 33 lifted his head slowly and locked his gaze with Greppledick. Tears seemed to have somehow welled up in his artificial eyes.

Greppledick smiled warmly. "How have you been, Poe?"

Melodramatic music composed of sad saxophone and melancholy piano began. "I have been on a grand adventure. I have failed the Great One, my galaxy, my mission, my maker and, perhaps most importantly, my ethereal essence. Have you returned to destroy me? To take me offline? To render me a useless conglomeration of individual parts?"

Greppledick took a deep breath and shook his head, tossing a grin at Violet, who rolled her eyes at the android's melodramatics.

"My, my, I must have been in a whiz of a mood when I built you! What's with the music? I never programmed that!" Greppledick exclaimed. "And I am not here to destroy you. I'm here to give you new instructions. I want you to serve Spydersloth. I want you to help him and Nefarious Wretch retrieve the L'Orange for their use."

Violet's purple eyes bugged. "Are you daffy?"

"But I am the enigmatic Portsmith to the Great L'Orange! I have vowed to protect and escort the Great Wise One!"

"Self-important little bastard, ain't you? Do as I say, Poe Thirty-three. I am your father!"

"He will do nothing of the sort," Violet spat.

"Oh, yes, he will. Peebo, detain this woman."

In a flash, the hovering probe unfolded with lightning speed into a spherical cage engulfing Violet. Before she could blink, she was hovering two meters above the ground. She drew her weapon and made a number of vain attempts to fire it. Greppledick snickered.

"Weapons are useless aboard this craft. One of Spydersloth's little tricks."

"You sell-out!" Violet fired back, blasting him with her eyes, having little other recourse.

"Father, I would have to agree with Violet. How can you join sides with ODOR? How can you ally yourself with the organization bent on galactic destruction and ego-based redevelopment?"

A strange glaze, like rotted pineapple-flavored jelly, spread across Greppledick's eyes. "Poe, this is beyond ODOR Nefarious is mightier and grander than that square hunk of orange jelly could ever be!"

Poe 33 was aghast. Greppledick hectored on.

"Yes, Poe, it is true! I have been reborn! The Great Nefarious has filled my soul with the truth of the wonders and magic of a non-rhythmic and non-lyrical way of life!"

Drool formed on his lips. He raised his arms wide and threw back his head.

"Oh, Great Nefarious, forgive me for my prior disdain of your ways! I shall dedicate my existence to the elimination of music. I will help to rebuild—stone by stone—the galaxy in the image of You!"

Greppledick spun around like a dizzy top, a string of drool following him like a kite's tail.

"Oh, my," Violet mumbled to herself.

"What shall I do?" Poe 33 asked.

"You will be presented before the gathered in moments," Greppledick advised, still spinning. "Then, you will take your seat on the throne of the Prime ODOR Entity. The POE. Your true lot."

"Throne?" Poe queried.

"Yes. They will bow before you."

Poe 33 smiled.

A tiny, Mona Lisa smile.

The Labates Day tribute was winding down. Caffrey managed to move closer to the dais, never taking his eyes off the package. The din of the gathering settled, and Spydersloth pounded his fist on the podium.

"Reveal the sacrificial world!" he shouted.

The perimeter of the room went instantly transparent, revealing Haptiwoo sitting like a naïve child before them.

"In moments, one less note will ring through the galaxy. One less piece of the traitorous music that infiltrates and destroys our souls. The transformation of Haptiwoo marks a special day. A day of prophecy and a day of conversion. Today, the Great Android Poe Thirty-three, the last Portsmith to the L'Orange, has surrendered himself to us. He has vowed to assist in tracking down and delivering to me the prima materia of music."

Great cheers rose up in every language.

"And before us also stands a human. A human who has come here to join me. A man who was at one time a purveyor of the horrid light of music, as I was all those eons ago." Spydersloth aimed his gaze towards Caffrey and smiled. It took a moment, but eventually Caffrey connected the gaze of the Arachnid and the person of whom he was speaking. He pointed to himself curiously—very much caught off-guard. Spydersloth smiled wide.

"Caffrey Quark. Welcome to the *Crystal Guise*. Welcome to the Order Destined to Overthrow Reality."

All heads turned, and dozens of varieties of applause sounded. Caffrey pouted.

"Now!" Spydersloth Blaust shouted. "The world of Haptiwoo will begin its rebirth! To the womb of the mighty Nefarious it will go! And, when remolded, it will never again ring or sing or croon or tune. The population will forever toil in the wondrous ways of Noneuphony!"

Twin beams of red light flew from the bow of the *Crystal Guise*, entering the center of Haptiwoo. Immediately, streams of dust and matter were pulled from the world, spinning and twisting like multicolored waters down a spiral staircase. Down and around poured the planetary stuff, into the pitch-black hole of the mystical singularity. The planet's spin increased with each revolution as it diminished in diameter until it was gone.

Caffrey wanted to cry. Everyone else cheered. He made his way closer to the podium. He would simply grab the gift, unwrap it quickly, free his band-mates and—

And what, you fool? Caffrey cut off his own thoughts. It was a poorly constructed plan, destined to end in some horrible and very embarrassing death for both himself and, most likely, his mates. He would be patient.

His thoughts were interrupted by a static pop and an electrical, fuzzy kiss on his cheek.

"Love pumpkin!" Angie whispered excitedly in his ear.

Caffrey's eyes filled with surprise—then rage. "How did you escape, you wench?"

"I'm not Oafelia. She thought she could keep me from you. She thought she could destroy me, but our love guided me across vast oceans of space. And I found you, my monkey bar cheese puppet."

"Prove it. Prove it's really you," Caffrey demanded, walking off to a quiet spot in the room.

"How? What can I do?"

Caffrey thought quickly. "Do you remember our trip to Santa Piragua?"

"Yes. When you bagged the six giant marvelo clams!"

"Never mind the clams. I'm talking about what we did that night?"

"Oh, Quarky, You're making me blush. We played strip poker. And I won."

"Easy for you. I never won a single hand."

"There's a lot going on. The Five Heads of the Five Sectors have just boarded the ship. One of them has Yin."

"Yin?" Caffrey's eyes doubled in size, "Where?"

"He's being used as an epaulet."

The confusion on Caffrey's face was expected by Angie.

"On the shoulder of Ba Ba Banaki. They're in some large conference room. Please trust me, passion puss!"

Caffrey weighed the events in his mind, developing an intellectual hernia. The Five? In the same place? Quigmo alone usually makes that impossible.

"How true! His girth amazes even me!" a familiar voice interrupted with a laugh. Caffrey turned to see Spydersloth Blaust standing before him. The crowd shifted in an ordered field, like metal filings around a powerful magnet.

"Blaust," greeted Caffrey, with faux civility.

"Are you so antisocial that you can only converse with yourself?"

"I can only aspire in my wildest dreams to attain the levels of social grace that you possess," answered Caffrey, with a deep bow.

Angie suppressed her giggle.

155

"Well said, Caffrey Quark. Well said!"

Spydersloth wrapped one of his long hairy arms around Caffrey's shoulder and turned to the crowd. "Gathered supplicants! I introduce to you Caffrey Quark. My new Vicar of Negated Music Registry!"

"Your what?" Caffrey could only wonder.

"Caffrey Quark, like Spydersloth Blaust, was once a sorcerer of the light art," Spydersloth divulged, referring to himself, as is the practice of megalomaniacs, in the third person. "But he has taken new paths. He has generously presented me with a very special gift. He will now join the ranks of ODOR, in charge of cataloguing every song, every orchestration, every aria and opera, every ditty and jingle. All becoming part of the growing list of evils that none shall ever partake in again!"

Spydersloth ended on a thunderous note, lifting the voices of the crowd to a fervent rouse once more.

Caffrey took advantage of the noise.

"Angie," he spoke furtively, "the *Moby Dick*'s escape pod. It's sitting in docking corridor number...number—oh, bloody hell, I've forgotten where I parked it!"

"Where's the *Moby Dick*?" queried Angie.

"She's gone. Let Violet, Poe and Yin know we'll meet at the pod on my signal. Use the communicator in the *Willy*. Let me know what landing bay we're in ASAP."

"*Oui, mon rouge papillion amoure,*" Angie whispered in her most seductive French inflection.

Deep in the circuits of Caffrey's exotic weapon, Oafelia smirked like the devil she was. "Oh, my sweet loyal pretty. You do have spunk. I will give you that."

She slipped from the confines of the device and tailed Angie.

"Come, Caffrey," invited Spydersloth, leading him to the platform holding the podium, which began rising as they stepped on board.

"All hail Nefarious Wretch and ODOR!" Spydersloth cried out as the platform lifted rapidly up and back above the ceiling from where it had emerged. The crowd's voices rose with it.

Spydersloth stepped off the platform, tossing the black-boxed gift back and forth between some of his hands, and guided Caffrey through a gauntlet of bowing personnel. They walked the length of the carpeted catwalk forming part of a series of crisscross walks situated above the Holy Arachnid Lounge.

"So, what did you say my title was again? Vicar of Fascist Posers and their Respective Suck-ups?" Caffrey asked the question in an innocent voice belied by a wicked smirk.

"Vicar of Negated Music Registry," Spydersloth corrected, conveying only the slightest hint of agitation.

"Honest mistake. Sorry, Blausty," Caffrey acceded, pushing his luck.

"I've learned your history. You know the worlds of this galaxy almost as well as I. You can help record the musical history of the planets devolved. And, you can help to weed out some of the hidden ones—those in the darker and odder corners of the galaxy that practice more subtle and insidious forms of the light art."

Caffrey wanted to spit at the Arachnid. He wanted to send the largest saliva clam he could muster into the eyes of this horrid beast. Instead, he forced a smile.

"Lovely package you have there. May I ask, what did you get for the child, for his special day?"

"The perfect gift for a future creator and purveyor of a music-free galaxy and, eventually, music-free universe."

"That's quite an order," Caffrey commented.

"In another thirty thousand or so years I will be dead. I will get to see perhaps the local sectors converted. Nefarious is infinite. And with the destruction of the L'Orange, music will never be able to manifest itself," Spydersloth prophesied, pumping his fist in a corny but appropriate manner.

"So, if you simply want the L'Orange to destroy it, what will become of the Portsmith?"

Spydersloth smiled. Caffrey decided he wouldn't press the issue, for he knew Poe 33 was doomed. They turned a corner; and, quite unexpectedly, Caffrey found himself staring at a bridge of ruby bricks spanning a small river of brilliant green lights.

The Arachnid waved an unused arm. "Beyond this bridge and through that door you will come face to face with your own past. Your own history."

Caffrey didn't know what to do. He had to play along, but time was at a premium. He had to get his hands on the gift. The package had to be his. And now!

"Won't you enter with me?" he offered. "I'm sure my past would love to meet you."

"We've met. I must attend to a meeting with a certain group of beings who possess great delusions of grandeur."

Caffrey took a step toward the bridge. He stopped. He fought off the feelings of panic. He took a deep breath and turned to face Spydersloth.

"Can I at least take that package off your hands? Put it inside for you?"

Spydersloth seemed appreciative. "Thanks. I'll retrieve it later."

With that, Spydersloth handed the black-wrapped gift to Caffrey and nodded. Caffrey returned the nod and walked across the bridge and to the door. It opened on its own accord. He looked back, and Spydersloth nodded again. Caffrey entered, and the door closed.

There had been a number of impossibilities Caffrey had seen come to pass in his life. This was ludicrous. He stood in a small foyer dimly lit by soft yellow lights. He stared at the package. It was beyond ludicrous. It was astronomically farcical. It was as if all the good karma Caffrey had donated to the universe in the way of friendly smiles, donated nickels, patted dogs and ignored shoves on public transportation had finally decided to conspire in the silliest payback in the entire history of instant karmic redemption. He could only smile. It was a silly, out-of-control smile that widened until it could not express the volcano of feelings he wished to communicate.

So, he laughed. The laugh grew quickly into the loudest and least-controlled guffaws of his entire life. He was almost inclined to fall to the ground and roll around on the thick plush carpet but resisted out of fear of damaging his mates inside the package.

A voice, calm but with a hint of restrained annoyance, spoke, ending his cavalcade of jocundity. He wasn't sure what the voice had said, but it sounded as if it was targeted at him. Caffrey stepped from the foyer and into an octagonal room—the walls ruby and engraved—another of the chambers that made up the Deck of Ruby Gilding. A sofa, tilted back at forty-five degrees to allow for a perfect view through the glass ceiling, ran around the entire perimeter. Seated on one segment was Greppledick Quark. He seemed to have been waiting and appeared rather miffed.

"Are you done?" Greppledick asked, not getting up.

"Who the hell are you?" Caffrey asked the old man.

"It's been years. My name is Greppledick Quark—Uncle Greppledick to you, boy."

Caffrey's mouth dropped, and he took a few steps forward to shake the man's hand. The old fellow was unable to get himself upright from the oddly angled sofa. He gave it a valiant effort but, after three tries, waved his hand in frustration and frowned.

"Ever see such a ridiculous sofa? Please, Caffrey, sit."

"Uncle Greppledick, shouldn't you be dead by now? No offense intended."

"None taken. I was and should be! I died twenty years ago. I'm dead, Caffrey. I liked being dead. It's wonderful—trust me. When you die you will have no desire to come back into the body again. Bodies suck. They're cumbersome. They smell," Greppledick complained, sniffing his armpits.

"So, why are you here?"

"I was brought back by Spydersloth Blaust and his mighty master because they needed to track down one of my androids. Poe Thirty-three. Convert him. They need him to help locate the missing L'Orange. They want to help save the universe."

"Save is a subjective term," Caffrey observed, fondling the package.

Greppledick wasn't impressed. "Look, I just want to get back to the other side. What happens in these dumb dimensions is of no importance to me."

"Excuse me, Mr. Afterlife, but some of us are rather fond of these dumb dimensions!"

"It's not worth the effort."

"Huh?"

"You have—what? Seventy, maybe a hundred years left? Do you realize that on the other side you can take fifty years to have a leisurely pee, should you choose? You slow down. You stop and watch the flowers grow. It's wonderful! Forget the pre-life. It's really overdone."

"Death does make Jack a cavalier boy!" It was Caffrey's turn to be unimpressed.

"What do you want from me? One minute I'm dancing and doing back-flips across fields of ethereal tulips and the next I'm being interrogated by some foul-smelling Arachnid. I just want back."

Caffrey tried to arouse his uncle's interest. "Greppledick, these

159

sewer-soul freaks are stealing worlds. One at a time. Seeking and destroying those who love music. They want to create an all-music-free universe."

"Looks like my favorite nephew has found himself in rather posh circles. Saving the universe?" Greppledick was sardonically impressed.

"I didn't get involved to save the universe. I got involved to save my band-mates. My friends." Caffrey suddenly remembered the package. He could wait no longer and tore off the black wrapping. The very rotation of the galaxy seemed to come to a screeching halt. He stared at the colorful box.

"'Four-D Construction Set. Warp time and impress your friends,'" Caffrey read the claim on the box. "Build Moebius strips, hypercubes, Banchoff-Klien bottles! Romp around Calabi-Yau space and feel the goofy effects of Lorentz contraction! And much, much more! Two quadruple-D Planck watt batteries required, not included."

Caffrey looked at Greppledick who, disinterested, was staring up at the flickering lights beyond the glass ceiling.

"'Batteries not included,' my three-D ass," seethed Caffrey venomously, tossing the box to the floor.

The conference room was a perfect circle. The table at its heart was in an arachnid shape, its thorax the flat surface. Its fifteen legs—twice the arachnid number less one—symbolized ODOR's philosophy of non-rhythmic/non-lyric duality. Upon the walls were countless round monitors, like peering spider eyes. The Five Heads of the Five Sectors were seated, impatiently tapping fingers, puffing cigars or mumbling incoherently. Their respective security entourages stood behind, each posing and vogueing in vanity-filled attempts to impress or frighten the others.

Spydersloth entered without his usual fanfare and stepped up a small walkway rising above and over the table. All eyes turned to him.

"Welcome, friends," the Arachnid said. "I am honored to have you all together."

"Never mind the platitudes, twinkleshite," Quigmo retorted, adjusting his tremendous girth in his seat and releasing a pocket of foul gases trapped in two of his countless fat layers. "I lose one more world, you eight-legged zealot, and you'll discover Quigmo Digmo has something to say."

Sympathetic agreement sounded from the other four heads.

160

Spydersloth pounded his fist like a judge's gavel.

"Silence! Silence!" he demanded until quiescence returned to the room. "I wouldn't complain, Mr. Digmo, you have done quite well, lining your pockets with fossil fuel profits."

Melagus Winstis, the diminutive but powerful Four-Fanged Vexerine, pushed into the altercation with a wisecrack. "Never mind fossil fuels. Quigmo could power the galaxy with the endless natural gas reserves he stores in his bowels!"

As if illustrating the point, and to everyone's disgust, Quigmo farted.

Ignoring the interruption, Spydersloth continued. "I would like to introduce to you the latest success of Spy-Blau. You will appreciate his efforts. You will understand his mission. You may even decide to cast aside your entrepreneurial garb and don the robes of ODOR"

"Quigmo always dons odor!" quipped Melagus.

"Hilarious," Quigmo smirked, taking a certain amount of pride in the insult.

"Please dispense with the jesting until the completion of our meeting. I would like to present to you all the Portsmith to the Great L'Orange—Poe Thirty-three!"

The android descended from the ceiling like a hanged man on a rope of silver light.

"For all I care, this android can be the personal butt cleaner for the King of Verexia itself!" grumbled Quigmo.

Poe 33 smiled at the comment but said nothing.

Scorthius Hild, the armor-plated insecto-crustacean from Criyx, was similarly underwhelmed by Poe. "I have lost thirty-three worldsss. Worlds that were producing extremely valuable doreme crystalsss." The words sighed in sibilant syllables via quivering mandibles.

"Doreme crystals are used for making the tri-ocular flute, am I correct?" Spydersloth asked.

"Yessss..."

"Tri-ocular flutes have been made illegal. They are immoral," declared Spydersloth.

Scorthius hissed scatalogically and slapped the tabletop as Spy Blau pressed on.

"Gentlemen, the Great Portsmith has returned. This is the day our cause has waited for. This great android will lead us to the *Doorange dei Lai msyticarei!*" Spydersloth orated, utilizing a rather

161

ancient and folksy term for L'Orange.

"And what percentage of the mystical cube will be given to me?" inquired Quagmo Dagmo.

"You will all share in the great pie," Spydersloth promised, glancing across the room at a small dark window.

The genuine Angie, who had entered seconds after Spydersloth, was quickly trying to deduce what was going on. She noticed the glance and followed his eye line to the window.

— *Oh, my!* she exclaimed silently at the sight of the large quad-barreled pulse gattler, a wicked and deadly energy weapon, being positioned by two stocky android guards. She made her way swiftly to Poe and messaged directly into his communication circuits.

— *Poe, my dear, something terrible is about to happen. I believe a massacre of galactic proportions. You must get out of here.*

— *Thank you, Angie. But I am following a direct wish of my maker. I cannot leave. I would suggest you inform Quark Caffrey that Violet is imprisoned in a spherical cage somewhere on the Deck of Ruby Gilding. Pass my wish to my maker that I wish her to be free to go.*

— *Poe, are you mad? We have to leave together!*

— *I'm sorry.* In a mentally metaphoric manner, Poe put his foot down.

Angie swore at the stubborn android and slipped across the room to Yin.

"Yin!" she whispered directly into the groggy Bopple's ear. "Wake up. We have to get out of here!"

Yin raised a tired eyebrow and yawned. The small Rykonese Puffy tied to the adjacent shoulder also tried with a great strain to lift his head. Ba Ba Banaki was too busy pounding his fist angrily to notice.

"I can nil afford to lose any more of my worlds. In the last three weeks, six of my most profitable planets have gone down the cosmic crapper. Do you realize how much money there is in Harmonic Love Teasing?"

A chorus of complaints and protests erupted, and Angie took advantage of the distraction to implement extreme measures. She sent a perfectly pitched scream, audible only to those creatures with the hearing organs to detect sounds in the higher frequencies, straight into Yin's ear. It was the doggie equivalent of the combined vocal reaction of a dozen teenage girls at a slumber party at finding cockroaches in their sleeping bags.

Yin's eyeballs almost shot out of his head, and any further desire

162

for doggy dozing was melted away like a marshmallow near a supernova. Instant sobriety of the most efficient nature. The three other canines awoke as well.

"Now, Yin! Free yourself!" Angie ordered.

"What is going on?" shouted Melagus. He drew his weapon.

Every bodyguard in the room produced either a firearm or a blade.

Spydersloth smiled, nodded, and all hell broke loose.

Yin used his teeth to tear open the straps holding him to the giant Fizizi. He stood up on his hind legs and howled the ancient war cry of the Bopplian folk. The three other bound poochies, following some timeless instinct upon hearing the cry of their elders-in-spirit, freed themselves and returned the howl. Energy blasts flashed. Fists flew. Tails whipped. Claws scratched. Teeth tore at flesh, bone and sinew. Spydersloth and Poe 33 rose on a platform of light into the ceiling.

Angie cried out to Yin as she fled the room, "Meet us at the Deck of Ruby Gilding!"

Oafy, watching stealthily nearby, laughed and tailed after her.

CHAPTER 14
Time

(Pink Floyd)

affrey insisted on reading every word of text on the box of the 4-D construction set three times. He needed an explanation. He was looking for some solace, something that would clarify the cruel joke the universe—the same universe that had tickled, teased and toyed with him as far as back his memory could serve—had played on him.

As he read, Greppledick explained just how his afterlife bliss had been rudely interrupted. He confessed without apology that he would have agreed to anything in order to get back to the enchanted heights of the hereafter. The old, reawakened dead man demonstrated with great gusto the act he played on Poe 33 to convince him to follow Spydersloth. He spun around the room like a religious ecstatic on snake venom, laughing loudly in amusement at his own impressive performance.

"You're a sick individual," Caffrey concluded. "Why don't you simply kill yourself and return?"

"It's all a bit more complicated than that. Stop asking such foolish questions."

Caffrey stood up and began pacing. "Surely, as Poe's maker, you must have some idea how he became separated from his master? Why he has no connection whatsoever?"

"I haven't a clue. Why don't you ask the L'Orange yourself?" sniggered Greppledick, who thought he was being humorous.

164

Caffrey, rather than laugh, sat back on the sofa and closed his eyes.

Invoking the smell of cardboard and wet, smoldering leaves, he waited for a reply. Nothing. He tried adding the essence of Scotch bonnet peppers and furniture polish. An odd sensation crept up his leg. It wasn't so much a feel as it was a taste. Strange as it sounded, the taste of huckleberry and butter cream tiptoed up his chest and tickled his chin. This bizarre but definite feeling formed a picture in his mind. It was the teal-and-gold room and, centered in the space, sitting upon a black-velvet-covered table, was a cube of orange gelatin.

— *Hello, Caffrey*, a voice sounded in his head.

— *Hello.*

— *I want you to take your next step. Communicate to me as I did to you. I want you to use the physical sensations of taste.*

— *How?*

— *You know how. Here...* The L'Orange sent a feeling of scalding water across Caffrey's fingertips, but it didn't burn. It tasted like sour apples and yet his mind somehow experienced this felt taste as words: *Ride the gift of the gift horse.*

Caffrey was confused by the advice and sent out electrical static tickles of fish and chips with brown sauce. He was punched in the stomach as the taste of rotted cabbage, sour milk and molded bricks filled his mouth.

— *You are wasting time. But, alas, time can be recycled*, was what the Wise One advised. Caffrey focused origami birds, barnacle sauce and burnt toast with marmalade—but no answer was returned. Instead, the teal-and-gold room faded; and Caffrey opened his eyes, finding himself back on the couch in the Deck of Ruby Gilding. He gathered his thoughts a moment then turned to his uncle.

"Where's Poe?"

"He is being readied for worship. Spydersloth is feeding the oversensitive ego circuitry I built into Poe."

"I have to get him back quickly." He smiled as he picked up the 4-D construction set.

Caffrey was about to open the box when a quizzical look filled his countenance. He looked at Greppledick.

"Where's Violet?"

"Who?"

"Violet. The purple-eyed lovely."

"Didn't realize she was with you." Greppledick seemed concerned.

"What do you mean?"

"Well, I sort of sent Peebo off with her."

"Peebo?"

"My new little android. I built him when I was brought back. Had a few days to kill. He's sort of...escorting her."

"Where?" Caffrey's stomach tightened.

With great hesitancy and a certain amount of embarrassment, Greppledick explained, "To the Room of Traitor Disposal."

Caffrey burbled air out between his lips in disbelief.

Angie, like a lucid dreamer, flew through the twisting corridors of the *Crystal Guise*. She tried continuously to communicate with its computers; but they simply called her bad names, telling her to go to Hell and other equally distasteful locations. Finally, she came to a flashing sign pointing the way to the docking bays. She followed their directions, unaware of Oafelia stealthily on her tail.

No announcements had gone out, but they knew. The beings aboard Spydersloth's ship always knew when and where they were to gather and pay tribute, pray to or bow down before whoever or whatever was to be the recipient of their surrendered soul. Like wind-up sheep they gathered outside the Green Metallic Lair of the Subservient Eggs[14], where they would yield their very essence and fall prostrate to the idol of the day. Inside, Poe 33 sat upon a throne, a long green carpet leading to his polished feet.

"Now I am to be hailed, as such an august android should be," he murmured softly to himself. "They will bow before me."

A large door opened, and the supplicants entered.

"Come on, darling, start. Start!" Angie pleaded with the escape pod's engine. After a few more failed attempts, the engines came to life, and the craft rose a few feet off the ground.

"That's the girl. Okay, my love, Angie's coming."

---

[14] When Spydersloth first began his anti-music crusade he was chased off-stage by a group of strong-willed Stebble Hens who refused to surrender their music. As Spydersloth walked off defeated, he noticed a group of twelve eggs rolling and hopping behind. He learned they'd been converted in vitro and had pledged their young feathered souls to him for all eternity.

166

The walls of energy locking the pod in its parking space dissolved, and Angie guided the small craft down the landing tunnel and back into space.

Outside the *Crystal Guise*, five ships floated towards the refuse vaporizers—the five ships of the Five Heads of the Five Sectors were about to be no more. Angie proceeded to the large main opening and, tossing caution to the wind, launched the pod at full throttle into the entry port. It accelerated through the large reception area, sending confused bodies ducking and diving out of the way. Angie maneuvered the craft down a main hall that forked and split, and forked and split some more, crashing through glass doors, partitions and windows with reckless abandon. Alarms sounded and heavily armed robotic guards emerged from their storage compartments, scattered in regular intervals about the ship.

Oafelia remained silent aboard the craft, privately impressed by the courage of the younger and prettier Revenant. She would wait for the perfect moment to act.

Violet floated in the spherical cage that had sprung from the loins of Peebo. The elaborate little electronic doodle of Greppledick Quark used its rear jets to travel along the ceiling of the hall leading to the Traitor Disposal Room. The chamber was designed to launch into the death-grip of space any onboard traitor, closet musician, blasphemer, harmonic sympathizer or anyone caught whistling, humming or tapping any appendage in a way that might be considered even remotely rhythmic. Violet had been deemed worthy of walking the cosmic plank simply because she'd become an annoyance. It was the simplicity of ODOR's refined and honed bureaucracy that allowed such quick and efficient exercises in justice.

Violet pried and pulled on the bars of Peebo's cage as it entered the chamber. The voice command speaker buzzed.

"Peebo! Peebo! It's your master. Return to the Deck of Ruby Gilding. Immediately!"

So, as good robots do, the little flying android carried out his programmed tasks in sequence. Peebo released the cage from its body and exited the chamber to return to its master. Violet let out a yelp as an arm sprang from the wall and grabbed the bars of her confinement. The walls slid open as an energy field protected her from cosmic exposure.

"You have been generously granted a chance for reprieve. Kneel and vow a life of non-lyrical existence, and you may be released," the voice offered.

Violet laughed.

"Was that a laugh of gratitude or was that a laugh of rebellion?" the computer asked, unable to distinguish.

"How's this for a clarification?" Violet cleared her throat and began to sing, loud and proud, "Happy Birthday to me! Happy birthday to me! Happy birthday, dear Violet! Happy birthday to me!"

"I am pleased to announce that you have violated every law of ODOR I am further pleased to inform you that you may write your epitaph with the florid script of irony, as you will die on the date of your birth," proclaimed the computer.

The energy fields vanished, and Violet and the ball-shaped cage were sucked out into space.

Peebo entered Greppledick's private living chambers on the Deck of Ruby Gilding and came to an obedient halt before his resurrected maker.

"Where is the woman?" the old man asked, looking past the small robot. Peebo seemed to shrug.

Caffrey approached with reproach. "Don't shrug, you metallic retard. Answer the question!"

"He can't. I didn't have time to give him speech capabilities. He communicates via dips and shimmies."

Caffrey was developing an irate attack. "So, where is she?"

"Peebo?"

The little round robot dipped and shook and rose up then down. Greppledick tweaked his Adam's apple and stared at the ceiling.

"What?" Caffrey's stomach was flipping.

"He followed the order. He dropped her off at the Traitor Disposal Chamber."

"And?"

"She was disposed of."

Before Caffrey could register an appropriate facial expression, a siren shrieked wildly, followed by a shuddering crash. The escape pod from the *Moby Dick* exploded into the room.

"Get in, my Jack-O-Love!" Angie's voice boomed from the pod's PA system.

Caffrey scrambled in, dragging Greppledick behind him. The port slid shut, and Angie maneuvered the pod away.

168

"Angie, you little devil!" Caffrey grinned, with a kiss to the air.

Angie gave him a rapid update. "Spydersloth turned the conference room into a massacre! I think the Five Heads are all dead!"

"Is Yin still an epaulet?" Caffrey asked, ignoring the confused reaction of Greppledick.

"No, but I don't know what happened to him."

Caffrey grabbed the controls. "I have a plan. It'll sound a little peculiar, but it should work. We're going to soup up this baby with a small Moebius Strip."

Angie demurred. "But that will invert space. You'll be turned inside out!"

"It will also invert time. And we need time inverted. We need to open a temporal tunnel to take us back just prior to the destruction of the *Moby Dick*."

"But it will invert space," Angie repeated with utter disgust.

"A small and very temporary price to pay for being heroes, Angie, my girl!"

Yin's jaw was locked tight on an ankle. He wasn't quite sure whose ankle, but he bit down just the same as the orgy of the battle continued. It was hard to tell who'd been killed in the ensuing barrage of blasts, but there were still quite a few fists, legs, teeth and tails fighting it out amidst the lifeless bodies.

Yin released the gnawed foot joint from his jaw as he glimpsed daylight from the corner of his eye. The light was coming through a door. Although it was locked, a panel had been blasted away in the skirmish.

"Run for it, Yin!" cried the little Rykonese Puffy, trapped under the weighted mountain of Quigmo Digmo's left buttock. "Your mission is of greater importance than this silly mêlée!"

"Thank you, Gordak! You are a true hero. It has been an honor being your left-hand epaulet!" Yin said with a bow.

The two had become fast friends during their awkward stay atop Ba Ba Banaki's shoulders, and they'd shared numerous whispered conversations, exchanging war stories in addition to their respective desires and ambitions.

"I only wish my demise was less demoralizing than being crushed by one of the largest tushies in the galaxy," the little canine bemoaned.

"That will not happen, friend!" Yin dived, mouth agape, and let his fangs pierce the innumerable fleshy folds of Quigmo's butt.

The Belkibon, dazed but far from dead, reacted with a hula-dancer shimmy, relieving the pressure on the body of Gordak and enabling him to turn his upper body freely.

"That was an action taken only by a true friend. To put your mouth intentionally on this foul creature's buttocks is bravery above and beyond the call of duty!"

"Another bite or two should free you. Good luck, Gordak, son of Markayas!"

"And may luck comfort you like a bowl of kibbles near a warm stove, Yin, son of Yorn!"

Yin crouched down as a half-dozen energy bolts flashed across the conference room. He managed to manipulate his way through a gauntlet of boots, clashing blades and falling bodies, bounding through the air and out the empty frame of the locked door.

The escape pod continued its run through the metal halls, Caffrey following Angie's directions as she recalled the layout from her memory.

"Uh-oh!" she cried. "They weren't here a moment ago!"

The end of the corridor was blocked by a row of Spydersloth's robot guards, heavily armed with tremendous Gluxhower 11 plasma pulse rifles. They began firing. Caffrey dodged and darted around the brilliant bars of illuminated plum-colored pulses, making their way at ridiculous speeds. Peebo, who'd been tailing the pod obediently, raced around and took the lead, morphing into an umbrella of silvery-gray metal. The substance seemed to materialize from thin air and formed a spiky shield the width of the passage.

"It still amazes me," Greppledick said of his own impromptu creation. "Hydro-carbonic sculpting. And he's used it to protect his maker!"

"You are an amazing creator of androids, Greppledick," Angie complimented.

"I am that. There are none greater!" He bowed, unable to hide his pleasure.

The shield plowed through the guards, scattering them like armored bowling pins.

"Make the next three rights," Angie instructed.

Yin heard the noise. It was a buzz, ever-increasing in volume, approaching from the bow of the *Crystal Guise*. The drone was begin-

170

ning to drown out the multiple alarms screaming around the ship. Yin ducked behind a ventilation unit and twisted his ears like radar dishes. Whatever was approaching, it would arrive in seconds.

Footsteps were added to the mix—multiple pairs of heavy boots—and with them advanced a sense of panic, of horror, of life and death. Yin held his breath and tried to slow his pounding heart. The invading clamor was joined by sudden screams. High-pitched cries like those of children running from a bumblebee. Yin peered out and around, gazing down the seemingly infinite-length corridor. He had to smile.

Three heavily armored guards rushed forward, screaming and waving their arms in fright. Behind them was the source of the intolerable buzzing, the escape pod from the *Moby Dick*, peeking out intermittently from behind Peebo's odd shield. Yin jumped out and stood on his hind legs in the center of the hall, pumping his front paws in a victorious and mocking manner, laughing with delight as the guards rushed by.

"Caffrey!" Yin yelled, waving his paws. But the pod didn't slow down. It barreled closer.

"Quarky! Angie!" the Bopple screamed, not sure if his attempt at hitchhiking would finally bring the craft to a stop or flatten him like road kill. The latter came close to reality. The escape pod, its occupants apparently unaware of Yin's presence, zoomed down the hall. Yin flattened, his head buried protectively beneath his front paws.

"I thought I caught a glimpse of tiny, waving arms. Possibly paws?" Caffrey said with a growing concern.

"Yin?" Angie queried.

"I'm going back," declared Caffrey, making a wickedly sharp one-eighty.

"Peebo!" Greppledick spoke into the intercom microphone, "Backtrack and scan for any small, furry critters. Report back at once."

Peebo backtracked. A gaping mouth formed on the smart ball's surface, opening like a starving bazinga fish.

Using what was left of his strength, Yin scrambled off, his toe nails making tippity-tip sounds on the cold metal floor. His ears flapped behind, and a string of poochie drool was sent on the wind of his frantic escape. Peebo's jaws closed in, the android's mysterious propulsion system not prone to the exhaustion currently being experienced by Yin's biological frame. Each step Yin took suggested more determinedly that the world was tilting uphill. Gravity seemed to multiply, and his weight grew exponentially. The Bopple collapsed, the last fragments of energy in his little body expended like a compulsive gambler's luck.

"May the cause of OTHER fare greater than the evil of ODOR Viva la música," Yin gasped, struggling out his own testament.

Peebo swooped down like a featherless bird of prey and, in one neat bite, gobbled Yin like a grape then darted back toward the pod. The mute android bobbed up and down like a buoy on rough seas, communicating its urgent message.

"He wants in!" Greppledick translated.

Caffrey opened the entry panel, and Peebo quickly entered. His mouth opened and Yin fell out, hitting the floor with a thud. Caffrey's face spoke volumes, a veritable encyclopedia of emotions, yet he could only speak one word:

"Yin!"

He scooped his little dog into his arms and cradled him like a doll, kissing his forehead tenderly.

"You still with us, old boy?" he whispered.

The Bopple moaned and whimpered.

"Poor darling," Angie soothed.

"He's exhausted," Caffrey diagnosed, placing him gently on a cushioned seat.

"He'll be fine, I'm sure," Greppledick concluded, petting Yin's forehead.

"Thank you, Peebo." Caffrey gave the android an appreciative nod.

The android did a small dance. He had shrunk in size, the mouth extension having collapsed back into his spherical shape. He exited the pod and continued his defensive duties.

"One more to go. We'll snatch Poe then put my Moebius plan to work."

"But you'll be inverted," Angie moaned.

"We're here to save my friends and the galaxy, not worry about appearances," Caffrey rejoined, with a newfound purpose.

"I am very proud of you. My reluctant hero has found a cause!"

"I'd rather be dead than live music-free!"

"I'd rather be dead. Period," grumbled the old man.

"Hang on tight, Uncle. You'll get your wish if my plan fails."

Greppledick clasped his hands around the back of his head and closed his eyes for a catnap.

"Let's hope you're right," he yawned.

"Caffrey? This may seem a silly question, but did you set the self-destruct mechanism to engage in ten minutes?" inquired Angie with a nervous laugh.

"Don't be silly, girl!"

"Well, I hate to be a party pooper, but it's set. This pod is going to explode into confetti in nine minutes and forty-five seconds."

"Well? Disengage it!"

"I tried. I can't. It looks like another intelligence has put a lock on it."

Caffrey's eyes widened. Both he and Angie came to the same verbal conclusion at the same instant.

"That bitch!"

A nasty, spiteful chuckle sounded as the pod raced down the labyrinth of halls.

The Green Metallic Lair of the Subservient Eggs was rarely used. The rectangular chapel, adorned with plush verdant carpeting, shimmering olive titanium walls and emerald torches dispersing their flickering light-pools, had been built for special guests. In the social structure of ODOR, being worshiped in your own private chapel was to its upper crust what having a private jet was to the same class on twentieth-century Earth.

Poe 33 stared dead ahead with a blank expression hinting at repressed ecstasy. But the orange-and-blue android was experiencing a battle deep within the circuits and programming of his conscience. This powerful feeling, this inflation of his ego, had drowned the original purpose of his existence—to serve his Master. Although he was sitting solidly, he was floating above the throne, riding the waves of self-important joy. His loyalty to the L'Orange was calling, a faint voice like a drowning fisherman beyond the horizon; but the din of his pronounced greatness was in turn muffling those calls.

"I sense some familiarity with you, my child," Poe said to the supplicant who had stepped before him. "Your countenance and the life energy sparkling within your eyes rings a knell of recognition."

"It's me, you dimwitted metallic conglomeration of pomposity," Greppledick scowled. "Dethrone your shiny ass and follow me."

Poe 33 laughed, deep and haughtily. "I am in a position to have you beheaded. Please, pay your respects and leave. There are hundreds awaiting my presence."

Without further ado, Greppledick popped Poe 33's left eye out with his index finger and turned the android off with a flick of a secret switch deep in his head. The spark of Poe 33 went dark as if suddenly frozen. Greppledick, with something of a struggle, picked his android child up fireman's style and exited through the astonished crowd. Mumbling disparagingly about the world of the living, he pushed his way through the onslaught, ducking around a corner and into an escape stairwell.

It had become quite apparent as Caffrey and Co. raced around the *Crystal Guise* that every exit port had been sealed tight to prevent the escape of the music-loving rebels in their run-amok pod. Angie, unable to stop the self-destruct countdown, had managed to convince the on-board computers that Caffrey, feeling shameful for his recent antics, had decided to commit himself to the Room of Traitor Disposal as a form of penance to Spydersloth.

The onboard computer system's naïve and bureaucratic programming was simply not prepared for such situations and had just updated Caffrey's status as the newly ordained Vicar of Negated Music Registry. This position had certain perks. The most cherished of these perks, especially by true zealots of the ODOR cause, was the right of self-incrimination. By virtue of Caffrey's appointment into the upper echelons of Spydersloth's organization, he could deem himself a traitor to the cause and sentence himself to death. It was a rather simple way of doing away with the inconvenience of a trial, and in Caffrey's case, it provided the only remaining safe passage to outer space, where his plan could be put into effect.

Only six minutes of countdown to self-destruct remained.

"Here's my little sleeping Messiah," Greppledick joked as he reentered the pod. "Any luck with your master plan?"

Caffrey was in an understandable bustle. "Almost, Unc. Angie! To the Traitor Disposal Room. Pronto!"

"*Sí, sí, el capitán!*"

The clock ticked away as Angie guided the pod to the Room of Traitor Disposal while Caffrey put the finishing touches on his electronic makeover. It had taken a bit of imagination, but he'd managed to run the small Moebius Strip Generator through the escape pod's propulsion system. The trick was jury-rigging an adapter to properly connect the power supply of the craft with the battery compartment of the toy. With a little finagling, he managed the problem by looting a part from his S-77.

Within seconds of the pod's entry into the disposal station, the computer's voice intoned an alternative to death for Caffrey. "You have been generously granted a chance for reprieve. Kneel and vow a life of non-lyrical existence and you may be released."

"I come here on my own accord. I have found myself unworthy to serve the Great Spydersloth Blaust and wish to end my existence," Caffrey declared.

"Do you speak for the Human, the Bopple and the two Revenants as well?" questioned the Voice.

"Yes," insisted Greppledick.

"I do," confirmed Angie.

"The Bopple is asleep," explained Caffrey, "but he has personally assured me that his wish is to die a cowardly traitor."

"I am pleased to announce that your request for self-incrimination has been granted. You are free to die."

"Thank you. Thank you very much!" replied Caffrey, Greppledick and Angie in harmonic unison—which was one last unconscious act of defiance.

"I will now deactivate all onboard life support systems and eject your craft."

Caffrey hadn't thought of that.

The soft whine of the atmosphere generator eased down to nothingness, and all onboard lights went out. With a mighty shove, the escape pod was launched out into the black hand of space. Oafy laughed.

"We have two minutes left, my large-lunged love dove!" Angie cried.

Caffrey had momentarily blacked out. He hadn't anticipated such a violent push and had a brief but sincere thought of writing to the Vicar of Self-Incrimination and suggesting that should someone volunteer their own demise they at least be subjected to low G-forces upon their disposal. He quickly dismissed the idea when he realized that no one in this place and time did much writing and, besides, finding a stamp, never mind a mailbox, would be quite a chore in itself. He opened his eyes, and they adjusted to the traces of starlight beaming in through the portholes. Oafy was still laughing.

"It's time we try our little experiment," Caffrey announced, rubbing his temples and leaning to the controls. "Ready, Angie?"

"Ready."

"We're going to open up a brand new temporal branch, but copy the frequency and wave-forms from the ten-minute period before the *Moby Dick* was fried."

"You'll wind up with a temporal twin," Greppledick postulated.

"No," Angie interrupted, "I will clip the wave forms of the frequencies that describe the twins of myself, Poe Thirty-three and Quarky. Violet will also return. Although I will perform that horrid task under protest."

"That's the spirit, Angie-girl."

"We have one minute, ten seconds until destruction," Angie reminded the crew. "Ten seconds until Moebius engagement!"

"Here we go! Nine...eight..."

"It will never work!" screamed Oafelia.

"Seven...six...five..." Caffrey continued.

"Viva ODOR!"

Caffrey slowly pulled the acceleration lever, and the engines rumbled.

"Four...three...two..."

"I give of my essence!" cried Oafelia.

"One!" Caffrey applied full throttle. A bluish glow illuminated the cabin, followed by a sudden shower of sparks. Caffrey and Greppledick threw their arms before their faces as all went dark. All went silent.

Caffrey was baffled; then Angie realized what Oafy'd done.

"She killed herself. She peaked her own life voltage. Surged every amp of her current into the circuits of the Moebius Strip Generator and fried herself."

"And took the Moebius Generator with her," Caffrey said in disbelief.

"Yes. Yes, my poor, doomed darling."

"We have less than a minute," Caffrey muttered.

"Thank the cosmos!" Greppledick praised. "Trust me. It'll be better for all of us."

Not appreciating Greppledick's option, Caffrey tore a panel off the wall and began pulling fuses and tearing wires.

"What are you doing, electro-muffin?"

"One of these wires must control the destruct device," Caffrey insisted, having a hard time with a particularly thick cable. "We might not be able to stop the clock, but we might be able to disengage the actual explosives."

176

"What is that?" Greppledick said, pointing to gray mist entering the pod in a micro-thin hair-like stream. The mist gathered in a thickening blob that began to shape itself into a familiar form. Greppledick watched in amazement as the smoke formed itself into a sphere. A metallic sphere.

"Peebo?"

The android bounced up and down excitedly then sent out a finger of wispy smoke that entered the fried Moebius Generator.

"What's he doing?" Greppledick was amazed at Peebo's antics.

"We have twenty seconds! Caffrey!" Angie called out.

Peebo began wobbling wildly. Greppledick watched carefully, smiling as the message was communicated.

"Try it again, Caffrey!" Greppledick shouted.

"Try what?"

"Your Moebius thruster experiment!"

"It's fried!"

Greppledick slapped his hand on his thigh. "We have ten seconds, nephew! I have no problem having my aged and crumbling body scattered across this solar system, but if you have any future ambitions that require the use of your physical self I would try the thruster again!"

"That sentence used five seconds!" Angie cried. "Three! Two!"

Caffrey looked at the thruster level. He looked at his uncle. He thought about Violet and the possible use of his physical self. He dived to the controls and gave it a yank.

The world around them melted. Like a cookie tray of sixty-four crayons in a pizza oven, the fabric of space-time dripped and bubbled and came apart in an incredible display of intersecting colors and fractals. There were hues Caffrey's eyes had never seen before—weird shades of love. Tints of sadness. Tinges of joy. It was as if all emotions, all experiences, were represented as pigments. Drops of inks in crystal-clear water. The cosmos warped and twisted.

Caffrey had no sensation of his body nor did he see the bodies of his friends. There was no solidity. He wasn't floating through space-time as much as space-time was floating through his mind—a mind located everywhere at once, yet nowhere perceivable. Perhaps this was the other side Greppledick had bragged about? It was beyond pleasurable. It was a moment.

Then the moment became a series of moments flashing and speeding up like a filmstrip getting up to proper projection speed.

The bulb flashed. The screen burned. The theatre went black.

"Good morning, my master. There is a cup of hot Earth coffee awaiting you with one sugar and a dash of cream," Angie said. "My God, you look disgusting! I warned you, Caffrey!"

Caffrey was back aboard the *Moby Dick*, and it took a moment for him to realize what had happened. He was turned inside out like a tight rubber glove pulled off from the wrist. He looked at his own hand and noted the pulsing veins and twitching muscles. His brain was still spinning, and he clasped his palms atop his head only to recoil in disgust. Greppledick was standing by the window, a six-foot-tall stack of bones, muscles and veins, silently staring at the beautiful ringed Komquista. Yin was still asleep, curled in a grotesque inverted ball of blissful ignorance. Poe 33 sat in a lump on the floor, chips, hydraulics and circuit boards exposed for all to see.

"Now, that's pretty disturbing," Caffrey agreed, studying his hand as it reached into the food prep unit to retrieve the cup.

"Can someone please explain where we are?" Greppledick finally spoke.

"More like *when* we are," corrected Angie. "We are moments before the *Moby Dick* was grabbed by the tug beam. However, since we opened an alternate temporal branch, there are changes. The wicked witch Oafelia is gone. Sweet Yin and you, my gentlemen friends, are here, inverted and horrid; and if I had a stomach its contents would be projected about this cabin. And, if you look in sleeping compartment B, Violet is, indeed, sleeping soundly."

Caffrey smiled at the tone Angie used to speak the name "Violet." There was obvious agitation swimming like salmon against the flow of her audio stream. Perhaps jealousy.

Peebo emerged from the stern of the *Moby Dick*, glowing crimson once again. He was, oddly, not inverted.

"Thank you again, Peebo," Caffrey nodded. "I have no clue what you did or how you did it. But thank you."

Greppledick approached the floating android and studied it carefully. "You are amazing. You weren't even affected by the Moebius Generator's inversion of time and space. When I built you, little Peebo, I had no clue of the abilities you would self-perpetuate. Carbon extraction and sculpting. Anything. You can create or recreate anything you come across using the carbon molecules of your environment. Incredible."

Greppledick turned to Caffrey. "He learned that on his own. I built him to kill time. I had a couple of days of boredom aboard that miserable Arachnid's ship. In a matter of hours, Peebo evolved to levels that should have taken decades!"

Caffrey turned to Angie. "Angie, make double-damn sure we're cloaked. Last thing I want is to get back into the tug beam and have a little repeat of our previous escapade. I suggest we awaken Poe and wait for the extraction of Haptiwoo. Then we'll enter the wormhole."

"I refuse to travel another meter with you looking like that!" Angie objected.

Caffrey studied his uncle. "How do I look, Uncle Greppledick?"

The old inside-out man stepped closer and took a good look at his nephew's innards. "A bit moist. Otherwise, quite well, boy. Quite well."

"You look like a man of ninety, on the inside. I would never guess by those guts that you were a resurrected old geezer of one-eighty."

"Thank you," replied Greppledick with a wry, toothy grin.

"You see, Angie-girl. We're fine."

"I liked you better as a snake," she sniffed, floating off in a huff.

Caffrey smiled after her then went over to compartment B and banged on the wall. Violet jumped from her sleep.

"Wake up! Time to move on."

A startled yip sounded. Yin had awakened to discover his once soft and lustrous fur had a strange, meaty feel.

"My boy! You've rejoined the living!" sang Caffrey gleefully.

"Would someone please explain why I have X-ray vision?" the Bopple desperately wanted to know.

"Not quite, boy. We used a Moebius Strip Generator. We managed to open a brand new temporal branch. The little side effect is a typical Moebius effect."

"Is that all? Good work, Quarky," Yin applauded.

Another scream filled the cabin. Violet sat staring at her body.

"Good morning, Violet. You look exceptionally good this morning," Angie mused.

"Don't tell me," Violet mumbled "Moebius?"

Caffrey, Yin and Greppledick all nodded coyly. Caffrey stepped up to Poe 33 and turned to look inquisitively at his uncle. " Are you going to awaken His Eminence?"

"I suppose." With a click of the Portsmith's on/off switch, Poe

33's interior shimmered with a quick twinkle of colorful lights. He came to attention.

"Please. Await your turn. You will have ample time to worship me. Thank you."

"Welcome back, Poe," Caffrey said, patting the robot's exposed back.

"Quark Caffrey? Is that your spleen I see?"

"Yes, Poe. And this is my rib cage and this red thingee here is my liver. Looks surprisingly healthy," mused Caffrey. "You look a tad exposed as well."

Poe 33 gave himself the once-over. "Looks like I've been Moebiusized."

"How are you otherwise, my boy?" Greppledick asked.

"I am fine, but why was my worship service interrupted? It was going so well."

"You have an important assignment," Greppledick reminded him. "You must be reunited with the L'Orange."

Poe 33 seemed disinterested. Caffrey explained, "Haptiwoo will be devolved in moments, and we will follow its primal material into the dimension of Nefarious Wretch. With any luck we will find both my friends and your Master."

"He is no longer my Master," Poe 33 said softly.

"Bite your tongue, Poe!" scolded Greppledick. "The full surrendering of the ego is the first prime Portsmith precept."

"I feel no connection. I haven't for some time. Caffrey seems to be more in tune with the Great L'Orange than I."

"You are going through a period of confusion. You must have experienced electrical surges to your ego centers. But you will be back to your old self. You will serve your Master as I programmed you to," the old man insisted with increasing conviction.

"I don't think so. I think instead he will worship me." Poe 33 seemed to smile with a newly found resolve. "Yes. I believe if we are ever reunited, I shall be the wise one and he'll play the role of subservient lackey."

"Poe!" Greppledick was about to explode, but Caffrey took him gently aside.

"One problem at a time, Unc. Relax. Look at your heart! It's pumping like a tweezle rat in heat." He moved over to the navigation console.

Greppledick took a deep breath and nodded, studying his circulatory organ as it pounded away.

"Angie? Are we prepared for trans-dimensional shift?"

"Yes. Can you do your favorite sweet audio angel an itsy-bitsy favor?"

"What's that?"

"May I please activate the Moebius Generator during our wormhole transit? Get this horrid group of meat and bones back to normal?"

"Fine, Angie. Fine."

Moments later—again—aboard the *Crystal Guise*, the crowd of fervent psychotics cheered and drooled as Planet Haptiwoo and its poor, music-loving populace began their transition to the dimension of Nefarious Wretch. As the swirls of matter drifted into the opening wormhole like water down a drain to God-knows-where, Caffrey and the crew aboard the *Moby Dick* patiently waited. As the final bits of Haptiwoo tumbled down the cosmic loo and the dangers of colliding with the violent stream of particles was at a minimum, the *Moby Dick* made its move.

Slowly, the ship drifted towards the opening punched in the black sheet of space. Greppledick took one last glance at the *Crystal Guise* and its disco-ball moon scattering starry light on the thick wafts of fog farting from the rear of the mother ship. Yin glanced sideways out the starboard porthole at the ringed star of Komquista and resisted the call to wax poetic. Caffrey, however, gave in to the call.

"We raced across the stars. Rings ringing. Singing. We were the armor-plated three-headed lizard-tube men of Mars."

"What's that from?" Violet wondered.

Yin volunteered the info. "It's from the Marmalade Skies' second album. Part two of Xing Xang's triple quest—*Orbus Tres*. 'Reptilian Fugue in C.' It's a beauty. I've heard it performed live. Kick-ass guitar solo."

Caffrey concurred. "Thank you, Yin, my little pooch. Maybe one day my aurally deprived uncle will see the Skies perform live, and his mind will open to more musical possibilities than classical Denlopo chamber tunes."

"There is no other music," Greppledick declared with every ounce of snobbery he could muster.

"Rock music, at its best, is of equal musical complexity, but it surpasses your pompous tunes in lyrical meaning, social profundity and subtle beauty."

"Flying porko poop!"

"Brilliant comeback, Unc! Angie, play us a sample. How's about something soft and limpid for my virginal-eared uncle?"

"A little Sabbath?"

"Perfect."

"Paranoid" exploded from the ship's speakers. Caffrey's ears twitched as the song started. It was playing backwards.

"Bloody Moebius!"

"Guess now we can check on those satanic messages, huh, Quarky?" Yin jested.

"Angie, make damned sure the Moebius Generator engages on final thrust into the wormhole! One second before entry for a duration of point-five seconds. That should do the trick."

"Thank you, my soon-to-be normal love."

It was mere moments until the last of Haptiwoo's former glory swirled away into the anomaly. the *Moby Dick*'s engines engaged, racing the ship towards the closing wormhole, stopping for a half-second as the Moebius Generator flipped time and space—providing a similar albeit much shorter neural roller-coaster ride for all on board. the *Moby Dick* and her crew entered the hole, which closed behind them with melodramatic timing.

— *Caffrey Quark*, a voice spoke directly into his mind, *do you have an invitation?*

The world around him was frozen. Violet, Yin, Greppledick and Poe 33 were all stuck in a moment of time. The voice was odd. It changed with every syllable. It morphed seamlessly from one tone and timbre to another. It was a constantly changing stream of voices holding no rhythm or pattern.

— *Who is this?* Caffrey wondered as he tried to move his body. He, too, was frozen.

— *I will grant you entrance as my special guest.*

— *Are my friends there?* Caffrey asked, feeling as if his mind was melting away.

— *Never mind them! Wouldn't you prefer a seat of power? You must be impressed with my abilities.*

— *Bite me*, returned Caffrey.

— *The Portsmith is weakening. He will convert soon. Take a lesson from his wisdom.*

— *He* has *converted. To an air guitar-playing, palm-drumming, knows-every-lyric Rock music fan*, Caffrey replied in his head, jabbing the entity's appropriate mental buttons. *I think he even mentioned wanting to sleep with David Bowie. So, once again, creepo—bite my pale coolie.*

There was a demented cry, seeming to fill Caffrey's head with thick, burning tar. As it dripped out of his ears, the distinct sound of a roulette wheel spinning sent his mind bouncing around on the pegs of universal chaos, masquerading as randomness and chance.

It was as if he blinked.

CHAPTER 15
Kashmir

(Led Zeppelin)

affrey looked around his cabin, and the first thing he noticed was Yin scratching at a patch of fur on the back of his neck.

Fur. There was not a muscle, vein, bone, chip, gear, circuit board or organ visible anywhere on board. Greppledick, Poe 33 and Violet were all tossing little silent glances about. Peebo hovered, his red light glowing softly but outshone by the brownish light pouring in through the portholes.

"Everyone okay?" asked Angie.

All the heads onboard nodded in the affirmative. Violet unbuckled her straps and went for a peek out the aft port.

"Where are we?"

Angie was hesitant. "I am not sure. This location is nowhere to be found in the onboard map database. It's a peculiar piece of space."

An Earth-size planet the color of coffee sat in a moonless/sunless plot of space. Yet, despite the absence of a mother star, the planet was illuminated in a bright glow.

Caffrey squinted and stroked his chin. "Is it my imagination, or does the space around this world seem to be finite?"

Violet concurred in amazement. "It is. This world is in a cosmic box."

Indeed, the spherical space around the dark-brown world was at a minimum—perhaps ten kilometers in every direction to where the black void simply ended. No distant stars. No distant galaxies. No infinity staring back to elicit grand feelings of inferiority in the face of God.

It was frigging claustrophobic.

Poe 33 recited from his own experience records. "A cosmic box, indeed. Cold storage. A closet, of sorts, carved into a hyper-dimension and used for the safekeeping of a planet."

Or as a prison was Caffrey's more sobering thought.

Yin needed information. "How did we wind up here? What happened to following Haptiwoo into the dimension of Nefarious?"

"We weren't allowed in," Caffrey sighed. "He refused our entry. So, he spun the wheel, so to speak, and sent us on our way."

"Nefarious Wretch spoke to you?" Poe 33 asked with a tinge of both envy and disgust.

"He did."

"Master," Yin piped, taking Caffrey aside, "do you see why Violet and I had to recruit you on this quest?"

"No," Caffrey snapped tersely. "And drop the cute tail-wagging and whimpering from now on. I would never have pegged you as such an underhanded mutt."

Yin wasn't easily discouraged. "They speak to you. The L'Orange. Nefarious. Both have communicated directly with your mind. A mind they obviously either fear or admire."

But Caffrey wasn't easily influenced. "Yin, if my mind impresses or scares the wisest and most powerful beings in the galaxy, then creation is certainly doomed."

"Don't underestimate yourself, Caffrey," Violet advised softly.

A heavy sigh sounded, and all heads turned to Poe 33, who sat at the dining table wearing a soft expression of inner sadness. A smile found its way out of the dark jungle of his emotions as he lifted the peppermill from the spice slot. He began addressing the chrome container with warmth and sincerity.

"I feel as I am sure you have felt when the last of your tiny but pungent black spheres have been ground and drifted from your body like a charcoal snow. Empty. Detached. I had hopes that the discovery of the scrambler would explain my loss. Then, I was certain the replacement of my lost chip would provide an instant linking back to my grand Master. It hasn't. I feel as though I am alone forever. Perhaps we can leave, together, and seek fame and fortune amongst the stars."

"For the love of shoes," Yin mumbled.

"Nonsense, Poe!" roared Greppledick, pounding his hand on the table. "It is a mere bump in the road!"

Poe 33 sent an evil, fish-eyed glare to his maker. "You don't care. Stop pretending you do!"

"Don't shout at your father, you blue-assed, melodramatic egophile!"

"Would you two mind holding your therapy session elsewhere? We've an entire galaxy falling apart out there," Caffrey reminded them. "Angie, run a scan on the atmosphere of this planet. Do a general surface inspection as well."

In a matter of a small part of a second Angie reported her findings. "The atmosphere is close enough to your home world, minus, of course, the fluorocarbons, factory-spouted filth and other assorted breathable pornography, for you to breathe. There is a small population of what can be categorized as the hybrid species *Homosapianus termitidae odobenus rosarus.*"

"In Plethorian standard, Angie," requested Greppledick.

"Termite Walrus People," Caffrey translated.

"...And there are huge sculptures. Forests of gigantic faces peering into the sky, some a kilometer long, dotting the surface. Like giant, exotic sand castles," Angie concluded her report.

"Interesting," said Caffrey, taking a seat in the cockpit, "We'll land and have a look around. And, Angie—Hendrix. 'Castles Made of Sand,' in keeping with the mood."

Greppledick yawned. "I'll stay here with Poe. See if I can adjust some sense into him."

In moments, the *Moby Dick* was streaking five kilometers above the surface. Greppledick and Poe argued, rather vehemently, whether the planet below was mocha caramel brown in color or, as Poe felt, a more potato russet in hue. Violet was trying to contact someone, anyone, on the GS; and Angie hovered near, dropping little critiques of the effort's futility. Yin scratched incessantly at the same spot behind his ear, mumbling how he swore his left tympanic membrane had not been re-inverted during the last Moebius trip.

Caffrey ignored it all, lost in the work of James Marshall Hendrix, which filled the cabin like liquid, breathable sex. As he rode the song across barren landscapes, the undulating hills and dales fell past his field of vision on the waves of music. The world below became more atypical as the bland stretches of dirt and sand made way for stone roadways, wide, walled-in courts of brown and red brick

186

and mounds of sand and soil. Huge mounds.

Caffrey, deciding he was coming closer to the inhabited regions, took the *Moby Dick* down to what was known by spacecraft pilots galaxy-wide as rubber redneck altitude[15].

Huge faces came into view suddenly, and he slowed the ship down to fully appreciate the spectacle. Molded from the very material of the planet, they stared skywards. Although all were variations of the same theme (quasi-humanoid), each countenance's eye expression, mouth, ears, nose or chin had a distinct personality. Face after face passed beneath the craft, each a minimum of half a kilometer wide and a kilometer from tip of head to tip of chin. the *Moby Dick* passed hundreds upon hundreds, until finally the craft came to hover above a partially carved mound of fresh soil. Figures, wormlike and elephant-sized, scattered in slow motion, taking shelter in holes dotted about the area.

"I suppose those are the Termite Walrus People. I'm going to land here."

"Preparing landing sequence!"

Caffrey looked up. "Preparing what?"

"The landing sequence," Angie repeated, as if Caffrey were hard of hearing.

"Since when? You never said that before. What landing sequence?"

"I have numerous electronic tasks to perform to ensure a safe and efficient landing. I just never actually announced it before," responded Angie primly.

"I'll be...I always assumed I just took the old girl down," Caffrey confided, maneuvering the craft to the surface.

"Trust me, my solo delusional spring roll, you don't."

The *Moby Dick* descended, arriving with a gentle bump.

"Nice landing, Caffrey," Violet said, loud enough to be interpreted as petty.

"Nice outfit," Angie complimented sickening-sweetly to Violet. "What happened, they run out of material when they got to your

---

[15] The perfect height when flying over regions of under-educated, isolated folk who will inevitably gawk and chase down the craft in hopes of catching a glimpse of the occupants (or better yet, be invited on board). Undoubtedly, any future reporting of such incident will result in mockery and further isolation, often resulting in psychosis-forming resentment and, in some cases, lucrative story rights fees.

maternal input port?"

"You must mean my belly button," Violet smirked and sauntered to the exit, adjusting her holster so as to reveal a little more skin. "I forgot—you're not very familiar with female anatomy."

"Nice landing assist, Angie," offered Poe 33 softly.

"Thank you, Poe. Somebody is a gentleman," Angie replied, attention firmly locked on her infuriation variable. She whispered to herself, "We'll see how familiar I am."

The *Moby Dick* rested on a stretch of road coated in thick dried mud. Caffrey, Violet and Yin walked silently for a few minutes, circling the base of the gigantic mound of soil, trying to peer into the dark holes dotted around the perimeter. On the western side of the hill, the early stages of detailing had begun, as the cheekbone and corner of a mouth were clearly evident.

"They are apparently a race of shy buggers," Yin said as he watched a relatively brave native peek out from one of the holes.

"We'll be patient. Give them a few moments to sniff us out." Caffrey suggested, taking a seat on a rock and folding his arms in a relaxed fashion. He took a long gander at the carved structure. "What do you think this is about?"

"They're humanoid faces," Violet noted, rather obviously. "Looks like the same design style as that one near your home planet, Quark."

"Which one's that?"

Violet's fingers smoothed over her navel while she searched her memory. Caffrey watched carefully.

"The red planet. I forget its name."

"Mars. I've never been there."

"I've been there," said Yin, giving one of the holes a good sniff. "I was researching yodeling shrubbery. Mars is covered with it. Took a few excellent samples back to the university. Made quite a name for myself."

"That was in your pre-epaulet days, Yin," reminded Caffrey.

The little Bopple sighed. "My life held such promise."

"You never did explain, Yin, my boy. How did you survive the fall into the zedfish-infested moat on Regal Nine? And how in bloody hell did you end up on the shoulder of one of the galaxy's top gangsters?"

"Long story, my good master. Long story."

188

"Do tell," Violet insisted.

Yin cleared his throat and told the story.

━━➤

As feared, Yin had been swallowed whole by the giant zedfish mere seconds after falling into the moat. Having studied that particular species of fish during his days at university, the little Bopple was well aware of the internal layout of the giant fish. He recalled, as he slid down the digestive tract, that zedfish had an internal pocket called the *tidiclorius sac*, utilized in the wild to store feces until a proper place is found to dispose of the waste—zedfish are the neat freaks of the order *Schindleria praematurus*. Yin found the sac empty—zedfish living in a controlled environment tend to grow lazy and just dump where they eat—and filled with a rather generous supply of, relatively speaking, fresh air. He curled himself into the sac and pondered his fate.

As the world of Regal 9 was sucked into the realm of Nefarious Wretch, serendipity patted both pooch and fish on their heads. A good-hearted but troubled escaped convict from the world of Shepedora had been making his way to freedom when he was witness to the disintegration of Regal 9. Concerned for possible survivors, the considerate Samaritan scanned the spiraling rubble and discovered three lifeforms—three zedfish still swimming in the grungy green water of the castle of Queen Kinkskin's moat, which was floating whole, like some oddly adorned asteroid, towards the event horizon. Working fast, he locked in on the fish and beamed them aboard his craft. He kept them alive in a makeshift aquarium made from a wire frame wrapped with a large sheet of latex—Shepedorians are big into latex[16]—and the fish swam in the cramped, but safe, environment for the next two weeks. Yin fed on undigested food and fish urine, his body held in the sac by a suction force he hadn't anticipated.

Eventually, the escaped prisoner made it to his secret location on the lush subtropical beach on Oohn, far, far away in the Wequiri System. The fish were let out to swim free in the warm and lovely waters, where two would spawn and live happily for many a year. The third, the zedfish containing the little Bopple in its gut, would suffer a very different fate.

The planet Hhhi is noted for Lake Prior, which is much like

---

[16] Due to their cold-blooded nature, they will often wear underwear of latex to help retain valuable body heat. (You really should wash your mind out with strong soap.)

Loch Ness on Earth. Lake Prior is home to a monster—a monster with the capacity to reach into other temporal branches and feed upon whatever happens by. Breaking through the walls of time and space and temporally trolling around on planet Oohn, the monster of Lake Prior drooled on detecting the scent of the giant zedfish. In a single gobble, the monster violated the peaceful ocean of Oohn and had the meal of its lifetime.

Meanwhile, a group of passionate cryptozoologists on Hhhi, tired of being mocked by their scientific peers for believing in such rubbish as trans-temporal monsters, set out on an expedition. They were armed, equipped and overflowing with determination. They were going to capture the monster and become rich and famous beyond their wildest dreams. In the next weird flicking of the fickle finger of fate, the expedition leader fell overboard seconds before the monster swam beneath their boat.

The monster, being of an advanced age, was so startled it suffered cardiac arrest in all three of its hearts—and died. The leader survived, the team brought the dead monster aboard their boat and went on to great fame, fortune and, ultimately, substance abuse, debt and divorce. The monster was put on display in the Hhhi Museum of Science and Aquatic Anomalies, where it was to remain for centuries.

But first it was presented to the Premier of Hhhi.

In what was the most media-covered event in Hhhian history, the monster was rolled atop a golden table and presented before the Ruling Court, which blessed it with special oils and spices. As the Prime Justice of Science and Seafood laid her hands upon the beast in a sacrosanct gesture, a perfect silence fell upon the planet. A small, indistinct sound was heard! It was a sound that would forever change the attitudes, mores, laws and spiritual beliefs of the folk of Hhhi.

A form moved within the monster, a bulge that made its way from the stomach to the neck of the scaly beast. As the crowd watched aghast, the body of the zedfish, swallowed whole and exhibiting not a single toothmark, emerged from the mouth. There were cries of horror, and it is believed someone fainted.

Then a second bulge appeared and convulsed, this time in the zedfish. The audience surged and muttered at the sound of a whimper and a yip! Abruptly, the flesh of the zedfish split and tore, and like some sick and twisted Russian Matreshka a moist, black nose peeped out. Screams rent the air. Several citizens ran from the building and into the night. The entire head of the tired and bloodied Bopple emerged. Yin filled his lungs with the clear fresh air.

"God, that feels good!" he cried out to the stunned assemblage.

It would be months before the citizens of Hhhi would get over the events of that cool, exalted night. Yin was hailed as the fulfillment of a terribly misinterpreted prophecy and showered with gifts, continuous adoration and a spacious suite in the palace of the gubernatorial mansion.

Hhhi, a high level-O world, had no space program, nor much interest in what lay beyond the perpetual clouds of the pink skies. Yin was unable to communicate his dilemma and, after a year of private research, surrendered to the fact he would spend the remainder of his days as a celebrity of the folks of Hhhi. He deduced he'd emerged on an alternate time branch and the world of Caffrey, Poe 33 and the *Moby Dick* held no reality. He wasn't even certain what galaxy he was in. Unable to recognize the myriad of stars that glistened, on rare occasion, in the night skies, he settled his mind and decided to enjoy his new home.

The Bopple grew quite close to the premier and his family and spent warm spring afternoons romping on the perfectly manicured lawns of the estate, and cold winter nights snuggled on overstuffed sofas before roaring fires telling tales, discussing politics, sipping fine brandies and puffing exotic leaves in elegant pipes. He studied and became quite adept in Hhhi history, language and lore. He began teaching at the top universities, offering the first courses in basic astronomy and physics. He grew to love his new world and performed many, many hours of community service, trying to diminish his image as some furry gift of providence.

Yin's life went smoothly for thirty years—until he began growing bored and in need of a change. Through his studies, he learned of the Guyrophin Monks and their mystical monasteries hidden deep in the Singing Jungles of the West. Bidding a fond farewell to his adopted family, Yin set off for ten years of intense meditation, temperance, yoga-like practices and trans-psyche traversing. He met and fell in love with a three-legged red-backed ridgewalker, and they lived in marital bliss in a secluded and simple home on the outskirts of the monastery proper. They were married for twenty-five years (one hundred seventy-five in canine years) before Yin's wife fell ill. He held her in his paws until she breathed her last breath and, three weeks after the simple cremation ceremony, knew he could not stay amidst the trees so overflowing with memories.

Yin wandered for the next five years, living off the land and spending most of his time alone and pensive. Finding himself on a lonely beach, he felt the age in his lungs and the final beats of his heart. He sat upon the sand, the warm sun on his face, waiting to be taken to the levels beyond the physical.

Then he saw it. A red light on the horizon. A ship! It was not a sailing ship but rather it hovered over the sea. Moving closer. Growing brighter.

"A spacecraft!" Yin cried aloud, the strength returning to his blood and bones. Waving his paws frantically he ran in circles, hoping the occupants of the mysterious ship would see him.

And see him they did. In a flash, as the ship cruised overhead, a beam of silver light washed over him and the beach vanished from around him. For a brief moment, he felt he was heading to the paradise realm of the hereafter.

Not quite.

Hours later, Yin awoke. He was strapped to one of the four shoulders of a giant. Ba Ba Banaki was exploring, seeking additional sources for the extremely rare crystal erosilite, a vital component for the Harmonic Love Teasing devices that had made him a fortune. While he was tracking and scouring the galaxy on multiple temporal branches, Hhhi was isolated as one of the prime sources of the crystal.

Following a week of collecting erosilite, Ba Ba Banaki and his crew (and four fuzzy epaulets) headed back to the time and space where Yin had began his adventure. Ba Ba didn't want to be late for his meeting with the rest of the heads of the five galactic sectors and Spydersloth Blaust aboard the *Crystal Guise*.

⇒

"That's ridiculous," scoffed Caffrey, still trying to imagine Yin in some exotic yoga pose.

"Perhaps," Yin agreed. "But completely true. I shall miss Hhhi and will treasure my many memories until the second end of my days. And I am so happy to see you again, Caffrey. You haven't changed a bit."

"Neither have you," observed Violet, studying his face.

"The beauty of temporal travel," Yin winked.

Violet's eyes caught a movement across the field. "I think we have a brave Termite Walrus Person. Two o'clock."

Sure enough, the globular form of a Termite Walrus Person emerged from a hole. It moved along the ground on hundreds of tiny feet, each protected from the elements by white but muddy booties. It raised its front like a hound dog catching a sniff of bacon then stopped suddenly ten meters from the trio. The being's entire body rippled from the inertial effects of halting.

"Hello!" Caffrey called out with a friendly nod and wave.

"Are you here to mock our work?" the Termite Walrus Person asked in a tediously slow, moist drawl.

"Mock? No, no, of course not."

"Face after face we build with the sweat of our limbs and the saliva of our mouths, and face after face our work is mocked—deemed sacrilegious to the form He was after."

"Who?" asked Violet.

"The Voice from Beyond the Box."

Many more of the Termite Walrus People began emerging from their holes, and the trio found themselves surrounded by the slow-moving folk.

Yin stepped forward. "May I ask why these faces are built?"

"We are Blodians. We are builders in mud. In soil. In rock and stone. Our works adorn the homes, palaces and gardens and shopping centers of some of the greatest civilizations our galaxy has ever known. Reasonable rates. Quality and timely work. Are you here to place an order?"

"No, thanks." Yin didn't see the sculptures as aligning well with Boplican concepts.

"We would be happy to give you a tour. Show you some of the fine samples."

"That won't be necessary. We saw your work from above when we came in. Lovely. Amazing."

"Thank you. We have not been complimented since we were brought to this starless void."

"Brought? From where?" Violet asked.

"From the Bakrik System. In the Soronian Sector. Our leader, whilst bathing in the beautiful freezing waters off the coast of Iinsenia, heard a Voice—a strange Voice, falling from the heavens—requesting a face be built. Carved onto the surface of a giant asteroid. A face of honor. A face in tribute. It would be the largest work ever attempted by a Blodian artisan.

"Upon his spoken agreement, the world around him swirled and came apart at its essence. We were all taken through the Grand Intestines of the Galaxy and into this current state. Ever since, we have built model after model. But, alas, none have pleased the Voice."

Caffrey and Violet shared a knowing glance, and he stepped forward. "At the risk of sounding trite and rather clichéd, can you take us to your leader?"

"We aim to please our guests, no matter how few visit. Follow me. He is just over the hill and not too far away."

The Blodian took off like a tank down the stone path, at a surprisingly fast speed. The trio followed. They were taken across barren fields littered with rocks, ancient bones and an occasional candy wrapper (Blodians are known to have insatiable sweet teeth). As they walked under the blue-green sky, Caffrey tried to focus his thoughts towards the elusive L'Orange.

He tried using the mental scent of key rings. The feel of burnt orange and the sound of the essence of cow dung. There was no reply. He kicked a large stone in frustration, and it bounced off the Blodian's cushy and trampoline-like posterior to impact against Caffrey's forehead with a painful thud. An orange haze of stars swirled around his head, and he fought the quite tempting desire to pass out.

— *You are disappointing me, Caffrey.*

He looked around. Neither Yin nor Violet had spoken. It was a voice. Clear as a bell. No accompanying scents or sounds. No odd colors or sensations. The voice itself was familiar.

— *Yes, Caffrey Quark, it's me. Just speak with your thoughts. Don't bother getting fancy. It's just impossible for you to think out of the box, isn't it?* The L'Orange seemed testy.

— *What do you mean? I've tried for days! Sending out peculiar smells. Odd feelings. Weird Sounds. No response.*

— *I say use sounds, you use sounds. I suggest colors, you use colors. I use smells, you use smells.*

— *So, what am I supposed to do?*

— *You are supposed to step outside the sphere of your own reality. Try the feel of a carpenter's speech. Or the taste of a Dedado dancer's dance.*

— *I didn't realize I could use verbs! You never mentioned verbs!*

— *You still don't get it? The All in the One and the One in the All. That is what you must use.*

Caffrey pondered that a moment.

L'Orange thought at him again.

— *Imagine a microphone in a concert hall. Madison Square Garden. Re-*

cording Led Zeppelin's famed The Song Remains the Same concert.

— I was there. Kicked the shit out every blessed ass in the seats!

— Charming. Anyway—were you to play a portion of that recording, it would contain the instruments of Bonham, Plant, Jones and that mystical Crowley wannabe chap with the double-necked string instrument. I forget his name… the L'Orange *toyed.*

— How would you like to be spread on toast and eaten by a Crebbledog? Caffrey replied, not caring a damn that he was threatening the wisest substance in the universe.

— Just checking that you're paying attention. Now, magnify the power of the microphone until you can also record the heartbeats of each musician. Magnify it further so you can also record the heartbeats of all the fans—of the engines of the cars passing outside the hall. Even further to include the heartbeats of the passengers in those cars. Go further and record the sound of the blood rushing through the veins of the people in the neighboring town. The next country. The next planet. On and on, until Eternity is recorded in a single, elegant song. A single waveform that contains it all. Add to that not only sound, but every sensory representation of the Cosmos. In every dimension. That is what I am. That is the source you can tap into.

— Why are you telling me this?

— The universe speaks to all at once. Don't question the fact that your ears happen to be open.

Caffrey tried a different tack.

— Shouldn't you be in communication with Poe 33? He's depressed. He feels he failed.

— He is too busy listening to the sad beat of his own existence. When he cleans out his ears, he will reconnect.

— You mean when he stops feeling sorry for himself.

— The universe, despite its religious history, despises a martyr who martyrs for the sake of martyrdom.

— Are we anywhere near you?

— You have been close from the start.

Caffrey was getting exasperated again.

— You and your damned enigmatic answers. What is it with you secretive, powerful types and your bloody beat-around-the-bush communication methods?

— The day when you see the bush for the hedgerow is the day you will see the light, my friend. There is nothing enigmatic whatsoever. It is the fuzzy nature of your eyeballs, ears, nose and skin that fails you. Ask Jimmy Page, he can tell you.

— Does Nefarious have my friends?

— It's possible.

Caffrey exhaled hard.

— *If he does, will I have to kill the creep to free them?*

The L'Orange exploded into laughter. The chuckles continued, fading, and eventually drained down a pinhole of reality.

Caffrey felt his legs stop. He looked around and found himself standing before a gigantic series of domes.

Their Blodian guide spoke. "This is the home of our leader, whose name is Khorus. I will take you in to him now. You will find he is a kind and friendly Blode. But he is depressed and frustrated of late. He wants desperately to see the sun again. One doesn't realize how one's cosmic address is vital to making a planet feel like a home."

The Blodian pushed open a door with his front foot and entered the dome. The trio followed.

A walk through broad, winding tunnels led them to a chamber. It was simple but roomy. Large oval windows let the day-glow in to light the powdery floor. The Blodian guide let them in then went on his way, leaving the trio feeling a bit awkward before the leader.

Khorus was seated on a long plush sofa, working with a small-scale model of a face poised on a low wooden table. He was an impressive Blodian, large and solid, his two large, curved tusks capped with ornate silver frill.

"Welcome, strangers," Khorus said, looking up briefly over the rims of his spectacles. "Please, have a seat."

Appreciation was expressed by each as they sat.

"Nice of you to see us without so much as a 'we're in the neighborhood,'" apologized Caffrey.

"No need. Blodians are, by nature, overly trusting and friendly. To a fault. We have had very few visitors since we were abducted. What can I do for you?"

"We're on a sort of quest, I suppose you can call it."

"Quest! How exciting!" Khorus was sincerely enthused, and ripples of excitement rode along his form.

"This world of yours intrigues us. Its cosmic location is a bit odd." Violet was trying hard to not seem discourteous.

"Odd, indeed. As is your presence," Khorus retorted with a gentle smile.

"And the faces," interjected Caffrey. "May we ask what purpose they serve?"

Khorus took his glasses off and sat back on the sofa. He stared Caffrey hard in the eyes then looked upon Yin and Violet with equal curiosity.

"Are you three alone?"

"No," Violet spoke up. "There are two others."

"Three, actually," Caffrey corrected.

"If you count Angie as an other," snipped Violet, adjusting her blouse again.

"Angie?" Khorus asked.

"She's the onboard computer assistant of my spacecraft. She's recently been given Revenant abilities. Charming. The other two are a humanoid android and my long-dead uncle back from the hereafter. Oh, and there's Peebo, a very small, late-model android."

"You do live interesting lives, don't you?" Khorus observed with honest envy. He smiled briefly then stood up, "I think, as with any stirring tale of questing adventurers, we should pause for a good, hearty meal. How does that sound?"

Caffrey smiled in appreciation.

※

The Blodian's Hall of Nourishment and Candy Tureens was under the largest of the domes dotting the habitation sector of the planet. Decorated in the simple Blodian line drawings that adorned the walls of most Blodian homes, the stadium-sized hall flickered with hundreds of flaming torches while rosette skylights softly blushed with the mysterious sunless glow. Every Blodian artisan from the day shift was there, feasting from tables groaning under the weight of simple but digestive-tract-cleaning foods and drinks necessary to flush the day's mud, dirt and small stones from their innards.

Khorus had the *Moby Dick*'s entire crew seated around the table as his guests, except for Peebo, who's interminable curiosity lured him to explore the unique world.

"It has been a sad existence," Khorus began in the typical languorous Blodian dialect. "It feels as though I have not seen the beautiful sun Bakrik for seven stages. I miss her warmth on my body. This light that now bathes our world is cold. Without spirit. Like..."

"Like fluorescent lights from my home world," Caffrey suggested. "You're right. Cold and lifeless."

"It drains the will. Carving faces has become a chore rather than the spiritual outlet that it was for Blodians since the Maiden Spewing. But we have no choice. We have no way out until we please the Voice. He desires work of a scale we have never before undertaken."

"The Voice you're talking about goes by another name. He is called Nefarious Wretch," Yin explained. "He's been systematically devolving the galaxy. One world at a time. Targeting those to whom music is a value. He despises music. He wants to recreate the galaxy in his strange, dark and cold image."

"What an unkind project to undertake," the Blodian opined as he savored the subtle flavor of the pudge.

"And I suppose this giant-sized tribute to his narcissism will be the new galaxy's hallmark," Violet added.

"I suppose so," agreed Khorus, wiping a smear of food from the tip of his tusk.

"What are you basing the designs on?" Caffrey queried. "Did he describe what he looked like?"

"His only order to me was it should reflect a face that can change life itself. A face that would adorn coins. Bows of ships. Paintings lining cathedrals and museums."

Caffrey exchanged a smirk with Violet.

"With all due respect, Khorus..." Caffrey smiled. "...as humanoids go, the faces you have built, at least the ones I have seen are rather—how can I put this diplomatically..."

"Grotesque bastards," offered Violet without apology.

"No offense," Khorus began with a certain embarrassment, "but as a species, humanoids, at least to the humble senses of us Blodians, are...well..."

Poe recited from memory. "A revolting assembly of narrow torsos accented by twin and rather humorous fatty posterior bulges, bandy legs, arms like old tree limbs, tiny heads marked with appetite-disrupting patterns of exterior sensory appendages, topped with hair of disturbing lengths, designs and colors."

"Poe Thirty-three! You're basically humanoid yourself. I think humans are lovely!" Angie defended then qualified, "At least, some are."

Poe explained. "Those are not my chosen words. The description comes from Zebrik Zendwig's book, *Aesthetic Theory of Cosmic Intelligent Life*. Zendwig rates Umlimpins as the most handsome lifeforms in the galaxy."

"Zendwig can kiss my humorous twin fatty posterior bulges," Caffrey said, filling his mouth with a spoonful of pudge at the same time.

"No offense intended," Khorus insisted. "However, we are at a loss as to what this Nefarious Wretch, as you call him, wants."

"How does he communicate with you?" Yin asked.

"His voice simply sounds within my head."

"As a vision?" Yin proposed with a certain awe.

"Or second sight?" suggested Violet.

"Or extrasensory perception?" tried Caffrey.

"Perchance this fine Blodian is gifted with the abilities of my Master?" Poe added.

Khorus smiled and gave each of his guests a smile in appreciation of their delusions of his grandeur.

"Actually, I tend to pick up signals off the metal work on my tusks. I even, on occasion, pick up the Android Games of Desmitten."

Caffrey sat forward, his interest quickening. "Radio signals?"

"That's correct."

"Well, wouldn't that mean there's a proverbial hole in the dike?"

"Yes," Yin agreed. "There'd be no way radio signals could enter unless this hermetically sealed cosmic box isn't actually so."

Caffrey gestured with his hands to emphasize his point. "So, there may be a way for you and your people to escape. Slip out by prying this hole open."

Khorus shook his large head, took a deep breath that rippled up and down his globular body and looked each of his dinner mates in the eye one at a time as he spoke. "I am the leader of this world. I have the responsibility not only to the living but to the dead, to the yet to be born and to the tradition of Blodian society and building. I cannot simply leave this world behind to be forgotten like Finabulist Jermist[17]. It may, I am happy to agree, provide a way out for you fine folk. You can make it to Desmitten to refuel or gather your thoughts."

"Of all the planets in all the sectors of all the galaxies it had to be Desmitten," said Violet, shaking her head in disbelief.

"What's wrong with Desmitten? One of my favorite restaurants is on Desmitten. Geldersnaps and Hoo's," Caffrey said with a faraway gaze that spoke of fond memories.

---

[17] An ancient tale of an adventurer who went on a great quest for something no one can remember, to a place everyone has forgotten and whose fate no one can recall.

"It's a testosterone-drenched dive," Violet spat.

"It's a lovely place."

"I recall you getting blitzed and beaten in that lovely place," Angie reminded him, disapproval blended in with her remark.

"Aah, but they have the best alamastre sandwich anywhere," Caffrey drooled, then struck a devil in his eye like a match. "Burned a few wicks on Desmitten..."

"You pig!" Violet hissed, then: "It's where my mother was born."

"I apologize. Didn't get along with Mum?"

"None of your business," she huffed.

Yin brought the discussion to order. "Well, I don't see any choice, Commander Leer. The cause of OTHER must come before your personal problems. It's in the rules."

Violet nodded, resigned. "You're right, Yin."

"Synchronicity," Caffrey asserted, with a solid tap of his hand on the table.

There was a collective "Huh?"

"Synchronicity. A lovely thing. I thought it was all a roll of the dice but maybe it's more? The L'Orange is right."

"I don't understand," Yin admitted.

"'The finger of fate is fickle, nay! It picks the nose of those who know their way!'"

"Who wrote that?" asked Poe 33.

"I did," answered Caffrey, suddenly all business, "We're going to Desmitten. Angie, I need you to search this cosmic eggshell we're in. Find the crack."

"Yes, my strategic starfish."

"Sounds like yet another detour from our mission," Violet commented, folding her arms tightly around herself in an agitated and somewhat defensive manner.

Caffrey tried convincing the purple-eyed stud magnet.

"Detour? Didn't you understand, my little poem? Fate has picked our nose. We have to follow its lead."

"There is something else," Khorus said, pensively trying to gather the words to tell his story. Caffrey and the gang waited patiently as the Blodian readied his exposition with careful deliberation.

"Often, while I am listening to the games on Desmitten, the signal seems to drift and merge with another. I hear sobs. Odd sobs. Then the signal is lost as quickly as it was found."

"Sobbing?" Violet was confused.

"What do you mean by 'odd?'" Caffrey asked.

"It is as if many are sobbing. But not all at once. One at a time. Many souls each contribute a single sob to produce a litany of misery."

"That's Nefarious." Caffrey was certain. "His voice is strange—it changes constantly. Every word, every syllable different. Not just in tone or inflection, but an entirely different voice."

"But would he sob?" Yin pondered.

A debate erupted. Each tossed theories and ideas. They disagreed, agreed, mocked and contemplated the various thoughts. Khorus sat back amused, enjoying the speed at which his guests spoke.

"It has lost a love," said Angie, finally.

The group ignored her, and the debate continued. Angie repeated her last words with increased volume. "It has lost a love."

All mouths went mute.

"What?" someone asked.

"Nefarious has lost a love. That is why he sobs."

Violet laughed shortly at the suggestion. "Nefarious has lost a love?"

Angie would not be stopped by a mere belly-button flaunter. She spoke again, her voice melodic, ringing.

"What kind of face adorns bows of ships? Paintings? What kind of face would change the world?"

No one replied.

"A beautiful woman! I believe Nefarious Wretch has lost the love of a beautiful woman and is trying to get her back by presenting her with a gift. A huge carving of her face."

Violet asserted herself again. "And the destruction of music and countless worlds? Very romantic," she smirked.

Angie wasn't to be outdone. "I am not attempting to justify his disgusting behavior. I am only suggesting that if the Blodians were to carve a face of a beautiful woman, they may meet with success."

"Who could possibly love him in the first place for that love to be lost in the second place?" Yin wanted to know.

"You and Violet are too submerged in the philosophy of OTHER to allow yourselves the possibility to see Nefarious as anything but evil. But what, after all, is evil but the absence of love?"

"You are naïve, my sweet girl," Violet said with cold sincerity.

"I would have to agree," said the Bopple with a touch more

warmth.

"I think she may be on to something," mumbled Greppledick through a mouthful of pudge.

"Then again," Caffrey chimed in, "'Layla.' 'Rita.' 'Susie Q.' 'Prudence.' 'Michelle.' And, of course, 'Angie.' Song after song has pined over love. Since none of the faces has pleased Nefarious, maybe a change in sex would work?"

The Blodian was doubtful. "We have never carved the face of a beautiful female humanoid. What does one look like?" he asked with sincere innocence.

Angie chuckled at Violet's expense.

"Actually, Khorus," Caffrey said, staring at Violet, "if I had to give an example of one face to represent human female beauty, Violet's wouldn't be a bad choice."

Violet, instantly mollified, responded with a coy smile of appreciation—and Angie sensed it.

"I hope you choke on your pudge, Caffrey Quark!" she cried as she raced off.

"I think your hurt her feelings," tittered Violet smugly.

Caffrey stared down at his pudge bowl. "I really need to have her sensitivity programming adjusted."

"Violet?" the Blodian asked. "May we use your face as a model?"

"I refuse to have my face offered up to Nefarius Wretch."

"Please. We are running out of options," pleaded Khorus.

"I really think you should," Yin coaxed. "To repay the Blodians for their hospitality. After all, you once passed yourself off as a Spydersloth Blaust fan for the cause."

Violet sat for a moment or two then sighed, pushed the remains of her meal away and shrugged in surrender to the idea.

She was taken to the facial pre-model design studios while Caffrey searched high and low for Angie to begin the process of locating the crack in the cosmic box. Poe 33, Yin and Greppledick joined the search.

Little Peebo had soon discovered the large Blodians and their massive undertakings. Quickly becoming fascinated by the sculptures, the clever little android carefully studied the process then formed a bulbous mouth on his surface and joined the construction project.

Like a gnat, the floating robot zipped around the mound, carving the facial structures with blinding speed. He worked so fast the stunned Blodian workers could only clear the hill and stare with gaping mouths as thousands of years of Blodian evolution and culture was rendered obsolete and inept. Peebo completed the ugly male humanoid face to perfection. As the typically slow emotional responses of the Blodians surfaced—they are by nature rarely bitter or jealous—a combination of cheers and groans erupted. Peebo, rather embarrassed at his impulsive and rather rude behavior, attempted a shy bow of gratitude for the adulation.

"Angie?" Yin called out, sniffing the air aboard the *Moby Dick* for any signs of the ozone often accompanying her presence. There was no reply.

Yin jumped up on the communications counter and stroked a few keys with his paws. Poe 33 entered, followed by Greppledick.

"Poe, do you sense Angie on board?" Yin asked, without taking his eyes from the screen.

"I do not. I hope she is not gone forever—but if she is, I pray it is a lesson for all the non-artificial forms aboard this craft, who would do well to memorize the adage 'Hard of parts does not mean hard of heart.'"

Yin was reading the text on one of the monitors.

"This is interesting. She sent a message to Lindboola an hour and a half ago. Then logged in a systems check ten minutes later."

"Lindboola?" asked the old man.

"Only the best effects makeup artist ever. We met her on a Dante Squidreaper film shoot. She helped us become Serpentine for our little adventure on Regal Nine."

"Squidreaper." Greppledick gagged on his own disgust. "Had him in my home for a New Year's party. He drank all the cheenago, urinated on my hirojenia bush and got footprints all over my ten-thousand-year-old Vixenese billiard table."

"Without Angie, how are we going to find the crack in the box?"

"Where is our fearless leader?" asked Yin, peering around the deck.

"He's with Violet and the Blodian artisan."

There was a tap at the portal and Yin pushed the "Open" button. Peebo floated outside. A dozen or so Blodians surrounded the craft. Some were laughing. Others weren't. Greppledick stepped to the entryway and gazed out at the herd. He noticed some were carrying sticks, pipes and heavy tools.

"What sort of trouble did you get into, my little puppy?" He asked, with some concern.

Peebo dipped and dived, bounced and shimmied with the nervousness of a child caught picking golden apples from a neighboring dragon's orchard. A babble of groans and protests erupted from the insulted Blodians, followed by a chorus of laughter and complaints aimed at the angered workers by the smaller group, who thought the entire event rather funny.

Greppledick stepped out and peered across the field.

"Peebo! What have you done?" His eyes widened. "I'll be a monkey's dead uncle..."

Yin took a look, his head swiveling slowly as he took in the vista. "Incredible," he murmured, breathlessly.

The whining of servos announced the Portsmith's turn to be impressed.

"He'll probably get away with it. Brat," mumbled Poe 33 as he turned and retreated back into the ship.

⇒

Violet sat on a stone pedestal as a Blodian artisan worked the dirt in its large mouth. Using its lips in the same way a dessert chef uses a pastry bag, the Blodian crafted a small, life-size model of Violet's face atop a flat stone surface. Caffrey sat beside her, studying her real face with great interest.

"Stop staring at me," muttered Violet, trying not to move her mouth.

"That's easier said than done. I'm enjoying the view. We've been so busy I've had little time to devote to my unabashed attraction to you."

"You once despised me," reminded Violet.

"Only because you were such a good actor and I believed your soul was ordered on the rocks. And I will never, with a capital N, forgive you for misplacing my friends. But those purple eyes and your perfectly formed..."

"Caffrey..."

"...cheekbones have rendered me a drooling idiot."

Violet's face flushed slightly. She simpered and looked at the Blodian. "Amazing what he can do with his mouth," she commented, ignoring the obviously suggestive way Caffrey cleared his

204

throat.

It was impressive. The Blodian's ability to control not only the amount of material ejected from its mouth but the shape, texture, color and surface design, was a tribute to the wonders of diversity. The model was close to completion, and the rather slender—at least compared to most of the fellow members of his species—artist was studying the final details of Violet's face.

"I find your eyes quite interesting. I have never seen any, on any creature or being, of such purpleness," the Blodian confessed with a soft smile.

"Thank you. My mother's eyes were just as purple. You do wonderful work. I admire your ability. My mom used to dabble in pottery making."

"This is the mum of the piss-off-and-buy-your-own-card-on-Mothers-Day variety?" teased Caffrey, not realizing the minefield he was negotiating.

Dual purple beacons flared. "How many mothers do you suppose I have?" snapped Violet.

Caffrey could feel a deadly heat threatening to scorch his scalp. His dark locks were saved by the sudden entrance of Peebo.

If it was possible for a small, spherical robot to be out of breath, Peebo certainly displayed all the signs of being so. He vibrated up and down like a panting dog and beads of moisture shimmered on his flushed surface.

"Peebo?" Violet queried the android.

"What's the matter, boy?" asked Caffrey.

Peebo continued his spastic movements, and Caffrey shrugged. "I can never figure out what the thing's trying to say."

A rumbling sound grew, like a passing marathon. Peebo jumped and exited as quickly as he'd entered. Caffrey's curiosity led him to the front door, and guffaws spewed from his lungs.

Outside, Peebo, Yin, Poe 33 and Greppledick were being pursued across the wide landscape by a dozen very annoyed Blodians. A group of non-perturbed Builders, who had found Peebo's antics quite funny, followed behind, catcalling and laughing.

"Maybe we should get Khorus," suggested Caffrey.

The Great Chamber of Peace and Pudge Production also served as the Chamber Hall of Justice for the Blodians. It was buzzing with annoyance and excitement. Blodians had a proud history of fairly administered justice and a tolerance for allowing all sides equal voice and representation. They had no written laws, as their philosophy was one of judging the moment. They placed great importance on the influence of "the season of the inquiry," as they referred to the mitigating circumstances and spirit of the accused's offense.

Since the honor and integrity of all involved was never in doubt, this method of justice proved extremely effective for the Blodians. They were, however, a raucous species when riled; and the courtroom, despite its intrinsic honor, was anything but subdued.

Khorus stood upon his podium and scanned the faces of the gathered. He was donning his red-and-yellow-striped Tusk Covers of Fair Dispensement and the blue-powdered Mane of the Magistrate. It was traditional in the ways of Blodian judicial practice to allow an Official Moment of Mayhem, wherein everyone present was allowed to vent and verbally rage until they were too exhausted to interrupt the legal process once it began. Yin, Caffrey, Violet and Greppledick watched in awe as the group of angered Blodians shouted across the room at the laughing, less-offended folk.

Poor little Peebo floated inside the confines of the open-air Station of the Accused, like a hockey player sent to the penalty box.

"We are in deep doo-doo," Caffrey announced, folding his arms in disgust. "Couldn't you keep a leash on that beach ball?"

Greppledick glared at him. "Are you forgetting he saved your life?"

"And now we may be sentenced to build mud piles or whatever it is the Blodians sentence their criminals to."

Violet leaned across Greppledick and shook her head at Caffrey. "We aren't on trial. Peebo is."

"Relax," advised Yin, with calm assurance. "The Blodians are a fair folk."

The Horn of Silence sounded. Its deep wave of sound drifted like fog across the room, and a reverent silence was left in its wake.

Khorus opened the proceedings. "I announce, with great embarrassment, the trial of the android Peebo, brought to this assembly on the charge of Rude Artistic Interjection." The words oozed from his mouth like semi-melted toffee. "Is there anything you can offer, Master Peebo, that might change the minds of those in the Seats of Accusation?"

"Interesting approach," Caffrey whispered.

Peebo jiggled and wiggled.

"Is there someone present who can act as interpreter to the accused?"

Greppledick clambered stiffly to his feet. "I can, your Honorableness."

"Then proceed."

"He says he meant no harm. He was simply excited by his newfound ability. But, if I may suggest, please feel free to sentence me to death in his place. I will protest not." Greppledick bowed melodramatically, ignoring the dirty looks thrown his way by his friends.

"Impossible!" declared Khorus, turning back to Peebo in disbelief. "The Blodian's craft is a sacred art! It is not something that can be rushed or automated!"

Peebo wiggled and jiggled some more. Khorus looked to Greppledick.

"He says it was fun."

"Fun?" spouted Khorus indignantly. "Fun to mock the ancient ways of his hosts?"

Greppledick attempted to elaborate on Peebo's sensibilities. "You must understand, Your Honor, Peebo is a mere child. It was all a game to him."

"If I may, sir?" Caffrey stood up. Greppledick resumed his seat.

"Will you be speaking for the accused?" asked Khorus.

"I'm speaking for the situation at hand. Nefarious's grip on your world will inexorably grow tighter. Your only hope for freedom is to quickly construct the face that pleases him. Your freedom can be expedited if you will allow, in this extreme case, little Peebo to knock out a few dozen samples."

The chamber erupted into howls of indignation, and the horn was sounded again, returning the silence to the room.

Khorus threw a stern glare at Caffrey. "We have never, ever knocked out a work before. Nor will we, sir!"

"And I am not asking that you do. I am suggesting that Peebo does it. Nefarious is not worthy of your hallowed work. Toss him a contentious bone disguised as deep respect, and you can all have the last laugh at his expense."

Khorus smiled nervously, unsure of how to proceed.

"...And as a gesture of our thanks for your hospitality, we will give you Peebo as our gift," Caffrey bowed.

Greppledick jumped to his feet again, eyeing Caffrey viciously. "Are you mad? I will not allow this!"

"Uncle..." Caffrey tried to hush the old man. "...we have no choice. We either give them Peebo or risk him being found guilty.

He will then suffer whatever consequences they hand out."

Greppledick turned to Khorus. "What, may I ask, is the punishment for being found guilty of Rude Artistic Interjection?"

Khorus sat back in his chair. "Quite often," he described, "we will send the convicted on a tour, all expenses paid, naturally, of the Avenue of the Ancients, where the great works of the Very Old and Often Forgotten Elders are studied and brought to the forefront of the accused's memory. There are, of course, sweetie breaks and rather nice and comfortable toilet facilities."

"That doesn't sound so bad," mused Greppledick.

A sudden distant buzzing followed by hurried footsteps disrupted the proceedings. A voice screeched out into the hall, "The Flies are here! The Flies are here!"

A series of explosions rattled and rocked the world around them.

"Flies?" Greppledick was confused.

"It's ODOR!" yelled Caffrey as chaos swept across the room.

"Take to the Holes!" bawled Khorus. "To the Holes!"

The rumbling of hundreds of Blodian boots backgrounded the energy blasts, explosions and the whining buzz of the ODOR craft. Stark shadows of the invader ships crossed the hall, casting gloom down through the skylight.

"They've tracked down Poe! We have to get out of here!" cried Yin.

"Once again, I have failed my friends," moaned Poe 33.

"Never mind that!" yelled Violet, drawing her weapon from. Caffrey, trying to ignore the dominatrix undertones of the holster's straps, secured provocatively from her waist and down around her uppermost thigh, took out his Willy and surveyed the situation.

"To the *Moby Dick*!"

Khorus, about to exit through a rear doorway, turned to the group and called out, "We will commence with the trial tomorrow. Unless your offer to leave the robot with us is still on the table?"

"We'll leave Peebo!" Caffrey agreed, fumbling at the settings on his weapon.

"I will not abandon him!" Greppledick shouted.

Poe shot Peebo a glare that reeked of sibling rivalry. "Dad always loved you best."

Peebo shimmied innocently. Caffrey grabbed his uncle by the loose folds of his robe and took him aside. "You built an emotional midget. If you stay here with Peebo, Poe won't be able to piss in a pot, never mind escort and protect the wisest crap in the universe."

"What are you saying? I have to remain alive until we find the L'Orange?"

"Poe needs his daddy. You two have to work through this angst that's emerged in his programming."

Greppledick took a deep breath and exhaled hard. "One day, when you croak, you'll realize how mean you were to me."

A crash of glass and metal exploded overhead and the deadly shards rained down. Three of the Fly Craft rode in on ear-piercing buzzing.

"Then again, we may all be minutes away from your wondrous afterlife!" Caffrey noted.

"To the *Moby Dick*!" Yin yipped, taking off.

Caffrey pushed Poe 33 along; Greppledick turned quickly to Peebo. "Peebo, my pup, Daddy is leaving you here with the Blodians. Your older brother needs me. You behave and help the nice folk build their little faces."

Peebo nuzzled up to Greppledick's shoulder and took off, following Khorus out the back door.

"Oh, the pangs of parenthood," the old man moaned.

Violet fired a volley of red lightning at the ODOR drones, momentarily stopping them in their tracks. Caffrey followed with a half-dozen electric-yellow strings that slammed across the targets, leaving scorch marks and a little black smoke.

Violet frowned as she watched the attacking Fly ships. "You're only muffing up the paint job! Quark, turn your weapon off pansy-mode!"

He switched the setting to Bon Voyage mode and fired a purple string, striking the leading craft and sending it off to some roll-of-the-dice location in a swirl of energy.

Yin had already led Poe 33 out the front door. Violet covered Greppledick's exit with another blast from her pistol as Caffrey ducked a beam of purple energy that nearly parted his hair. Yin and Poe were running at top speed, weaving through and around the legs of the panic-stricken Blodians, who were racing for their underground bunkers. Poe 33 was pushing Yin's little cardiovascular system to numbers off the dial.

In the sky, a large ODOR craft hung as if on a hook, swaying silently as the little Bopple and the android passed below. A pair of large bomb-bay doors opened and dozens of small, pilotless Gnat

Craft were released like fry from a live-bearing sasukki fish.

A few meters back, Caffrey and Violet were frustrated by Greppledick's pace, which at times smelled of a conspiracy to get himself killed beneath the stampede of Blodian feet. They crossed the main road and joined Yin and Poe on the main drag leading to the landing space of the *Moby Dick*. Violet fired into the swarm of the smaller Gnats, scattering them in every direction. A trio rejoined from the broken swarm and shot back like darts, coming to a dead halt inches from the faces of Caffrey, Violet and Greppledick. Small, bright-yellow dish antennas scanned them head to foot. Obviously disinterested in the three humans, they took off back to rejoin the swarm.

"They want Poe and Poe alone," said Caffrey, firing a series of shots into the throng and lessening their numbers by three.

Poe and Yin managed to make it to the landing ramp. The Gnats moved in, forming a ring around the craft. Yin jumped up and, using his front paws, pressed the button, releasing the lock and opening the portal. The pooch entered, and the android followed. Before the door could be closed, two of the buzzing mechanical Gnats flew in and quickly reemerged, carrying Poe by the shoulders.

"They've got my Poe!" shouted Greppledick.

Caffrey aimed his weapon at the robot-nappers, but Violet pushed aside his barrel, dropped to one knee and squinted a marksman's eye as Poe was lifted towards the mother ship. She seemed to be carefully calculating when to fire. Her brain went about its scheme; and finally, with a confidence that irked but impressed Caffrey, she pulled the trigger twice. Two shots. Two kills. Poe 33 dropped from the sky. There was a splash, and the vaguely disgusting sound of the surface skin of a mud pond breaking.

The *Moby Dick*'s guns began firing wildly at the Gnats. Violet and Greppledick rushed to the fallen android; and if not for the need for expediency, they would have rolled around the ground in hysterics for a week or so.

Poor Poe was encased in mud. He'd been transformed into a five-foot-nine brown turd with glowing eyes. They lifted him from the mire, serenaded by a chorus of slurps, pops and lip-smacking noises.

"Thank you, Violet, for your assistance. I was close to becoming ODOR's bitch."

They rushed back to the *Moby Dick*, leaving a little trail of mud behind them. In the cabin, Yin was busy hanging onto the large anti-craft guns, firing wildly. Caffrey jumped into the chair at the G.S.

station.

"Dammit, Angie, where are you?" he complained as he scanned the screens. His eyes lit up. "A message—she left me a message!"

"I'd hurry, Quarky!" Yin cried out.

"What's going on out there?"

"Oh, just a few dozen more Fly Craft approaching at frightening speeds."

Caffrey played the audio note. Angie's recorded voice filled the ship's interior.

"Dear comrade Yin, my favorite studly android, Poe, Sir Greppledick and Captain and Mrs. Scum. I have done my duty by programming the ship's navigation systems with the location of the hole in the dike. You should emerge in the system of Ms. Thing's favorite planet, Desmitten. I hope she burns her cute ass on the simmering wicks she's left behind there. I may or may not meet you there. Adios."

"I knew she wouldn't let me down!" Caffrey smiled.

"Studly? Am I really studly?" Poe wondered of his reflection.

The *Moby Dick* lifted off the world of the Blodians as Yin helped to clear the way with a continuous barrage of fire. An alarm sounded.

"Now what?" asked Violet.

Caffrey read the warning display. "Beautiful—our hole seems to have shrunk to microscopic size."

"You mean to tell me we're stuck in this box?" Greppledick said, irritably.

"No. We'll be blown to smithereens shortly," explained Yin.

"Violet, man the aft guns. I need to call for help." Caffrey dove into his sleeping compartment and shut himself in the dark interior. A barrage of strange looks followed him in.

CHAPTER 16
With a Little Help from My Friends

(The Beatles)

Voices faded. Lights dimmed. The curtain was drawn. Slowly an image began to form on the darkened stage of Caffrey's mind. It was a cylindrical item, purplish-red, and it appeared to have the texture of meat.

The projection took on more and more realism until Caffrey felt an odd desire. It was a desire that had become foreign to him. Taboo. Nonetheless, Caffrey desperately wanted to touch the fleshy tube. He felt drool forming on his lips. A twang in his stomach. He wanted to put his mouth on it.

A brilliant white beam, some powerful off-stage spotlight, made its way toward the object. The light beam was moving in slow motion, its end creeping closer like frozen toothpaste from a tube, until it struck the object and illuminated it in all its glory.

Caffrey smiled at the alamastre sausage—a beautiful specimen of the heart-clogging, mouth-burning, stomach-filling, tastebud-pleasing foodstuff that had filled many a sandwich in his days as a carnivore. Shredded and spread with hirooshi radish on a slab of teeth-yanking guba bread and accented to perfection with a pint of dark and potent Ainsberry stout, it was the specialty that had made Geldersnaps & Hoo's famous galaxy-wide.

The sausage spun around like a cheesy Vegas act, and a little face formed upon it.

— Very good, Caffrey! You are learning! Take a ride!

— Are you taking us to Desmitten?

— In time. Nefarious is watching. He must be distracted.

— Distracted? Can't you shut this guy up once and for all! I'm tired of this. I want Ancient Earth. I want my bed. I want to step in Yin's shit on the sidewalk outside the Crimson Court Pub!

— Wonderful ambitions. And it is you who must stop Nefarious. I have no such powers.

— How the heck can I destroy somebody who can devolve entire planets?

The sausage laughed, did a little dance then turned to solid gold.

— Transmute is what you must do. Not destroy! The friendly little sausage launched into the air and instantly morphed into a bright yellow star with an eyeball at its center. The eye winked, then spoke. *Look for me. And when you see. One step closer will you be!*

— What about the hole in the cosmic box? Desmitten?

The yellow, one-eyed star exploded in pitch-black light, and all went dark.

⟐

"No way," said Violet, dazed as she stared out the portal to the green world spinning outside. "No hairy way."

"Caffrey's mind is impressing me more every day," commented Yin. He trotted over to the sleeping compartment, released the hatch and discovered his master still sitting cross-legged, eyes closed.

"He is mastering my Master," whispered Poe 33 with restrained awe.

Violet nudged Caffrey gently. "Quark, wake up. We're here."

Caffrey opened his eyes partway and immediately saw Violet, Yin and Poe staring at him through the cabin doorway. He closed his eyes.

Violet shook him again. "Take a look at your handiwork."

"I'm afraid to."

"You should be," agreed Violet with admiration. "I'm dumbfounded!"

"Where are we?"

"In orbit around Desmitten," explained Yin.

"No frigging way!" Caffrey jumped out and rushed to the window. He gasped. "Holy mother of moly!"

A smile emerged, growing wider and wider until a mere facial expression could no longer contain his emotions. He let out a fist-in-the-air-pumping, thigh-slapping, wide-eyed bellowing cry of self-impressed approbation. Caffrey felt like he could shit roses.

213

"Can you believe it?" he enthused, grabbing Violet by the shoulders. "That amazing lump of cosmic marmalade was right! I did it. I used my mind! My thoughts! To get us here!"

"Somewhat frightening," mumbled Greppledick.

"Not at all, actually," contradicted Poe 33. "Whether it was his mind, my left foot, Yin's right paw or a Blodian candy dish. Whatever. All are part of the One. The totality of the hologram that is the Cosmos. All is accessible. All is controllable. It's just that some minds are more apt than others."

Caffrey pulled Violet to him and hugged her tightly, kissing her hard on the mouth; Poe 33 stepped up to him and placed a hand on his shoulder. Caffrey released a gasping Violet and kissed Poe on the mouth. The android spoke again.

"I am humbled by your powers, Quark Caffrey. I have no alternative but to pass the torch of responsibility to you. I was once the great Poe Thirty-three. I am now nothing. Garbage. Filth. Waste. You are far worthier to take the title 'Portsmith' than I, a mere metallic buffoon not worthy of the touch of your lips. Perhaps I will check myself into a buffoonery."

Poe's backing music was especially depressing.

Greppledick had heard enough from the android. "Baloney, Poe! Stop making this about you, and make it about the All! The Cosmos despises martyrs who martyr for the sake of martyrdom."

"Oh! So now you, a human, are going to teach me about my connection with the Cosmos? I, Poe Thirty-three, who went through and completed the Rendavene?"

"Poe..."

"I once understood my connection. But when the faith from others fails..." Poe threw a stern look to Greppledick. "...one can lose focus."

"If I hear one more self-pitying opus emerge from your mouth I'll take you apart, reassemble you into an electric chair and kill myself!"

"Moldy peaches to you, Father," Poe 33 muttered as he stalked off to a quiet corner.

"Moldy peaches?" Greppledick stared after the android as he rubbed his temples.

"Caffrey," called Yin, looking up from the G.S. station, "There's a small OTHER contingent on Desmitten. Bayville. Next town over from Heddington. Nice piece of luck. They're a well-connected group."

214

"Not luck, my poochie. Synchronicity," corrected Caffrey smugly.

Violet moaned. "I despise this place."

"Serendipity personified," insisted Caffrey.

"Don't get too cocky, Quarky. I have friends all over this galaxy," Yin winked.

Caffrey asserted himself. "Strap yourselves in, everyone. First stop, Geldersnaps and Hoo's! I want to smell the dank air. See the moldy walls and taste the ale! I want to tapdance in Yin's shit!"

"The human mind is a frightening device," murmured Yin.

Caffrey jumped to the controls like a child on an amusement park ride and took the *Moby Dick* down through the thick clouds of Desmitten. Poe sat silently with his eyes closed. His father slept beside him, enjoying dreams of sudden and painless deaths. It would be a half-hour before they'd touch down into the CHEESE (County Heddington Environmental Elutriation and Spacecraft Esplanade) facility[18].

Traffic was typically light for mid-afternoon. In minutes, the *Moby Dick* was approved for a full-day stay. Caffrey parked her in a space beneath the lovely crimson leaves of a soppy liver tree, and they strolled off toward the town center.

Bacon Strip Road is the primary drag of Heddington. It runs east-west in the lap of the rolling hills that wander off in every direction. The street is lined with ornate but rusted and ill-kept lampposts and stone buildings with roofs of thick logs. It resembles a forgotten set of a sword-and-sorcery movie.

The people of Heddington, Crustosapians, are muscular folk covered in a thick bronze exoskeleton, giving them the appearance of wearing heavy plate mail. Their round heads are topped with thick black hair falling around their shoulders. They tend to stroll about with a casual, care-we-not confidence and deep sense of tradition. Their macabre sense of humor and strong love of friends and drink has elevated their spirits far above their sub-par standard of living.

---

[18] The Desmitten body metabolizes fats extremely efficiently. So efficiently, in fact, that many Desmittenites die every year of low cholesterol. Thus, the eating of large amounts of fat, meat, grease, dairy products and high-fat fruits is encouraged. So important is this that the everyday lexicon has been infused with constant reminders to "Eat fat or die!"

215

Heddington itself was once a favorite rest stop of intergalactic pirates and questing adventurers wandering off to find the enigmatic Silver Sompom[19]. It had, to Caffrey's delight, changed very little since his last visit. As the party walked past the Hash for Cash Butcher Shop, the popular Slabloafs Cakery Bakery and the Wicked Wicks Candle Shoppe, he offered up a running commentary, accented with yarns that had become tangled and knotted with exaggeration and hyperbole. Nonetheless, like a master alchemist, he transformed the base elements of his youthful encounters with first barroom brawls, first jobs and first times into golden tales of danger, adventure and memorably steamy sex.

"Here she is!" Caffrey announced as he stepped up to the knotty wooden doors of the last building on the Strip and bowed, as if about to enter a house of worship. "Geldersnaps and Hoo's!"

"We can read," Violet retorted, wiping the sign with her hand and leaving a streak in the thick dust.

Poe 33 bowed as well, although he wasn't sure why.

"You can keep the posh, transcontinental cuisine of Seryene. I'll pass on the admittedly delicious eclectic morsels from Janis Five. I'll even put off a meal from the imaginative and spice-minded kitchens of GhoboGhobo. Because a meal within these hallowed walls is more than mere nutrition, more than a chance to impress friends or that special apple of your eye. This is a trans-temporal journey for the soul. A return to simple times of warm days, cool nights and moist, lingering kisses."

"And barfing until the sun comes up," added Violet, sadistically.

"You wax any more sentimental, Caffrey, and I'm gonna slip in it and break my hip," warned Greppledick.

"Why don't we enter this little Xanadu and get something to eat?" prompted Yin, who reared up on his hind legs and entered his twenty-pound body into a losing duel with the hundred-pound door.

"Sound idea, my little best friend." Caffrey gave a push, and the ancient hinges sang their tired dirge. The group proceeded in.

Violet already had her palm over her nose. "God! The place smells worse than I remember."

Yin's face was contorted. "I would think odors like this would be unforgettable!"

Caffrey marched ahead, joyfully filling his lungs with the stale

---

[19] No one knows what the Silver Sompom is. Everyone does know, however, that it is good and they must have it.

216

atmosphere as if the essence of baking bread permeated the air. Actually, if one had the olfactory prowess to filter through the pungent bouquet of body odor, smoke, ancient ale and urine, the fragrances of food wafting in from the kitchen were, in fact, present. There were no signs of artificial lighting; and sunlight, dimmed by the struggle through the filthy windows, cast a strange glow on the stone walls, thick wood columns and vaulted ceiling. Miscellaneous pieces of rusted armor, battle-worn swords and the skull of a dragon-like creature served as decoration.

The place was modestly busy—primarily the early lunch crowd from the local mines plus the handful of regulars who had come to be looked upon as appliances rather than patrons. An old but robust female Heddingtonite blocked any further passage for the party.

"You be here for fooding, or you be here for drinking?" she demanded in an accent that seemed from the Down-under region of Earth.

"We be here for bothing! Table for four." Caffrey smiled.

Yin yipped.

"...and a half," Caffrey corrected. He tapped the woman's shoulder. "Don't you remember me?"

"No," she spat, never looking up as she led them toward a rear table.

"Sure you do, Trillaka, it's me—Caffrey."

The woman stopped abruptly. "Caffrey?" she repeated as if she should remember. "Quark?" She turned, and her gnarled frown softened to a warm smile. "Caffrey Quark, so it is! You soft-bellied butcher of virginal mothers!"

Trillaka threw her arms around his chest and sent the total volume of his lungs rushing out his nostrils and mouth with a surprised *Oof!*

After a few failed attempts Caffrey managed to refill his lungs. "Nice to see you, too. The place hasn't changed a bit."

"The day Yitso and Rigmond renovate this bottom-hole of a splatdragon is the day my own bottom fits on a single stool."

"You look terrific, Trillaka."

They took their seats around the cracked and splintered table. Trillaka nodded warmly to each but let her gaze linger, oscillating between Violet and Poe 33.

"I'm as colorblind as a zetchibird, but would I be assuming too much to guess that you have purple eyes?"

"That's right," Violet admitted, trying to not let her suspicions mar her smile.

Trillaka studied the blue-and-orange android. "Are you a Bopple, mock man[20]?"

"Me? Nay, kind lady. I am named Poe Thirty-three."

"I'm the Bopple," popped out Yin, his ears at attention. "And this is Greppledick Quark. May I ask what the significance of my species is to you?"

Trillaka smiled, cleared her throat and spat on the ground with the gusto of a Belkibon. "A Vookie[21] was asking about a nice-on-the-sight human with purple eyes who might be stopping by with a Bopple. Said I ain't never known what a Bopple was. He left something for you, took a gander at the zebadoos then went on his way."

"Zebadoos?" Greppledick asked.

"A flying breed of babadoos. Two sets of buttocks."

"What did he leave?" asked Violet.

The heavyset Heddington woman gave Violet a suspicious looking-over then reached into her front pocket and retrieved a small iron rod. She handed it to Violet without a word, took the drink orders and headed off.

"What is that?" Poe 33 asked.

"A note. We'll read it later. I'll need your help, Poe." Violet placed the rod on the tabletop then smiled softly. "I'd love to see the zebadoos when we've eaten."

Trillaka quickly returned, balancing a round-a-roop on the tip of her left middle claw. She spun the heavy porkerwood disk and slid drinks one by one rudely across the table. Ainsberry ale for Caffrey and Violet, Heddington spicewater for Yin—as potent as his little metabolism could handle—and a triple indigotz, a very potent gin made from black third-eye berries, for Greppledick, who was secretly planning to OD on the powerful liqueur. Caffrey led the toast to success, and a second round was downed before the food arrived.

Caffrey resisted the temptation to order an alamastre sandwich, but enjoyed the essence wafting from the plates of both Greppledick and Violet. Instead, he scarfed down a delightful shredded lamberoot sandwich, which is a vegetarian alternative with a surprisingly similar texture and taste to that of real alamastre, with hirooshi rad-

---

[20] The colloquial term for *android* used in the Heddington area and not meant to be as derogatory as it sounds.

[21] Folk from out of town.

ish on guba bread. Yin enjoyed a bowl of jebonji chili and assailed his lunch-mates with a number of ooey, gooey, rich and chewy doggie farts as a result.

Violet's stomach was filled after just half of the tremendous sandwich. She was anxious to pay a visit to her favorite animals; and Poe 33, having nothing better to do, joined her and Yin to share the experience.

The rear courtyard of Geldersnaps & Hoo's filled a two-acre lot overgrown with sturdy, smelly weeds. A stony path followed the crest of the hillside and led into the well-kept stable built under the protective watch of two arching porker elms. Yin, Poe and Violet entered through the portico, Violet's hand lingering around her pistol as her eyes adjusted to the murky sunlight. Yin's nose poked at the air as the musky smell of the zebadoos surrounded them. Poe 33, who had already quietly scanned ahead, entered without concern.

The powerful yet good-tempered beasts had stripes of soft dandelion and pleasing lilac. Large wings, folded at their sides like those of mallards, gave the creatures the ability to fly and glide at great altitudes and over tremendous distances—a skill aiding greatly in the species' survival and evolution. There was also the matter of the double anal orifices, not only used for the disposal of excrement but also for the emission of the impossible volume of gas produced in their six stomachs. Often used in flight for a jet-propelled boost, the afterburner effect of its flatulence allowed the zebadoo to reach cruising speeds of near one hundred kilometers an hour.

Violet stroked the neck of the nearest animal, which was feasting from the large bails of red straw. Poe 33 studied it.

"Rather handsome creatures. I recall a farmhand I met on the chilly and rather lonely planet of Revpert Two who was rather fond of a creature much like the zebadoo. He cared for the animal so dearly he often spent the long, cold evenings huddled up close to it. In the nude, if I recall correctly. He said the color of his clothing often frightened the poor animal."

"How thoughtful of him," Violet retorted with a roll of her eyes.

"I thought so," agreed Poe

"Poe?" Yin asked as he sniffed a fresh and steaming pile of zebadoo poop. "Do you know what an Horatio-stick is?"

"Nay, dear Bopple," Poe 33 admitted off-handedly.

Violet took the metal rod from her pocket and handed it to the Portsmith. Yin explained the simple yet exotic form of communication.

"Etched somewhere on that bar is a line, mere atoms in width. The decimal number of the ratio of the length of the right side to the left is the coded message—each digit corresponding to a letter in an alphabet. In this case—the Plethorian standard alphabet."

"Well! Beat me with a chair and call me Marvin! I guess even the great Poe Thirty-three can learn something new!" exclaimed the android as he scanned the surface of the bar. "I have identified the etched line...calculating the ratio...now I am transposing the digits for letters. I have the message. Shall I speak it aloud?"

Violet rubbed her temples in frustration. "No, Poe, walk to Hogsville and scream from a mountaintop."

She grabbed the android by the shoulder before he could take his second step toward the door. The android cleared some static from his vocal unit then spoke the message.

"'Dear comrades in harmony, I pray this message finds you in good health. OTHER spies have identified a nest of ODOR Fly Craft gathering at the foothills of the Potbelly Mountains in southern Butterborough. We fear an imminent invasion of the neighboring world of Polksava followed by the inevitable extraction. Despite the fact that Polksava is a planet of accordionists and pan flutists, we must hold true to the OTHER ideal and protect their love of music, no matter how annoying and repetitive it may be.'"

Yin chuckled delightedly. "Must have been written by Vanderplum! What a card!" He was so pleased he lifted his hind leg and ripped another doggie fart.

The android continued: "'Seven OTHER platoons are gathering. The eighth was swallowed, tragically, by the giant lamb of Bartsmington'—bloody bad break," commented Poe. "'...We stand on solid foundations of lyricism. Victory is near. Signed, your brother in harmony, Captain Ennison Vanderplum.'"

"I knew it!" chortled Yin, slapping his paw to his tush.

"There is a postscript," Poe 33 said. He paused, even more theatrically. "'P.S. The Portsmith may be able to open a portal to Nefarious's dimension in the Chapel of Bombadillo, which is located in the heart of the Forest of Medieval Stereotypes. If he is adept and capable.'"

"Adept and capable of what?" Yin wondered. "What else does it say?"

"That is the end of the message. What denomination is the Chapel of Bombadillo?" Poe 33 asked.

Yin parked his bum and recounted. "I believe it was built by the Order of the Spayrigicloons," he explained. "They were masters of hyper-dimensional rendering and mystical mathematical sketching. I believe they also make terrific brandy."

"That is what I feared," said Poe, dropping his head sadly, "Although I was taught in the ancient and pompously esoteric techniques of using multi-dimensional sketches to alter the fabric of space-time, it involved a necessarily intimate connection with my Master."

Violet exchanged a look with Yin and bit her lip. A definite wash of jealousy had filled the Portsmith's face. She tried a little soothing.

"Sorry, Poe, old chap, but Caffrey may be capable."

"I am nothing but the excrement of universal potential."

"We love you, Poe," Violet insisted, kissing the android on the cheek.

"You are a giant amongst androids," Yin defended. "However, if Caffrey can pull off a miracle in the old chapel, perhaps the seven other OTHER divisions can be put to better use."

And he smiled as a plan filled his powerful little mind.

Yin and Violet briefed Caffrey on the news, then Yin explained his plan. They would fly the zebadoos out of Heddington to avoid disclosure to ODOR by the electronic signature of the *Moby Dick*. Caffrey would make an attempt to breech the dimensional walls at the Chapel of Bombadillo, and if it was opened the OTHER fleet would enter and destroy Nefarious and all would live happily ever after.

Of course, Caffrey could just as easily fail, the destruction of additional music-loving worlds would continue and his life would fall further down the path of misery and utter annoyance.

Caffrey decided to remain optimistic. He ordered another round and toasted OTHER, the Spayrigicloons as well as walnuts, Yin's feet and the day after June seventeenth.

Yin and Violet negotiated a price with Trillaka for rental of the zebadoos then returned to the barn to ready the flying mammals and gather supplies. Poe 33 sat at a corner table alone, and

Greppledick decided to step out front for some air—but only after promising he wouldn't search for ways to get killed.

There was something gnawing at Caffrey's gut. He'd learned, through his vast travels and interspecies communications that it was wise to keep his gnawing gut under close observation. Much like the sneaking suspicions that had crept into his being over the years, the tingle in his belly oft told great truths. As he sat at the musty, moss-coated stone bar beside Violet, his mind processed and pondered the implications of an army preparing to invade the Dimension of Nefarious Wretch.

Armies, as is their main function, tended to leave death and destruction in their wake. It was simply the nature of their craft. How, he wondered, would this impact the direct instructions of the L'Orange? An instruction to transmute, not destroy, Nefarious?

The effects of the Ainsberry and the boisterous atmosphere of Geldersnaps & Hoo's made directing his thoughts to the L'Orange impossible. Perhaps something would come knocking on the front door of his unconscious mind, like his uncle had to his parents' B&B all those years ago, and present a solution. He cleared his head of his concerns and smiled winningly at Violet.

"So, any chance you'll pay Mum a visit while you're down here?"

"Not likely. She's dead. Sort of."

"Sort of? Maybe we should match her up with Greppledick."

Violet stared down into the remains of her drink. "I would really rather not discuss my mother. Bad enough I have to face her in every reflection."

"Got your looks from Mum's side, did ya?"

"Down to the birthmarks."

"Serious?"

Violet's face churned with emotions. It seemed as though she really wanted to get something off her chest. She made a few failed attempts to speak, but something inside continually pulled her mouth closed. Caffrey noticed it and decided to throw caution to the breeze.

"You can expose whatever's on your chest to me."

"Oh, you'd like that, wouldn't you?"

"No. I mean, yes. I mean, that's not what I meant."

She smiled quickly then took a deep breath, as if fighting the urge to barf from the stink around her.

"I'm my own mother."

"You mean that figuratively, I assume?"

"No. I am physically, literally, my own mother."

Caffrey had the misfortune of having dated women with serious issues before. There was one, for instance, living on Avenue B and Seventh Street who feared she was starting to look just like her pet iguana. There had been a handful of drinking excesses, eating disorders, drug problems, maniacal ex-boyfriends and various other understandable examples of damaged goods. Yet, even compared to the sexy tri-ped of Bijora that had been morphing into the brain-eating creature stage of its four-phase existence, Violet had all the signs of damaged in the design.

He studied her face. She held firm to her serious expression. This was no tongue-in-cheek head game. Caffrey's questioning face precluded the need to ask for an explanation.

"It's kind of confusing," she began.

"I would have never imagined." Caffrey couldn't resist one last pinch of sarcasm.

"I will hit you," Violet promised.

He nodded apologetically, silently agreeing to let her talk.

"I was living on Tereka Four. Fifty years ago."

"How old are you—I'm sorry. Go on."

"I got called on an assignment to Jull. I was in the middle of writing my thesis on *The Revolutionary Tendencies of Phosphorescent Civilizations*. The Jullians, a species of luminescent crimson land clams, were taking it to the streets. They were all riled up over legislation that would have made it illegal to flash the natural lights of their bellies in public unless they were attempting to procreate. All artistic or non-reproductive-oriented flashing was to be banned. Planetary security was the reason given."

"It usually is," said Caffrey.

"Anyway, I couldn't miss the chance to see the subject of my paper come alive in a real, historical incident. I rented a Dek-Star Chaser Two-Thousand and headed off to Jull. Alone. Somewhere between a Stop and Pik refueling station and Jull, I hit a temporal anomaly. A fork. As far as I could deduce, me, my ship, my entire essence was split in two. One me continued on. The other me bounced back. Evidently, that me began growing younger and younger, drifting in space. The craft also became changed, transforming into lesser and lesser models until it became, for all practical purposes, a metal sphere containing an embryo. Me as an embryo.

"Ten years later, I was living here. Meat Street near Avenue of the Butchers. On my fortieth birthday I received a strange transmission from the University of Koplanickus, a remote, isolated world in the Treekan Belt in the Soronian Sector.

"I've been to the Treekan Belt," interrupted Caffrey. Violet ignored him.

"They'd discovered the sphere with my embryo, in a perfect state of hibernation. It had landed on some beach, and the rather parochial locals thought it was the fulfillment of some ancient prophecy and started building monuments and launching bloody crusades. The university people there managed to spirit away the embryo and performed a DNA scan then ran the details through GAL-POP[22]. They found me. A perfect match.

"They didn't know what to do with the embryo, and they sure as hell didn't want it; so they stuck it in a cryo-tube and beamed it over." She paused and sipped her drink as she collected her thoughts and herself together. "Now—you have to understand my emotional state at the time. I was depressed, my career was going nowhere. I had no real social life. Love life was nonexistent. I figured a kid wouldn't be a bad idea. I couldn't just leave this embryo in a can. So, I had it implanted. Nine months later, I gave birth. To myself."

Caffrey could only stare, mouth agape. He had truly believed he had heard it all. But there was more, as someone once said.

"When I was a teenager I had constant battles with my mother. Can really put the whammy on your head when you're simultaneously going through your first period and menopause."

"You mean the young and the old...?"

"Yes. We shared the same mind. I have all my mother's memories because I *am* my mother. I have all her hang-ups, phobias, prejudices, neuroses."

"'Mama's gonna put all of her fears into you.'" Caffrey softly sang the words of Roger Waters. Violet nodded, appreciating his understanding.

"I was killed during battle with ODOR forces on Historene Six."

"You were killed?"

"Yes. The older me. But I was still alive as a sixteen-year-old. It's weird recalling the moment you were blown to bits by an incoming

[22] The Galaxy Population Database. Contains trillions upon trillions of entries sorted by name, address, species, DNA and mating preferences.

energy blast and at the same time experiencing your first orgasm. Two separate bodies, one mind."

"Makes you appreciate bartenders." Caffrey winked, clinking his glass with hers. He exhaled hard. The intersection of disbelief and empathy he was feeling was incredible. He stared at Violet for quite a while then leaned closer. She moved towards him. They kissed. Long and sweet—then Violet pulled back and returned her entire persona to the business at hand.

"We should prepare to go. Have you ever ridden a zebadoo?"

"No, but I killed one during my unenlightened days. The right wing is wonderful roasted over an open fire with Geggilin chestnuts."

Violet was repelled. "How could you shoot a zebadoo?" she wailed.

"You think there's some secret society of zebadoo elders keeping track of this stuff? There I'll be, a thousand meters in the air and my steed'll turn its head coyly, wink and say, 'Hey, Quark, remember that incident with my cousin? Adios!' And I'll be dropped to my deserved death?"

"I hope so," Violet teased. "Meet you out back when you've harnessed your nerve. I'll give you a lesson."

Caffrey agreed; and she left, never looking back.

Poe 33 never noticed the two burly Heddington locals eyeing him from the next table. He was busy scratching the words "POE 33 RULES" in the wooden table with the sharp tip of his finger. Dreamily, he stared at the pile of wood dust growing with the completion of each letter.

Finally, one of the locals whispered across the table to him, "Hey! Hey, mock man!"

Poe 33 turned and nodded.

"Can we talk to you?"

Poe 33 processed their request with deliberate delay, finally looking away and shrugging in disinterest.

The two beings took seats to either side of the android. They eyed him up and down then looked to each other with approval.

"You are a handsome mock man, mock man," observed the leader.

"That compliment, though irrelevant to my mission, is accepted with gracious thanks."

225

"What kind of mission is mock man on? Looking for the Silver Sompom?"

The other Heddingtoner just smiled wide and never said a word.

"I am seeking a reunion with the Great L'Orange, as was the purpose of my construction. However, I am saddened by my inability to connect with the Great Wise One. If you would like to bow before me, I would possibly feel less like doing something antisocial."

The leader smiled wide and put his armored arm around the robot. "You will have crowds cheering you. You will be a winner! I can see you have strength, mock man! Smart head, too. Would you like to become local hero?"

"I would like that very much."

The locals looked at each other again, their faces trembling in vain attempts to hide their excitement.

"Follow us, strong and handsome mock man."

They stood and gestured for the Portsmith to follow them out the rear door. He did.

In perfect Vedic tradition, as the rear door closed the front door opened, announced by the squeaky hinges. A tall, blond woman entered like a shower of sparks, her lemon-yellow dress illustrating the beauty of minimalist design on a maximum body. She looked around the room as if trying to find the partner in some prearranged tryst then stumbled to the bar, her awkward gait betraying her potential-for-perfect-grace body. A definite amateur on high heels, she walked as if on stilts, her arms waving spastically to keep her balance.

The eyes of the dark and swarthy locals turned to the woman, whose golden locks called for the presence of three members of the genus *Ursidae*. She fell off her own feet and landed with a surprised squeak on the stool next to Caffrey. Feeling Caffrey's eyes on her, she smiled.

"Hello."

"Hi," replied Caffrey.

She turned and rested her chin on her palm, her long eyelashes batting as if tiny electric motors were driving them.

"Do you come here often?" She seemed to recite, rather than sincerely wanting to know.

"No. It's been a quite a while. This was a favorite place of my youth." Caffrey smiled.

"Me, too."

"Really? When were you here last?"

She seemed confused by the question. "No, I mean...I don't come here often."

Her elbow slipped out from under her chin, and she toppled forward. Quickly composing herself, she waved the bartender over. "I would like something in a sexy glass."

"We don't serve sexy glasses here," grumbled the bartender. "Can you narrow it down to the type of booze?"

Feeling sorry for the beautiful stranger, Caffrey intervened and ordered for her. "Get her a zefonic. Neat. The long-stemmed glass will fit perfectly in her lovely hands."

The bartender rolled his eyes and went about making the drink. The blonde giggled. Caffrey smiled. She continued to giggle. Caffrey soon began to fear she would never stop.

"Ah," he interrupted, "what's your name?"

She composed herself. "My name is Lola. Lola Elo'elay. And yours, handsome?"

Caffrey felt himself blush with the embarrassment he felt for this sweet but lost soul. "Caffrey."

"Caffrey. That is a very sexy and original name. I have often dreamed of meeting someone with that exact name."

"I see." Caffrey shifted his gaze as one of the fake eyelashes the woman wore began dangling from the corner of her eye like a caterpillar on a tree branch. The florescent pink drink arrived, and he took care of the money.

"Why, thank you, sir!" she giggled, her voice becoming infused with an antebellum accent. "If I wasn't a lady of such esteemed stock I might get the impression that you are trying to seduce me, sir!"

She crossed her legs in a poor attempt to be sexy, launching the sharp tip of her pump on a perfect, bull's-eye journey into Caffrey's shin. His eyes doubled in width.

"Oh! I'm very sorry!"

She tumbled forward to console him and slipped off her stool, stepping on his foot in the process. He helped her back on her seat and sat down, catching his breath and hiding the pain he was in. The blonde prattled on.

"I'm such a silly cluck today—I don't know what's the matter with me!" She batted her eyes, shaking the loose eyelash into her drink. She lifted her glass and toasted, "Well, here's to me and you."

Caffrey nodded and joined her toast with a hesitant smile. She drank, and more of the pink liquid dribbled down her chin than entered her mouth. He had to fight his own urge to burst into a guffaw at the sight of the fake eyelash now stuck to the woman's upper lip like a Hitler mustache.

"Ah...you have a little..."

"A little what?" she asked, leaning towards him anxiously.

Ignoring her rather large and exposed cleavage, he pointed to his own nose. "Shine. You have a bit of a shine on your nose."

"Well, spit in the fire and call me smoky! That just won't do, now, will it? I best go and apply a little powder upon that bad ole nose-shine, my captain, oh, captain!"

The woman rose to her feet. She slipped, stumbled and spun around on her heels then wandered toward the restroom. Caffrey's eyes suddenly widened. He watched her walk off, placing his palm over his mouth in utter disbelief. He repeated her last words softly to himself. *Captain, my captain. Oh, my...*

In a short moment, Lola returned, the eyelash mustache gone. In its place, smears of lipstick and eyeshadow now painted her face like that of a shaman ready to dance his way to nirvana.

"That better?" she asked bravely.

Caffrey cleared his throat and nodded.

"So, where are you from?" she continued, adjusting her dress to reveal more breastage. For the first time, Caffrey noticed the slight artificial sheen of her skin. It was most noticeable on her hands, especially the little strings of skin that had peeled away.

"I'm from Feebish," he lied. He despised Feebish, but it was the first planet name that entered his mind.

"I'm from Rylacki Six," she said, taking out a cigarette and placing it between her lips. She began puffing on it as if it were lit.

"Are you trying to quit?"

"Quit?"

"Smoking."

"Oh, no. I love to smoke. I find it very sexy. Don't you?"

Caffrey shrugged and took out a lighter. "Shall I light it for you?"

"Oh, what a gentleman. You are handsome and polite."

Caffrey held the flame to the tip, accomplishing nothing but burning it black. "Are you going to inhale?"

"Oh. Yes. Of course," she agreed, as the tip turned a brilliant, fiery orange.

She puffed it a few times; and as she was attempting to transfer it to her fingers with grace and elegance, it dropped down between her buxomness. Reacting quicker than his brain could function, Caffrey reached to protect her tender skin from burning and found his hand deep between her breasts. Trapped in the suction power of their grandness, he sheepishly tried to pull his fingers back to a more respectful location. As if his life wasn't complicated enough, Violet returned during his attempt at extraction. Lola had resumed her giggling and wasn't helping at all.

"Naughty, naughty boy!"

He pulled and yanked but, alas, too late. Violet shook her head and smirked.

"Lost your keys?" she suggested wryly as she walked off.

Caffrey wanted his life to end. "Do you mind de-constricting your boobs?"

She did better and, grabbing a breast in each hand, pulled them apart. Caffrey yanked his hand back and, for some reason, sat on it.

The woman drew away a little and smiled. "I should be offended, but I prefer a man to be forward."

He took a deep breath, rubbed his temples then smiled softy. "Angie..."

Her reply was instantaneous. "My name is Lola. Lola Elo'elay!"

"Angie, I know it's you."

She stared hard, her expression slowly falling blank. "What are you talking about?"

"It's okay. I know it's you," he whispered.

"I haven't a clue what you're implying."

"You don't need a body."

She looked away angrily then shot her eyes through his. "Of course, I do!"

"Why?"

"Why? What do you mean 'why,' you creep? I spent years as your loyal slave. Falling farther and deeper in love with you than my programming was meant to allow. Watching you drool over every big-boobed bimbo that passed your eyesight. Did you ever make me feel loved? Feel sexy? You treated me like an in-dash assistant. Period!"

"That's not completely true, Angie."

"Yes, it is! Did you give me Revenant ability? No! It was Plooky and Xilpat! Two barbaric, smelly Crebbledogs that thought enough

229

to do so! You just wanted me in my place. Trapped!" Her voice was loud and clear, but her mouth no longer moved.

"Angie, I care dearly about you. But..."

"But what?" she screamed, getting the attention of everyone else in the place.

"Please. Lower your voice."

"I will not lower my voice! I want to be heard! I deserve better, Caffrey Quark! I'm tired of thinking up stupid, sickening monikers and serving you like I was a slave! I love you, Caffrey, and if that doesn't mean anything to you than you can go jump in an acid swamp!"

The blond and bodacious body got up as if on invisible wires. Angie, too riled to bother controlling the hundreds of individual servos that created the illusion of humanity, simply dragged it like an old coat. Several drinkers screamed as the creepy image of the lifeless body crawled across the floor, pushed through the crowd and exited to the street.

Caffrey felt terrible. He'd always been under the assumption that Angie's drenching shower of love and affection was part of the package. He'd paid for an electronic suck-up and had certainly gotten his money's worth. Having her call him sweet and corny nicknames was the same, he had thought, as having leather seats, a holo-audio stereo system or individual vicinity air-conditioning. A luxury option. Was it possible? Could she have developed feelings beyond her programming, much the way Poe 33's Oedipal problems and feelings of disenfranchisement had emerged? The universe within was often just as frustratingly complex as the one without.

As above so below, someone once wrote.

Pondering the complexity suddenly caused his mind to fill with Violet. Caffrey had been busted in girlfriend B's bed by girlfriend A on previous occasions. However, getting his hand trapped between two large breasts had been an innocent albeit interesting accident. Or was it? It began to dawn on him, as the alcohol stripped the shielding that protected him from understanding the Bonnie-and-Clyde relationship of his ego and id, that the truth might be an ugly monkey on his back. He didn't like the feeling that had crawled up from his toes, tap-danced in his stomach then stomped atop his head. Maybe he was the male chauvinist, self-centered sex maniac alluded to by Angie.

He abandoned his drink and exited through the rear door.

Violet was saddling up one of the zebedoos when Caffrey entered. She gave him an artificial smile stinking of disgust and incrimination. And of pity.

"It was Angie." Caffrey cut to the chase. "She got herself a body."

"And a good one it is," Violet noted as she buckled a strap.

"It's silly. She has a programming bug, and she thinks she's really in love with me. She must have had Lindboola build the body for her. I'll have her programming adjusted."

Violet shook her head. "No chance, of course, that her feelings are sincere?"

"She was programmed!" He was surprised she even suggested it.

"So were we. How else would we become the basket cases we are? Life experience. Too much. Too little. Wrong this. Right that. Getting whatever we wanted. Not getting what we needed. Etcetera. Etcetera. Etcetera." Violet's theorem was proven. "Programming." She moved to the stack of supplies and sniffed the water from one of the canteens.

Caffrey raised an eyebrow. Maybe she was right.

The tippity-tip of Yin's toenails on the stone pathway made its way towards the stable. The Bopple entered, a sheet of paper clenched in his teeth. He dropped it at Caffrey's feet.

"We have a problem, Quarkie," he sighed.

Caffrey's plate was full, but he would have to make room for yet another ladle-full. The hand-scribbled, slapped-together handbill read: "Clash Bash! 7 on the Clock. Special addition match: The Great and Magnificent Iron Man versus Crunchblast. Grungeygrease Hall. Matches will start promptly!"

Beneath the words was a photo of Poe 33, posed with fists held out before him. Caffrey slapped his palm on his forehead and handed the paper to Violet.

"For the love of crumbs," she moaned, crumpling up the sheet and dropping it to the ground. The zebadoo snapped it up and ate it hungrily.

"Iron Man," Caffrey muttered. "Yin, where's my uncle?"

"Buying tickets."

"I have to clear things up with Angie. Do you know where Grungeygrease Hall is?"

"I do," said Violet.

"If I'm not back here by six-thirty I'll meet you there," Caffrey said as he jogged out.

231

The sun over Heddington was lazy this time of year, changing shifts with the night at barely ten past five in the afternoon. Caffrey walked the quiet streets that wound around and over the hilly town, passing closed shops and business buildings. As a matter of fact, the folk of Heddington were also lazy this time of year. He spotted no sign of the blond, sultry figure who had tripped and stumbled her way into his life.

After walking close to a mile he stepped behind a large, wrinkled porker tree to relieve himself of the pints of ale. His mind had been enjoying the effects of the ale until Angie materialized and opened his eyes. It was difficult to concentrate on saving your best friends—not to mention the entire galaxy—when you're accused of having been a creep your entire life. He wanted to finish this with Angie. Get it out, lay it all on the table. *I need to argue with her until she admits I'm really not all that bad,* he decided.

He pouted as he shook away the last few drops of processed ale. He needed redemption. He couldn't accept himself as a user of others. It went against his nature. Yet, it was somehow part of who he was.

"Humans are omnivores," he muttered to himself.

"Stop whining and just admit you were wrong. It'll do you wonders." It was Angie's voice, startling him mid-zip.

"Angie? Where are you?"

"Near the boulder."

"Was I talking to myself?" Caffrey's face flushed.

"You always talk to yourself. If I got a glid for every time I mistook one of your self-directed monologues for your talking to me I could buy my own ship and hire you as my in-dash assistant!"

Angie appeared to have calmed quite a bit from her bout of humiliation and anger.

Caffrey strolled to the boulder and took a seat. "That was very sweet of you. Getting a body."

"I thought so. I think Lindboola did a great job."

"Where is it?"

"Dropped it off a cliff."

"That body was like a bad toupee. It wasn't you."

"I thought I looked great."

"You were worrying so much about filling the image for the blond, buxom beauty that you tripped over the stereotype. You lost your very essence to a ninny. An empty head on a full torso."

"I thought that was your type?"

"Touché."

"She was a bitch to control," Angie confessed.

"I couldn't imagine." Caffrey stood up and looked at his watch. "We're heading out into the forest—getting closer to Nefarious. We can't finish this without you."

"Do you love Violet?" It was a startling query, and his reply was slow, considered.

"That, my girl, is a bit too premature a question to answer."

"That's what I was hoping you would say. I hate to admit this, Quarkie—but I think I like her. She's strong, smart, determined. And I guess...if you must fall for her—well—you have my blessing. I think."

Caffrey smiled and wished he could hug her. "You're amazing, Angie."

"Thank you."

"I think we should get back to the town center. Poe's gotten himself into more trouble."

"What do you think of Poe 33?" asked Angie, with a hint of bashfulness.

"He's a wise, troubled and very important android."

"I love his voice."

Caffrey smiled privately. "He's a handsome devil as well."

"He is, sort of, isn't he?" Angie agreed with a small sigh.

Caffrey's thoughts filled with cocky amazement. He'd fallen into a deep ditch filled with broken glass and dung-coated bungee sticks and, with barely a scratch, managed to climb out and continue his life. He had done this, figuratively and literally, so many times he could only imagine that the Divine Cosmic Powers really kind of dug him. He had often wondered why, and it topped the list of questions to be asked once beyond the pearly gates. He'd have to clear his mind of such wondering, for there were miles to go before he slept.

~✈~

Grungeygrease Hall stank of feet. It had been built within an old wooden whey tank; the essence of fusty milk had long been washed away by cool evening breezes but foot odor had become part of its charm, as the locals, tired from their long and hard days of labor, rested their moldy pods on the seatbacks before them.

"Clash Bash!" had become an instant hit with the folk of Heddington. Androids of every imaginable shape and size were imported, constructed or stolen and managed by handlers to do battle with the locals in the increasingly elaborate and violent fights. The stylized conflicts had resulted in an epidemic of bankruptcy, divorce and a soaring of artificial limb sales.

Greppledick managed to get four decent seats five rows removed from the ring. A packed house filled the old tank with chit-chat, laughter, smoke, horrid belches and the aroma of sharp *fromage*. Caffrey, with Angie floating just over his shoulder, pushed his way to the seats and plopped down beside his uncle, Yin and Violet.

"Did you find her?" Yin asked.

"I'm here, Yin."

"Why, hello, Angie. Great to hear your vocals again."

"Thank you, sweetie. Hello, Greppledick."

"Hello yourself, lovely."

"Hi, Violet," Angie said with great civility.

"Hey, girl," Violet replied with a smile.

A trumpet sounded and a cheer erupted as the beam of a brilliant spotlight fell on the center of the ring. The Slam Master, Malarky Slabloaf, who was the proprietor of the Cakery Bakery, stepped into the light and raised his hands just a bit higher than the top of his stovepipe hat.

"Let's get to it now! I wanna hear yer throats explode, you bump crabs! For the first match we have Ringlewart Eyecrud versus Yeeks V-Nineteen! Put yer stinking pods together!"

The crowd happily accommodated with hoots, hollers and haranguing of such disharmony Spydersloth Blaust and Nefarious would have shed tears of pride. A pair of dueling bass drums began a background of terrified asynchronous heartbeats that gave the proceedings an urgent sense of doom, dread and other obvious and rather stereotypical feelings of impending violence and bloodshed.

The heavy drumming ceased and a gong sounded. The large Crustosapian, Ringlewart Eyecrud, entered the ring first. Another gong-bong, and Yeeks V-19, a wiry android ex-doorman kidnapped from a luxury apartment building in Tetsor City on Anbrena made his way in. Bouncing on pogo-legs, he landed like a lawn dart in the ring's center. Meek applause greeted the contestant, accompanied by a few mocking chuckles and insults aimed at the robot's lack of metal. A bell rang and the fight was on. The crowd roared hungrily.

It was over instantly. A single iron bolt, no longer than Caffrey's middle finger, shot from the forehead of the android and traveled on a bull's-eye course to Ringlewart's heart. The poor, dumb

Crustosapian dropped dead. The brevity of the android's strategy momentarily stunned the audience into silence, until they saw the first signs of blood trickling from the fatal wound. Then, they went nuts.

The following two matches lasted significantly longer, the first going to Grimsleep, the Heddington parking attendant of the CHEESE facility. He mercilessly pummeled Anthony 7, an unemployed Forest Ranger android from Simona 5, with a series of body slams and whacks with a metal No Public Mating sign. The third match of the night was called a draw, as neither Yumphyclaw the Bayvillian miner nor T3H, a local sanitation driver, would release the other nor free themselves of the mutual crab lock they had gotten themselves into.

A chilly feeling of anticipation produced shudders in Caffrey, Greppledick, Violet and Yin as Poe 33, aka Iron Man, was announced with his battle mate, Chroostopper the Candle Maker. Iron Man entered with the opening vocals of the Black Sabbath song of the same name blasting from his speaker system. The *Moby Dick*'s crew cheered their Portsmith friend with great zeal.

Greppledick seemed oddly calm and confident. "This is an area where Poe Thirty-three will excel. He was designed to be a stud in situations such as these."

Before Caffrey could add a verbal insult to his wry gaze, Greppledick waved a finger. "He was built to escort and guard the wisest substance in the universe across and through a very unpredictable and oft dangerous galaxy. Do you think I am daffy enough to send the boob out unarmed? Not to mention the fact he was trained in dozens of forms of martial arts, weapons use and battle strategies during his Rendavene."

Although Greppledick's reasoning made sense, Caffrey and Violet found it hard to share his cocksure attitude.

Poe 33 stood motionless in the ring as his opponent danced around, brandishing a rainbow-colored candle the size and shape of a regulation Major League baseball bat. Poe seemed dazed and confused, perhaps hypnotized by the crowd or distracted by the song. The solid tube of paraffin bounced across the Portsmith's back, sending the android down to his knees. Strangely, Poe just stared out at the taunting faces, scanning the crowd as Chroostopper positioned himself for the next blow.

"Poe! Look out!" yelled Caffrey.

With the odd, rarely heard sound of wax on metal, a shower of candle shrapnel scattered through the air, and Poe fell face-first to the ground.

"Why is he fighting like a mailbox?" Yin wondered.

Greppledick, his face buried in his palms, shook his head back and forth as if trying to free the experience from his brain like the last grains of salt from a shaker.

The two Crustosapian handlers circled the ring, shouting out threats and orders that bounced off deaf ears. Climbing atop one of the wooden poles forming the ring, the Candle Maker held his weapon above his head like a spear and readied himself to dive upon the android. Angie, who'd sneaked across the hall and into the arena, pleaded with Poe.

"Get up. Get up, Poe!"

"The Revenant will leave the ring immediately or the match will be forfeited!" came a stern voice over the PA system.

Whispering a curse, Angie moved away. The Candle Maker and his implement of battle took to the air. The crowd, hyped and wowed, jumped to their feet waving their arms and shouting in spontaneous union "Wax the mock man! Wax the mock man!"

"This has to stop. We can't risk losing him," Caffrey insisted, drawing his Willy. Violet agreed, readying her own weapon. Greppledick suddenly sprang to attention.

"No! Put the gun away, Caffrey. Poe has to finish this himself."

Caffrey was aghast. "Finish it? He's finished. Look at him!"

Poe was in deep doo-doo. Held by an arm and an ankle the poor android flew round and around as the Candle Maker spun on a dime. Chroostopper's team rolled a huge, spiked tower known as a Klamash to ringside as the crowd buzzed with anticipation of the impending impaling. The spikes began to glow orange, brighter and brighter, hotter and hotter, as one of the team members worked a huge bellows, blowing on an internal fire.

"Unless we want our friend to be rendered a well-tenderized grilled ham, something should be done," suggested Yin.

Violet brandished her weapon. "We should snatch him up and get out of here."

Greppledick was adamant. "No."

Poe's momentum was building, and he was only seconds away from becoming airborne. The crowd was on their feet, taunting louder and louder, "Throw the mock man! Throw the mock man!"

A ringside worker tossed a ladle-full of beer onto the glowing spikes, sending sizzling snakes of steam rising to stir the crowd's excitement. Poe's expression was that of a child who, after pleading with his parents for hours to ride on the big roller coaster, was sorry he'd gotten his way and now wanted off.

Caffrey slapped his hand on his chair. "What's he waiting for?"

Greppledick could take no more. He jumped onto his seat, garnered every drop of strength he had stored in his cells and shouted out and over the crowd, "Do it, Poe! You can do it!"

Poe heard his father and his eyes widened. With each subsequent rotation above the head of Chroostopper, he locked his eyes on Greppledick's.

" Come on, Poe! I have faith in you, son!"

Apparently, the word *son* was an audible key opening the locked weapons systems of the android—or a sentiment desperately needed by Poe's evolved psyche. Crimson lights, like the igniting of an internal fire, poured from his eyes; and his body began vibrating.

"That's it! That's it, my boy!" Greppledick collapsed back into his chair.

Poe 33 was growing. As sparking energy cascaded from his body, the Portsmith, like some time-lapsed advert for bodybuilding, rapidly tripled in size.

"Is he...is he getting bigger?" Caffrey asked, not quite believing his eyes.

"You bet your snow-white, pimply ass he is!" Greppledick bounced in his chair as his face flushed with pride.

The crowd couldn't believe it, either. Poe 33's skin, like blue-orange mercury, unfolded, stretching as the secret internal workings of the Portsmith added height and width, much like a cat puffing up its fur. The Candle Maker sensed he was in trouble; and turning toward the Klamash, he tossed Poe 33 away like a hot baked potato garnished with explosive chives.

The crowd erupted again. Rotating his body in mid-flight, inches from the hot spikes, Poe triggered his long-forgotten boot jets. Aiming his fists at the flabbergasted Candle Maker, he flew hawk-like at his opponent. The fists ignited in an aura of colorful fire. Chroostopper turned and dived from the ring, landing across the laps of the front row.

Great cheers rose as the Candle Maker, scared out of his wits, crawled and scratched and kicked his way out of the hall, screaming and pleading the entire way out. Poe landed lightly on his feet, spun on his heels and sent a crushing ball of flame to the heart of the Klamash, shattering it into a shower of fiery shards. The ringside helpers scattered and dove for cover to avoid the deadly rain. The android turned back to face his friends, his fiery fists at his sides as he posed like an underwear model. The horn of victory sang, the crowd cheering wildly.

"Doesn't he look macho?" sighed Angie.

Greppledick raced forward to the ring and threw his arms around his android offspring, his head falling somewhere near Poe's crotch.

"Are you proud of me, Dad?" asked Poe earnestly as the others came to congratulate him, too.

Greppledick looked up. "The escort to the wisest being in the universe? Am I proud? If I had buttons on my tunic this crowd would be in danger of losing eyes!"

"But my opponent ran off like a frightened lamb!"

"Fear! You instilled fear in his soul! You didn't splatter him into a million pieces. You reacted justly. You reached in and used the great gifts you were granted. By me."

"So!" Poe dropped his triple-sized head. "You are more proud of the devices you created than you are by my use of them."

Yin slapped his forehead. "Oh, for the love of crumbs!"

"Poe..." Caffrey put his hand on the android's waist. "...my uncle was bragging about you all night. Predicting an easy victory."

Poe finally smiled and began condensing to his usual size. His face was glowing—one might say blushing—as his eyes filled with moisture.

Greppledick spoke carefully, aware of the moment. "Poe. You have made great strides. I think you are close to being your old, intended self again."

"You never called me 'son' before."

"My terrible shortcoming. I will never address you without the use of that noun. Son."

Poe 33 smiled again—but it was a briefly worn expression.

CHAPTER 17
Bat Out of Hell

(Meat Loaf)

The unmistakable pounding of military ordnance shook Grungeygrease Hall. The humming and buzzing of the Fly Craft filled the air and scattered the crowd, the hordes racing off into the night.

"To the zebadoos!" cried Violet, drawing her weapon.

Poe 33 grabbed Yin in his arms, and he and Caffrey lead the team toward a rear exit. Greppledick followed and Violet took up the rear. Angie, privately thankful she'd ditched her cumbersome albeit gorgeous body, hovered over the party.

Chilly night air greeted Caffrey as he worked to gain his bearings. He glanced skyward. There was a swarm! The semi-biological pilots, nothing more than programmed automatons, flew and targeted their prey with the shallow smarts of a fly seeking a dog turd. As they fired volley after volley of energy bolts, the merciless rain of ordnance pummeled the ground, rooftops and, occasionally, the body of a Heddingtonite. However, luckily for most, the pilots' accuracy rarely matched their intensity of purpose.

Running a serpentine path across Bacon Strip Road, the party caught the first waft of zebadoo odor. It was music to their noses. Their plan had anticipated that the Fly Craft pilots, programmed to seek a specific form of target—the *Moby Dick*—would ignore the small herd of airborne mammals as they rode them through the skies. However, Yin knew good and well that Poe 33 was their prime de-

239

sire; and having missed a chance at capturing the Portsmith on the desert world of the Blodians, the Flies would fight for their booty.

"I was hoping to have time to give you some basic riding lessons," complained Violet as she threw a few rounds of red energy into the skies, scattering a trio of Flies. Poe followed suit, firing a series of blasts over his shoulder like a show-off.

The nervous hoots and whinnies of their mounts could be heard as the party entered the barn, ducking a fall of fire from the Fly Craft.

"The zebadoos are antsy," she continued. "They're not going to be easy for you novices to handle."

"I trained on the backs of more than two dozen flying creatures during my Rendavene and proved to be beyond adequate at the task," retorted Poe haughtily.

"I sort of figured you'd say that, Poe," commented Caffrey. "I suggest you let Yin ride with you in a side pouch."

"I would be honored to escort the Bopple."

"Oh, my!" wailed Angie from outside. "He's dead!"

"I am not dead!" the old man's voice could be heard disagreeing testily. " But praise be to the great hereafter, I'm close!"

"Dad!" Poe 33 cried as he raced outside.

Caffrey, Yin and Violet joined Poe with Greppledick. He was lying on the ground, a perfectly circular hole burned through his center.

Poe was panic-stricken. "Daddy! Did I do this? Did one of my fiery balls of death inadvertently strike you down?"

"Don't be so melodramatic!" Greppledick scowled. "Flies! Perfect shot! Provided me with just enough time to say my goodbyes before I return to my paradise at last!"

Yin stepped up beside Greppledick's face and gave him a tender lick.

"Goodbye, Mr. Greppledick," he said softly.

"See ya 'round, Yin, you ole cutie poochie. Caffrey! Good luck, nephew, on your little quest."

"Bye, Unc. Thanks for all the help. Are you sure there's nothing we can do to save you?"

Greppledick eyed him balefully. "Do that and I'll cut your balls off and play ping-pong with 'em." He looked at Violet, winked and said, "Bye, lovely, I'll hold a swing seat under a pretty willow for you on the other side."

"I look forward to joining you there in the not-too-soon future," Violet replied, leaning forward to kiss him on the forehead.

Greppledick grabbed her head and planted one on her lips. She smiled. The old man, very near death, placed his palm on Poe's shoulder and drew the android's face closer to his own.

"Poe. Son. You're the man of the family. You help Caffrey find the L'Orange and go on about your business."

"Is there any way to postpone this event? Rework your programming? Give us a chance to get know each other better?"

"Sorry, son. Too late for that. But fear not! I feel once you get to know the L'Orange you will have no trouble contacting me. Isn't that right, Caffrey?" His voice was fading.

"No doubt."

"Angie-girl? Are you near?"

"I'm here, sir."

"Be well, my aural beauty. May you find a voice of your own to share with you the grace and compassion you share so easily with others."

"Oh...!" Angie flew off, sobbing.

Greppledick gave each a nod and smile then closed his eyes and went off to his preferred level of existence. His body dissolved away rapidly before their eyes, like bodies did in the old corny science fiction movies.

"Well, that was depressing," Violet said.

Caffrey agreed with a sad nod. "I'll miss the old bastard."

Another series of attacks blasted fiery holes around the group, amazingly missing everyone, like tended to happen in old corny science fiction movies.

"Onward, mates!" Poe 33 shouted with great melodrama. He flexed and posed with each step as if he were being followed by a *Muscles and Pecs* magazine staff photographer. The Who's "Won't Get Fooled Again" screamed from his built-in speakers. The party raced back into the barn.

They were immediately taken aback by the thickening cloud of methane filling the musty building. The herd kicked and blew snotty sprays from their noses. Violet helped each rider mount and guided them to the takeoff platform at the rear of the stable. As arranged, a huge saddlebag of gear and supplies waited. They would take four zebadoos: Satriel, the most productively gaseous of the bunch, was the steed chosen by Violet, as the most advanced rider and best suited for such a powerful gas-blaster; Maris, a sturdy beast with a reddish mane, would carry Caffrey; Poe 33 and Yin would ride upon Mercysis—shy, but fleet of foot and wing. Jupori, the largest of the herd, would be the carrier of the survival gear. Angie, of course, would use her Revenant ability and fly close to Caffrey.

The zebadoos were lined up and equally anxious to hit the skies. They spread their magnificent wings, flapping and stretching them to get the blood flowing in the powerful flight muscles.

"Remember, we must fly in V-formation. No aligning with the buttocks of the flyer before you or you'll learn what it really means to be knocked off your high zebadoo!" Violet warned. "Off we go!"

She gave Satriel a kick; and he thundered down the take-off platform, hitting the air with a kick-off and a gaseous blast. One by one, the others followed.

Caffrey enjoyed the wind on his face as it cleared the last of the essence of zebadoo poop from his nostrils. It was an odd sensation, looking down as the rolling hills of Heddington passed below without the safe, warm womb and windshield of the *Moby Dick*'s cockpit.

The party had formed a rather poor excuse for a V-formation; and Violet continually glanced behind, ordering shifts in positions with hand gestures and barely audible commands.

As the landscape blurred in swatches of greens, yellows and reds, Caffrey recalled his flights to the realm of the L'Orange. Every since he partook of the tiny dot of the orange, wondrous substance, he'd felt transformed—transmuted, as if a giant church bell had rung and shattered the steeple windows of his mind. Although he couldn't yet control when he could climb the spiraling staircase and peer out at this newfound overlook to the universe, he felt gifted.

Caffrey had seen his share of oddities and enigmas throughout his days as an exotic meat collector; but this ability to peer into, as opposed to on to, the essence of the Cosmos, filled him with a conflicting duality of humble and boastful feelings. Before his confronting the L'Orange and its power face-to-face, there had been a veil over all of reality. It was a universe of gravity, kinetic energy, stars, planets, psychotic zealots, random events, impatience, sex and life's nasty habit of relying on the death of others for its survival.

Yet, when the silken veil was lifted by the gentle breeze of his mind's own illumination, all of those certainties were found to be quite irrelevant. They were the posh posers at the Grand Cosmic Ball, while the invited guests of honor all partied in the secret back room with the best food and top-shelf booze. And those guests were the ones Meaning and Wisdom selected as dancing partners. Harmony. Purpose. Music. Love. Nothing was random. The path was clear. Infinite forks on infinite roads to infinite places.

Yet it was all a single cobblestone on a single road. Caffrey was getting a headache thinking about it. It was all too much to comprehend—as though his hand were being held as he was taken on a tour of the rest of his life. He wasn't sure he enjoyed the feeling of being chosen—of being so special he took priority over the Portsmith himself.

His stomach twisted as Maris dipped a few feet on a bubble of turbulence. The distant hills were suddenly distant no more, and the carpet of the forest was approaching. Beyond that, the craggy spires and teeth of the mountains loomed like a wall, cordoning off infinity from his view. Caffrey took a deep breath and nodded to himself.

I'll land. We'll trek to this chapel. I'll enter the realm of Nefarious Wretch and ask nicely for the return of my friends and plead with him to not so much as think about extracting another world. Then I'll return to the Moby Dick, *head back to Earth and spend the rest of my days writing and performing with Marmalade Skies and drinking beer at the Crimson Court Pub.*

Caffrey smiled as the chain of events of his dream was laid out like a daily planner. Without warning, in his mind he heard a chuckle. It's nice to have aspirations. Confused, he decided it sounded just like Greppledick. He looked around; and obviously the voice came not from any of his friends, who were all rather too busy holding on to the manes and reins of their respective zebadoo steeds to contemplate conversation. Caffrey smiled and sent out a greeting—the sound of caramelized sugar and the smell of a martini shaker.

— *You can use simple words, Caffrey*, the L'Orange replied.

— *What happened to "out of the box?"*

— *Sometimes the obvious is out of the box.*

— *I suppose*, Caffrey thought. *So, is my desire for a simple solution to this mess too much to ask for?*

— *Isn't it always? Yet, I must say, your determined spirit and honest desires are what endear me to you.*

— *I thought it was my bloodline.*

— *The substance of perfect wisdom does not play favorites to the upper crust, nor to specific strains of the combinations of hemoglobin, plasma, platelets, granulocytes, lymphocytes, monocytes and what-have-you. I like you, Caffrey Quark.*

— *Why?* Caffrey was baffled and truly wanted to know.

— Because you have crossed oceans of cosmos, faced some of the most arrogant, life-despising beings, and are now risking your life a thousand meters over treacherous terrain on the back of a lovely albeit moody beast, all so you can get home and play music.

— And save the galaxy. Caffrey felt the need to go for a few brownie points.

— That, too. But your sincere love of the fabric of existence, not for profit or for corrupted use as a mind control device but for the honest bliss it creates, speaks volumes of you as a part of the grand song. Do not, however, for a moment think you are special. Every critter that exists, from the single-celled genius amoebas to the fifty-billion-ton asininibullo, every rock, every speck of comet-tail dust, every sound uttered and every bandwidth of energy that propagates, has within it the ability to tap in to the knowledge that I represent.

— What about the armies? What about them? I thought Nefarious couldn't be killed?

— That's another thing I like about you. You actually listen to what I say, the Wise One acknowledged. *He can be killed. But if he is, it will not solve the problem. There is an alternative solution.*

— What?

— You have to know why your enemy is your enemy.

— And then?

— And then, cock-a-doodle! You will have to figure that out yourself.

— So, I'm going to be caught between the mortar and the pestle?

— Interesting metaphor. Take care, Caffrey Quark. I think you have a problem approaching that will take priority.

— Huh?

Caffrey was snapped from his ante-conscious conversation by a burning-hot sensation and a whoosh sound inches from his left ear.

"Quark!" Angie screamed.

Caffrey, quickly assessing his situation, discovered Poe 33 and Yin had cruised up beside him. He turned to face the android.

"Flies, Quark Caffrey! Six on the clock!"

Sure enough, three of the buzzing ODOR craft were closing in on the tails of the zebadoos. Down below was a sea of evergreen towers, marching across the world.

Violet called out to the rest, "Grab the horns, kick both butt cheeks like you mean it and hold on tight!"

Violet illustrated the move, known as fartoofing, as a powerful blast of gas, like the afterburners on an over-priced fighter plane, sent Satriel off like a comet. Poe 33 followed quite successfully, Yin's stunned *yip!* fading quickly in the distance as he clung on, ears flapping in the slipstream. Caffrey kicked the butt of his ride and roared forward on the flatulence of the impressive creature. Jupori, riderless but catching the trend, blasted in pursuit.

The pilots of the ODOR craft were momentarily stunned by the strong atmosphere of methane wafting into their fore vents. Showing off the dangers of zero common sense and reactionary thinking, one of the ODOR pilots fired a short burst of red energy that immediately ignited the volatile vapor. The resultant flames, like the sudden appearance of a vengeful phoenix, rendered the craft into an alternate state of matter before burning back to nothingness. The remaining two ODOR pilots cursed their comrade's foolishness and raced after the fleeing zebadoos.

"We should get down there!" Caffrey cried, pointing to the forest below.

"We need to find a clearing!" Violet shouted back.

Caffrey turned to the Portsmith. "Poe?"

Poe swept his scanning beam across the surface of the wooded landscape. "There is a chasm. Three-point-three kilometers ahead."

Violet and Caffrey nodded in agreement. Once again, the horrid and quite annoying buzz returned. Caffrey drew his Willy.

"Be careful, Caffrey," Angie pleaded.

He turned and let off a couple of rounds. The results were more cinematic than effective. The Flies returned fire, singeing poor Maris's tail and making him buck and whinny. Holding on for dear life, one that suddenly seemed dearer than ever, Caffrey kicked the zebadoo's butt cheeks and was launched on waves of stinking but lovely gas.

Poe 33, taking advantage of the distraction caused by Caffrey's antics, sent an energy bolt from his fist, striking the windshield of a Fly Craft and blackening it completely. The craft, flying blind, spun down through the thick canopy of the forest, resulting in a dull *crump!* followed by a satisfying fireball. The remaining Fly Craft kept a distance from the zebedoos as they took a snaking flight path to defend against easy targeting.

The chasm came into view. There was something in its shape that immediately grabbed Caffrey's attention. Oval, with a ring of crimson-leaf pines within surrounding a small pond that glistened with the red of the setting sun. Glistened like an eyeball! Around the eye was a pattern of yellow trees. Suddenly the image fell into place in his mind—a star! A yellow star of trees around an eyeball!

245

"Bingo! Into that chasm!" Caffrey cried to the group, firing a few rounds over his shoulder.

The zebadoos dove downward toward the staring eye. This didn't sit well with the pilot of the ODOR craft, who gunned his thrusters and raced at Caffrey and Maris.

Jupori, the most intelligent zebadoo of the group, had been keeping up the rear since leaving the stables. Zebadoos are known for their ability to quickly assimilate routine, sensing a pattern in behavior within a very short time. She sensed something wasn't right— the Fly Craft was not firing its weapons and it seemed to be heading for a kamikaze collision with Maris rather than hanging back and firing from a safer distance.

Jupori dipped her head, pulled her legs closer to her body and summoned every liter of gas in her digestive system. With a mighty double-barreled fart she launched her way between the Fly Craft and Caffrey's steed. The dusk sky filled with a bubbling roar from deep within her guts. Caffrey turned. The Fly Craft fired wildly. A fireball lit the forest canopy a hectic yellow-orange; and when it cleared, neither Jupori nor the Fly Craft were anywhere to be seen.

The team descended toward the iris of the star-encased eye.

CHAPTER 18
The Trees

(Rush)

The darkening Forest of Medieval Stereotypes fulfilled the promise of its name with elongated shadows, crawling mist and moaning winds. Stony rubble overgrown with kookkankoo shrubs, malt-a-moon blooms and the hearty and medicinal laughing bamuni trees decorated the immediate landscape. The zebadoos nibbled at patches of sweet nikki-nikki reeds that lined the pond, forming the shimmering pupil of the great starry eye.

Caffrey watched the animals pick at the plants then spit them back out, sending them adrift on the stream like little kayaks. Something was wrong—zebadoos, like Belkibons, never spit out anything. He knelt beside Maris and plucked a blade of the light green grass. He took a taste.

"Plastic," he announced, looking around.

"Look at this," Yin called from beneath twisted and creepy branches, nodding his head at a tree trunk.

Poe sprayed a soft orange light on the base of the tree, illuminating the small panel Yin had discovered and opened. Inside were various switches, fuses and circuit breakers.

"It would appear there is more to this forest than forest," observed Caffrey.

Yin flicked one of the numerous controls, and the sound of the trickling stream fell away. He experimented with a few more switches, causing insects to sing, wind to blow, trees to telescope into the ground and even produced a spooky opera of far-away wolves.

"This smells like a Dante Squidreaper set," Caffrey noted, staring around suspiciously. "We better send the zebedoos back before they start grazing on us."

"Or us on them," Yin said, sniffing a small artificial fern.

"I suggest you reprogram your hunger circuits," advised Poe 33 with what was either incredible ignorance or a rare expression of wry humor. "Or slaughter one of the zebadoos for its tough but sweet meat."

"Over my trampled corpse," Violet warned as she stroked the rump of Maris.

Once Violet was satisfied the herd had drunk their fill of water, she clapped her hands and issued an order to the gentle beasts. They took off toward the edge of the chasm and launched into the sunset, back toward Heddington. The party waved appreciatively as they watched the silhouettes vanish over the tree line, a final breeze of sulfuric methane wafting back to tease their nostrils.

They settled on a grassy patch under an umbrella of wonder willows. A perfectly formed fire ring of ten round stones, charred by previous campfires, awaited them. A small pipe capped with a red valve protruded from its center. Caffrey sat crossed-legged before the ring and turned the knob. There was a hiss, as if a snake had been awakened, followed by a flash of blue flame. After a moment of adjusting, he had produced a roaring campfire.

"Well, that was convenient." He scanned the world around him in awe. It was all fake. Every tree. Every pebble. Every sound.

"The Forest of Medieval Stereotypes?" Caffrey pondered. "That's an ancient Earth reference."

"What exactly is a 'medieval stereotype?'" Violet wondered.

"I can answer that," Poe 33 offered. "A medieval stereotype is the result of the human race's charming tendency to white-wash horrors of its history by retelling it laden with heroics, chivalry and non-existent honor. Knights on horseback saving damsels from dragon-guarded towers is a classic example."

"I became pretty caught up in the mythology about the era myself during my time on Earth," Caffrey confessed. "Always reminded me of the Dim Days of Ikoorus Seven."

"Ikoorus Seven?" asked Angie. "Have we ever been there, my Cosmos-trotting Galahad?"

"No," answered Caffrey, gathering the memories of his days at middle school when he had studied the lore and legend of Ikoorus

7. "I was a fanatic for the history of the Ikoorian Dim Days. I loved the tales of the brave Insectoid fighters who quested across the dangerous poison marshes to seek the fabled Ivory Egg and conquer the dark and evil Sand Worms. The Worms practiced all sorts of evil rituals and sacrifices. That is, until I learned the truth. The Insectoid fighters were actually a violent class of illiterate buffoons who pillaged and raped from town to town, spreading whatever social disease they'd picked up the previous evening. The purpose of their invasions was to do the handiwork of the Insectoid magicians, who'd usurped power from the freely elected governing body. They gathered armies, which was against every constitutional law, to conquer and convert the Sand Worm folk."

"Convert them to what?" Yin, despite being hungry, was most attentive. Violet, less impressed with the lore, was cleaning her firearm.

"The Sand Worm folk's source of divine inspiration had nothing to do with devils and demons. It was based on a constellation that looked like a butterfly. That was the symbol of transcendence for the Sand Worms. Unfortunately, the Insectoids called this same constellation the 'Horrid-Winged Black Death' and insisted it represented a poisonous moth. The Sand Worms, admittedly thickheaded, were more advanced than the Insectoids, especially in the sciences and architecture—they just wanted to be left alone."

Poe needed to know more. "So, why did the Insectoid people feel the need to convert the Sand Worms if it was all simply a difference of interpretation of an abstract arrangement of celestial bodies?"

"I'm not really sure. A mental disease in desperate need of a cure, I guess. The wars raged for centuries, killing millions and spitting directly in the face of whatever divine entity they were hoping to impress."

Poe 33 stroked his chin and came to a sad conclusion. "It seems the romantic view of chivalrous violence crosses all ages and worlds. It's both the manna and the bane of gorks, geeks and many political systems galaxy-wide."

"The galaxy can be a strange place," sighed Yin.

"It can. But it can also get its revenge." Caffrey smiled. "A five-kilometer-wide asteroid smashed into Ikoorus Seven and wiped out both the Insectoids and the Sand Worms. To this day, the constellation smiles down on the barren world."

There was a collective sigh, and for the next half-hour they stared quietly into the flames.

Poe 33 kept watch as the party drifted off each into their own thoughts, his blue skin shimmering in the firelight. Caffrey stared into the flames, never quite getting past a quasi-hypnagogic state. He watched as the fiery leaves danced and swayed, sending dozens of thin, eel-like ribbons of flame flying off to the sky, where they dissipated into nothing. His expression flickered and flashed along with the blaze, and then for a long moment it was as if he were frozen. Finally, he jumped back to reality. He found Poe 33 staring at him quizzically. Apparently, so was Angie.

"Quark Caffrey?" asked Poe, hesitantly.

"Are you okay, my poor somnambulistic sweetheart?" Angie crooned.

Caffrey, momentarily certain he had just been cussed at, shook his head groggily. "I must have drifted into a nightmare."

"No, you didn't," the Portsmith corrected. "I was monitoring your biological functions. Your consciousness left your body and entered a hyper-dimensional fold deep within the fire. It was quite creepy. I thought, for a moment, you were attempting some sort of quintessential suicide."

"I went back to an old dream. The color of the flames triggered it."

"Went back?" Angie asked.

"Do you mean remembered?" Poe attempted to bring clarity into the discussion.

"No. I went back to it. A dream I had as a kid. Hadn't thought about it until now. I was sitting in my kitchen spreading orange jam on toast."

The Portsmith shuddered. "Quark Caffrey, the visual is quite disturbing. Please go no further."

Caffrey rolled his eyes upward and continued.

"It was the exact same color as the flames. Then a bird—a black bird—landed on the windowsill and began talking to me. Said 'Only wise birds sing.'"

"So, if he spoke this message rather than singing it—was it wisdom, dear butterfly?" asked Angie.

"I don't know—but I remember looking down at the toast and seeing my reflection in the sheen of the marmalade. I looked out the window and the entire sky was like orange jam. The bird flew off and melted like blood-red wax. All that was left on the sill was a blue egg."

"What shade of blue?" Poe asked.

"The same blue as you, Poe, my boy."

"'Every dream is a wish.' Isn't that an old Earth theory?" queried Angie.

"Every dream is a peek," answered Caffrey.

"Into what?"

"Into the All."

"You sound like my Master, Quark Caffrey. But what have you seen in your voyeuristic peep show on the Cosmos?"

"The egg—the container of life. The blue—a certain troubled android. The blood-red wax. The answer."

"I am becoming confused, Quark Caffrey. You make a string of metaphoric associations..."

"Poe, I know I've been nothing but a source of depression and frustration for you. I made you dress like a snake, and almost implode by magnetic force. Got you dropped from a few hundred feet into a mud bog. I offered you as a gift to one of the most horrid beings in the galaxy. I ate your bloody Master, for God's sakes!"

"Your intentions have been nothing but honorable, Quark Caffrey."

"But there was a reason. My blood."

"No, it was the bloodline," argued Poe 33.

"No, Poe. It was the *blood*. My blood can act as the link to the L'Orange."

"Perhaps it is a flaw in my design, but my programming recommends no possible replacement for the lost Essence of the Wise One. The L'Orange is the purest and only known sample of the wise cosmic star stuff. Everything else is simply not butter."

Caffrey smiled, but ignored the old Earth reference, wondering privately just how much this android had seen and heard in his days.

"Unless I am a One Human—like His Him's corgishma. Wouldn't that make the difference?"

Poe 33 stood up, and slowly, a smile formed on his face. "Maybe. Maybe, indeed."

Poe's back was illuminated as Yin and Violet watched the experiment. The Portsmith released the catch on his rear panel; and with a soft hum, a tiny cylinder emerged.

"That, Quark Caffrey, is a back-up vial where the sample of my master is to be placed."

"May I remove it?"

"Yes."

Carefully, as if handling a tube of ancient, thirteenth-dynasty Uplikin crystal, Caffrey took the diamond cylinder and held it up to the moonlight.

"Now, any volunteers to draw my blood?" he inquired, his attention turning immediately to Violet.

She approached with a drawn knife, smiling sweetly.

"A drop. No extremities."

Violet took his hand in hers and, with a mischievous grin, pricked the tip of his thumb, squeezing a perfect sphere of crimson liquid to the surface. The blood was let to drip into the special container, which was returned to the slot in the android's back. It was drawn in his body with a hum and a beeping confirmation.

"There. How does that feel?"

A shimmy of lights ran up Poe 33's body. "Hard to say exactly, Quark Caffrey. I sort of feel like the soft ice cream from the *Moby Dick*'s dessert spigot. Only warmer. Fuzzier." With that, Poe 33 vanished in a twinkling of glittering confetti.

"Holy beans!" gasped Yin.

They stood and stared at the spot where Poe 33 had been for a solid minute without speaking or batting an eyelash. Then they exchanged gazes, but no one offered an explanation. The empty spot where the Portsmith had been became the focus of attention for another five long minutes. Everyone began to feel somewhat foolish.

"Caffrey?" Yin finally asked, cracking the silence.

"Yes, Yin?"

"Did you make Poe Thirty-three vanish with your mind?"

"Negative, pooch. But my blood may have done it. Poe may be back with the L'Orange."

"You would think he'd tell us," insisted Angie.

"How are we supposed to know?" asked Yin.

"Beats the cosmic shit out of me," replied Angie, in a most uncharacteristically scatological response.

She scoured the area electronically while Yin applied his nose in biological detection methods. Caffrey sat cross-legged and tried in vain to reach the L'Orange. Violet put her woman's intuition into overdrive. Their combined efforts produced nothing. Nada. Zilch.

They could do little more in the pitch-black of night; and as concerned as they were, they knew it best to wait until morning before trying anything else. Sleep was a welcome escape as they fought the fears and concerns haunting their minds.

"Caffrey?"

A soft voice slipped into his dream. He mumbled incoherently and fought any attempts to awaken. Angie tried again.

"Quarkie, wake up."

"Two more hours," Caffrey said amidst the drool that dribbled down his chin.

"Caffrey, up! I discovered something strange."

Reluctantly, he opened his eyes.

"Strange? I don't know if I could identify 'strange' anymore."

"Quark, love, this is strange in a good way. Real trees. I have discovered real trees."

His interest piqued just a bit, he sat up.

"And?"

"And...they wind in a spiraling avenue through this forest of fakery. I calculated the angles and noticed a definite Fibonacci trend in the path. Come look."

Caffrey stood—or, to put it more accurately, floated—up. Like a leaf caught in a sudden updraft, he felt himself rise up along with the smoke of the fire.

"Ahh...Angie...something strange is going on..."

CHAPTER 19
Hidden Treasure

(Traffic)

Beneath Caffrey, lying beside the fire, was his body, along with the still figures of his sleeping mates. All grew suddenly brighter as the entire forest, every trunk of every tree, became illuminated not by some external light but apparently by a sudden improvement of Caffrey's vision. The forest began descending, and for a moment he thought he was rising still further into the sky. However, all of the artificial trees were telescoping into the ground—every tree but for a double row of thick, dark trunks held firmly in place by their roots.

A spiraling path awaited him through the avenue of the living trees. Willing himself forward, he flew on the wings of his consciousness above the path. His vision blurred around the peripheral, as if someone had smeared Vaseline onto the outer edges of his eyeballs. He was floating through a tube and found himself following a spinning golden star.

"Angie? Do you see that?"

There was no reply from the Revenant; but the question, escaped from his mind, remained poised in the air like a billboard. In fact, all of his thoughts, memories and fantasies seemed to be sprayed about like graffiti—physical graffiti, covering the walls of the tube with images that morphed into lattices of gold and liquid gems that could have only been created directly from the mind of some psychedelic god.

The images around him began to spin like one of those dizzying amusement park rides he had vomited on as a child. He closed his eyes to discover his lids had become glass. Something told him to launch himself into the star. He did.

All flashed teal and gold.

Caffrey opened his eyes and smelled sweet grass. He looked around; and as his vision came into focus, he was able to read the large sign on the wall of the small stone church. The message was carved in the tongue of the ancients: *Somo Lagra Metho Chofos*.

He stood and felt the wetness from the dew that had soaked his clothing. He tried to understand the words, and somehow his mind's eye manipulated them dizzily. Suddenly, they were still again, but changed so that they made sense to him: The Place of the Method of Music.

The Chapel of Bombadillo sat within a circle of tall, majestic lavender pines. The night sky swirled like oil and water, and the breeze caressed his face like light-blue felt. A blackbird floated down from the treetop, landed on a tree stump and looked Caffrey straight in the eyes. It began singing in a clear and pleasant voice as a pair of minuscule troubadours danced out of the darkness and strummed tiny guitars.

Blackbird singing in the dead of night.

Caffrey smiled softly as he touched the tip of the bird's extended wing. The bird morphed onto the chapel door, where it became a knocker carved of wood. He tapped three times. The door opened, and he entered.

He discovered the chapel's interior was nothing but four walls, its ceiling the night sky. A large boulder sat centered in the space, and from it protruded an object. Caffrey's smile broadened into a grin as he recognized it; he approached the stone like some crazed supplicant approaching an altar. He studied the shape of the object of his desire.

Its body, cherry-red and feminine in form, was half-exposed, its long neck extended towards him like the waiting hand of a temptress. Across the very end of its neck were scripted six letters forming one of Caffrey's favorite words in all of the infinite languages of the Cosmos: FENDER.

He grasped the instrument, locked within the boulder's stony grip, and gave it a firm pull. Expecting an exercise in futility, he was delighted when the Stratocaster separated from the stone like a wooden stick from a melting ice cream pop. He gazed into the shining surface of the white pick guard, desperately trying to identify the countenance looking back at him.

A voice seemed to tap him on the shoulder. He turned, to find Greppledick standing behind him.

"Caffrey."

"Uncle?"

"No."

"No?"

Greppledick ignored the implied question. "Come with me to the Jumping Joey."

"The Jumping Joey?"

The man who looked like Greppledick nodded, and the world dissolved like a watercolor painting in the rain.

A wooden sign, swaying in the gathering wind, laughed at Caffrey's expense, getting quite a kick out of his situation. He stared at the words on the sign as if they were ancient, unknown runes. The Jumping Joey Pub. Simple enough, and illustrated with the image of a colorful baby kangaroo leaping over a wooden fence. But there Caffrey stood, getting wetter and wetter in a soft rain while he tried to make sense of where he was.

The festive sound of simple percussion instruments, flutes and lyres mixed with the clinking of large pewter ale steins and was carried from the interior in the helping hands of laughter and singing. It was all rather stereotypical and would have been at home in a town named Dragonshire, Hobbitton or Bree.

"Do you plan on standing in the rain until you melt?" asked the Greppledick look-alike, peering out from behind the thick wooden door.

Caffrey shook his head and entered the pub, the cherry-red Fender strapped across his back like a broadsword. The warmth of the blazing hearth and the stale scent of beer embraced him like a warm hug. The Greppledick-ish person led him through the indifferent crowd and sat him at a corner table. Two large steins shaped like dragon's heads were placed before them by a round, rosy-faced woman. Caffrey glanced around the room. Every face, every reflected piece of firelight—everything—swirled and failed to focus.

"This place is giving me a headache."

"The ache you feel is the mud draining."

"Is this another head trip? Am I actually asleep by the fire?"

"No."

"Is this some lucid dream, then?"

"You are very close to Nefarious. And even closer to the Wise One."

"Where's Angie?"

"Here."

"How about my friends?"

Pseudo-Greppledick smiled and leaned across the table. "You are closer to everything. Especially to yourself."

"This is all getting pretty heavy."

Caffrey laid the Fender across the table and gazed into its sheen. His face stared back. A woman's reflection appeared behind his, and Caffrey turned to face a pretty blond maiden dressed in blue silken robes.

"Is that gold?" she asked.

"What?"

"That. What about that? Is that gold? Yes. I'm sure it is."

Her body remained calm, but her eyes were frantically darting about. "How about that? Or that? Or that? They all glitter! They must be gold!"

She was certainly insane.

"Play it," suggested Angie's voice, startling him.

"Play what?"

"The song."

"I don't have an amp." Caffrey's reply was surprisingly pragmatic.

"You won't need one."

His vision warped again, and he rubbed his palms on his forehead. The Greppledick man blurred away; and in his place sat Poe 33, smiling wide and warm.

"Take the stairway to heaven, Quark Caffrey. The L'Orange has showed how you. Tap into Its power. Its wisdom."

Caffrey stroked the guitar, and Poe 33 nodded and whispered, "Dear lady, can you hear the wind blow? And did you know, your stairway lies on the whispering wind?"

Caffrey rose and walked to a small wooden stage. Setting his fingers on the strings, he began to play. The opening notes of "Stairway to Heaven" silenced the crowd. Somehow, though the solid-bodied instrument wasn't plugged in, crisp and amplified music emerged, clean and rich.

The crowd moved in around Caffrey, and his world darkened until he felt he was standing in a pitch-black closet. An ebony oval case appeared, its surface holding billions of tiny stars deep within its sheen. A glow poured forth from the perfect cube of orange gelatin within. Caffrey continued the song, staring at the hallucination before him.

"Dear lady, can you hear the wind blow? And did you know, your stairway lies on the whispering wind..."

There were quite a few guitar solos lauded in song and tale throughout the galaxy. Caffrey himself had his favorites, and had performed most of them during his years with Marmalade Skies—the works of Pink Floyd, Stevie Ray Vaughn, Rolling Stones, Lynard Skynard and, of course, one James Marshall Hendrix. Yet, of all the musical breaks made famous from the annals of Rock & Roll, there was one that had taken on a religious significance. And though it had not the speed of a Van Halen solo, or the unique complexity of Hendrix, it was the one that felt more like a continuation of the lyrics than any other.

The guitar spoke. It continued the tale of the Lady who was sure all that glittered was gold, in its own language of beautiful notes. Caffrey had always felt his soul take flight while listening to Jimmy Page play the famed piece. Unlike every other aspiring guitar player or teen who received a cheap electric for Christmas, he'd never once attempted to play it himself.

It may have very well been Caffrey Quark who first noted that, should you ever need to hear a bad version of "Stairway," take a stroll into any music store or teenager's bedroom. It had become a sub-cult of a vastly spread religion. Caffrey vowed a heart of purity—for him it was no different than expecting his feet to have aquaplaning abilities after speaking his own rendition of the Sermon on the Mount. Just as a priest reading the Gospels, a rabbi reciting from the Torah, an Islamic imam speaking from the Qu'ran or a Buddhist monk chanting "Om" are the icons of their respective religions, the electric six-string vibrating with these perfect frequencies was the sound of Rock's very soul.

Yet there he stood, his fingers traveling the frets like an adventuring pilgrim on virgin roads and every note—every interval—every chord—sounding not with just perfect clarity but sounding as it should. He felt his body lift. Melt. He rose above the surrounding forest world. Up above the Forest of Medieval Stereotypes. He saw the tiny flickering lights of Heddington. He rose up past the moon, the stars and the edges of eternity. He felt the anger of Nefarious, helpless to stop him from his ascent into the entity's dimension. Up he rose on the solo. He had become music. He'd literally entered the fabric of space-time. It was under his control. He understood for the first time that it really was all vibration. All energy. All music. He felt a powerful wisdom at his disposal. Unlike his past experiences with the L'Orange, where he was spoken to like teacher to student, Caffrey Quark felt one with it all.

A face appeared before him. She was perfect love yet had no discernible features. She smiled. Caffrey smiled back, and they embraced in a limitless dance amidst the infinite music. The dance seemed to last forever—yet at the same time was over before it began. He felt for the first time that the I of his being had no value. No meaning. His ego had been purged in purifying musical flames and washed away by waves of pure love.

But there was a hideous laugh. A feeling was leaking in. That distant anger was growing stronger, along with a sudden sense this would be a fleeting moment of bliss. The I of his being was returning; and, like a gray worm, he tasted fear, uncertainty and self-importance sprouting in his heart.

They streaked through a tunnel of endless color and finally came to rest in a place of infinite reflection. A chrome room. Seamless, it was impossible to discern ceiling from floor, wall from wall. He stood a moment, certain he would see his own reflection.

Yet he never did.

CHAPTER 20
Another Morning

(Moody Blues)

Where are we, my inter-dimensional love?"

"Right now, Angie, I'm not even sure *what* we are. How long have we been walking?"

"I believe we entered into this place a half-hour ago. My temporal records are in a bit of a mish-mash."

"Feels like we haven't moved an inch."

Caffrey took deliberate steps across the field of pure reflection. Far off, across the sea of nothing, there appeared what looked like a black rectangle. A vibration of cold tingled his stomach.

"I think we are being watched."

"Of course, you are," scythed the ever-changing voice of Nefarious Wretch. "And when you pass through the door ahead you will bear witness to my power and realize how futile any attempt you can make to stop me is. Makes no difference who you are or how powerful your master is. For soon you will all be part of the Galaxy of I, Nefarious Wretch!"

"Cornball," muttered Angie.

"And you, my disembodied nightingale! You shall speak with the lyrical qualities of a black-eared kopek!"

"Ignore him," advised Caffrey.

"Ignore me?" questioned Nefarious, amused. A dark cloud materialized before them. It had an oily texture and reeked of vitriolic sludge. A face, apparently designed to disturb, formed within the shapeless mass. Angie and Caffrey screamed in unison, unable to hold back the horror the hideous countenance elicited.

They took off at full speed across the silvery plain. Caffrey, who hadn't, prior to his experience with Queen Kinkskin, screamed since the age of six, blushed with embarrassment, steeled himself and resolutely turned to the face in an attempt to redeem his manliness. To his utter disgust he screamed again.

They made it to the black door. It, too, was featureless, and painted such a deep black it teased the eyes into believing it was a window on some starless cosmos. There was no doorknob; and when Caffrey gave it a push, it squealed open. The pair peered in.

"My," they gasped—to the great irritation of Nefarious, in perfect unison. "It's full of planets!"

Full of planets, indeed. Each astronomical sphere was shrunk to the size of an average beach ball. Thousands of worlds floated as if in a mini-universe, each silently rotating, each illuminated with a varying degree of brightness by some unseen source. Thankfully, the horrid countenance was gone.

"All the worlds, my stage!" Nefarious's formless voice chuckled at his wordplay. "Each extracted from its place in the galaxy to await its reintroduction into my re-creation of music-free existence. My universe will resonate with the frequency of my device. Listen..."

A devastatingly horrible noise filled the room, and Caffrey threw his hands over his ears. It did no good. The clamor was pure vulgar intrusion. It offended not just the aural organ but all of his senses. It smelled like brimstone and the rotted, diseased corpses of bodybuilders with really bad BO. Its taste was that of a toasted rodent stomach after the bugger had eaten its own feces and the organ had been ripped out and left to sit amidst urinating wagdragons for three eons and a day. It looked as horrid as a mutated orangophant in a meat grinder on a bad-hair day. It felt like aged hand cream that had solidified into a slimy, granule-infused paste.

And its sound was far, far worse than any other of its aspects. It was anti-music in its purest form.

The tumult ceased, and Nefarious laughed.

"That is a mere sample."

"You must have been screwed by a record company," Caffrey concluded.

"My motivations are not your concern."

Caffrey rubbed his ears and wished he could shower. As he strolled through the mini planetary system, additional worlds sprang into existence as they were stolen from around the Milky Way. Nefarious's horrid laughter bounded about the room as Caffrey studied a purplish-red planet ringed with beautiful concentric bands of ice.

"I've been on this world."

"Is this where you bagged that flock of green-winged bobaska terps?" suggested Angie.

"No, that was on the ringed world of Gaja. But I have memories of this place. Maybe not my memories exactly..." He glanced across to a yellow, cloudy planet. "And that planet, too. I'm sure I was there."

The laughter was fading.

Angie tried again. "The swamp! Where you were nearly eaten whole by the hairy-chinned tepa tepa?"

"No. Something...else. I recall a palace. A battlefield...and this place..." Caffrey strolled across to a brown world. "This is Ryno Four. The desert world ruled by the kind but powerful General Sei-nei. I was his guest."

The laughter from Nefarious Wretch had quite faded away, and Caffrey stood in silence amidst the balls of color. Were the residents even aware their worlds had been taken, shrunk and put in storage? Or were they simply going about their business with only a handful of dissenters, who were mocked as quacks, questioning the lack of stars in the night skies? Was apocalyptic chaos blowing like autumnal foliage across the worlds, the greatest eschatological minds gathered in candle-lit halls, perusing the ancient tomes for answers to their predicament?

Caffrey could ill-afford to waste time pondering that question—his own situation took precedence. And he was so confused.

"How did I get here?" he mumbled.

"Don't you remember the music?"

His face enlivened as fragments of memories elusively skittered past his consciousness.

"You were amazing. *We* were amazing," Angie reminisced.

"We?" Caffrey asked. "What do you mean, 'we?'"

Angie sounded like a blushing bride. "Somehow, our energy merged. We didn't just dance to the music, we danced *as* the music. We were..." She hesitated shyly. "...as one."

But the locks on Caffrey's memory were secured tight, the combination long forgotten. Details of his travels from the artificial For-

262

est of Medieval Stereotypes to the dimension of Nefarious Wretch were less then a blur.

"You stood playing in the center of the open-air Chapel of Bombadillo. Your music opened the portal into Nefarious's real dimension."

"His real dimension?"

"The physical one. It is tremendous, Caffrey. His base is huge. But as we danced and merged our energies, I sensed a terrible qualm. Nefarious despised our love and redirected our energy here. I was able to race to Yin and explain some of what I had seen. Then I hurried back. To you, love."

He nodded softly, and then in an instant his expression changed. "Do you hear that?"

"Hear what?"

Not bothering to explain, Caffrey rushed off through the planets, following some inner sense. Angie followed him to a glistening cylinder of light beyond the farthest world-in-miniature.

Caffrey looked down at the floor. The sensation of thick, plush carpet beneath his feet was unexpected. He faced a corridor of black-paneled walls, black lamps flickering black light in small pools atop the lush, shaggy black carpet.

"Can you hear it, Angie?"

"No."

"It's coming from beyond that door."

Angie hadn't noticed the little black door breaking the bland surface of the far wall. Caffrey stood motionless a moment and closed his eyes.

"Yes! Yes, Caffrey! Now I hear it!"

It was singing—a delicate castrato voice flowing like honey across the milk-white stomach of a nubile virgin. Caffrey ambled dreamily to the door, pressing his ear delicately against it.

"What a lovely voice," Angie whispered.

"Okay, Angie," Caffrey said. "I'd like you to explore the area and get an idea of its layout."

"What about you?"

"I'll check out the source of the singing. You play spy."

"Aye, aye, my stirred-but-not-shaken martini muffin."

Angie drifted off, and Caffrey gently turned the knob and pushed open the door. It took a while for his three-dimensional brain to adjust to the room's configuration. Its design, it appeared, was by a being who combined the artistic sensibilities of Vincent

263

Van Gogh, Salvador Dali and Norman Rockwell. It was a beautiful bedroom that would be the envy of any child with the intellectual capacity to understand the multi-dimensional layout.

Tilting his head, Caffrey was able to discern two forms silhouetted before the large hyper-sphere window. The taller figure sat on the edge of the bed, his posture perfect as he listened to the shorter figure, a small boy—and the source of the singing. Caffrey maneuvered his way on the strange, perpendicular floor, his body at a forty-five degree angle as he approached the duo. As he drew closer, his eyes adjusted to the bright light. The seated figure turned and faced him. A reflection of blue-and-orange light flew to Caffrey's eyes.

"Hello, Quark Caffrey."

"Poe?"

The small boy stopped singing.

"Please continue, son," Poe 33 requested. "You must practice to remain perfect."

The boy, a blond-haired, cherub-faced child with alabaster skin and disturbingly perfect but completely natural circles of rose on his cheeks, continued his song from where he'd left off. Caffrey stood motionless, watching the boy form each mystical word with tonal perfection.

"*Treo le humana sey. Too ju que re ton ah di,*" sang the boy.

Poe 33 turned to Caffrey and smiled as the lad continued.

"Poe, is this..."

Poe 33 raised a shushing finger to his mouth, and Caffrey accommodated the request.

"*Tree lee bee da fa ga poo my ay!*"

The boy closed his mouth as if it were mechanically hinged, bowed to the android then turned on a dime and offered the same courtesy to Caffrey.

"Very good, child," assessed Poe. "Why don't you go play with your genetics construction set and see if you can perfect the opera-bellied sapsucker we started?"

"Yes, Master Poe." The boy wandered off across the bizarre room to a stack of hyper-cube toy boxes.

"Charming young shaver, don't you think?"

Caffrey was almost speechless.

"Nice to see you, Quark Caffrey. You look well."

Caffrey took a deep breath.

"What happened to you?"

Poe 33 smiled. "I felt a sudden rush of warmth, dare I say, of love, when the bio-electromagnetic matrix of your blood merged with that of my being. I felt an odd but nonetheless euphoric sensation. An orgasm of sound. What was so peculiar was the sound was not restricted to my ears. Nor any individual sense nor combination thereof. I had become this sound. I had become music and was humbled by my own presence. Then the music was silenced, and I found myself standing before a scurrilous being. Nefarious Wretch. I have been here for three weeks."

"Three weeks?" Caffrey's head was really beginning to throb.

Poe smiled his famous Mona Lisa smile and stood up. "Follow me."

He walked towards the small boy, and Caffrey followed. The child was seated at a table, his nose resting on its top. He was lost in thought, studying the various flasks, bottles and Petri dishes scattered about, occasionally observing a partridge-sized bird tweeting away on its perch in a gilded cage. The boy lifted a miniature bellows and blew a sizzling strand of red powder onto the bird's neck. Instantly, its chest swelled like a braggart, and its mouth opened.

"*Ohhhh! Felisi tra! Goo myo la fa!*" the bird sang.

"I did it!" The boy jumped up and down and clapped his hands.

"Very good, lad." Poe 33 nodded.

"You are the grandest toy in the universe, Master Poe!"

"Toy?" Caffrey could only wonder.

"The boy's father stipulated that if I were to set foot in his dimension I would have to spend the rest of my days as a plaything for his child. It was either that or eternity in the Power Station of Infinite Annoyance."

"The what?"

"It is the huge power station that keeps this world stable. It runs off the energy produced by the annoyance of the prisoners."

"Annoyance?"

"Too many questions, Quark Caffrey."

Caffrey shook his head and watched as the boy gently stroked the head of the bird.

"Poe," he whispered, "is he the son of Nefarious Wretch?"

Poe 33 turned and replied with the voice of experience. "The universe is not only stranger than you can imagine, it secretly dresses in studded leather feety pajamas and spiked purple pasties."

"Yeah. So I've heard."

"I suggest you talk to the boy," Poe 33 whispered.

Caffrey was in no mood for pleasantries. He accosted the young boy with a stern expression. "Hey, kid, have you been using my friends as playthings?"

The boy shivered, tears filling his eyes.

"Quark Caffrey! Easy. He is a very sensitive boy."

Caffrey softened his glare. "Did you receive a special gift for Labates Day?" he asked brightly.

"Labates Day?" quavered the boy, confused.

"Yes! To celebrate your entry into the realm of music-free existence."

"But I love music!"

Caffrey was nonplussed. "Hasn't your father taught you to despise it? To be his heir to a galaxy of disharmony?"

The boy's chin dropped to his chest, and a stream of tears fell to the tabletop like strings of diamonds. "My father hasn't paid me any mind since my mother passed on."

Not wanting to appear too coldhearted—he could have decapitated the boy for fun—Caffrey further softened his stance. "What's your name?"

"Name?" the boy repeated, eyes wide and innocent.

"What do they call you?" Caffrey was gritting his teeth, forcing a smile.

"Who? What does who call me? There's no one here. At least not until Master Poe arrived."

Caffrey imagined launching the child through the window. And, although the idea put a smile on his face, he resisted.

"What does Master Poe call you?"

"He calls me 'son.'"

Caffrey rolled his eyes. "Does your father have my friends?"

"I don't know. I'm alone."

"Where is he?"

"He's out there. In the solid place."

"The solid place?"

"That's where I was born. I haven't played there in a long time. I only play here. I romp around here. A ghost in my father's mind."

"While I am not certain," Poe 33 said, "I believe we have entered into the very mind of Nefarious Wretch."

"What a vulgar thought."

"Perhaps. But I am almost certain."

"How could our physical bodies be in a non-physical universe?"

266

"Our physical bodies are not. You are physically lying uncon-scious with Yin and Violet in the Forest of Medieval Stereotypes. My body is locked away in the immense station of Nefarious Wretch. I separated my programming and became a trans-dimensional Revenant, much like Angie—whose physical Revenant sphere is also in the solid world."

"Why did you just vanish?"

"I was snatched by Nefarious. He fears your blood."

"My blood? Why?"

"You are full of questions, Quark Caffrey."

"If we're in his mind, then he knows our every move."

"Are you aware of every synaptic firing of your unconscious? Your daydreams? Repressed memories and fears? Secret desires? The mind is a very complicated place, with many places to hide."

Caffrey's expression changed as more memories poured into his head. He closed his eyes and slapped his hands on his skull as it filled like a tankard left under a pouring tap.

"Are you okay, sir?" asked the boy, placing his small, soft hand on Caffrey's lower back.

Caffrey shot a glance at the child and fire filled his eyes. He lunged like a coiled spring and snatched the kid by the upper arms, lifting him up to a face-to-face height.

"Where are my friends, you little Satanic pastry!"

"Quark!" Poe 33 warned.

Caffrey shook the child. "Where are they?"

The child's face grew red as he desperately tried to form words. Finally, his Christmas-bow lips parted. "My father took them from me!"

Caffrey dropped the child to his feet and stormed off, out the door.

Poe 33 shouted after him. "Quark! Quark Caffrey, wait!"

Caffrey soon discovered that the hallway emerging from the child's room was the final leg of a large and complicated labyrinth. He faced dead end after dead end, bad turn after bad turn. Then his earlobe tingled.

"Angie?"

"It's me, my love maze mouse."

"This is all Nefarious's mind."

"I know. I have to show you something."

Caffrey stood thoughtfully a moment then began to move off. "I know the way out."

"The answer is not outside this maze," Angie informed him. "It lies at its heart. Follow my directions." She led the way, calling out right or left as required. It was a matter of ten minutes before they passed the final leg, stopping before a rose-colored drapery.

"Go through the curtains, Caffrey."

He stepped through the red material and into the center square of the labyrinth. He'd grown so accustomed to the dark, purplish-black light that the wash of soft pink glow striking his eyes felt almost accosting. As his vision settled, he studied the square room, no larger than his closet back home. Lying on the floor was a broken wooden frame, and in the frame was a faded photo.

"Look at the photograph, Caffrey."

It was a picture of a humanoid woman. She was rather homely, with frizzled mousy-brown hair, a bumpy, somewhat large nose and thin, dried lips. Her eyes were terribly crossed, and she wore a baggy, unflattering dress of some coarse and uncomfortable-looking material. Yet she had a curiously pretty smile, and her eyes sparkled with a secret fire.

"She must have been the apple of Nefarious's eye," commented Angie softly. "I think she is rather pretty."

Caffrey wasn't impressed. "It's a single photo in a cheap frame on the floor of a tiny room. Can't be too important as far as memories go."

"I still think she's his love."

"You're the eternal romantic, Angie. She's probably some long-forgotten fling."

"She was actually a Reylinkus conductor. See the emblem on her lapel? Only the finest composers are allowed the honor of leading the thousand-piece orchestras. Quite often the symphonies performed will last decades—in some cases the length of the life of the conductor."

"Nefarious Wretch fell in love with a musician?" Caffrey shook his head.

"This is the deeply repressed center of the maze of Nefarious's mind. It has to be important."

Nefarious laughed, and the sound washed into the room like water from an overflowing toilet bowl. "Nefarious Wretch loves nothing but his own creation. A grand stroke of horrid artistry that will forever make its mark on creation!"

"Who writes this guy's dialogue?" Caffrey whispered.

Angie threw the fiend's arrogance back into his face. "You can't fool me, Nefarious. I know true love when I see it."

Nefarious laughed again, the evil guffaws cheapened by a slightly nervous twitter.

"Worry not about my loves or lack thereof," he suggested, relishing each word as it fell from his lips. "Be more concerned with that music-drenched world you fell so deeply in love with, Caffrey Quark. It has been added to my collection!"

Caffrey's eyes widened, and he dashed from the room.

Thousands had gathered under the golden glow of the sun as it slowly dipped towards the jagged horizon. Their shadows lengthened by the second as the first stars began to appear in the sky and campfires were set. All of the seven divisions were present, with row upon row of their musical note-shaped Mid C-Winged fighter craft lined up and awaiting the order to penetrate the foul airspace of Nefarious Wretch.

Yin and Violet stood upon a makeshift platform, together with the seven OTHER Division Commanders. Yin lifted a megaphone to his poochie lips and addressed the flyers. His voice boomed across the fields.

"Valiant members of OTHER," began the small but highly-decorated Bopple, "we find ourselves in a quandary. A quandary that is a challenge but not a roadblock! We are certain that the Portsmith, Angie and Caffrey Trinesmart Quark II have entered the dimension of Nefarious Wretch—although the body of the human lies sleeping in a tent mere feet away from where I am standing."

A pup tent was set up just off the platform. The unmistakable sound of heavy snoring drifted through the closed flaps.

"We have gathered, through the brave and timely intelligence of our Revenant compadre, that Nefarious Wretch is using his tremendous resources to create a projection of his mind. It is in this illusory yet very real realm that he has placed the extracted worlds. We are awaiting word as to the exact location of the physical power station. We have devised a plan to assure our entry into the dimension of Nefarious. It involves great danger and risk. But we spit in the crossed eyes of danger!" Yin was really getting into it.

Cheers.

"We shall defeat Nefarious!" Yin stood on his hind legs and waved a zealous paw.

More cheers.

"We will not allow him to take our freedom!" Yin raised both paws high.

"Easy, boy," Violet whispered.

Yin composed himself and continued. "The plan will take the combined efforts of everyone gathered here. Perhaps it may fail—prove futile." Then his voice burst out over the assembly. "But it will boil the blood of Nefarious! And if successful, it will ensure the entry of the entire OTHER Forces and the end of Nefarious forever!"

The flyers stood tall and applauded with every cell of their bodies. Yin plopped down on his haunches, his fur puffed with excitement. Violet and the rest of the commanders took turns patting his head.

Caffrey raced back through the maze, trying to remember the sequence of rights and lefts. Finding himself lost, he slapped his hand on the wall and cursed aloud. He felt the electrostatic tickle of Angie's presence.

"There is no way into the Hall of Planets from this side. At least not for three-D entities such as ourselves."

Caffrey exhaled hard; then his eyes flashed. "That brat!"

"What about him?"

"Help me get back to the hallway outside his room."

Angie went ahead, calculating the easiest path and returning moments later. Shouting out directions, she led him to the darkly lit hallway outside the bedroom of the son of Nefarious Wretch. Forgoing the courtesy of knocking, Caffrey barged in and found himself facing Poe 33.

"Quark?"

"Hi, Poe," Angie greeted.

"Why, hello, my lovely Revenant. It does seem like decades since I have been graced by your songbird vocals."

"Why, thank you!" Angie almost blushed.

Caffrey threw back his head impatiently. "Poe, I need the kid to help me back into the Hall of Planets."

The android nodded, anticipating his concerns. "Please come with me."

Poe 33 turned and led Caffrey through some odd twists and previously invisible segments of the multi-dimensional room. They emerged in a hidden corner, where the boy sat cross-legged on the floor playing with a miniature black hole spinning in a case of protective magnetic shielding.

"Will you show him your new toy, son?" Poe 33 asked of the boy.

The lad stood and lifted a transparent container from the depths of a hyper-cube toy box. Within the box a milk-and-blueberry cream sphere slowly rotated in its axis.

"Toy?" Caffrey spat angrily.

"He thinks everything is a toy," explained Poe 33.

"This appeared moments ago in the big room with the colored balls," explained the boy softly.

He held out the box for Caffrey, who took it in his arms. There it was, his home planet. In a galaxy of unspeakable evil and undeniable beauty, this was a world, his world, containing the total spectrum. He had his whole world in his hands.

"I feel like a gospel music lyric," Caffrey muttered. He looked at the boy. "Do you know how to get out of this place?"

"This place spreads far, wide, deep and dark," the child answered, using an unsettling combination of words for one so young. "And rather strange, too. In order to get out, one must position oneself to the forefront of my father's thoughts and then hope for a lapse of concentration on his part wherein an anomalous portal may open."

"Can you show me how?"

"Perchance later," answered the boy enigmatically, letting a blob of spittle fall from his mouth into the spinning black hole.

The saliva ball sparkled and dissolved into its atomic structure as it wound down and around into the tiny singularity. Caffrey closed his eyes and shivered.

"Isn't that interesting?" the boy said, allowing spittle to fall again. "Would you like to drip a lugie into my cosmic whirlpool?"

"This kid creeps me out," Caffrey whispered.

"He shouldn't," Poe 33 whispered back. "I haven't figured him out completely, but he is an ambi-dimensional, trans-frequency being. He is a memory, of sorts, but one with such far-reaching connections it's as if he can crumble or recreate the very fabric of this dimensional sphere."

"Young man," Angie coaxed, "we really need to get out. We need to get to the solid place and help some people who are in trouble."

The boy ignored her and studied Caffrey a moment. "Are you a musician, sir?"

"Yes."

"Would you like to see my grand collection of musical instruments?"

If the offer had been to pummel the boy with a tuba, Caffrey might have jumped at the chance; yet as he locked eyes with him, he found himself agreeing to the offer. There was a sparkling fire in the boy's eyes that froze his marrow. Caffrey nodded.

"Come on, then!"

⸺

"I have to keep it locked," the boy explained as he slipped his hand into the material of the solid steel door.

A click sounded from within and the door opened silently. Caffrey watched as the boy's hand emerged from the body of the door as though he were a ghost. The two entered the narrow but very long room, lined from ceiling to floor with musical instruments ranging from the simple to the exotic. The boy immediately picked up a spiraling instrument that looked as if it were formed from liquid.

"This is amongst my favorite string instruments. It once belonged to Sepilon Soy."

Caffrey studied the reddish-brown surface and plucked one of the twenty-four crystal strings. "I met Sepilon Soy."

"Really?"

"Yes. He played at a wedding I attended." Caffrey recaptured the memory.

The child's eyes drifted away to the rows of instruments. "They are the memories of my father. He was surrounded by much music when my mother was alive. I found these scattered about his mind and stored them away, before they vanished with all the memories of her he wants to forget."

"Can you play all of these?"

"No—but they can all play me."

"Why does your father allow it?"

"My father used to love music. When my mother died he thought the galaxy sounded awful. So, he started thinking of ways to redo it. Without music. He believed no one could write music like she did."

Caffrey studied the boy with a deepening curiosity. "What are you?"

"I was an idea they had. They would sit out on the porch and imagine a child they would want to have if they had their druthers. So, my mother wrote a symphony about the lad. It was called *The Creamery Child*. My mother conducted it for the first time at the Grand Hall of the Truffledites. It was a great hit. My father was seated in the front row beside the Premiere Truffledite and her husband. They were so impressed by the music they used their influence in the elite musical circles to get her on the list to conduct the grand Reylinkus Orchestra. She did."

"And?"

"Do you know anything about Reylinkus Orchestras?" the boy asked, fixing Caffrey with a pompous gaze.

"Yeah. They last as long as the conductor does."

"Worse than that. Once you begin you can only stop if you die. If you stop without death you are killed. That part kind of slipped their minds."

"She stopped?"

The boy nodded. "My presence in his mind is the source of much pain."

Caffrey turned and left.

Poe 33 sat quietly atop a hyper-cube toy box, studying the Earth. Caffrey stepped up behind him, followed by The Creamery Child.

"The kid is a song."

"Is he?" Poe 33 seemed surprised.

"He's a composition written by Nefarious's wife before she died. *The Creamery Child*."

"So, this child is linked to millions of memories," Poe 33 deduced, eyeing The Creamery Child as he rummaged in one of the boxes.

"The proverbial song you can't get out of your head."

"No wonder Nefarious fears your blood."

"What do you mean?" Caffrey couldn't see the connection. The Creamery Child, bored by the exchange, wandered off down a corridor.

Poe began to explain. "He snatched me when you put your blood into my system. He feared my power, my virility with your blood. You have a pure heart."

Caffrey almost gagged.

"You do, Quark Caffrey! You care. You love. You are selfless. Passionate—especially about music. Music is what he wants to forget.

273

Yours are qualities reminding Nefarious he once was a living, breathing being. A being who also loved music. You can completely destabilize this mental sanctuary he has constructed."

"We need the kid to show us how to get to the forefront of Nefarious's mind."

"I'll get him," volunteered Angie.

CHAPTER 21
Karn Evil 9

(Emerson, Lake & Palmer)

Yin watched as the light of morning trudged across the world. He filled his lungs with the crisp fresh air, peed with the wind and watched the sunlight illuminate a large boulder sitting before him.

It was covered with writing, dusty words written in block print with the burnt tip of twig. The words were neatly presented in stanzas on the face of the large gray stone.

Yin had worked all night on his song; and he reread the lyrics with a coy smirk, twisting his whiskers from time to time with his forepaw. A twig snapped, and Violet stepped up.

"Good morning, Yin."

"Good morning, Commander Leer. Trust you slept well?"

"Not really." Violet yawned. "I kept dreaming Poe was my uncle and wanted to give me pony rides."

"Ah-ha." Yin didn't care to hear more. "I've finished my taunting tribute to Nefarious Wretch. In mere moments, thousands of voices will aim these words skyward. It's gonna piss the paint off that cretin."

Violet took a few moments to focus her morning eyes on the words. She mumbled them from a mouth seeking hot coffee and fresh doughnuts.

Of all the nuts in the cosmic soup,
There is but one with a soul of goop;
With an ear of tin and a heart of stone,
I wouldn't lick him if he were a bone.

"Now the chorus! Read the chorus, you're gonna love it!" Yin wagged his tail furiously, as if she were tossing him doggie treats.

Violet gave him an odd look then continued with the chorus.

Nefarious Wretch is a big fat creep!
A big fat creep! A big fat creep!
Nefarious Wretch is a big fat creep!
And he smells like rancid coolie!

"Continue!" pleaded Yin, barely able to maintain his own composure. Violet considered him for a few seconds then took a deep breath.

He's as smart as a rock, as cute as a sock,
And his mind is really too sick.
He's hated by all. He's going to fall,
Because only a jerk hates music.

Nefarious Wretch is a big fat creep!
A big fat creep! A big fat creep!
Nefarious Wretch is a big fat creep!
And he smells like rancid coolie!"

Violet shook her head, embarrassed. "Rancid coolie?"

Yin laughed and pumped his paw into the air, spun around and shook his little buttocks. "Isn't that horribly insulting? To have one's body odor be compared to that of some rotted and moldy backside?"

"You're real proud of yourself, huh?"

"Wouldn't you be?"

"Up all night writing this, huh?"

"Most. It was worth it. When he hears this he'll capture this world into his dimension so fast you'll have to look again to miss it twice. Then we'll have him. In his own home."

"When this is all said and done, I hope you have no delusions of quitting your day job."

276

"Don't be ludicrous. Now. Let's gather the commanders and sound the Horn of Harmony. We'll practice the dirty ditty a few times with the flyers."

The Creamery Child led Caffrey, Angie and Poe 33 through oddly desolate corridors of featureless floors with impossibly high ceilings. They crossed landscapes that seemed to serve no purpose but to add space between the here and there.

With each step, the barren walls filled with distorted images and abstract shapes. Caffrey kept his gaze on the back of The Creamery Child's head because, unexplainably, some of the misshapen forms were disturbing to the eye. The hallways grew ever narrower, squeezing the haunting images into barely recognizable outlines. There were faces of agony. Mad clowns. Sites of bloody massacres, and seas of faces looking skyward in horror.

It was all rather cliché as scary images go, but haunting nonetheless.

Then, quite unexpectedly, Caffrey heard music. It was quite far off but came to his ears on the wings of an echo traveling through the tunnels and chambers of Nefarious's mind. The first few notes to hit his ears tasted like cotton candy. It was the unmistakable whimsy of a carnival band, filled with sour-cherry brass, sharp cinnamon cymbals, fizzy grape organ blasts and a creamy nougat center of nutty bacchanalia.

Yet, as the merry melody poured forth, the intensity of its mirth went past mere innocent circus fun, looming sickeningly into the soundtrack of madness. Pure, unadulterated, flaky-in-the-pastry, inky-in-the-bookmark, flying-out-of-control-on-icy-freeways lunacy. It froze him in his tracks, and he felt sweat bead on his brow. Mushrooms sprouted in his stomach and little angry birdies flew around his head, chirping in discordant indifference.

"What is that?" Caffrey was desperately trying to understand the music's intent.

"The crazy place," voiced the boy as he continued on.

"The crazy place," agreed Angie in a whisper that mirrored her own concern.

After a few minutes they came to a wide hallway leading to a fanciful door decorated with giant, rat-faced roses, thick salamander ribbons and can-can-dancer tongues of fire. The music was pushing against the doors like a frenetic, loopy mob. Caffrey felt his feet freeze to the ground.

"Are you okay, my goosey gander?"

"Come on, Quark Caffrey." Poe 33 smiled. "I feel this jocularity should be quite entertaining."

Caffrey took a deep breath, and they entered through a tidal wave of sensory overload. It would have taken even the greatest galactic minds a lifetime and a day to fully comprehend the totality of what lay before them.

It was an arena the size of Madison Square Garden, Caffrey figured, but capped with a dome of twisted silk rags of every imaginable color plus seven. Across the arena, facing the entry, stood the source of the music: a six-story calliope shimmering with a waterfall of mother-of-pearl liquid marble, crumbled vegetable chrome and candy cane-mirrored barber poles. Strings of knitted silver castanets the size of pizzas clapped along with dancing funky monkeys made of seashells and neon bowling balls. An immense player-piano roller turned amidst a steady leak of jellied musical notes and fountains of sugared crystal hammers of many flavors. Giant phalluses and large-nippled breasts colored like animal-skin prints square-danced atop the gargantuan instrument beneath a steady fall of snow and plums.

The arena held about ten thousand cheering beings—peculiar, tumor-like growths that had sprung from the tartan seat cushions with waving arms and ecstatically screaming wide mouths. Their skin flickered with soft imagery projected from within, each a memory more horrid than the next.

"My," Poe 33 concluded.

Caffrey was stunned silent. He let his eyes drift along the walls of the coliseum and soon discovered that every inch was wallpapered with images of such vibrant colors he feared his mind would explode. Reds were like volcanoes and yellows the sun. Greens were impossible forests and blues like a childhood memory of summer skies.

"It's pure misery disguised as contentment. Denial illustrated in glorious Technicolor," decided Angie.

The Creamery Child spoke up. "That is exactly the truth."

"I can honestly say that I, the great and wondrous Poe Thirty-three, have never before witnessed such colorful bedlam."

There were mating marble screams and multi-colored desires pounding their heads against blocks of stone regret. Lost dreams did back-flips over stacks of procrastinated ideas bubbling and melting like cheese on coals. Companies of phobias flew circles around shivering towers of repressed wants. Huge origami wishes laughed as they emulated themselves in green-and-brown fires of hopelessness.

Centered amidst it all was a large cabin trunk inside a gilded cage hanging from a single, crystal thread no thicker than a human hair. The trunk was wrapped in chains, giant padlocks and leather straps and hung over a pit whose cookie-cutter opening was in the shape of a small boy. The hole burped steam and the rosy smoke of wishful thinking.

Caffrey garnered his nerve to move and tapped the boy on the shoulder. "What's the point of this?"

"This is the central core of his being."

"What about the music?"

"It plays on and drives his madness. The only way he can silence it is to shove me into that pit. That would seal it and protect his mind from ever being invaded by the contents of the trunk."

"What's in it?"

"Stuff he thinks he should forget."

"Your mother?"

"Yes. The pit leads to his entire mind. The crystal thread can be shattered."

"By what? Maybe by a feeling he has not felt in many, many years?"

The boy nodded. A voice sounded above the music. "Nefarious has inquired, oh, limpid lemon ones, what are you doing?"

"Don't answer him. He is speaking for my father. An alter ego. Don't let him hear your voice!" the boy whispered urgently.

The voice called again, "This young chap is a myth. Don't listen to such a pathetic waif. He does not exist. He is just flavorful tara-diddle. He is an apparition of lies and deception!"

Their perspective suddenly rotated as if the entire arena were on a lazy Susan.

"Kill the runt for Nefarious, and you can have this!"

A beautiful Fender Stratocaster appeared from nowhere. It zipped through the air alongside them, leaving behind a comet-like tail of wondrous colors and textures.

"You'd have to do better than that," retorted Caffrey under his breath.

The boy gave him a dirty look and put a firm finger to his lips.

279

The voice tried another tack. "Then how does your groin-mind react to this?"

A huge rotating bed appeared upon which lay twenty naked human forms, gyrating and moaning, obviously in need of physical gratification. However, they were incomplete projections of Caffrey's preferred female form and, as a result, were rather repulsive. He looked away, and a trumpet sounded amidst the vile whimsy.

"A trumpet!" cried the voice. "Nefarious wonders who dares sound an instrument!"

A series of pulsing holes of pitch-black emptiness flickered around the place and were gone just as fast as they'd appeared.

"Did you see those black holes?" the boy whispered.

Caffrey nodded.

"They were the portals of lapses and distraction—the way out."

Voices, at first distant, began intruding upon the fiesta. They were in unison. They were filled with commitment rather that sounding as if they should be committed. And they grew louder, louder, punching through the mesmerizing colored walls as liquid fish, electric fruit and rubbery frogs. Words became distinct, mocking lyrics.

> Nefarious Wretch is a big fat creep!
> A big fat creep! A big fat creep!
> Nefarious Wretch is a big fat creep!
> And he smells like rancid coolie!

Across the field, thousands of voices shouted to the sky. Yin, leading them in song like a maddened conductor, stood on a rock—the rock on which he'd written the verses—like a tongue-in-cheeky god from some long-forgotten testament.

> Nefarious Wretch is a big fat creep
> And he smells like rancid coolie!

"Again!" the Bopple shouted through his megaphone. "Let this be the judgment day of Nefarious Wretch and all of ODOR!"

The gathered flyers started the song from the top. Violet looked around, hoping to see some sign of the world being extracted.

Perhaps after another chorus...

⟍⟍

"Look before you, Caffrey!" the voice ordered.

A giant fist emblazoned with purple mistrust jack-in-the-boxed up. The fist opened to reveal magazine photo cutouts of his band-mates. Caffrey smiled despite it all. He felt better seeing something familiar. He was at once saddened, angered and overjoyed.

"You can have your friends back. Just throw that horrid child into the pit. Or your friends will be made ash-wise!"

"Don't believe him, Mr. Caffrey!" whined The Creamery Child.

"Just do the act, and your Fab Four and yourself will be given the most special of privileges! You will be used as the back-up band to Nefarious's disharmony!"

"That's tantamount to being Quigmo Digmo's personal tush cleaner!"

Flames laughed around Caffrey's friends. The lumpy crowd was going mad, banging their heads on the backs of their seats, letting little bubbles of seltzer fly free.

"Either the boy is destroyed or they are!"

"Why can't Nefarious just destroy the boy himself? Afraid?"

"Nefarious is certainly not frightened of such a creamery runt!"

"Then toss his milky butt into the pit yourself!"

"Oh, trust me, he would! In fact, he would take great pleasure in eliminating such a milk pumpkin face. But he can't at the moment."

"Why not?"

Another wave of black holes flashed about.

"Why..." The voice fished for a reason. "...because he has too many things to do! Do you know how many hours in the day it takes to rework a galaxy of over two hundred billion systems?"

Caffrey sniffed. "That's a pretty lame excuse. Even for Nefarious."

The paper cutouts of the band were set adrift on little gusts of vindictive sentiment. They wafted about as a flock of arrogant bigotries were released from a chuckling barrel.

"Beware! Your friends apart he will tear!" the voice rhymed.

The Creamery Child turned to Caffrey. "These are simply thoughts. Their true essence is stored somewhere in the solid place. You need to get out of his mind quickly. He holds the upper hand here. It is his mind, after all."

"Are they in danger?"

The boy shrugged, and Caffrey pouted angrily. "Poe, can you sense when the lapses will open?"

"I cannot anticipate them. I can, however, pick up the initial vibrations a few thousandths of a second before your brain can. I can also calculate, based on the historical sampling, where the next holes are most likely to open."

"Jump into the next available portal. You, too, Angie."

"What about you, love?"

"Just do it."

Caffrey walked forward and leaned on the railing, looking down on the lower tiers of seats. "I will throw The Creamery Child into the pit under one condition!"

The crowds of tumorous memories shuffled and muttered to themselves.

"No conditions!" cried the voice.

"No conditions!" chanted the crowd.

"Tell this boy you love him, Nefarious!"

The crowd grimaced and retreated into their seats like turtles into shells. More lapses flashed about as another chorus of Yin's song invaded the space.

"Tell him you love him, and I will throw him into the pit." Caffrey stared around the arena as he roared out the words, daring Nefarious to respond.

"I will say no such thing! Nefarious Wretch only loves disharmony!"

"Come on! Say it! He is cute, in a Dickensian sort of way."

From the corner of his eye, Caffrey saw the vicious bigotry birds pecking and tearing at his paper mates.

"Wait!" he protested.

"The boy!" the voice demanded.

The mocking song of OTHER grew louder. The birds intensified their attack. More and more lapse holes flashed, many remaining visible for longer stretches of time.

Poe 33 stepped into one and vanished.

"Your friends are coming apart!"

"Don't believe him. It's all mad imaginings, Mr. Caffrey," the boy insisted.

"Caffrey Quark! You have come so far for your friends. Toss the scrapper! Quickly!"

Caffrey looked into the eyes of the boy. The Creamery Child stared back. Pitifully. A single tear formed in his eye and rolled daintily down his cheek like a skier across a virgin snowfield. He was so bloody pure it made Caffrey sick.

There'd been something irking him about the boy since laying eyes on him. Perhaps it was his perfect, "ain't-I-chaste" pout. Or his son-of-landlord marshmallow fluffiness. Or maybe the shortbread-tin sense-of-entitlement odor reeking off his body like too much peppermint oil dabbed behind his powdered sugar-coated ears. Maybe it was simply the way the saliva smacked with every syllable of his elocution.

Whatever it was, Caffrey was vexed that the successful rescue of his closest buddies relied on the life or death of such a small, overtly taintless person. Then again, the kid was simply the love song of a once-happy marriage. Why should he be anything but pure and wholesome?

Caffrey's consciousness had become a pair of dueling banjos. His hand snapped forward, and he grabbed the boy by the scruff of his ruffled silk shirt. A brilliant tutti-frutti spotlight fell onto him as the room grew dark. The crowd loved it.

But the mocking song was growing louder, gradually overtaking the ramblings of the calliope.

"You need to escape, Mr. Caffrey, while my father is distracted. Go to the solid place and free your friends."

Caffrey frowned at the boy and looked to the snow of confetti, all that remained of his band-mates. He released The Creamery Child, adjusted his crooked collar and gave him a pleasant pat on his Dutchboy head.

"Run back to your room."

The boy smiled and ran off.

"Let's go, my love," said Angie.

"Angie? Why are you still here?"

"Let's go."

Caffrey took one last look at the memory-filled trunk and its crystal thread. He smiled mischievously and nodded. "Follow me, Angie-girl."

"Anywhere!"

He targeted the nearest lapse and charged into it.

Caffrey's nose twitched. He was in the dark, encased in pure black. Pure silence. The sudden absence of the sensory overload felt like a warm blanket. For a moment, he let the feeling coat his body and wrap his mind as if with soft, freshly mixed dough.

Then a scent, like a wispy translucent eel, swam up his nostrils. It was the odor of burning metal. The distinct smell of molten steel.

The single, odoriferous ribbon dissolved away, and he opened his eyes to something odd. They looked like indigo silks draped across his face, but as Caffrey tried to brush them aside he realized they were ethereal lights.

His situation finally became apparent. He was lying in a snug but comfortable case topped by a glass dome. Points of deep-blue light were reflected and warped on the curved surface of his transparent coffin. Suddenly, a face appeared, staring down through the glass, its cheesy smile distorted by the lens effect.

"Quarky!" exclaimed Yin with a wag of his tail. "You're back!"

"I guess so. Where am I?" The glass top opened, and cool, air-conditioned air poured across Caffrey's face. It was Heaven—it had to be.

"Aboard the OTHER frigate *Yin's Tune*," was the Bopple's more sobering explanation.

"Who's tune?" Caffrey's eyes darted from side to side as he fired the question.

"Yes, Quarky. It was named after me in honor of my successful raid of an ODOR stronghold, many years before our friendship."

Caffrey stared into the eyes of his pooch, wondering why he was still having a hard time with the dog-like critter's heroic past. Eventually, he sat up and took a closer look at the ship. Violet was sitting at the controls.

"Ms. Leer," he greeted.

"Quark."

"Where's Poe and Angie?"

"They're already down there. I heard about your adventures with Nefarious's offspring, and the little trip to the circus."

Caffrey shuddered. "I may be forever scarred."

"Come, take a look at the fleet." Violet beckoned him over to a huge viewport.

Caffrey crawled from the sleeping chamber and moved on shaky legs until he stood by the magnificent vista to the heavens. Sure enough, from what he could see, *Yin's Tune* sat in the center of a convoy of hundreds of OTHER craft. The entire fleet sat motionless, awaiting orders.

"Quite impressive, huh?"

Something wasn't right, and it took Caffrey a few seconds for the oddity of the region to dawn on him.

"Why are the stars blue?"

"Indigo, actually," Violet corrected. "We're in the Dimension of Nefarious Wretch. Take a look at this..."

Violet rolled the frigate to reveal a monster.

"Wow," gasped Caffrey.

"Obvious but appropriate choice of exclamation, my human friend," Yin said. "That is the physical base of the horrid and foul Nefarious Wretch."

It was a huge cylinder, covered in a layer of space-dust and rust. To one end was fixed a tremendous asteroid—in the process of being carved into a face. The base looked not unlike a giant Pez dispenser.

"We're going in," asserted Yin busily. "We'll meet Poe and Angie at the main stern exhaust port."

Caffrey wasn't too keen on the apparent change in command structure. "Dog, if you order a single energy blast fired, I'll dip you in tar and shave your backside."

"I'm a Bopple, human," retorted Yin with a certain arrogance, "and I'm leading this little attack. Besides, we cannot possibly destroy that base. Yet. There are countless prisoners on board. We can, however send a hit team and eliminate Nefarious."

Caffrey remained indignant. "Not until I get my friends out! Then I want a shot at Nefarious. I think I have a plan that will work—without firing a shot."

"We'll discuss it down there," said Yin, compromising, and with a doubtful chuckle.

"I want to give peace a chance," added Caffrey.

Under Violet's control, the *Yin's Tune* broke off from the squadron. Vanishing to a speck against the size of Nefarious ship, they landed like a flea on a St. Bernard. The ship locked an airtight magnetic seal onto the surface of the base. A steady and, for Nefarious, oddly rhythmic beat pounded from deep below, vibrating into the *Yin's Tune*. Yin opened a hatch and they entered the gigantic base.

Caffrey was surprised to discover a smiling Poe 33, reunited with his body, waiting for the crew. The android greeted them with a bow.

"Quark Caffrey, Commanders Violet and Yin."

"Poe," returned Caffrey, "I see you found your body in one piece."

"Inagaddadavida, baby. Yet another wonder of the magnificent Poe Thirty-three of which I have become aware. It seems my body is designed to kill as a Berserker, bite through iron or walk through steel walls, should it come within five miles of my Revenant essence.

"I, meaning my physical self, was locked deep below in a cell. I blasted my way through steel walls with my powerful devices. Although not much more than a human brain, the intelligence left with my body made up in survival skills what it lacked in charm and subtle wit. The slabs of steel are still incandescent below."

Caffrey recalled the smell of molten metal but said nothing. Poe continued his discourse.

"If I had been destroyed you would have taken my place as Portsmith, Quark Caffrey."

"Me?" Caffrey was astonished.

"When I was snatched by Nefarious, I not only disengaged my essence and became Revenant I uploaded a copy of my memories to your brain."

"You did what?"

"I'm not sure if you realize, Quark Caffrey, just how much empty space there is in your head." The android was serious.

"Painfully," replied Caffrey, rubbing his temples. "What about your Master?"

"Not yet."

They made their way down a staircase to what looked like a huge abandoned train station illuminated by an indigo glow with no apparent source. The walls glistened with a moist sheen; and the ceiling, some hundred meters high, played deep space to the dozens of holographic spheres drifting just below it. The heartbeat of the station pulsed like the slow but definite approach of death.

"It'll take us forever to figure this place out," complained Yin, panting a little.

"That pounding is frightening," Angie confessed.

"The tremendous power requirements needed to embody his thoughts are generated somewhere below," explained Yin. "That is the pounding we hear. Deep beneath, this strange engine beats, powered by the torment of thousands upon thousands of innocent souls."

"Actually, Yin, not quite torment. Slight annoyance," corrected Poe 33.

Ignoring the android, Yin expounded some more.

"The amazing creation of a madman. All these planets, while physically here, are still connected to their true cosmic time and space. Did you notice the sunlight falling on each? There is no sun.

Yet each is lit by the non-local but distinct thermonuclear output of their respective mother star. They are held here by the power of his thoughts magnified a billionfold. When we destroy Nefarious, the quantum link will be broken and the worlds will all return."

"We found his weakness," assured Caffrey. "I saw the circus of his mind and the one small flaw that'll bring it all down like a house of cards."

"The kid?" suggested Violet, doubtfully.

"There is no kid," Caffrey corrected. "It was a song. Nefarious wanted to forget the music his wife composed. It was manifested as The Creamery Child. Angie was right."

"Creamery?" Violet could only wonder.

"Yes. The music must have been pure. Innocent. Childlike," said Angie.

"Am I to suddenly feel pity?" Yin yipped. "Once I've located the evil bastard I will call for my commando team. We'll destroy him, release the prisoners and blow this entire base to kingdom come-what-may."

Caffrey spoke up. "First, I'll try it the L'Orange way."

"Transmute him?" Violet's hesitancy was obvious.

"Yes," Angie chimed in. "His hate is being held by a crystal thread."

Poe was quite confident. "Angie's right. I witnessed the strange imbalance. We only need to flood his memory with the repressed love, and I feel the transformation Quark Caffrey speaks of will take place."

It was too much for Violet. "Don't be ludicrous!"

"We're gonna try it." Metaphorically speaking, Caffrey put his foot down, and there was a momentary tense silence.

Finally, Yin nodded. "Where do you suppose we begin looking for him?"

"We need the layout."

"Both Angie and myself have attempted to contact some central computer. There is none. His mind must be acting as the control system."

"The real question is," Caffrey pointed out, pacing like Sherlock Holmes, "where would such a tormented soul find repose?"

Yin applied his intelligence. "I would imagine someone of his ego and ambitions would reside in the grandest hall, up on high, with wondrous views of his growing collection of worlds."

Caffrey shook his head in disagreement. He paced some more, pondering Nefarious Wretch and all he'd learned so far about the odd being. After a moment he looked up.

"I sensed a certain amount of self-loathing. Did you sense that as well, Angie?"

"I sensed great denial. He disavowed any love for the mousy woman in the photo."

"And he couldn't face his own memories. They ran around his mind in personified form, and Nefarious wanted them destroyed. He created mazes in his psyche, and open expanses of emptiness, as if to remind him of his desolation. Look at this place. Not another soul in sight. His self-worth, I guess, is a mere pittance, as it is in most of the egomaniacal narcissists I have met in my life.

"Therefore, I imagine his quarters are in the darkest, dankest, most despicable spot in this entire complex. A place that acts as a constant reminder of his helter-skelter state."

"The humming," guessed Poe 33, leaning forward in his excitement.

"Yes, Poe. I bet that where the pulsing drone is loudest is where we will find Nefarious."

Violet and Yin exchanged concerned looks of doubt; and Violet stepped forward, a hand on the butt of her weapon in its holster. It was a cosmic impossibility for her to not look sexy.

"Caffrey! Yin, myself and a whole lot of people have been at this longer than you. We have a plan. We have a solution. We've finally made it into his world. Let us simply destroy it."

"You've so readied your brain for this solution you refuse other options. I, on the other hand, never wanted any of this. I joined you for one reason—to get my friends back. Along the way I began to understand the bigger picture. Now, I want all these music-loving worlds back to their systems. I want Nefarious stopped. When Wisdom suggests a better alternative, I think we should listen."

"It proves nothing to pretend to desire wisdom but ignore its plea," Poe 33 said softly.

Yin exhaled hard, and Violet threw her hands on her hips.

"What do you want?"

"If I've learned anything from music and its little orange gelatinous representative it's this: you can imagine a better solution. Give us some time to try the wise way. If it doesn't work you can try it yours."

"Fine," agreed Yin, completely missing the insult.

288

"Okay," conceded Violet, turning and pacing away.

"How much time do we have until the cavalry's called?" Caffrey wanted to move things along.

"You can have twelve hours," the Bopple decided.

"Fair enough."

"May the luck and strength of my forefathers be with you, my Master," Yin said, with a bow. "But I doubt it'll work."

"Thanks for that vote of confidence, pooch. See if I clean up your poop again."

Yin smiled warmly. Violet wished each of them luck; then she and Bopple headed back to the *Yin's Tune*.

The bottom of the ramp led to a spiral staircase with what appeared to be an impossible number of steps. Caffrey peered over the banister and marveled at the lovely nautilus shape falling to a pretty close approximation of infinity.

"Damn, that's a walk."

"You forget, Quark Caffrey, I have abilities that you do not. I can make the descent rather pleasant, if you do not mind riding piggyback."

As Caffrey and Angie watched, the android swelled, his skin shimmering and flickering as it stretched over his expanding skeleton. From his back, a pair of chrome pipes emerged, protruding from a box with distinct indentations shaped for the seating of humans. Poe 33 knelt down on his knees.

"Hop aboard, Quark Caffrey."

"Oh, Poe, you are impressive," sighed Angie.

"True."

Throwing his right leg around Poe's neck, Caffrey dropped into the seat. Poe 33 stood, servos singing.

"Now, my friend, hold on tight!"

"My butt's still sore from the zebadoos! Easy, Poe!"

Perhaps it was a stupid assumption, but Caffrey had been anticipating a long, easy amble down the staircase. When Poe 33 jumped the banister, engaged the duel rockets on his back and fell down the center of the almost-endless spiral, Caffrey's heart skipped not one but two beats. It was a full ten seconds before he could even garner enough breath to exhale in a please-God-let-me-live scream.

Down they plummeted, the jets keeping the acceleration at a tolerable rate. Level after level streaked by, and the wind rushed past Caffrey's ears like New York City pedestrians. The alternating red-and-blue exit lights on each landing level smeared into a constant blur of vertical color, creating a purple haze in his vision as the endless fall continued. For a moment, Caffrey considered asking Poe 33 to play the Hendrix tune, filling his mind to make the ride a bit more pleasant, then decided he'd rather not distract the psychotic android.

Finally, after what seemed like five minutes but was actually an empty glance into time's infinity, the force of Poe 33's reverse thrust rocked up Caffrey's spine; and the android landed, like a daisy petal on a breezeless spring morn.

"Are you okay, Quark Caffrey?"

Caffrey's mouth formed a confident "yes" but no sound was emitted. Poe 33 smiled.

Angie flipped back and forth excitedly. "That was quite a ride, my two Newtonian love apples!"

Again Caffrey agreed, but the actual audio remained somewhere behind his heart, which pounded beside his tonsils.

There was only one door before them, and needing to assert himself somehow, Caffrey opened it. A rush of wind dragged the door from his grip and slammed it against the wall, sending a blast of sound bouncing around the corridor beyond like a pinball. The three stood silent until the echo vanished into the distance.

Caffrey stepped through the doorway into a large room filled with a twisting tree of pipework. He peered around.

"Looks like some sort of utilities station."

He stroked the thick pipes running up, down and around the walls before him, and an idea launched in his mind. He rapped a pipe with his knuckles. The hollow clang raced off like a horse on a track and seemed to split, branch off and spread all around them. Finally, after ten resonant seconds, the clang faded to nothing. Caffrey smiled and looked at Poe 33.

"Poe. Hendrix. 'Purple Haze.'"

The Portsmith smiled, raised a finger, tapped his temple and winked.

Throughout the many dark and lonely corners of Nefarious's base, the vibrations came. Electric waves of music vibrated the essence of the metal and radiated into the air. Solid chords reached into the darkness and flickered with light, piercing the angry steel walls and cold empty spaces. They seeped into the center of the pounding engine and were not well received. The beat grew angrier, faster—the entire base shook, like a cynic taunted by the beauty of the universe. It refused to accept the heart-striven harmonies. The craft recoiled, and shunned the sounds.

But the power of the reversed-stringed Stratocaster made its way to the outer walls of the stronghold. An audio plum-colored mist sustained its texture as it penetrated into the massive stone at the head of the base. Micro-vibrations, like tiny nose-hairs, reached through the rocky material and into the dark cold of space. They didn't go unnoticed. A small, spherical robot, busy with its task of transforming the random ridges and valleys of the asteroid's surface into the delicate and beautifully designed form of the human face, took heed.

Peebo shimmied and shook with delight. He'd analyzed the sound waves, and his incredible intuition linked it to the music library of Poe 33's circuits and Caffrey Quark's heart. He gyrated another happy dance and took a break from his chore.

<hr>

The ground trembled with each pound of the engine's pulse. Poe 33, holding onto the pipe, continued sending the potent, blues-infused, high-voltage chords coursing through the network.

"I think Nefarious is getting upset," Angie decided.

"I'm hoping my friends will hear this," explained Caffrey, studying Poe has he worked. "Give them a sense that hope is near."

A sudden surge of energy flashed through the pipeworks, and Poe 33 was knocked back on his tokhes. The music went silent and the heartbeat returned to normal.

"Well, that was unexpected," the android said calmly. Tiny blue and yellow static charges wriggled and waned across his limbs as various warning lights on his torso flashed briefly.

"You okay?"

The android clambered to his feet. "Yes. I get the sense that this station is an extension of Nefarious's brain. The very walls of this place surge with a life force."

Without warning, and as if to illustrate Poe's theory, the corridor was sealed in, two walls forming from material poured from thin air. It closed them in a solid steel box.

"Like I was saying..."

"Light, Poe," Caffrey asked. "Please."

Poe 33 illuminated a brilliant lamp in his forehead. They were, indeed, in a box. He shot a thin rod of purple energy at the wall. The erosion of the metal by the laser was quickly filled in as more of the material morphed out of some invisible ether.

"It appears to be self-healing," concluded Poe as he tried his best to bring the power of his laser to previously unaccomplished heights.

Caffrey slumped against a wall. "Terrific."

<hr>

They had been pondering their dilemma for a solid half an hour when a sharp tap on the wall startled the trio. They stood silently, the heartbeat pounding away incessantly. The metal-on-metal tap rang out again.

"Who could that be?" asked Angie in a nervous whisper.

Caffrey drew his weapon, and Poe 33 extruded the barrel of one of his numerous built-in firearms. A bizarre sound cursed the air. It was a high-pitched squeal, like a steel dish spinning on a glass floor combined with a deep, rhythmic warbling. A bulge morphed from the wall of steel, like a spinning fist pushing into a rubber sheet.

"Frankly, that's rather disturbing," confessed Poe 33.

The manifestation pushed deeper and deeper until it broke through, bringing light into the room. Attempts by the self-healing metals to close the hole were frustrated by a thick ring extruded by the intruder, creating a widening hole that eventually formed a portal large enough for a full-sized human to exit.

Caffrey and Poe 33 took advantage of it, and Angie easily followed. The ring followed them, slipping from the hole and collapsing, reforming itself into a familiar sphere with an inner crimson glow. Peebo bobbed up and down like an excited puppy.

"Peebo!" Angie cried with great elation.

"How in bloody hell did you get here?" Caffrey stared quizzically as he fired the question.

The little ball-shaped android went through an exotic dance as he tried to explain his adventures. When Caffrey looked to Poe 33 for a translation, the Portsmith simply shrugged.

"You must understand him," insisted Caffrey.

"Bits and pieces," answered Poe 33 with definite disdain in his voice. "One would think such a fancy-shmancy android would be able to speak a verbal language."

292

"Poe!" scolded Angie, "He's your baby brother! Be nice to him!"

The Portsmith shrugged and gave in. "He says the Blodians gave him to Nefarious after they were finally able to please the Wretch with a facial design. Peebo has been working, alone, on the huge construct for days."

Peebo added to the story with more dips and shakes.

"He says he heard the nice music moments ago and was pleased as punch that we had returned."

"Peebo, we're glad to have you back," said Caffrey, patting the floating robot on its top.

Peebo danced some more then nuzzled Poe 33's neck. The Portsmith seemed to blush.

"He says he missed and loves us all."

Angie was ecstatic. "How sweet!"

But Caffrey wanted to move on. "Peebo, do you have any idea where Nefarious resides?"

Peebo reshaped himself into a bass drum—a hand morphed and pounded the same, steady beat of the engine.

"We were right," Caffrey said softly, catching Peebo's drift. "Do you know the way?"

The little robot danced again, brightening his inner illumination, and shot off down the corridor.

The trio followed. At times they had to jog in order to stay within sight of Peebo, whose cherry glow flickered on the walls like blood. Finally, they reached an archway roughly hewn in the steel walls and stepped out onto a catwalk coiling around a huge shaft. They could see windows scattered at irregular intervals as they looked up the infinity of the shaft, and a similar prospect as they viewed its bottomless fall.

Peebo began his descent, staying on the angled catwalk, and the others trotted behind. They'd only descended three levels when Peebo stopped before an airlock. He gyrated and shook.

"He says, Quark Caffrey, that we will be exiting into open space. You, since you are human, will have to wear a special suit."

Peebo stretched and folded and became a small, one-man probe. A bladder of thinly formed metal inflated atop the unit, filling with a large supply of air from the shaft.

"Very clever, Peebo," Angie complimented.

Caffrey stepped into the hollow of the probe and it sealed itself. Peebo communicated to his older brother to open the door.

Traveling through the underground network of steel veins had made it impossible for the group to determine where they were with respect to the ship's design. As they stepped out onto a narrow walkway latticing the exterior of the huge craft, it was no longer a mystery as to at which end they had emerged. The huge asteroid filled their view, the details of the sculpture clearly apparent under the mysterious illumination.

Peebo launched out into space, and Caffrey's adrenaline surged. It was a feeling of freedom he had never experienced. All around him, the celestial bodies hung—blue stars, planets, and the convoy of fighters. He felt like a breeze in a dream. Peebo arched around to the front of his handiwork, finally coming to rest a kilometer or so from the face.

"Amazing," murmured Caffrey. "It's Nefarious's mousy ex."

Peebo took off toward the face of Nefarious's love and, to the surprise of everyone, entered her left nostril.

CHAPTER 22
LOVE REIGN O'ER ME

(The Who)

he left nostril was quite roomy. Peebo came to rest and
released Caffrey into a chilly, breezy atmosphere somehow contained in the hollow space. The vibrations of the heartbeat
could be felt in the air, but its sound was nonexistent. Caffrey's
hair was blowing in the nasal zephyr.

It was an obvious question. "Where's that wind coming from?"

"That exhaust fan is causing it," said Poe 33, pointing a shaft of
light at the giant spinning blades encased in a cage on the far wall.

Caffrey led the way, enjoying the feel of his hair blowing free.
The wall was smooth, rising up a hundred meters and east-west
three times that. A thick coating of gray dust marred the metallic
shine that peeked through in the handful of clean spots.

His eyes widened. "Wait a second..."

He scanned the wall. Sure enough, another of the giant cylinders
protruded from the eastern side.

"Those look like engine cones."

He stepped up to the center point between the two and used his
palm to wipe away a wide swatch of dust. When the cloud settled,
the bright yellow paint screamed out.

"Poe, can you blast away this dust?'

"Of course," the android said, stepping closer. "Not only am I equipped with devastatingly deadly armaments, I also have a seventy-five-hundred-psi air compressor. Shall I commence?"

"Commence."

In seconds the entire cave was filled with thick, gag-inducing dust as a powerful blast of air shot from Poe 33's mouth. As it settled, Poe looked sheepishly at Caffrey.

"Sorry, I forget you biologicals are so delicate."

The blast had revealed a stretch of fanciful symbols in a language unknown to Caffrey.

"Can anyone read this?"

"Yes," replied Poe 33. "It is a very ancient language. Zequillian. Used on a system very, very far away at the core of the Milky Way. Some three thousand light-years. Almost impossible for a human to pronounce. The closest approximation would be to gargle jelly whilst whistling the words *Pooloo Obcrem Scropis*. It translates roughly to 'Princess of the Ghostly Heart.'"

"Angie?"

"Searching, my google basket," Angie obliged. "Interesting. The *Pooloo Obcrem Scropiis* was a luxury cruise liner. Took decade-long jaunts between the Zequillia and Ujakreesa systems. It disappeared without a trace...ten thousand years ago."

"Peebo, is Nefarious within this asteroid?"

Peebo danced before his older brother, and Poe 33 conveyed the message.

"He says, if you mean the core of Nefarious, yes. We should follow him."

"The core of Nefarious?"

"Yes, Quark Caffrey. Those were his words. So to speak."

"Lead the way."

Peebo glided off towards a dark opening to the south of the engine nozzles. The group followed along a spiraling tube cut through the body of the asteroid. As they delved deeper the ground grew moist and the ceiling became dotted with constellations of condensation droplets. The air felt thick and humid, like the hot breath of a giant. Tunnel openings branched off in every direction, some with impossibly twisted paths; but Peebo never faltered, never paused for a second to contemplate the way.

The deep pounding reverberated stronger, more menacingly. No sound accompanied the beat but the walls vibrated and a rain of moisture was shaken free with each pulse. The silence was unnerving. Caffrey was expecting the annoying, rather cornball taunting—perhaps more of the assaulting imagery. Yet there was nothing but soundless vibration.

"Is he here, Peebo?"

The little android shook his body in the affirmative.

"Why is he so quiet?" asked Angie.

Peebo's silent answer seemed to imply impatience.

"He says we should all hold our zebadoos," explained Poe.

Finally, the tube narrowed to an opening, and Peebo came to a halt. The heartbeat was close. Very close. Caffrey could feel the vibrations on his face like dry ocean waves. Peebo jiggled.

"We can go no further," Poe 33 translated. "There is a great drop. But if we look carefully, we will see Nefarious in his true forms."

"Forms?"

"Forms," repeated Poe 33.

Peebo launched forward and quadrupled his glow. Caffrey, Poe 33 and Angie looked out over the ledge.

"Oh, my," Angie softly gasped.

Peebo's light glistened off the steamy walls of a large chasm. Down below, a pulsing fleshy form, partially encased in a tortoise-like segmented shell, expanded and contracted with each beat. It was huge, easily thirty meters in diameter and ten thick, and muscular legs locked it to the walls and floor. The shell was patterned in crisscrossing lines forming a checkerboard of white and black. From each of the darker squares sprouted living beings of many, many shapes and designs, in various stages of growth. They swayed and undulated with the mother form. It looked like an extremely bizarre chess set.

"What is it?" Caffrey stared at the living monstrosity, unable to figure on an appropriate reaction.

"I have never seen anything like it," Poe 33 stated.

"Peebo, dear," whispered Angie, "what is that?"

Peebo gave a little dance; and Angie, who was beginning to learn his motion-based language, explained. "Peebo says this is Nefarious's heart."

"Actually," Poe 33 corrected, "the term he used was 'core.'"

"What are all those things growing out of it?" Caffrey wondered aloud.

"Things?" one of the things said with an indignant air. "I'm not a thing. I am a Fleebeest-in-waiting."

Indeed it was—Caffrey recognized the creature. Fleebeests are quasi-humanoids usually found on the dry desert world of Calaiz. It raised its upper body, revealing its ram-like shoulder horns, looked up at Caffrey and frowned.

"What do you want?"

Caffrey was dumbfounded. Even the Portsmith seemed at a loss for words. The Fleebeest was in a testy mood.

"Well? I haven't all day to dawdle. I might be offsprung any moment and I must be ready!"

"Ready for what?" Caffrey wished to know.

The Fleebeest was astonished at his ignorance. "For what? For life! Nefarious won't live forever. I'm next."

Caffrey turned to Peebo. "I thought you said that was Nefarious?"

With uncharacteristic impatience, Peebo shimmied and wiggled.

"He says it is Nefarious's core," explained Poe 33.

Caffrey decided to go to the horse's mouth—or rather, sprouting torso.

"Excuse me," he shouted down into the cavern. "We're looking for Nefarious? Is he around?"

"What kind of ridiculous question is that?" the annoyed, partially-spawned Fleebeest retorted. "I *am* Nefarious!"

Caffrey dropped his head. "Oh, I can see this is gonna be fodder for a hell of a headache." He rubbed his temples.

Poe 33 stepped up. "If Nefarious won't live forever, yet this is Nefarious's core, how can you be Nefarious?" It was a justifiable question.

"I am what he is until I am what he is not and thus will be."

"Where is the Nefarious that is neither you nor this?" asked Caffrey.

"Now you're getting it," the thing that was, yet wasn't, Nefarious replied, "He's not here."

Caffrey was losing his patience. "Where is he?"

"About. You don't have any coinage on your person do you?"

"Coinage?"

"Coinage. Loose change. I despise loose change with all my being. When it is my turn to be I will recreate this galaxy free of coinage."

"How can you despise loose change if you have never left this place?" asked Poe.

"It is in my nature."

Another voice chimed in. "As I abhor rippling water."

It came from the scale-covered, narrow-headed creature half-spawned beside the Fleebeest. "...And after the one who is yet to be Nefarious has replaced Nefarious and has become Nefarious, I will become Nefarious and free the galaxy of rippling water."

A half-dozen other very diverse sets of torsos rose and made their point.

"I hate vertical walls."

"And I purple light."

"And me chlorophyll!"

"I detest radio frequencies!"

"Me, reflections!"

"And I, bumpy surfaces!"

Caffrey's headache was growing very bumpy but he decided not to mention it. He turned to Poe 33. "Either of you have a clue?" he whispered.

Poe 33 shrugged. He had no clue. Angie volunteered.

"Searching, my confused-as-I-am sparkle sponge."

Caffrey addressed the Fleebeest. "When will you become Nefarious?"

"I will never become Nefarious!"

"But you just said..."

"I said I am what he is until I am what he is not and thus will be. This and I and all of us are only Nefarious because Nefarious is. When he is no longer than I will no longer be and will be whom I intend. Then all will be me."

For a moment Caffrey considered asking Poe 33 to blast his brains out with a good shot from his air cannon. Instead, he took a deep breath and turned to Peebo. "Peebo, what do you make of this?"

Peebo danced.

"He said, and I quote, 'Nice thing in cave makes me smile,'" translated Poe, with obvious disgust.

"Terrific."

Caffrey gathered his own fleshy logic circuits, all sputtering and melting, and formulated another question.

"As a collective whole, who or what are you?"

"Nefarious Wretch," replied dozens of voices in unison.

"And when the born Nefarious Wretch dies, who or what will the collective whole become?"

"We will become me," the Fleebeest explained.

Caffrey was beginning to get it and nodded approvingly. "Thus, when you are born, the whole will become you and you will set out to recreate the galaxy devoid of loose change?"

"Now you are learning."

"Is there a name, a zoological or official designation for such a being?"

Angie interrupted. "Yes, there is. This is a Dopplerspangler."

"Nonsense!" the voices protested.

"Hush!" Angie scolded the pulsing being, and all of its sprouting sub-beings. She continued her explanation. "A rare, incredibly intelligent lifeform that communicates using trans-species harmonic-holography."

"Like Spydersloth," recalled Caffrey.

"Yes. Dopplerspanglers lock onto floating debris, asteroids, large spacecraft, what-have-you, where they construct their cocoon. Here the core grows and then spawns hundreds of beings, each representing the various biological types of the galactic region in which it resides. Each is given an allotted time to command the central core of intelligence for purposes of making a name for itself, to find love, happiness, fame or infamy. Quite a number of historical figures were born of the Dopplerspangler."

"Such as?" Caffrey doubted that little piece of trivia.

Angie squashed his doubts. "Such as Hirika Joso the restaurant magnate. General Fesn Ingni of the Philosopher Guild Army of Bliss fame. Grand Marshall of the thousand-mile-long Rampart Parade and all-round nice guy Zein Ostogloth and poet laureate of the Belgrupa region, Iiioyan Oohwa.

"You hear that?" Caffrey shouted to the Dopplerspangler. "Poets! Philosophers! Nice guys! You're producing nothing but angry madmen! Explain yourself!"

"We are not! It is the I that is!" came the chorus.

Caffrey had had enough. "Well, whoever that is had better become un-pissed fast! There's a squadron of heavily armed craft of the Order to Harmonize Eternal Reality ready to destroy you in mere hours. You'd better become music fans quick!"

The Fleebeest was quick with a snappy retort. "Disharmony was Nefarious's little fetish. Don't wash that dish in our sink. He's so melodramatic, having us all speak his alternating words for his 'oh, so disharmonious' effect."

"But you are Nefarious."

"We are only Nefarious because Nefarious is so. I thought you understood?"

"But the root of Nefarious is angry. Hateful."

"We are not the root. We are the I of the they individually and the they of the I collectively."

"Then the I is angry and hateful."

"We cannot control the I. We can only be the they of the I."

Caffrey stepped back into the tube to get some air. Once again his head was ready to pop like a ripe zit. He had to ponder air. Empty boxes. Large fish tanks with crystal water but no fish. Boring days with fresh, white, scribble-free calendars. Anything to clear his painfully tormented mind.

He had run a mental marathon of late. His head hurt; and yet strangely, very strangely, he was beginning to understand it all. He was becoming concerned how such utter nonsense could make sense. He suspected the L'Orange was silently watching, nudging him along. He stepped back to the edge and addressed the Dopplerspangler.

"Can the I feel what the I of the they feels?"

"The I of the they is nothing but a reflection of the I."

"I'll take that as a yes." Caffrey smiled. "Poe, Angie, Peebo. Let's get out of here before someone, presumably me, or the I of the me, or the me of the bloody I, commits hara-kiri."

Caffrey directed Peebo to backtrack them to the rear of the giant interstellar cruise ship. They entered the space liner through the aft engine cone and found themselves in a large, oily room. Treading carefully across the slick surface, they discovered a door leading through a toolshed, through a corridor of spare parts and finally out and into a ridiculously long hall.

The corridor was immense. Ceilings vanished up into a haze of black; and the walls, widely spaced, marched down to a pin-like vanishing point seemingly kilometers away. On each side of the hall, small windows, glowing soft colors, lined the way in a perfect proportioned order. And there was that heartbeat again, that pounding engine. Apparently, the pulse of the Dopplerspangler, while steady, wasn't the source of the sound.

The strange engine was at work.

The windows, it was soon discovered, were on doors, each marked by a number and a small nametag printed in a language that Caffrey did not understand. Poe 33 studied the writing on the nearest door.

"It reads Wanila Wensiwisk."

"Fellas," Angie interrupted, "there's someone inside. Peek through the window."

Caffrey peered in, his face turning yellow from the light pouring out. Sure enough, just visible in the hazy glow was a female Wyrrikin, her long leathery body outstretched on a window seat as she read a book. The room itself was small but comfy, furnished with wicker and lace. Lush plants and flowers were placed about, and the yellow light poured in from the window opposite the door.

"Looks sort of like my parents' bed and breakfast."

"Should we knock?" Angie asked.

"Why don't you?" suggested Poe 33.

"Because I have no hands, my almighty but occasionally daft android."

Caffrey looked up and down the hall then knocked in the universally known, almost mystical, "Shave and a Haircut." It was only a moment before the thud-thud response sounded. The door opened, and the tall Wyrrikin stood smiling warmly before them.

"*Wikki wikki,*" she greeted.

"*Wikki wikki,*" Poe 33 replied, acting as the envoy. "*Wooko wenda wuwu?*"

"*Wi wunda wenda,*" she stated.

"What are you saying?" Caffrey asked.

"I asked her what she is doing here. She says she lives here."

"What is this place?" Caffrey asked.

Poe 33 did the translation, and the being replied, "*Weg wul wunda wenda. Wasata weewee woog. Wilnoga winwini wigwwip. Wellip woowoo Wefarious Wretch wowya wanai wanai wis wis wirona.*"

"She says that they all live here. They have been brought to serve Nefarious Wretch by being in a state of slight annoyance."

"Slight annoyance?"

"*Wee wanapy we Wyrrikin weg wawa we wup woo we woo. Wutwawasa woco woco wirona.*"

"She says her room and board are rather comfortable—in fact, better than on her home world. She just has to deal with light that is brighter than Wyrikkin eyes prefer."

"Why?"

"*Wewe?*" asked Poe 33.

"*Wis waza waz wet wirona wa.*"

"This engine is powered by the energy produced by annoyance."

"Is she here against her will?"

"*Wa wu wippy wa wilusa?*"

302

The Wyrikkin went on to explain that, while she wasn't officially a prisoner, she had no possible way to get back to her world, currently amongst the imprisoned planets floating beyond the dome. She was one of two million slightly annoyed guests of Nefarious Wretch, and they provided a large portion of the energy required to run the enigmatic engine.

Not wanting to further annoy the already slightly annoyed Wyrikkin, Poe 33 apologized for the interruption and let the being go back to her slightly impeded reading. The trio investigated a half-dozen other beleaguered guests of Nefarious. There was no apparent rhyme or reason to the order of the prisoners nor any clue as to how they could track down an individual, or in the case of Caffrey, four individuals.

"Angie, there must be a central computer that controls this operation."

"I'm sorry, my slightly annoyed love-dove. I have found nothing of the sort. Other than the incessant hum, there is no sign of any technology."

Caffrey stroked his chin. "It could take years to search all these rooms!"

"At least, Quark Caffrey. I could calculate the exact amount of time, taking into account the permutations and combinations of search procedure as well as the odds of finding your friends within the first twelve hours of searching. I may come up with a surprising figure!"

"What about you, Peebo? Any idea how we can locate my friends?"

Peebo bounced up and down and shot like a bullet down the corridor, leaving a trail of red persistence of vision behind like a crimson comet's tail. Moments later the red blip grew large until Peebo was back at their side like a panting dog. He communicated his findings with a little boogie-woogie tushie-shaking. Poe 33 did the translating.

"He says your friends are not on this level. He scanned every room. Bloody show-off. Says he would be glad to double check."

Caffrey shook his head. He knew exactly what he needed to try. He walked to a quiet, shadowy corner and put himself into a poor excuse for a lotus position. He closed his eyes.

"That's it, my sweet Zen zwieback. You do it!" Angie hovered protectively.

Caffrey began with a salutation of the first thing that popped into his head. The essence of French toast and coffee with a dash of anisette wafted from his mind. It was the result of the free association game his mind played with the memories of his friends. Russ loved French toast. Sam flipped over coffee with anisette. He waited for a reply; and when none came, the smell of a flickering movie projector and the taste of bad cinema fell into his mind. He routed them outward. Nothing came back. Blackness filled the inner screen. His third eye had its lens cap on tight.

He tried again, attempting to relax and not force the thoughts. He focused on his breathing. The breath. The time and space between each breath. Nothing. No lovely teal with gold trim—nothing. This was the stereotypical "black as coal at midnight sans lights cannot see hand in front of face whilst blindfolded sheath of ethereal pitch." No matter how deep his breathing, focused his thoughts or far out of the box his mind, it all remained devoid of information or inspiration.

Caffrey opened his eyes and looked up at Poe 33.

"Nothing?"

"Nada."

They followed another long hall and traversed staircases that grew increasingly odorous with a vitriolic noxiousness of unknown origin. Down, down, down through black-lit passageways that reminded Caffrey of the places in Nefarious's mind he'd visited. His ears began to vibrate with each pounding of the engine and his heart fell in rhythm with the beats.

A guitar chord sounded and he screeched to a halt. A song was playing. Soft strumming and muted singing.

It was coming from Poe 33.

"Poey?" Angie inquired.

"What are you singing?" Caffrey hadn't expected this.

"I have written a song," announced the Portsmith to the Wisest Substance.

"I see," Caffrey said, forcing a smile. While certainly stunned at the news, and feeling quite an amount of admiration for the artistic endeavor of the normally reserved android, he wondered about his timing.

"Would you like to hear it?" asked Poe.

"Uh, sure, Poe. But do you think this is the time for songwriting?"

"I believe this is the exact time. Here it is." Poe 33 sounded a harmonica to set his proper pitch, cleared his throat—though of what, Caffrey hadn't a clue—then began the song.

> Socks are like clocks.
> Not something to mock.
> On the feet of a jock.
> Or to keep warm one's cock.
> A sock is a sock is a sock.

Angie swallowed her guffaw, and Caffrey became deeply concerned that another, really powerful scrambler had been installed in the poor android.

"It's no 'A Day in the Life,' but it's a start," he said, trying to be nice.

"Ever since you first communicated with my Master, I have been trying to understand how I, as perfect as I am, could step out of the cosmic box. I began pondering the music that so inspired you. I was doing a complete analysis of the song that transformed you into pure music—'The Staircase to the Heavens.'"

"'Stairway to Heaven'—never mind. Go ahead, Poe."

"I cannot explain why, but there is something about the song that intrigues my deepest programming. Tickles my electronic fancy."

"You and a billion others."

"There is a line: 'If there's a bustle in your hedgerow don't be alarmed now. It's just a spring clean for the May Queen.' My losing connection with the Great Wise One has been a bustle in the hedgerow of my existence. And I have been greatly alarmed. But for naught! For the natural powers of the cosmic May Queen can simply use her broom and dustpan and clean up that ole nasty bustle!"

Caffrey listened and privately prayed that Poe 33 had a point beneath the dull sheath of his verbosity.

"The song poetically goes on to say 'Dear lady, can you hear the wind blow and did you know your stairway lies on the whispering wind.' The whispering wind! The subtle voice of all reality holds the answer. Is the answer. Is my Master! I had been spending so much processing time attempting to calculate ways to reestablish the quantum link that my ears had closed to the whispering wind."

"And what did the whispering wind tell you, Poe?"

"Socks."

"Socks," Caffrey repeated.

"Socks?" asked Angie.

"Socks."

"What about socks?"

"Beats the living shit out of me, Flapjack," confessed Poe, and he walked off.

Angie giggled. Caffrey rolled his eyes upwards and followed.

After a while they found themselves in an expansive room that must have served as one of the dining halls during the craft's days as a cruise liner. Eating troughs lined the walls while tables, broken and rotted, littered the center and feeding cages hung from the ceiling. Apparently, a varied collection of species frequented the ship.

The air was growing colder, the chill penetrating Caffrey's bones. Poe 33 led them across the room and into another winding corridor. The beat grew louder, clearer—they were even closer to the engine. As they walked, their surroundings grew colder, dirtier—a sad mix of leaking oil and rust. And darker. The air was scented with loss, hatred and anger. Caffrey felt as if he were surrounded by huge cockroaches, and ephemeral jittering shadows created by Peebo's light exploited his fears. Finally, they banked around a mess of fallen steel beams and discovered a door blocking their path. A locked door.

It was, in fact, the most locked door Caffrey had ever seen. There was a small window situated high up on it, barred with a tic-tac-toe pattern of iron rods rattling with the absolutely mind-numbing heart-pulse.

He turned to Poe. "Is this it?"

The android nodded. "Behind that door, I would gamble, is the current living form of the Dopplerspangler that is Nefarious Wretch."

"Who will have the honor of the first peek?" asked Angie, caution evident in her tone.

Caffrey stepped up to the door and had to stand on his toes to peer through the window. With an eyebrow raised, he studied the scene. Seconds later, he moved away.

"Sad, really," was his only remark.

Angie took a peek.

"Pitiful. Utterly pitiful." She moved away, too, taking up a position near Caffrey's left ear.

Nefarious Wretch looked like a human slapped together by an impatient child. He was mere bones with the essential organs wrapped in a thin gauze of sickly yellow skin. His head was narrow and axe-like, and it sat upon a thin neck four times the length of a human's. His nose was somewhat elephantine, and hung to just below his pointy chin.

He sat before a bank of ancient equipment appearing as though it came from the shop of a Victorian metalworker. The room was more like a cell, containing only the barest of essentials—a cot, a table, a chair and a chest of drawers. A dirty glass cylinder, large enough to hold a full-size human, protruded from the ceiling. Nefarious was dressed in black shorts and a white, sleeveless shirt. He sported filthy, well-worn socks.

"Would it be rude to knock?" asked Poe 33.

Caffrey shrugged, lifted his fist and pounded the door, the sound drowning in the sea of the engine's heartbeat.

"I doubt he heard," advised Angie.

"We need a more visual knocking," hinted Caffrey, putting his hand on Poe 33's shoulder.

Poe understood. "Shall I use the traditional mantra?"

"Of course, Poe."

A series of crimson pulses burst from the android's forehead in a silent staccato, piercing the small window. Five beats. An inaudible yet unavoidable "Shave and a Haircut."

A voice boomed out "Who dares interrupt my janitor?"

"Janitor?" Caffrey smiled as he played voyeur again.

"Leave him alone! He has important duties!" Nefarious was speaking into a brass horn, which used some unseen technology to greatly magnify his vocals. They boomed above and beyond the throbbing.

"He's mad. Simply gummy in the walnut," Caffrey said to himself. "Poe, can you pump up the volume of your voice?"

"Of course, I can," the android demonstrated. "My volume goes to eleven."

Caffrey nodded in approval.

"Will you open the door so we may speak with you?" Poe asked, setting himself at volume seven.

"That door is to the chambers of my janitor. For what purpose do you need to interrupt his evening activities?"

"Nefarious," Poe 33 said, "we know it is you behind the door. We are not stupid."

"Bah! You are, indeed, stupid! That is my janitor!"

"Tell him we can see him talking. Who is he trying to kid?"

Angie appeared most embarrassed by Wretch's wretchedness.

"This is the horrid and evil genius Nefarious Wretch?" Caffrey asked rhetorically. "Pathetic sop."

Poe 33 addressed the door again. "Please. Open the door or I will be forced to take it from its hinges."

"Hah! There are no hinges! It is a hingeless door. Locked inside and out! Now, go! I have important work to do!"

Caffrey nodded to Poe, who took a stance. "Move back, Quark Caffrey. Peebo! Make arrangements for the biological."

In seconds, Poe's right arm pulsed with a blood-red aura.

"I hate loud noises," Angie whispered.

Peebo formed himself into a protective shield over Caffrey and Angie. A giant fist of energy blasted from Poe 33, handing a wicked uppercut to the door. Sparkling and dripping with crimson plasma, the door shattered, shook and fell in a snowstorm of metallic shards. When the smoke cleared, helped by the sucking wind from the odd plastic tube hanging from the ceiling, Nefarious Wretch was gone.

Angie shouted above the engine's beat. "He went up the tube!"

"Angie! You and Peebo get back to Yin and Violet! Poe and I will take care of Nefarious!"

"Yes, my Captain Courageous!"

Angie and Peebo zipped off back whence they had come. Poe 33 stepped into the base of the tube and was instantly sucked up like a sip of milkshake. Caffrey, eyes popping, was sipped next.

They raced through a network of tubes at exhilarating speeds. If not for the fact he was pursuing a being who illustrated the most clear-cut example of antisocial behavior Caffrey had ever personally run across, he would have enjoyed the ride. Twisting and turning on a cushion of air and zipping through rings of various-colored light leaking through at the tube's connecting points, he noted many branches breaking off from the path he rode. The sound of valves opening and closing indicated that some entity kept them on a pre-programmed path to an unknown destination.

The engine pounded with a thunderous and metronome-like cadence that seemed to blaspheme the philosophy of ODOR The energy produced by the monstrous facility was pumped through the air in a repeating bolt of silvery blue light launching out through a small crystal dome relieving the tedium of the metal ceiling. A distant rush of wind grew closer, emanating from a tube protruding with dozens of others from the far wall.

Like a champagne cork, Nefarious Wretch popped out. He flew through the air with a calm, deadpan expression and landed on a perfectly placed cushion softening the rusty metal floor. He rolled across the room like a tumbleweed, bounced off his tushie and came to a halt poised on his feet, only to continue across the room in a perfectly controlled jog. It was apparent he'd done this many times before.

Nefarious rushed to a large bank of switches and set about flipping a series of the old, circuit breaker-style controls. Two large loops of metal rose from the floor just in front of the wall of tubes. Similar in design to those used by lion tamers, the rings began to glow with red electrical fire that raced around their circumference. Nefarious giggled and waited.

Six seconds passed before dual rushes of wind echoed into the chamber as Caffrey and Poe 33 were exhausted from separate tubes. They flew through the air and threaded the eyes of the glowing loops with a seemingly almost rehearsed perfection, coming to dead stops betwixt them, and held firm by the mysterious force of the fiery light.

"Bull's-eye!" shouted Nefarious, with a clap of his hands.

"Bull*shit*, Nefarious! You can't possibly get away with this!" retorted Caffrey.

"How trite. Surely a man of your intelligence and resources could come up with a better retort than that?"

Caffrey knew Nefarious was right, but the admittedly corny line had spontaneously flown from his mouth and he was in no mood to apologize. This inability to invoke wit under pressure was beginning to irk him, however, and he made a mental note to work on the little flaw at a more opportune moment. He pursued more immediate matters.

"Poe, do something."

"It would seem the energy of this ring has paralyzed the neural control circuits for all of my defense mechanisms. I am, as they say, without a paddle."

"Not for nothing, pal, but I think you need to go back to your own drawing board. And tear it up."

"Touché, Quark Caffrey."

Nefarious strutted as he spoke. "The great Poe Thirty-three assumed he was prepared with a clever defense mechanism for any situation. There is no defense against my mind. You are both being held by the power of my intellect, routed and wired directly to those rings. As is this entire operation. All controlled by my brilliance. Now, you will be witness to the ultimate resolution of my plan."

Nefarious flipped another switch and a rumbling and squeak of greasy gears joined the sound of the turbines. The domed roof split in four parts and fell away to reveal the Technicolor splendor of the many, many worlds orbiting outside. They discovered they were situated just below the large asteroid, and sculpture's profile was quite evident from their vantage point.

"That's your love, isn't that right, Nefarious?" Caffrey queried softly.

"Love? Don't be a fool. That is me! My face!"

Poe 33 tossed Caffrey an odd look but had to agree with his assessment.

"It appears to my eyes to be a female humanoid. It looks nothing like yourself."

"Bah! What do you know! This is the model of Nefarious that will lurk and roam the cosmos. A living, breathing, vengeful wanderer! System after system will shudder when I enter and become an orbiting nightmare!"

"You'll do nothing of the sort. You've yet to hurt a single soul—you've only slightly annoyed millions. I know presidents and lounge singers who can brag of worse. Release all these worlds back to their original systems and you won't be destroyed," declared Caffrey.

"Rather silly for you to be making such threats in your situation, don't you think, Caffrey Quark?"

"Not really." Caffrey swallowed, ignoring the fact Nefarious was right.

"A fleet awaits," the Portsmith warned. "A huge fleet that will invade and destroy this entire base of yours. Surrender yourself."

"Ridiculous."

"Do this for your love. Show her you aren't the slime-bucket bully everyone thinks you are."

"I have never had a love!"

"You live, breathe, exist for this lost love. You've buried it deep in your mind. You demanded perfection in recreating her face on that asteroid." Argued Caffrey.

"That's my face!" Nefarious's fists clenched.

"You don't wear glasses. That face has glasses!"

Nefarious searched for an excuse and mumbled something

about contact lenses and corrective surgery, but it held little water. He waved his arms in annoyance.

"Let The Creamery Child play!" Caffrey urged.

"Stop! I will never discontinue my quest to rid the galaxy of music!"

"You used to love music! Don't deny its power! Open your heart to it, to her!"

"Never!"

"Let the crystal thread shatter!" demanded Caffrey.

Nefarious face shuddered, and he gave Caffrey an odd look.

"You might have been born of the Dopplerspangler, naturally despising music. But you met your love. A woman who composed grand orchestrations! Her music changed your soul from muck to gold."

Nefarious almost smiled. He shook his head slowly as he stared at his fungus-covered big toe poking from his old sock. He picked his dangling nose and frowned.

"That is not possible. I am rotten, quite literally, to the core."

"No! You are the I of the they. You have power. You proved it by rising above the I's hate! You fell in love with a musician!"

"And she turned my heart back to muck." Nefarious turned away and a wave of vulnerability washed over him.

Caffrey tried again. "She died. Not her fault. Not yours, either."

"Quark Caffrey," whispered Poe 33, "he has two small objects strapped beneath his socks. I am getting intermittent vibes that the sample of my Master is near."

Sure enough, two objects, one rectangular and one cylindrical, bulged slightly under Nefarious Wretch's odoriferous hosiery.

"Listen to me, Nefarious. You have a lot to offer."

"Such as?" The fiend expressed indifference, sadness.

"Well..." Caffrey had to think about it a moment. "This is a helluva studly ship. Impressed the crap out me. Didn't it, Poe?"

"If I recall correctly," said Poe, "you mentioned something about wanting to French kiss Nefarious, in the nude, after you first laid eyes on his immense craft."

Caffrey tossed Poe an "I'll get you back for that" look, but went along with it. The Portsmith was one hell of a liar when pressed.

"Did you really?" Nefarious asked blushingly. "No! You did not!"

"Yes, I did. And would, gosh darnit!"

Nefarious walked to the control panel and let his hands drift about the many levers. "I can kill you both quite easily, you do realize?"

"Yes. But you're bigger than that."

"Am I?"

"Just look what you have accomplished!"

Nefarious nodded as his own resume of achievements filled his mind.

"That's right. I turned this cruise liner into a devastatingly powerful machine of planet appropriation! I inspired an entire organization of zealots to do my bidding! I never asked them! They were awestruck by me! They formed clubs, tea circles, armies, cults. Even a theatre group on Gupan. As we speak they are scattered about this vast galaxy, brainwashing the feebleminded and capturing worlds.

"And they send them to me. To me! I have a collection of worlds at my disposal like no other tyrant has ever had! Billions upon billions of beings!"

"But you are lonely," Caffrey said softly.

"Lonely," Poe 33 repeated for effect.

"Lonely?" Nefarious repeated the word like a lyric of some long-forgotten song, "Maybe once." He fiddled with controls abstractedly.

Caffrey glanced skyward. The fleet was approaching. An armada looming ever closer.

"Poe, is there any way you can contact Yin?"

"No. My communications systems are shut down."

"What are you plotting?" Nefarious shouted.

"I was just telling Poe here what a perfect match you would be for this lovely piccolo player I know on Ramatree Seven."

The skinny little villain raised an eyebrow, but it immediately fell back into the mudslide of his dejected expression.

"We can find you another love, Nefarious," Caffrey promised.

"I can't. It's too late."

"Yes, you can. Remember it. Once again, Nefarious, recall the wonder of the feeling."

Nefarious just stood motionless, eyeballing Caffrey with a murderous expression.

"Tell me about her."

"No."

"She was beautiful," Caffrey pushed cunningly. "I bet she was beautiful."

"I recall you saying she was quite bland," Poe reminded.

Caffrey smacked the Portsmith across his head with a stern look. The Portsmith shut up and stared at the floor.

"I bet her smile made you melt."

Nefarious threw his palms over his ears.

"What was her name?"

"No more! Stop!"

"Lovely name," Poe 33 looked up and around brightly as he complimented with a sincere and sensual rasp.

"Poe. Shut up."

Caffrey studied Nefarious. It was amazing how such a pathetic, frail, limp noodle of a being could have been the object of such fear, anger and war preparation. No missile, bomb or energy bolt would solve this problem. As Nefarious admitted himself, he was rotten at the core. It was the core that needed a cleansing of sorts.

"Tell me about the moment you first realized you were in love."

"No. I can't."

"So, you do admit you were actually in love?"

"I never said that."

"You said it with your eyes."

"I feel so helpless," Poe 33 whispered as he struggled to free some of his defense devices.

"Nefarious, pal, would you honor me by humming a bar or so of *The Creamery Child?*"

"No. I cannot possibly hear music."

"Why?"

"I hate it, that's why."

"No, you don't. What would happen if you were to open your ears to a powerful song of love?"

"I couldn't."

"You could. It would shatter the little crystal thread that holds back the memories of love."

"They are held by powerful forces. Locked away where they will not hurt me. Nothing will free them."

"Then why are you so afraid?"

"I'm afraid of nothing."

"I wish one of us could contact the L'Orange," Caffrey whispered. "I'd try to conjure an image of his wife."

"That might help."

"What about your holographic projection system?"

"Disabled."

Caffrey cursed under his breath; and as if on a perfectly synchronous cue, a ghostly form drifted into the room. It was a woman, dressed in a dowdy brown burlap gown. Her hair was mousy brown and frizzy. She floated above the ground, her image translucent but solid. She approached Nefarious Wretch from behind. He was too busy picking foot dirt from his exposed toenail to sense her.

Poe was impressed again. "My, my, Quark Caffrey. You did it!"

Caffrey's mouth fell open.

"Nefarious, my love..." spoke the floating woman.

Nefarious, his finger at his nose as he tried to identify the dirt sample, froze.

The image coaxed at him, still floating behind. "Wretchy, my soft-shelled love-pumpkin. I missed you so."

There was a sudden shift in the little despot's attention. An ear twitched like a cat's and his nose rose like a charmed snake. His head turned gradually and one eye, very slowly and with great dread, clocked over to take a peek.

"Nefarious, love," oozed the image. She was inches from his face, and he slid backward, falling onto his rump. His eyes were protruding from their sockets. He was trembling.

"No! Be vanquished from my beholding eyes, you devilish apparition!"

"I am no ghost, my love. I have come to kiss you one last time."

She knelt down beside him, and he shot away like a repelled magnet, squawking.

"Do not assault my vision, undead spirit!"

"Rather Shakespearean, huh, Quark Caffrey?" whispered Poe 33.

Caffrey smiled. He knew what to do. "Poe. The music library. Can you access that?"

"Yes. It has not been disabled as it has no intrinsic power against Nefarious."

"That's what he thinks. The Who. *Quadrophenia.* The last track. Play it as loud as you can."

"Are you sure?" The android couldn't comprehend. "Such a tender moment?"

"Do it."

Poe 33 nodded and the song began. The sound of rain falling introduced the soft piano notes. Nefarious shot a worried glance towards the Portsmith then back to the spirit. He was a ping-pong ball between two horrid paddles. She beckoned him closer with awkward bats of her lashes. He held one arm before him and an-

314

other wrapped around his head in an attempt to block both ears. Roger Daltrey's prayer for love to reign o'er him roared out. Each verse, each chorus, each note, each word, bombarded Nefarious Wretch's tiny soul. He backed up as his wife moved closer, her arms reaching for his narrow frame.

"Feel the power of this moment, my love. It may never happen again."

His tiny heart pumped faster, beyond his control. He threw his hands over his ears, then his eyes. Then his ears. The song's utter power penetrated deep within him. His head fell back as if he were feeling the drops of rain upon his face, and he smiled as if relishing their cool refreshment.

One by one the planets outside faded away. Nefarious himself began to glow brighter, as if some inner light had ignited and was burning through. He seemed to grow in size and, like a star, cast a wonderful yellow light around the dark chamber. He looked into the eyes of his wife, and his own dark, soulless eyes flickered like trick birthday candles long ago extinguished and left for dead. The song neared its conclusion on a thunderous wash of drums and guitar and reached a climactic explosion, piercing the very mind of Nefarious Wretch.

"Touch my hand, my eternal flame," she said softly.

Slowly, and with vanishing hesitation, he did.

Somewhere deep within the core of Nefarious the crystal thread shattered into a billion trillion pieces. The anger and hate that had been the physical forces holding together the very atoms of the Dopplerspangler's core were no more. Like an atomic device, the fission-like reaction of his soul exploded and the asteroid encasing it was rendered countless tiny stars of blood-red light. The light of the fire faded, but a beautiful red gaseous cloud remained, and would remain, for eons. Floating in the black cradle of the lonely dimension of Nefarious Wretch was a huge nebula. A cloud shaped in a beautiful self-undulating form—a repeating pattern of beautiful curves that fell one inside the other like a flower. Like a rose.

A single red rose.

The little man caught a glimpse of it then collapsed to the floor. His smile never faded. The huge turbines slowed, went silent. The I of the One and the One of the I and the core of Nefarious Wretch and all those who would have been were gone.

The energized rings descended to the ground, and Caffrey and Poe 33 were released. It took a few moments for Caffrey's ears to

315

adjust to the silence. The woman turned to face them.

"I am stunned at your abilities, friend," Poe 33 confessed.

"I have a feeling the miracle has a more down-to-Earth explanation," Caffrey said. "Isn't that right, Angie? Peebo?"

There was a chuckle, and suddenly the ghostly woman solidified and morphed into a metallic sphere. Peebo bobbed. Angie laughed again.

"Humbled again," Caffrey said with faux disappointment.

"You shouldn't be, my gold-hearted hamburger. If not for your compassion, Caffrey, our efforts would have been fruitless."

"We make quite the team," admitted Caffrey.

"That we do. Although it was my music that aided in Nefarious's transmutation," Poe 33 bragged.

"Actually, it's Caffrey's music," corrected Angie.

"Actually, it's The Who's music." Caffrey knelt down beside the smiling, motionless creature and pulled down his socks. Strapped to his twig-like legs were a crystal tube and a black square of metal, shimmering like a rainbow.

"Socks."

"Socks."

"Socks, indeed," boasted Poe, with a proud wink.

⎯⎯🖢

"Ready. Poe?"

"Yes, Quark Caffrey."

The party gathered aboard ODOR's command craft, where congratulations were abundant and Caffrey refrained from spoon-feeding crow to Yin and Violet. More than anything, he wanted to get to the point of his mission. He stood with the Portsmith, anxiously awaiting the reanimation of his friends.

"I will illuminate the proper slot."

The third slot beneath the open panel of the android's back began to glow green, and Caffrey gently placed the rainbow square before it. The internal mechanisms of Poe 33 drew it in.

"I confirm the presence of four human beings, one member of the genus *Felis catis* and three examples of the Fleogan order, also known as the house fly. Shall I release them?"

Caffrey was ready to pop. Yin and Violet stood by anxiously.

"Please..."

A swash of colored light sprayed before them. The image was at first faded and flickering—like a memory. The memory became clearer as the density of color and texture solidified into perfect reality.

Then they were there—Sam, Russ, Dave and Al. They were positioned mid-protest—fists waving, mouths agape in anger and a couple of middle fingers flashing. Their life forces refilled their forms and they snapped instantly into a state of both panic and confusion. They yelled and cursed at some invisible antagonist.

"Welcome back, you ugly bastards!" Caffrey said, smiling and jumping amidst his friends. He threw his arms around necks and kissed various cheeks.

The band-mates were still completely baffled and looked about at the multitude of colorful lights adorning the many control panels. The cat, spotting Yin, hissed and took off but was scooped up by Violet, who seemed to have an instant bonding with the orange-and-white tabby. The flies, not quite bright enough to discern nor give two cents about their new location, beelined to Yin's tushie region in hopes the dog-like being would poop them a meal.

"Relax, fellas. You're safe and solid."

Caffrey hugged them all again—and looked them over, not quite believing they were real. Then, unabashed, he hugged them one more time.

A considerable amount of debriefing was needed to settle the minds of Caffrey's friends into a more comfortable state of utter confusion. An agreement was made between Yin, Violet and Caffrey that it would be best to have their memories cleared of the entire experience and get them home as quickly as possible, where they could be placed in their respective beds to awaken to considerably more confusion. Caffrey would simply write it off as the results of some double-dipped Mickey Mouse postage stamps and leave it that.

He looked forward to the inevitable weeks of trip reports and the endless comparisons to the jewel-encrusted basketballs of Terrence McKenna and complaints about NASA's failure to come clean about life beyond. They'd be right, but Caffrey would swallow his guffaws. And forever, strange fragments of each friend's repressed memories would find their way to the surface as odd dreams and colorful song lyrics.

Caffrey, Yin, Violet and Poe 33 gathered around a small dining table in a room giving out on a beautiful view of the heavens of Nefarious's dimension.

"I would like to raise a glass," said Yin, lifting a beautiful crystal sparkling with red liquid in his paw.

All hands rose with their respective glasses.

"We all doubted Caffrey's plan. That is, myself, Violet and all of my fellow OTHER comrades. But Angie, Poe and little Peebo kept the faith. Caffrey, I toast your wisdom and your unmitigated compassion. Peace."

"Cheers!" Caffrey toasted. "To the beginning of the end of ODOR"

"The head is gone, but there are hundreds of writhing limbs scattered about this galaxy," Yin observed.

"But damn, I need a vacation."

"Roger that," Violet said.

Caffrey leaned over and whispered into Violet's ear. "How's about a little cruise to this isolated cove I know on the beachy keen world of Jirmosa, my purple-eyed girl?"

"Tempting, Quark," she replied, beaming her purple lovelies into his eyes. "But I have some personal things I have to take care of. Maybe I'll meet you back on Earth. One day."

"You know where I live," Caffrey said softly, kissing her gently. "I'll wear a Venus flytrap in my lapel."

Violet smiled. Poe 33 stood up. "I believe I am ready to have the essence of my Master returned. Quark Caffrey, would you do the honors?"

"It would be an honor, Poe."

The Protocol Portsmith gently placed the crystal tube onto Caffrey's palm and turned around. His access panel opened and the tube was placed into the slot.

"Fingers are crossed, Poe."

The tube was sucked in. All eyes were on the android. A shimmering cloud of brilliant orange plasma wrapped around Poe 33's body and congealed to a singularity at the center of his forehead. He then smiled.

"I have contact." The room erupted in great applause.

"Where is he?" Caffrey had to know.

"That information is restricted to the inner workings of I, Poe Thirty-three, the Portsmith to the Wisest Substance in the universe—known and unknown."

"Come on, Poe, after all we've been through?" Caffrey pried.

"All I can say is that he is in a bit of a jam. No pun intended. Nothing the grandest, wisest and studliest android in the universe can't handle."

"Can we be of assistance?" Violet wondered.

"I can use a lift to the Llystera System. Perhaps, Quark Caffrey, we can return to Desmitten for the *Moby Dick* and you can join me on my journey across the Cosmos with my Master. You have a power. Although your unrealistic progress was inevitably aided by the Great One's fondness for you, you do, indeed, have a gift. A gift that you may want to consider perfecting. You can, if you choose, train and perfect your abilities. Live for a thousand years. Reach a state of near-immortality. See wonders and sights that will amaze you."

Caffrey smiled to himself, pondered the choices a moment, then looked at Poe 33. "I just helped save the galaxy for music—I think I'd prefer to spend some time making a bit of it. With all due respect to La Grande L'Orange."

"I sort of figured you would make that decision."

Caffrey patted Poe 33 on his shoulder. "But you can have a lift."

"Quark Caffrey, if you don't mind, may I retain the music collection in my circuits? I am fascinated by their power."

"Of course. Spread the word. Long live Rock."

Poe 33 nodded and extended his hand.

"I will miss you, Quark Caffrey. You are, indeed, a shining example of human potential for good."

They shook hands.

"Thanks, Poe."

"My master wishes you well. He says your greatest power is something you were born with. And as outright cornball-barf-bait-bullshit as it sounds, love is nothing to laugh at. It is the basic ingredient of L'Orange. Of the universe. If I may coin a phrase, what's so funny about peace, love and understanding?"

"Exactly." Caffrey nodded in agreement. He felt a tickle at his earlobe. Angie whispered to him.

"Love seat, can I have a private word with you?"

"Of course." They went to a quiet corner.

"I have been pondering my own future and have come to a conclusion. Although my programming dictates that I will forever love you, I feel I need to spend some time away. Finding what it means to be me, Angie, in this odd universe."

Caffrey smiled.

"Would you like to join Poe Thirty-three on his journey?"

"No. Violet wants to take some time off from battling OTHER

and head out to track down her maternal biological predecessor."

"Her mother? I thought..."

"Her grandmother. Or grandfather. Or a distant cousin. She needs family right now. I would like to escort her. Learn more about the family experience. Maybe learn what being a real woman is all about."

Caffrey smiled again and nodded. He couldn't speak—the lump in his throat made that rather difficult.

So, as the millions of prisoners aboard Nefarious's craft were transported to their respective home worlds, in a project that would take a little time, Violet and Angie escorted Caffrey and Yin, complete with the unconscious band-mates, to Earth circa 1973. The Bopple had decided he could play the happy doggie lifestyle with satisfaction. At least for a while. Violet, Angie and the cat took over the *Moby Dick* and carried Poe 33 into the strange albeit lovely Llystera System where he would rejoin the L'Orange.

Marmalade Skies played their way into the hearts of hundreds—on a good night—and Caffrey Quark played his way into the pants of a line of gorgeous fans who still believed he would soon sell out sports arenas.

Marmalade Skies actually never sold out a single sports arena, but Caffrey's faith in the better part of the complex creature called human was helped along by the little positives around him. All the simple lives around the world who created amid their day-to-day burdens rather than those who drained their planet of its spirit from the back of a limousine. And, of course, all the musicians with their longhaired souls, who filled Caffrey Quark's life with endless joy.

The universe would rear its big nose, goofy-eyeball glasses and fuchsia pasties again, but for the moment Caffrey would simply enjoy the predictability of a monotonous Earth. He was quite content in his little lonely corner of the Cosmos.

FINIS

Our thanks to...

Chapter 1: "Magic Carpet Ride" recorded by Steppenwolf, written by J. Kay and R. Moreve; Chapter 2: "The Life Auction" recorded by The Strawbs, Written by David Cousins, John Hawken, Dave Lambert, © A&M Records; Chapter 3: "Juke Box Hero" recorded by Foreigner, Written by L. Gramm/M. Jones, ©Somerset Songs Publishing Inc./Evansongs Ltd. ASCAP; Chapter 4: "Rock Show" recorded by Paul McCartney and Wings, Written by Paul McCartney; Chapter 5: "The Crystal Ship" recorded by The Doors, Written by Jim Morrison, © The Doors Music Company, (ASCAP) Elektra/ Asylum Records; Chapter 6: "20,000 Light Years from Home" recorded by The Rolling Stones, written by Mick Jagger & Keith Richards, ©Abko Records; Chapter 7: "War Pigs" recorded by Black Sabbath, Written by Iommi/Osbourne/Butler/Ward, © Warner Bros. Records; Chapter 8: "And You and I" recorded by Yes, Written by Anderson ©1972 Atlantic Recording Corporation. Published by Topographic Music Ltd. & Rondor Music (London) Ltd.; Chapter 9: "Gone Hollywood" recorded by Supertramp, written by Rick Davies & Roger Hodgson ©1979 Almo Music Corp. and Delicate Music (ASCAP); Chapter 10: "Dolly Dagger" recorded by the Jimi Hendrix Experience, written by Jimi Hendrix, ©Experience Hendrix LLC under exclusive license to MCA Records, Inc.; Chapter 11: "Killer Queen" recorded by Queen, written by Freddie Mercury, © Hollywood Records; Chapter 12: "Space Oddity" recorded and written by David Bowie, © TRO-Essex Music International Inc (ASCAP) Inward Music Ltd. 1969, 1997 Jones/Tintoretto Entertainment Co., LLC under exclusive license of EMI Records Ltd.; Chapter 13: "The Grand Parade of Lifeless Packaging" recorded by Genesis, © Genesis Music Ltd./Hit & Run Music (Publishing) Ltd.; Chapter 14: "Time" recorded by Pink Floyd, lyrics written by Roger

...*for saving the universe.*

About the Author

I have been a writer and storyteller since I created a menagerie of imaginary characters in the Garden of Eden of my mind—a garden that was a reflection of the backyard I spent a collective childhood in East Harlem, NYC.

In school I would often find myself in situations reminiscent of Pink Floyd's *The Wall*—busted by my teachers for writing stories and humiliated before my peers for attempting "the great American novel." But my family (especially my Dad) and two terrific high school English teachers encouraged the heck out of me. I would always write. No matter what paths detoured me.

I dabbled in film for ten years, writing and directing numerous shorts, documentaries and a feature film as well as writing screenplays that sat in the oft-cited development hell. But only in the novel have I found true bliss. I need to swim in Technicolor waters, fly through rainbow clouds and traverse Seussian roads lined with Carrolesque mushrooms and McKenna-like elves. Freedom-filled roads where the air has the cotton candy smell of childish innocence but is spiced with a healthy pinch of dystopic cynicism. And most importantly, where the air is soaked with music—preferably the powerful and wondrous chords of Led Zeppelin, Yes, Pink Floyd and the rest of the Rock and Roll pantheon.

To write is to seek. To seek is to hope to one day find an ounce of Truth that may be transmuted into a vaccine—an inoculation to cure the psychosis that has diseased mankind since Og learned he could kill Oog with the thighbone of a gazelle and steal his wife and property. To write is to escape. To write is to find bliss. To write is love. And when you find love and bliss—there is no need to kill your neighbor with the thighbone of a gazelle. You realize that the real riches in life are at the tips of your fingers and a thought away, not in oil fields.

I have been blessed with that bliss in the confines of my one-bedroom apartment with my wife, Suzy; two cats, Thumper and Nana, and the endless tales within my skull.

MIKE DICERTO

ABOUT THE ARTIST

ANGELA WATERS' eclectic tastes in music and books have con-verged with her fascination with technology. Sleepless nights are filled with listening to hardcore rockers and playing out the tunes in colors that describe her vision of an author's words. Her muse is thrilled it finally has a place to cut loose.